JOHN D. HEDERMAN

FIREDRAKE

To my parents, John and Josephine

"We have a new and original writer on our hands."
SUNDAY INDEPENDENT

JOHN D. HEDERMAN

FIREDRAKE

Science Fiction
As You Have Never Read It

ERRIS BOOKS

This edition first published in 2021 by
Erris Books
Dublin
Ireland

First published in 1982 by Frederick Muller Limited,
London
England

Paperback ISBN:	978-1-78846-206-8
Ebook ISBN:	978-1-78846-207-5
Amazon paperback ISBN:	978-1-78846-208-2

Typeset by Dinky Design
Cover design by Andrew Brown

One

Come away O human child!
To the waters and the wild
With a faery, hand in hand,
For the world's more full of
weeping than you can understand.

W. B. Yeats

Bobby Weston was eight. A split second ago he had been preoccupied with his own badness and now he was dead. At least that's what the police and the doctor said as they waited for the ambulance to take his smashed body off to the morgue. Nobody knew who he was and they would have to keep him on ice until his parents reported their child missing.

"Jesus!" the cab driver who had hit him whispered over and over to himself, as he hunched sweating and trembling over the steering wheel. The doctor couldn't do anything for Bobby Weston but he could try to sedate his unfortunate killer. The cab driver had never stood a chance; there were lots of witnesses to the accident and they all agreed on that point. The cab had been cruising down the street close to the kerb and, since the driver had been on the lookout for a fare, he had not been attentive. Bobby Weston had run out in front of him just as the cab was passing a parked van. There was nothing anyone could have done to save either of them.

Ten minutes after he had been declared dead the ambulance pulled into the morgue and they opened the back doors to put the boy's body on a slab. The body bag was still there strapped to the stretcher – but it was empty. Bobby Weston was gone. The inside of the ambulance stank rankly of hound; there was a large, fresh dog turd on the floor, the blood stained body bag and nothing more.

"The child's bin et be dogs," an Irish attendant moaned, moved more by the prospect of the inquisition that must follow than by the fate of the body.

"Don't be ridiculous," the driver snapped. "The ambulance doors were locked – nothing could get in or out ... We've been had, that's it! There's a joker abroad who should be locked up."

The police never solved the mystery of the missing corpse. It had never been identified and no one had reported a child missing in New York City that day, at least none that hadn't been found. The 1950s were busy times and with no one pushing for an explanation the matter was shelved until it was forgotten.

Mud, tar, darkness and dying seaweed. That's all there was at the bottom of the pier. It was like the time he got the toffee apple only to find that the apple was rotten. Bobby moaned with disappointment and the nagging guilt that he had held off all day smothered him. At once he was aware of the tar on his Sunday suit and the salty mud on his shoes and socks. He had done so many wicked things today – and all for nothing.

Mummy and Daddy had talked about this holiday for ages, but from the start he had wished it were over. He hated New York. He hated everywhere new. Where was the wicked Baron and his hateful dogs?

Firedrake

"Hounds, boy, hounds!" The old man had puffed his moustaches and growled at him, but he was a Baron and everyone knew that Barons were bad. Granny Seavert had read him lots of stories that were full of witches and Barons. And this one had tried to poison him, like Snow White, only with poisoned sweets instead of with an apple. Bobby Weston had dashed the bag of boiled sweets to the ground and had run as hard as he could down the streets until he had reached the pier. He didn't know if the fat Baron, or the big hairy hounds, were following but, while he ran, he had heard the old man shouting magic spells after him, dreadful words like "Yoiks, tally-ho and view-hallooo!" But he had escaped and was alone on the pier. He had been too fast for the bad Baron and the red-mouthed, panting hounds. He looked around and saw no one. A seagull screamed and the feeling of loneliness was almost worse than being chased ... He hadbeen a very bad boy and Granny Seavert had, told him time and again, that the devil had power over bad boys ... The devil was after him now – and it was all Mummy and Daddy's fault. Bobby had explained it all to the Baron. He hadn't wanted to talk to the horrible old man and he couldn't understand how he had come to be trapped by him and the two panting hounds.

The road to the pier was on the other side of the street. Bobby had begun to run across it when there had been a scream of tyres, a bang and he had felt dizzy. Then he was walking down the road to the pier beside the fat strange man, who called him a careless idiot, kept clicking his fingers and growling at the hounds "to heel, Sir."

The Baron had dreadful eyes and once they fixed Bobby he had had to tell him everything: why he was going to the pier, why he hated New York, why he loved Granny Seavert and wanted to stay in New England – everything. He was covered in blood but the Baron's eyes still made him talk and while he talked the hounds slobbered all over him licking his hands, face, legs and clothes clean. What had happened to him? Where had all the blood come from? But the Baron wouldn't let him think about these things and made Bobby tell him all about himself. He was very stupid and Bobby had had to explain things over and over until the Baron grunted, "go on, boy".

Bobby had told him that Daddy used to be in the diplomatic service. The Baron asked what his father did but Bobby didn't know except that they were always travelling, meeting strange people, living in new homes. Mummy and Daddy liked this, especially the parties they were always giving and attending, but for Bobby it had meant new schools, hostile children he never got to know, and strange houses that were never home. All that changed when Granny Seavert, Daddy's aunt, got sick and gave Mummy and Daddy the farm in Rhode Island, New England. They had a real home at last. The big old house in the magic countryside was his – it had to be.

While he was there he forgot his anxieties, except at night when trains and ships sped him to lonely places and cold eyes watched him. Before coming to live there, Mummy and Daddy had been too busy for him. They kept buying him things he didn't want and yelled at him when he tried to explain what was wrong – they were overtired and he was always in the way, whining or getting sick. Now *they* were lonely, cut off from their friends on Granny's farm while Bobby made his own new friends and explored the countryside. New York worried him. It was just as barren as all the other places he had been to before: the nightmares were real again and home was now the dream.

...What if Mummy and Daddy decided not to go back to the farm again? Granny Seavert was better now; that was why they had been able to take this holiday. Bobby shivered and the horrible old Baron laughed and made him explain further why he was afraid of the city. Why was he out in the streets alone? Bobby told him that New York was a prison. By night he was sent to bed early while Mummy and Daddy went to the shows. In the day time he had to stay in his room until they got up. Even then they wouldn't let him out on his own. 'Too dangerous!'

"As you have just proved," the Baron snorted.

"What do you mean, Sir?"

"You got yourself killed, boy. Fortunately for you I was able to do something about that. I have a task for you and I believe that I have adequately recompensed you ... Pray continue. You still haven't told me why you are here."

Bobby explained that once his parents had taken him to the pier. That had been great, but they wouldn't let him go down to the seaweed and thick barnacles underneath. The pier was built on huge black trees rising out of the sea. There were little boats painted in all the colours of the fall dancing underneath and he thought of the starfish, shells and treasure down there. But Mummy had said that he would get his shoes dirty and that had been that. Living with parents was difficult. You had to be careful never to let them know what you were doing or thinking because when they found out they would stop you. It was a good thing that boys were smart.

This morning it had been raining. Mummy and Daddy were sick– their breath smelled funny and they both had headaches ... There would be no walk today. So he sat in his room and thought up the Plan.

Creeping downstairs into the kitchen, he found all the sugar and hid it behind the coat stand in the hall. Someone would have to go for more and he could go too. It was lunch time before they found out there was none, and then the best thing of all happened – they sent *him* to buy more in the small food store around the corner. He had been dashing off towards the pier to investigate its clammy treasure when the cab had crossed his path.

"So," the Baron laughed, his great white eyebrows thrashing around his forehead like a white cat's tail, "You want to find treasure! ... Well treasure you will find!" Then he had produced the bag of boiled sweets and Bobby had run from him in terror. The hounds, who had licked all the blood off the boy, crouched to give chase but the Baron commanded them to "sit!" Laughing, he shouted after Bobby, took a small brass horn from his pocket and wound a blast on it, but when Bobby cast a terrified glance behind him there was no one there. Baron and hounds were gone.

It had taken him most of the day to get to the Long Island pier and now the dark world below among the wooden piles was a disappointment. He lifted a strand of slime-covered wrack with his toe, but it was dead and covered nothing.

"Amazing how scum thrives near humans. You won't find any shells here – the Indians made them all into wampum. And as for anything else ..."

It was a rich strong voice with a lot of laughter in it and for a moment Bobby thought it was the Baron back again. But it was a very different man.

"We don't need scum at all, yet it cannot live without us and we do not let anything else live near us. Don't you think that remarkable, Bobby?"

He had never seen anyone remotely like him. He was old, perhaps as old as Joe's father who was nearly forty. His mouth was smiling, but there was an expression in his eyes he had seen only once before – in old man Baxter's, the day the window came down on his fingers. He had straw gold hair, bright blue eyes and wore the black dress of a superhero, all medals and silver flashes. He looked much more glorious than Superman, Captain Marvel, or Batman. He said that he was Hauptstürmführer August Neurath, 33rd Waffen Grenadier division der SS Charlemagne. He had somehow known Bobby Weston's name.

But all this was for thinking about afterwards. Now, all Bobby could focus on was the blood oozing over the rims of the stranger's shiny black boots and the smell of burnt meat. He walked behind Bobby and from then on, no matter how Bobby turned, he was always behind him.

"Yes Bobby ... I must thank you for being so prompt. I will never be a convinced masochist."

"I don't understand Sir ... Why are your legs bleeding, why do they smell burnt, Sir?"

"You're a country boy Bobby; ever see a chicken climb back into its eggshell?"

"No, Sir ... It wouldn't fit – besides they usually eat the shell."

"But if the chicken tried, and succeeded, it would hurt. It is too big and the shell too small ... Verstehen?"

"Ver ...? I hope that horrible Baron doesn't find us here, Sir!"

"Baron?"

Bobby told him how he had tried to cross the street, but couldn't remember how he had done it. The bang, the noise and then he had been across the street, walking, all bloody, down the road with the Baron and two monstrous hounds beside him.

"They licked you clean." Neurath examined him. "There's no blood now."

"Yes, Sir ... but my clothes are dirty again – Mummy will be furious ... Where did all that blood come from?"

"It was yours," Neurath answered. "You owe Hildemar more than you know ... Don't worry about the Baron, Bobby. He's gone home now. Someone had to see that you came to no harm."

"You were expecting me to come, Sir?"

"No. Anyone would have done, provided he was male, prepubescent, of a reasonably well-to-do background and sufficiently insecure. You meet all the requirements, Bobby."

"I don't understand, Sir?"

"Natürlich. You came to find treasure!"

"Yes, Sir."

"Well– there it is."

It was the most beautiful thing he had ever seen and it really was treasure, not stones nor shells that lost their glamour when they dried, not something that would die and stink like fish or seaweed; this was real treasure.

It lay in the bottom of a green-scummed pool, a band about three inches wide and over a foot long. It was a thin strip of some forty brilliantly coloured strings laid out in a row and all joined to each other along their whole length. At one end, the strings merged into a red plug with bright gold teeth, while the other end of the loom was capped by a gold-jawed socket into which the plug fitted.

He snatched it from the pool and held it up to the setting sun. It was a necklace, but one of a kind he had never seen before. The strings were made of a soft plastic and no one strand was the same colour as any other. It reminded him of a wampum bracelet he had seen in a shop which Daddy said was worth a fortune.

"You can be sure that it's quite priceless," the man informed him dryly, but Bobby was too excited to wonder how he seemed to know his thoughts.

"What is it, Sir?"

"Itself."

"I know what it is. It's Treasure – it's mine."

"As long as nobody else wants it, Bobby."

"Do you want it? I found it!" Bobby's face clouded.

"I have everything I need ... But remember, when the Dutch came here first, they bought this island from the Indians with similar ahh ... treasure. How long did the Indians stay rich?"

"Are they rich, Sir?"

"No ... Everything of value was taken from them."

"Everything, Sir?"

"Everything that people knew they had."

"Then I will keep my treasure a secret. I won't tell anyone."

"Surely you will show it to your parents?"

But Bobby shook his head.

"It is getting dark. I will walk back with you. They are no longer angry with you, they are so worried."

On the way home Bobby tried to get his big friend to tell him how he had won his medals, what had happened to his legs, would they ever stop bleeding. Neurath talked freely but his answers somehow turned out not to be answers.

They mounted the steps together and Neurath gave Bobby a bag of sugar.

"Mission accomplished ... Sugar you were sent for and you return successful ... Strange, I have never tasted sugar – there was only saccharine."

Bobby took the sugar and wondered if Neurath had been carrying it all the time. He turned his head to ring the doorbell and when he looked round, he was alone.

A year passed before anyone learned that Bobby was a fluent German speaker. A lot of foreigners, refugees mostly, had moved into their district. Most of them had settled in comfortably but a few, especially the old, had been broken by the war. Granny Seavert and other local matriarchs had tried to make the strange land less terrible for them and it was on one such visit that the old lady discovered Bobby Weston's achievement.

Old Mrs Pjorsky was a German-speaking Czech. Being an ethnic German, neither she nor her family could be sent to the extermination camps; instead her grandchildren had been seized by the Lebensborn, her daughter and her husband murdered, she had been clubbed unconscious and left for dead in her wrecked home. She had never seen nor heard of her children again and the horror of the Lebensborn had broken her mind. She was one of the host of agonized parents of fair-haired, blue-eyed children who had been stolen by that organization to be experimented on, bred from or, if lucky, re-educated and enrolled into the ranks of the SS – drained of goodness to die for the Führer. Now Mrs Pjorsky was crazy and dying.

Granny Seavert visited her often, but this was the first time she had let Bobby come; children were mad enough without seeing it in their elders. But Granny wasn't as young as she used to be and Bobby was strong enough to carry things now. He adored his Granny and haunted her kingdom – the kitchen. He loved the pies she was forever baking, the strange rich-smelling herbs she gathered and hung to dry everywhere and, above all, her stories of witches and magic. He followed her where and when she let him and, on this occasion, he was carrying a basket full of eggs, bread, wine and pie when old Mrs Pjorsky folded him to her bosom and began to croon to him in German. Bobby knew that she thought he was one of her grandchildren. He tried to tell her who he was but it was no good – she wasn't listening.

Granny Seavert didn't understand what was being said. But she knew what was happening. She made Bobby stay in those withered arms until Mrs Pjorsky was asleep.

"Where'd you learn that foreign talk?" she asked him on the way home.

He told her about the dreams. At first they had been frightening; everything was so harsh and he couldn't understand what was being said. He remembered every detail of the dreams each morning. They were never the same and they followed a sequence just like the Lone Ranger movies.

He never noticed Granny Seavert's worry. In the dreams

he was always one boy – an older boy who was rough, fighting all the time, getting hurt and he didn't care when other boys screamed in pain. After a while he learned that his name was Manfred Burk. Later, as he learned more words, he recognized that Manfred was in an orphanage – a horrible place where there was always hunger and masters and boys to beat anyone who was different or afraid.

"You have fine parents," Granny Seavert reminded him, but she was only thinking out loud.

"Yes, but Manfred's are dead. His father was an Oberbootsmann. I don't know what that is. Do you Granny?"

"No. What happened to his mother?"

"I don't know. Manfred doesn't know either. His father died in something called a Luftschiff which went on fire."

"Loopshift? Fiddlesticks – ain't no sech thing," Granny muttered. "Is there?"

"Gosh yes, Granny. It's a type of aeroplane. They're huge and fat and they float in the air like a string of barrels joined together. They're the colour of sand and they make noises like motorcycles breaking down. Sometimes they're called Zeppelins ... Oh, something happened to Manfred's mother a few weeks later – she's dead I guess."

"Hmm – go on."

"Last night they beat Manfred unconscious, but Mr Neurath and the Baron made them stop it."

"Who are these people, Bobby?"

He told her about the Baron first. Granny would have burst out laughing if she hadn't been so worried about the dreams.

"Don't you worry none about him, Bobby. He wasn't nothing but a fat old fool walking his dogs in the park. I know his type – they like skeering kids ... You dream about him because he skeered you ... Now who is this Mister Neurath?"

"Hauptstürmführer August Neurath, 33rd Waffen Grenadierdivision der SS Charlemagne."

He told her about the day he had gone to look for treasure under the Long Island pier and his meeting with Neurath. But he didn't tell her about the treasure he found – that was secret.

Perhaps if she hadn't been so worried Granny Seavert might have detected his sudden reticence and interrogated word of the treasure from him. There was something terribly wrong. People did not learn foreign languages from dreams, neither did they dream in sequence and remember the dreams as well. Besides, who ever heard of a nine-year-old boy remembering a name like Howstormfoofer, or whatever it was. Instead of re-examining the incident at the pier, Granny Seavert concentrated on Neurath. She made Bobby describe him and, when he had, she was certain of what had happened.

Now all there was to learn was – why. She made him tell her about Manfred – about the dreams.

Manfred felt no pain now – unless he moved, and he had to go to the lavatory. What on earth had got into him to make him take on the whole orphanage? He would have won too, if the masters had kept out of it. A wry grin split his drawn face as he remembered Snämund's face. The head boy had learnt the speech for the Minister's visit. No wonder Herr Hofmann and Herr Gruber had beaten him raw; Snämund could only slobber teeth now – not platitudes. But why had he stood against them all? That little snot Martin had cheered with the rest of them when Herr Hofmann and Herr Gruber had him across the horse in the gym.

They had flogged him until the blood ran down his legs because he wouldn't let them beat up Martin, a snivelling little toad who had asked, had pleaded, with him for help. Well, he had helped ... How he hated himself, not the battle nor the pain – but the foolishness. Martin knew all along that he was a fool and had laughed.

Manfred drew up his arms to press himself off the bed, but a hand pushed him back and something freezing cold was slid under his stomach.

"Work away there Manfred!"

He looked up. He had thought the splendid soldier who had stopped the beating had been the delirium before he fainted. But, he was real. What was he – he had never seen that black uniform before, nor all those medals, wound badges and silver insignia. The cold thing under his belly intensified his need.

"Please, Sir, I want to go to the lavatory!"

"You're lying on one."

Steeling himself against embarrassment, Manfred stared hard at the pillow and worked away. This must be the Infirmary he thought. I must be really sick.

"You were – they almost killed you." The soldier took the bed pan and sluiced it down the sink.

"Why did you answer my question – I didn't speak it?"

"*Why* and not *how*? You are incisive, Manfred! But then you always were ... Would you like some chocolate? It is very good chocolate – Amerikanisch."

Manfred took the thick, paper-wrapped bar with its strange script and meaningless legend. He forced himself to eat it slowly and all the while he studied the soldier. He must be as strong as Papa had been. He was as huge, but didn't have a big belly. The most important looking medal on the black tunic was a black cross with silver oak leaves and a sword.

"Knife and Salad," the soldier prompted – again unasked. "Knight's Cross of the Iron Cross with Oak leaves and Swords."

He had thin lips and hard blue eyes. There was a stubble of almost white hair creeping under the high-peaked black cap whose cockade was a malevolent silver skull and crossed bones. This was a man to behave in front of ... Why was he so kind? He looked at the face again and realized that the soldier's lips weren't naturally thin, nor the eyes hard – the man, like him, was in pain.

"Did they beat you too, Sir?"

The soldier roared with laughter. "They wouldn't dare. They think we are from the Ministry. There is a military presence on the board."

"You stopped them flogging me!"

"No, that was Hildemar – the Baron. He's gone now!"

Manfred had a hazy memory of a huge old man and a deep growl, "Cease this outrage!"

"Why, Sir? I mean why me?"

"To save my life ... old comrade," the soldier whispered as though he were answering a thought. His eyes stared past Manfred at a memory.

In those few moments of introspection Manfred looked him up and down to see if there was anything he had missed. There was – those silver lightning flashes on his collar. Lightning, death from the air ... A Zeppelin man? A friend of Papa come to take him away from this hell! Oh please God yes!

"I can't Manfred ... I would not rob you so shamefully."

The soldier's voice was cracking and Manfred was awed by the emotion in his eyes, something deeper than he had ever seen in his father's, but often in his mother's all those years ago – love.

Manfred couldn't deny that, nor the disappointment. He burst into tears and inner fury at his own weakness only fed the anguish. The soldier held him to him and gave him his handkerchief. Eventually Manfred was calm enough to wipe his eyes in it, blow his nose and be curious about the gothic red-embroidered legend on its hem: 33rd Waffen Grenadierdivision der SS Charlemagne.

"I'm sorry, Sir. I've ruined your handkerchief."

"August ... August Neurath ... And don't worry about the handkerchief – they annihilated the Charlemagne ... Listen to me Manfred. I can't take you with me because if I did it would destroy you. If you had a baby brother who pleaded with you for a hand grenade, would you answer his love by giving it to him?"

"Of course not, Sir!"

"August ... Your baby brother will weep with disappointment!"

"Of course ... August. But he wouldn't understand."

"Precisely– no more than you can."

"I'm sorry August ... I thought ... I had hoped when you came ... that I wasn't alone ... that there was still someone left."

"I came Manfred ... No one is ever alone."

"Then why am I always aching?"

"Because you listen with your ears and not your heart, and you return illusion for love, words for emotion and *how* for *why*. The universe exists because of many laws, events and their consequences. To dare to ask why any of these laws exist, or why they work the way they do, is to know that you are cared for. Cared for so deeply that to know it now would consume you."

"Is that why you are here? To tell me this?"

Neurath groaned and, as he tried to move his legs into a less painful position, Manfred saw the leather boots bend right over. August's legs had to be broken in several places. Blood welled over the rims where the bending dragged a gap and there was a smell of burnt meat. Neurath managed to straighten his legs and when he looked at Manfred his face showed only a little pain.

"Mein Gott, August ... You need a doctor!"

"For this!" He stood up and walked easily up and down the stone room.

"How can you do it ... the pain – why?"

"It is for you Manfred ... It was the least I could

do."Neurath's voice was soft, then he was cheerful again. "Well, I can't take you with me but I can spring you. What would you like to be Manfred?"

That was easy – he had always known. "A Zeppelin man – like Papa."

"Hmmm ... What you need is a fairy godmother. Come to think of it, that wouldn't do. Your command might turn into a pumpkin like Cinderella's coach."

"Don't joke August ... It's too serious. Your poor legs, how can you walk on them – they're broken."

"Like this, Manfred! Aufwiedersehen, old comrade." Neurath marched to the door, flung it open and was gone. Manfred froze in the bed, grief and pain overwhelmed by shock.

The door August had opened so easily wasn't a door at all! It had been once, but it had been bricked up and the door itself was only a panel bolted to the stone. Waves of sleep beat him down and Manfred had time to wonder if the chocolate were drugged, and August only a dream, before sleep conquered him.

"He can't have been a ghost though, Granny. Mister Neurath got Manfred out ... He's in the Naval Academy now." Bobby finished his account and tried to run off to play with a group of his friends further on down the road.

"You comin' home with me Master Bob!" Granny Seavert grabbed his arm and held it tightly.

She's mad at me – she always calls me Master Bob when she's cross, Bobby thought and wondered what it was.

In the kitchen Granny Seavert gave Bobby a silver dollar and a horseshoe nail.

"Now, Bobby, listen to me carefully ... That Mister Neurath is an elf. Stands to reason – he's not human and he's not a ghost... He's a sperit. Now I' m not saying you did good or bad

– but you shouldn't have taken that sugar from him. He's got power over you now! He could take you and leave us an ailing changeling in your place. But he can't touch you when you're protected by silver and iron. They are holy metals – poison to the elves – so always keep them with you."

"Yes Granny ... Granny ?"

"Yes child."

"Will I ever see Mister Neurath again?"

She clipped his ear and sent him upstairs to look for her teeth, but as he ran out of the kitchen she called him back.

"Don't go telling anyone about this y'hear. Especially your Maw and Paw – the sperits don't like being talked about ... Now, where's m'teeth?"

Two

They had been ignorant young men perhaps, and the things which they died for had been useless. But their ignorance had been innocent.
They had done something horribly difficult in their ignorant innocence, which was not for themselves.

T. H. White, *The Book of Merlyn*

The command car's bumpers slammed on the turf when the docking trolley was swung clear.

"Here he comes – the youngest 'old man' in the service," Izzy whispered and swung the wheel nervously. Oberleutnant Jurgen von Lüth, SL17's second watch officer, shrugged in disgust and assumed station at the helm. The 'old man' looked amazingly steady as he paced across the mown acres towards his command.

"Poor bastard!" Oberleutnant zur See Manfred Burk hissed, swinging the gondola door open and pulling the drunk Kapitän-leutnant into the car.

"Ship 'by and ready for lift off, Sir," Manfred saluted. "Five hundred pounds free lift."

The lunatic eyes of a terrified octogenarian tried to focus

on Manfred while the thirty-five-year-old face they were set in blenched. Kapitän-leutnant Heinrich Schorn had been a seasoned mariner. He had rounded the horn eight times in leaky clippers and never shown fear. Earth and water had been his elements before they put him in command of SL 17. The knowledge that she was a city ship, a present to the Navy from a patriotic community, didn't help. The Navy would never have commissioned another Schütte-Lanz type "c" into the service – but they had had to accept the gift.

They had done so with bad grace evidently. Other ships bore the coat of arms of their subscribing cities and were often named after them; not so SL 17. She was bare of any insignia and no one at Ahlhorn seemed to know her origins. She had sailed west from her original field, Jamboli, Bulgaria, and docked in Ahlhorn one day, to bring her within range of London. Ahlhorn hadn't wanted her, but she had been hung up in shed Aladin and the transit crew had taken the train east before the paperwork refusing SL 17 shed space could be completed.

That had been that. A recent accident had left Ahlhorn with more crews than ships so SL 17 couldn't be returned until she had been replaced. In the meantime no request for the ship's papers would be made – they must remain in what Ahlhorn insisted was her home base, Jamboli. There was a bad joke in the mess – that SL 17 had been a present to the Luftkriegsmarine from the Englisch.

Schorn stumbled, but Manfred caught his arm before his Kapitän lost his balance.

"Thank you, number one."Schorn's voice was as slurred and deliberate as his walk. "What do we do when it happens, Exec . . . Jump or burn?"

"No reason to worry about that, Sir." Manfred secured a folding chair to the duck boards by the for'ard windows and helped him into it. "After all, this is only a reconnaissance ... Shall I take the watch, Sir?"

Schorn glared at him half questioning, half insulted, and on the verge of tears. Damn his Exec – he couldn't read the man at all. How dare he patronize him – or did he? Was he Germany's last good man, not a laughing vulture like the rest?

If Burk was that decent then he was unendurable. The constant certainty of agony and death had robbed Schorn of courage and dignity, leaving him only his pride and his Exec's intolerable pity.

"No! Up ship, number one . . . I'll stand the first watch."

"The old man's never been this bad before, Manfred," Izzy, the ship's third watch officer and navigator, whispered once they had climbed up into the gunner's nest to get a fix.

"Mathy died two days ago, Iz. The news came in last night. Also, they turned down Schorn's request for a transfer to the surface fleet."

"Oh my God ... Did Mathy jump?"

Manfred shrugged: "Who knows. But he was torched at thirteen hundred feet and he was alive when the Englanders reached him ... The others can fool themselves into believing it won't happen to them, but Schorn can't; he knows Mathy was the best ... And his ship was a modern height climber, not a lumbering old watering cart like this one!

"What are we doing now, Manfred?" Panic crept into Izzy's voice.

"A reconnaissance patrol over our own waters."

He didn't tell his friend that something was torching airships within sight of the German coast and their mission was to find out what it was. Somewhere in the North Sea the British were deploying a new superweapon, one that consumed the highest, fastest airships and the German Naval Airship Service had sent their most expendable, obsolete craft to investigate.

Izzy was happy again. Manfred looked at his tubby little friend and wondered how anyone could live like him – a life of permanent happiness punctuated by intervals of abject terror. There was something wonderful about the way Izzy could divorce intellect from intelligence. He was clever, could absorb, store and produce learning wherever it was necessary. But he never tormented himself with questions, never doubted himself nor his future, and he refused to recognize the war or allow it to manipulate him as it had the rest of the country.

How had it started – their friendship? In the Naval Academy of course, but why had Manfred stuck to Isador Ißenquhart to the eventual exclusion of all others? Manfred had been popular at the academy whereas Izzy had been mildly persecuted, partly because he was a Jew and partly because he wasn't brave and was therefore good sport. But Manfred and Izzy had become friends and Izzy always hauled him back in the times of bleakness and introspection. Someone, who obviously didn't think, had said that man was superior to all the animals because he thought.

Thought was not a survival characteristic, rather it was an incentive to suicide. In his case it permitted him to jump or burn when SL 17 died. Schorn had carried it to a further stage of futility by trying to keep himself too drunk to care.

The only survivors in this world were those with the confidence of stupidity, or those very rare people, like Izzy, who could think, as deeply as was required, along restricted lines and consign the rest of his life to beauty and belief. Why were they friends? A happy accident of the past, like Neurath and the Academy? And who was Neurath? Was he good or evil? He had shown Manfred hope with the Academy, friendship with Izzy, but he had also given him despair.

"Oh God, Neurath ... Why did you ever torment me ... I could have been happy with what you gave me ... If only I had never met her ... Where are you Gräfin – do you think of me, remember me at all ... remember your Kapitän Harsch?"

"What's that ... I can't hear you above the wind," Izzy shouted.

Manfred waved 'forget it' and Izzy followed him down the ladder into the heaving cathedral of cotton and netting inside the ship's envelope. Life had its compensations and if this mission proceeded carefully, he and Iz would be attacking one of Momma Ißenquhart's magnificent dinners within a month.

And then the alarm sounded.

"Exec to bridge!" Jurgen 's voice sounded shrill down the speaking tubes just as the men began running down the walkway to the gun posts.

"Flugzeug!" the after look-out screamed down the speaking tubes as Manfred, closely followed by Izzy, hurled himself down the open ladder into the command car.

"Height and bearing ... Confirm the aircraft's height and bearing," von Lüth spoke into the tube with the patience of a bored school master.

"Probably a seagull with arthritic wings, what? ... By the way, Oberleutnant Burk, you're in command now."

"Where's Schorn ... the Kapitän–leutnant?"

Von Luth pointed to the blackness of the North Sea far below.

"Drink does help one to make decisions ... In his case perhaps it was the correct one."

"It was an accident ... He must have fallen ..." Manfred's response was automatic and loyal.

"If you like ... Heinrich Schorn 1883–1918," von Lüth shrugged.

"Now we must learn if there is a seagull, or a cremation, threatening us!"

"Flugzeug!" the speaking tube wailed in confirmation. "Port fifteen ... Mein Gott – it's above us!"

Manfred thrust himself against the cellulose windows of the command car and stared into the grey heavens. Impossible! How could there be a plane here, just off the

German coast? It had to be one of their own, perhaps a Gotha returning from London?

It couldn't be the Englisch, it mustn't be ... That would mean they could get a seaplane up to sixteen thousand feet, and more, in a matter of minutes ... An unthinkable rate of climb! A few short years ago the Zeppelins had been free to scourge England, as free as their defective engines would permit. Now that the engines were good the British had better planes and incendiary ammunition. It was getting harder and harder just to keep an airship in the sky, never mind bomb London.

During the last few months airships were being torched off the coast of Germany – another new weapon? Schorn had given up. SL 17 was Manfred's ship now – his first command. Would it also be his last?

As he stared out into the overcast twilight he prayed that it was a mistake; but he knew that something was out there – a monster that left a trail of new widows and orphans in its wake.

Then he saw it. It was a flying boat and definitely not a German silhouette. The watch was correct; the plane was a good thousand feet above them, coasting in silently on dead motors to burn his ship before he could use the radio to warn Ahlhorn.

"Hold your fire!" he shouted, but he was too late. The twin Spandaus in the engine cars, and the look-out's nests, sprayed thin trails of tracers at the gliding sea plane. It was one thing to shoot at a plane and quite another for the pilot to realize that he was being shot at. Besides, torching a Zeppelin was not without grave danger to the burner. Manfred prayed that his enemy was an experienced pilot who would know these things. That would give him time.

Running for home was out of the question. SL 17 was an obsolete wooden ship that rolled like a bitch and moved like a tortoise. She had a rate of climb that compared in inches to what that plane could do in metres. Neither could he scramble for height. SL 17 was already at her operational ceiling and the enemy was above her. But she could fall. Pray God her damp soaked plywood frames would hold.

"Exec! Von Lüth ... Take command ... Telegraphs obey bridge." Jurgen glanced at Izzy, accepted the promotion and stepped from the plotting table into the centre of the command car. Manfred had always considered him to be a supercilious bastard, as shallow as an oil slick, and he was surprised to see the calm on the man's face. Didn't he know he was going to die, and in agony? Poor Izzy knew; his face was the colour of sweetened cream.

"I'm going up top, Exec ... The ship will fall by the bows. Use the engines to sustain dive. Level off at a hundred feet and only then dump ballast ... And run for home. Understood?"

"Yes Sir." Jurgen answered. "Sir ..."

"Yes."

"What if she breaks up?"

"Then you will give the order to abandon ship. You will hold the ship off the men in the sea before you dive yourself and you will fire the ship before you go."

"Yes Sir ... and good luck." There was concern in his Exec's face now, but for Manfred, not for himself.

As he hauled himself up the narrow, rail-less ladder from the command car into the interior of the ship Manfred called to the Petty Officer at the ballast station, "Vent cells one, three and eleven. When they are empty, seal them tight."

Inside the clear-doped envelope of cotton and cellon, Manfred groped his way down the cathedral-like ship, feeling the netting of the lift bags, until he had reached cell seven. Here there was a ladder leading to one of the upper look-out nests on top of the airship. Something was wrong up there. He could hear Petty Officer Zeitel screaming at a rating above the wail of the wind and sleet.

"Piss on it, Dummkopf."

"I can't sir. I can't open my flies ... My hands are frozen," the watch sobbed.

Manfred emerged into the driving sleet just as the Spandaus began to stutter again. The breach of the twin-mounted machine guns, named after their place of manufacture, steamed as a result of Zeitel's emergency maintenance and the Petty Officer was still fumbling with his buttons. He saw Manfred and tried to come to attention.

"Breech jammed, Sir. Ice!"

"Thank you, Mister Zeitel ... I want you and rating Brück back inside. 'By to abandon."

"Sir!" They shouted in unison and Zeitel practically kicked the frozen, half-paralyzed Brück down the ladder, shouting after him as he descended, "Yer'll freeze the water for us all, Dummling. How dare you let yersel get this cold!"

Panic seized Manfred ... Damn Schorn – why had he deserted them? It had been easy to play commander with the Ka'leut on the bridge, albeit incapable. That had been command without consequence. Now he was on his own. Schorn had refused responsibility – had *he* usurped it? No other commander had dreamed of what he was going to try now ... If he were wrong then twenty-one men would die for his presumption.

The valves were still whoosing hydrogen into the storm. SL17 bucked like a harpooned whale and began to fall by the bows. What was he doing up here in the dark and gale? He remembered the old legend of Siegfried. Siegfried had dug a pit to slay the dragon Fafnir and had hidden in it, stabbing the mighty firedrake to death as it had crawled over him. In size, this seaplane was to SL17 what Siegfried had been to Fafnir, but the seaplane had all the dragon's might while SL17 was as vulnerable as any Siegfried and didn't even have a pit to hide in.

There was another whisper in the gale. Manfred looked

up and saw that the seaplane had started up its engine and already the faint sparkles of its tracers had begun. The pilot was certain and the kill helpless. The roaring of the cells died and he saw the vent lips close as they were drawn tight under the envelope. Trembling in a sweat of determination and fear Manfred raised the signal pistol and lobbed a magnesium flare high into the air over the ship's stern. Pray God the empty cells' seals held. They were often jammed open by ice ... If the fire got into the cells ...

There was an explosion like a giant gas oven being lit and the whole sky blazed with light. Dazzled and scorched, Manfred lost his footing and fell back into the ship. But the veterans had guessed what he was going to attempt and there were two of them at the foot of the ladder to catch him before he could plunge through the cotton skin at the bottom of the ship and out into the sea below.

"Status ... A status report," Manfred gulped when he got his wind back.

"You did it, Sir ... Saved all our bacon, crackling and all," Kornbloß, the chief rigger shouted, worship pouring from the huge ex-docker's eyes like a gundog just before a shoot.

They were still falling, dangerously fast now. Manfred moved to go for'ard but Petty Officer Henschell held him back. He was right of course; if Manfred had been on the ladder when Jurgen levelled off nothing would have saved him.

The walkway seemed to tilt before him and all at once there was an explosion of noise. Cotton skin split and roared as the longitudinals pressed it apart; wooden rings jetted fine sprays of compressed damp as they were distorted. All the wood moaned and some of it broke. The engines rose from their usual throbbing roar to something like screams and everywhere water ballast flushed and gurgled as it was dumped into the sea. Just when it seemed that the whole ship was about to founder, she levelled off and the noise subsided into the normal throb of engines and slapping of the cells. Manfred made his way for'ard.

"Home, Manfred?" Izzy asked hopefully when he climbed into the car.

"No ... Our mission is to find out why the patrols aren't returning. We know why. But we still don't know how. Damage reports, Exec?"

Damage reports were still coming in as he asked but, by the time Jurgen had finished, the tinny voices from the tubes were silent. SL 17 still had operational status, but only just. When Manfred had vented the three cells he had created a huge volume of hydrogen gas in the sky which its own lift, and the wind, had taken far enough away from SL 17 before he lit it. The fire and the explosion had blinded the pilot of the seaplane who, assuming he had torched the Zeppelin, had dived for safety.

SL 17 was safe now as it lay a hundred feet above the sea camouflaged by the mist. But she had lost two-thirds of her useful lift, had sustained severe structural damage in pulling out of her dive and was losing more lift from leaking cells.

"I rather think we can go home, Sir," Jurgen drawled. "Graatz followed the seaplane as it broke away. It was operating from a cruiser. We have it all on film."

So that was how the British did it! No magic planes with fantastic endurance, speed or rate of climb. Just a cruiser operating off the German coast! She would have several sea planes and one of them would be in the air and high at all times. That close to home, airship commanders would be weary; a bomb run on London could keep them as long as fifty hours in the air, vigilance would be lax and the seaplane would torch them – it was a rotten war.

"Izzy, plot a course for Ahlhorn."

"Will you radio a report ahead, "Jurgen asked.

"No, I will want all electrical apparatus shut down."

"But the gyrocompass..?"

"All apparatus ... We are leaking gas, Mister Lüth."

Izzy passed their new course to the steersman whose stand controlled the rudder and the ship's course. The helmsman on the elevator wheel kept height station, holding the ship low, a hundred feet above the sea and just under the mist.

Docking was a nightmare, one of the savage conflicts imposed on him by his command. Manfred hated the clumsy Schütte-Lanz class airships and longed for the day when they would be given the real thing, an all metal-frame Zeppelin. The SL ships were little better than lumbering crematoria. In flight, their damp-soaked members dried out and got soaked again by rain, so a stable trim was impossible. They required a larger crew just to maintain air stability and they had less lift, less speed and could only carry a fraction of the load of a real Zeppelin. But Germany had plenty of wood, whereas aluminium had to be imported – past the British blockade.

If Manfred could wreck his command before it made him, and his crew, part of its inevitable suttee, they would have to give him a new one. He wouldn't be the first SL officer to get a Zeppelin that way. And here was the perfect time to write the bitch off. Half broken, and digging splintered members into the turf, SL 17 wallowed before the doors of her shed. There were a hundred men on the lines trying to walk the sprung, imbalanced ship onto her trestles. One grab at the breeches, or a pull at the venting panel, could send the wooden monster splintering against the walls. But that would be a shameful thing to do to a lady, albeit a graceless old dame who wallowed through the air instead of dancing – and she was his first ship!

Inside the shed, the gangs struggled to ease SL 17 over the trestles while ground crew with knives and axes cut away the trailing spars and cotton. Manfred pumped 500 litres of water ballast for'ard to bring down the bows and the ship was tied down onto her moorings. The gondola bumpers hit the floor and shook the command car roughly. Manfred dismissed his crew and, while the ground crews swarmed over the ship, pumping the cells full, stripping down the guns and replenishing the ballast, he made the final entries in the deck log and ballast sheet.

Manfred and Izzy walked out the gaping doors of shed Aladin and set out for the barracks over a mile away. Ahlhorn depressed him. It was a place of fear, correctness and little soul. Everywhere fields of neatly cut grass and swathes of scrubbed concrete stretched out into the mist. There were no trees; the only skyline was provided by the enormous sheds and the hydrogen gasometers built between them. Underfoot lay vaults of oil, gasoline and hydrogen-generating plant, making the manicured fields as vulnerable to fire as the great ships themselves.

There was something obscene about this war, something that robbed it of the glory of previous ones; or was it that all battles were vile, romanticized by veterans and historians? But he couldn't think of any other war where beauty had been pressed into terror's service.

Airships were never meant for war. They were ornaments for the sky, expressions of delight to ferry man from this earth to his dreams. But now all the dreams were nightmares and his people had made the airship the 'Kulturgeist' of the nation. Only those, like him, who sailed in airships could know their frailty. There was nothing 'Kolossal' in the bombing of terrified civilians and only tragedy in the least combat. Today he had been lucky, as he had been yesterday, but to what point when tomorrow he and the crew must burn and scream in a sinking pyre?

"I wish you'd transfer to the surface navy, Izzy."

"Will they confirm your command Manfred?"

"Perhaps."

"If we got a transfer, they'd drown us in a U-Boat. I'd rather burn – it's quicker."

They skirted the green-painted walls of an enormous gasometer which would sink below the ground at the next weigh-off, and the low sprawling barracks lay ahead of them.

Three

O love they die in yon rich sky,
They faint on hill or field or river:
Our echoes roll from soul to soul,
And grow forever and for ever.

ALFRED, LORD TENNYSON

In a tower of crystal reaching high above the turmoil of the city two emperors talked.

Neither one had the sensitivity to realize that they were the stuff of fairy tales. One was emperor of the air and the other of fire, for the former was chairman of one of the world's largest airlines while the latter built the aircraft and the motors that thrust them through the heavens.

For two days each man had probed the other guardedly for breakdowns of current trends and growth projections. Their futures were hazardous, not only because of the enormous investment it would require, but because the product was shrouded in fear and uncertainty. But, if both their cartels were to continue to expand, something revolutionary would have to be invoked. Otherwise they were faced with the prospect of zero growth and eventual extinction.

The removal of air controls had resulted in a massive

increase of air passengers which had, in turn, been reflected in greater aircraft production. But cheap air travel had been achieved at the expense of universal customer dissatisfaction, cramped flights, plastic service and interminable waits at airports. Flights were up by another thirty-seven per cent, while complaints had soared to one hundred and seventy per cent. Air travel, while available to all, had become an ordeal and the airlines were now losing more customers through long delays in answering the booking inquiries than they were gaining on bargain flights.

"There is a real market for a luxury service today!" the airline director pronounced.

"Sure ... For the illusion of luxury ... Those who expect the real thing go by sea ... But it can't be done – not with present airport facilities." The Lockheed director sounded tired.

"Could you build airships?"

The Lockheed director jerked in his chair, slopping his drink onto his $500 suit in contrived surprise.

"I don't think we've anything more to discuss!"

"Hear me out!"

The airline director produced two folders, gave one to the other man and, without opening his own, began his sales pitch. Airships had the advantage of zero cost lift. The only fuel that would be required would be a low grade diesel for drive. They hadn't anything like the number of moving parts of a commercial airliner, would require a much smaller technical staff and, if constructed according to modern computer-assisted technology, would be a lot safer than conventional craft. An airship could be kept hung up in its shed for a fraction of the cost of a weather-grounded airplane. If built for diesel and helium, and sheathed in modern synthetics, it would be virtually fire proof.

"But it will come apart in the first weather it runs into," the Lockheed man protested. "Look at what happened to the

Shenandoah, the *Akron* and the *Macon* – they all came apart."

"All built too big, too soon, too weak and they were the wrong shape," the airline chief countered. He opened the dossier and took out a photograph of an extraordinary craft – a model of an airship that had never been seen aloft. It was a gigantic, oblate spheroid resembling two deep soup plates stuck together rim to rim. Eight propellor shafts protruded from the lower hemisphere, pointing down to give vertical lift and canted at an angle to deliver forward drive. The centre of the lower hemisphere was a cylindrical chamber of alloy and perspex, ribbed internally by rows of luxurious pullman seats which ran from the panoramic hull to an inner promenade encircling a lounge, kitchen, sleeping accommodation and cargo holds. The upper hemisphere of the ship was an astrodome that reached over another circular promenade enclosing a dining room, ball room, shopping arcade, swimming pool and a solarium. Inset in the prominent equatorial rim was a tiny bubble of perspex, the ship's bridge and titular bows since it was on the other side of the ship's rim to the battery of eight stabilizing fins.

An impressive artefact, the Lockheed director conceded, but he kept his interest hidden. A ship like this would fly quite low and consequently fill the sky. The colour scheme for its hull would have to be researched carefully to extract the maximum benefit from that effect.There was no doubt that airships dominated the sky, completed it in a way that even the biggest aeroplane couldn't hope to rival. And people still remembered them with the same affection as for steam trains. Children still preferred their train sets to be models of steam engines even though they had never seen one except in old movies. Steam trains, sailing ships and Zeppelins had burned themselves indelibly into the memories of man.

The air king lifted a performance specification from the dossier and began to itemize the details. With modern alloys, a ship with an intercontinental endurance and a nominal useful lift of 50,000 kilos, a hull that was aerodynamically stable and capable of withstanding a 200-mile-an-hour gale, was well within present day capabilities. What was being considered were two schemes: one was an inter-city service where luxury wouldn't be a major consideration, but direct flight city-centre to city-centre, would be the major attraction. Too much present day flying time was wasted in getting to and from city airports. Most cities were built on rivers where mouldering warehouse properties could be picked up for a song and converted into an airship terminal.

The second projected service would be an intercontinental one where a ship would carry a nominal one hundred passengers to Europe in absolute luxury on a flight of around eighty hours, at a projected rate of a thousand dollars per passage. Lower fares and higher speeds could be realized if passenger numbers were increased and luxury reduced. However, the air lord felt that this course would be self-defeating.

"Too slow," the Lockheed director pronounced.

"Too fast, you mean ... Just think about it. An eight hour cruise at panoramic heights in the most luxurious surroundings that can be devised, a menu and a wine list that a king couldn't have commanded a hundred years ago. Add to that the facilities, literally under the stars, and finish the picture with a ship's crew specially trained in old world courtesies ... It's got more going for it than Heaven has."

The Lockheed director pretended to study the dossier. It was a précis of material his staff had gathered, or been fed, over a month ago and it contained nothing new. He performed the ritual of consideration as a courtesy; the decision to merge with the airline in this venture had already been made. However, the investment would be enormous, more so in the acquisition of sites for terminals than in the development and construction of the ships, and it was important to check that no extra expense was being considered.

Karma – that was the problem. What had the old airships got that had made his grandparents save 'til they starved to buy a passage on those dangerous hydrogen bombs?

... Hydrogen bombs! – that was a good one; he filed it in his memory for a suitable board meeting.

"What if the public aren't interested?"

The air king produced another folder, one to which the Lockheed man's investigators hadn't been privy, and read from it. The airline's market research department had analyzed the charisma of airships and suggested three possible factors: Shape, Size, and Position ... huge, phallic, aloft–and dominant. The new, flying saucer type airships would fill the sky by their nearness to the ground in a manner no Jumbo could. But the essential symbolism – its virility – must be induced by association: publicity flights by conventional Zeppelin types and a hard sell by soft ladies. And there lay the principal danger – the instability and fragility of the conventional ships. If any of them failed, no one would give the stable oblates a chance ... Unless they were built and flown by the military. That way success could be harvested and disaster circumvented.

Could the public be regimented that easily? the Lockheed man wondered. His prosperity insisted on it, yet he hoped that mankind was more enlightened. However, the airline's psycho-sales strategy agreed in broad outline with that of his own company. The only question now was which branch of the armed forces would make the best 'Patsy'. With the combined clout their companies carried, the government, any government, must co-operate.

It would have to be the Army – only they were sufficiently lacking in an airship tradition to commission and fly an *Akron* or *Macon* type ship with confidence. Also, their ignorance must make them compliant and less meddlesome than any other service. But, of course, that had already been taken care of. The Lockheed man was angry with himself for not having anticipated that.

"Yes – the Army has been given the job," the airline director confirmed.

"The New York Zep?"

"Yes."

"But it was broken up for scrap!"

"Yes, but by us – and we have subcontracted it to the army for reconstruction."

"Reconstruction – that junk? It's ancient, inefficient alloys, high weight penalty, metal fatigue ... At best it could only be used as a model," the Lockheed man objected.

"Negative!" The airline director was triumphant. He had been devising this plan long before the New York Zep had been discovered and when the Navy raised it his idea had crystalized. Later, when the anomalies began to mount up, he accepted them as manna from heaven.

An echo of an extremely large, though rather tenuous, object, had been discovered in Long Island Sound and a team had been sent down to investigate. Buried in the mud, they found the skeleton of a metal and rag monster, huge rings of hole-pierced girders joined together by hundreds of metres of perforated longitudinals. One of the divers became entangled in the tattered shroud peeling off one of the rings, found it immensely strong and almost drowned before his colleagues managed to hack him free.

The giant airship had been raised and displayed in Central Park, before being bought and transported in secrecy to a shed in New Jersey. It had been a seven day wonder – the Zeppelin which had come within an ace of delivering the only precision attack on the States in either world war.

The media lost interest in it soon. For one thing, speculation on the damage it might have inflicted was out – the wreck contained neither guns, bombs nor cannon. Nothing of the slightest military or tactical importance had been salvaged with it. The Japanese Fu-Go bomb attacks on the USA in the winter of 1944 , had been more effective and who wanted to hear about them? Major General Sueyoshi Kusaba's Fu-Go bombs had been the first intercontinental missile attack ever. They had consisted of ten thousand silk tissue paper balloons armed with 12kg incendiaries and 15kg anti-personnel bombs. They had been launched into the prevailing easterly winds from Honshu Island. An electrical system released ballast during the fifty to sixty-hour flight and eventually the bombs dropped somewhere over the North American continent. But, apart from the fact that over nine thousand of them were still unaccounted for, the Fu-Go balloons had none of the enigma of the New York Zep.

There was a billion-dollar joker somewhere and until he could be identified, and the how, the motive, and the why explained, the New York Zep posed an awkward dilemma.

How could a wreck, which had been positively dated as having lain in the Sound for around sixty years, be so modern? Its members were cast from high tensile alloys that had only been discovered within the last five years. The engines were modern lightweight diesels. The remains of the lift bags and the envelope were polythenes, so modern that they weren't being produced commercially yet. The lifting agent had been helium and in the smashed command car was found evidence that all flight functions had been subordinated to, or been routed through, something similar to, if not identical with, a microprocessor. No trace of the computer had been found either in the ship or in the vicinity of the wreck. Further contradictions were still being discovered and the military was worried. But the airline director was intrigued. Despite her dating, the ship was modern – and viable.

"Reconstructing simulacra won't hurt us – seeing as how the development and research have been done for us," he told the Lockheed man. "Besides, several ships are nearly as cheap as one – especially if the army's footing the bill for the prototype. "

"You planted the New York Zep!" the Lockheed director accused him.

The airline director shook his head and the Lockheed man had to accept the denial. It was inconceivable that something as big as a super-Zeppelin could be built and flown in secret – not with spy satellites with resolutions good enough to read the headlines of your newspaper. Besides, how could a ship that size have been secretly planted that close inshore? Coastal radar was so good now that you couldn't drown undetected a hundred kilometres out if you had metal fillings in your teeth. Something as big as this Zeppelin must trigger every screen from here to the DEW line! No! The chemical and physical dating results had to be correct – the New York Zep had to have been in the mud *before* the radar defences had been built.

"It had three wheels in the command car," the airline director told him. "One would be the elevator and another the helm ... I wonder what the third wheel was for? Guess we'll never know. They were all routed through the missing computer and the drive chains were iron and they were rusted off their sheaves."

Interesting – but not pertinent. The Lockheed man clarified his last doubts.

"Have you got Congress to secure the Army contract with me? And are we certain that the Army is our best alternative?"

"Yes – on both counts. Thanks to a healthy interservice rivalry you can rest assured that the Army will bring their problems to us and not to the other services. After all, *they* have a tradition in airships that the Army must be jealous of," the airline director assured him. And so the pact was sealed.

The series of graphs and projections displayed on the VDU froze on a still-frame map of the North American continent. The map was a radiation projection that showed the entire continent sterilized. Superimposed on the chart, a character generator flashed in angry red: YOU WILL LOSE!

Three star general, Gerry Bascombe, dumped the computer into 'store' and when the magnetic card was extruded from the outlet he placed it with the programme breakdown in the file. There seemed to be no way America could survive a pre-emptive strike on the East. But what if the Reds attacked? They weren't into microprocessors, all their policies being labour intensive. What if they had no computers to tell them that they couldn't win – that no one could? That was the essential dilemma – what to do if the East went lemming. And what would the President do? Attempt to roll with the punch, or join in the poisoning of the whole world? Either way America would be doomed.

Bascombe opened a drawer in his desk and pulled out a thick folder labelled TACTICS OF NON AGGRESSIVE WARFARE. He pulled the full sheet from his typewriter and put it in the folder. Nearly done, but would it ever make the curriculum of West Point? He replaced the folder as the buzzer sounded.

Major Bob Weston brushed a crease out of his tunic arm and entered the office. Both men regarded each other carefully.

"Sit Major ... Bob isn't it?"

"Yes sir."

"Name's Gerry."

"OK Gerry!"

Bascombe pretended to examine the Major's file. There wasn't anything outstanding in it – there never was in peacetime. Bob was a safe bet, but was that what was wanted now? Age 37 ... Height 190 ... Weight 70 kilos ... Hair, black ... Eyes, brown ... And so on. He was a New Englander, heterosexual, Episcopalian, psychologically stable if over neat and somewhat unimaginative. Political awareness zero.

All in all, nothing on which to base an exciting new department, except that Bob Weston had written a book on the feasibility of lighter than air transportation. He wasn't married. The General frowned; independent men couldn't be trusted – there was nothing like marriage to make a man consider his future. Still, the Major had a girl ...

Bascombe's fingers chased across the page until he had her ... Susan Harmon, age twenty six, graduate summa cum Laude, and now librarian in the college; political affiliations – none; religious denomination – none. A clever, uncommitted dame; what did Weston see in her? The photograph showed a pretty girl with the dress sense of a chimp. Height, 160cm, weight 126lbs, vital statistics, 36,26,36, hair light brown, eyes blue, face oval, distinguishing marks, none ... Bob must be just another dope bright enough to appreciate the body she hid under those sacks, and dumb enough to miss her brain ... Thinking broads were a pain in the ass and this one thought plenty ... Still, until Weston shacked up with someone more suitable, she was the only handle on Bob the general had.

And what about her? The file was no help: female, white Caucasian, parents dead, no living relatives. No, the Harmon broad was truly independent – even her job was secure. Colleges were notoriously hard to squeeze – should it ever become necessary to apply pressure on Major Weston through her.

The general glared at the girl's photograph, closed the file and dropped it on the desk. America had degenerated into a nation of liberated freeloaders. Articulate ignorance was rife, shouting down the honest efforts of those who held national integrity dear. If only the Army would assign him to a role where he could influence strategy! A position at West Point was all Bascombe had ever wanted; there he must be listened to and no pinko loudmouth in the world could demolish his arguments ... But West Point must wait – they'd assigned him to '*Firedrake*' .

The General's long silence had begun to unnerve Bob and Bascombe missed none of it. When the major had changed his position in the chair for the third time the general smiled and redirected his attention to him.

"Settling in here, Bob?"

"I'd have preferred to work nearer home, Sir."

"Gerry ... 'Country boy?"

"Yes, and New England could do with a government contract."

Bascombe nodded.

"It has to be New Jersey. This is the only state with a tradition in airships ... Do you know what you will be doing here?"

"Reconstructing the Long Island Zep."

"Yes ... but there's more to it than that."

The triumphant smile of a chess master who has broken out of an apparent zugzwang spread over the general's face as he explained. The primary function of the American armed forces was to defend the American way of life, the democracy which, year by year, increased its stranglehold on the defence budget. The Reds had no such disadvantage and, for every ton of military hardware the West built, they built a hundred. Europe was as good as lost – the Soviets could take her any time and would do so when America lost the strategic lead.

Fortunately the Reds were a suspicious lot and that weakness was being exploited.

The joint US Armed Forces were engaged in a series of projects – mare's nests – which were leaked to the East. And the Reds were certain to misinterpret them, and rush to squander their resources to counter the 'threat'.

"Given a situation where fuel is in short supply, where we might contemplate a non-nuclear strategic strike and were observed, by satellite, to have constructed at least one modern airship ... what do you imagine they will do, Bob?"

"Build an armada of airships of their own?"

"Yes! Security feeds on its own fear!"

The Soviets would have to be paranoid to believe in a threat from airships, Bob thought. Surely their position wasn't that weak?

"Will it work, Gerry?"

"The Navy have convinced them that we have a heavier than water ballistic submarine... The Red fleet are losing crews every day now thanks to engine failure... And we have them shovelling their roubles into many more fantasies."

"So this project is cosmetic only?"

"No!"Bascombe drummed his fingers on the desk and his face clouded. "It's not just the Reds who're being given the run around ... We were manoeuvered into this project by the Civil Aviation gang ... The Army is footing the bill for their research."

Bascombe laid three large folders on the table and pushed them over to Bob. They were all titled PROJECT 7431 DMI FIREDRAKE and classified 'Top Secret'.

"I'm only E4, Gerry. 'Secret' is as high as I'm cleared for."

Bob kept his hands clamped on his knees and wouldn't look at the folders.

"You've been screened for *Firedrake*." Bascombe opened the folders and showed Bob his name, rank and serial number on the enclosed lists of cleared personnel.

"The name of the operation is appropriate – no?"

"What' s a 'firedrake'?"

"A fiery dragon in German myth. It stayed coiled around its golden hoard and harmed no one – except the greedy!"

"Will this ship have hydrogen lift?" Bob was alarmed .

"Helium ... No, the harm is for the Reds – let's hope our firedrake burns them, financially that is."

Back in his apartment, Bob emptied his briefcase onto the table. The last thing to slide out was a bright rainbow, his 'treasure' – as magnetically colourful as it had been on the day he and Neurath had fished it out of the pool. There had been two moments in all his life when delight had surprised him; finding his treasure had been one of them and the other the day he had met Susan. Up to then, Bob had formed a vague opinion that, in an ideal society, men and women would live apart from each other, only meeting on mutually agreed terms. There was no doubt that girls were good fun, and they probably felt the same about men, but that was where communication ended. Men and women were incompatible. Everything that men did or valued was either dismissed or despised by women whose own goals, if they existed at all, men found incomprehensible. But Sue was different. Why, Bob couldn't explain, except that somehow her occasional dismissals of him, and his ideas, were a challenge, while her chaotic priorities were cute. Would she still hold him, decades later, as his treasure had?

They had met in the Park the first day the New York Zep had gone on display. There had been several artists filling canvas and paper with interpretations of the wreckage and Bob, who was just another rubberneck himself at the time, glanced at all of them. One of the paintings was quite evocative, grossly inaccurate, but still beautiful. The artist had painted a silver airship, of extremely unstable design, aloft against a splendid sunset. It was shaping a course overland and out to sea. To the right of the canvas, on the water, a schooner of improbable sail capacity caught the wind while, on the land to the left, a brass and iron steam train billowed smoke in the wrong direction. Here was talent crying out for enlightenment. Bob saw his duty and didn't shirk it. The paint-smeared artist introduced herself as Susan Harmon. She listened to his criticism gravely then pointed out that if the smoke went the other way the schooner would be obscured, and if she increased the airship's diameter to one that would enable it to steer without breaking up it wouldn't look right.

That kind of logic demanded coffee and while they were drinking it she accepted his offer to take in a show. Bob was hooked, so much so that when she gave him the picture he had it framed and hung in his apartment.

Four

When, when shall I meet you
When shall I see your face?
For I am living in Time at present
But you are living in Space.

J. AIKEN, *DENZIL'S SONG*

Reporting to Förstmann was always an ordeal. Perhaps it would be easier if the Adjutant were a true aristocrat like the majority of the ship's officers, but the Fregattenkapitän had achieved his present rank despite mediocre origins and he worshipped the etiquette that the aristocratic Junkers set could afford to put aside.

Manfred perplexed him; his pedigree was appalling yet he had graduated with honours from one of the best academies in the country – though how Burk, the orphan of a Warrant Officer, had been admitted there in the first place was a mystery. Fregattenkapitän Förstmann's attitude to the upstart sub-lieutenant had initially been hostile, but Manfred had never provoked him. He never permitted himself the liberties enjoyed by the rest of the Luftschiff service. He was always neat, sober and correct and, above all, he was superb aloft, completely reliable and of proven integrity.

What Förstmann hated most of all was the surrender of virtue to a war which recognized the insolent, and encouraged men to strive against each other, and their superiors, to the detriment of fidelity. But, apart from his existence in a gentleman's service, Manfred had honoured all Förstmann's values and so, after a year, the old man had conquered his prejudice and promoted Burk to Oberleutnant. But that didn't mean that Manfred could report to him, unshaven and in combat dress.

In their quarters Manfred and Izzy washed and dressed, the latter in an expensive hand-tailored uniform that he usually kept flung over a chair. What would have happened to him if he had never met Izzy? Manfred wondered as he knotted his tie, grateful for the promotion that allowed him the luxury of a soft collar and tie rather than the starched horror he had had to wear as a Leutnant.

He had been given a lot more by the Ißenquharts than just friendship – they had made him family. Momma had bought him the 'blues' he now put on. The buttons and the two cuff-rings were real gilt, as was the gold thread. This rig wouldn't turn green as any uniform he could have afforded must have done, and the same applied to the crown and oakleaf cockade on his night-blue peaked cap.

"Come on Manfred ... I've been ready for ages!"

"There's no point in making a report until the snaps are developed."

Manfred looked his friend over in cynical approval; he looked like a crumpled million deutschmark note – worthwhile, if not worthy. He set the pork-pie shaped cap carefully over his close cropped, brown hair and dabbed a stypic pencil into the cleft in his chin. It was getting harder and harder to shave without cutting himself; the lines in his face were growing deeper with each mission and his hands shook. Should he grow a beard and moustaches?

What kind of face did he have? Mouth too large, chin cleft slightly like a baby's bottom, nose too short and eyes all bloodshot from cold and altitude and sunk too deeply in his head. Was he ugly? He couldn't make up his mind and the girls wouldn't tell him. They tended to confide in him and love others ...

There was a knock on the door. "The stills, Herr Oberleutnant!"

He took the envelope, broke the seal and flipped through the photographs. Thank God! It was all there! He thanked the corporal and tossed the stills onto the fire. All film, once processed, went up to the top and he had no business receiving copies. They had been necessary up to now in order to brief Schorn after sobering him up for his de-briefing with Förstmann. Fortunately Stills department had been discreet and sympathetic: it seemed a pity that Schorn had never known how many people had cared.

He walked down the corridor towards the Director of Operations' office while Izzy waited for him in the officers' mess.

"Grüss Gott, Herr Oberleutnant!"

"Grüss Gott, Herr Fregattenkapitän!" Manfred returned formally. "Herr Fregattenkapitän I must report a casualty ... "

"Sit down Burk ... I know all about Schorn ... He was a traitor. He could have died for his country – but no ... Nevertheless, his family mustn't suffer ... So ... he was killed in action!"

He considered Burk carefully. Was the boy a man or a fool? Despite the double element of surprise – the sudden appearance of the enemy plane and Schorn's unforgivable suicide – he had saved the ship. No, Burk wasn't a fool, even though he had denied himself the command of SL17 while he had stood double watches and, in general, covered up for Schorn. Anyone else would have had the Kapitän-leutnant cashiered, and considered it his duty to do so. All his life, Förstmann had prized loyalty above everything. Burk's background was a pity – but not unforgivable.

"I have recommended you for Schorn's command, Burk. The FdL will confirm it in the next despatch – he agreed to this over the phone ... Now, these photographs ..."

It was a 'Short seaplane' that had attacked SL17. Three more of them could be seen on the water beside the armoured cruiser. Förstmann shuffled through the photographs and the enlargements, but couldn't find anything to help him identify the cruiser or its class. But he was pleased with Burk, very pleased indeed. Terror was meaningless once it had a name. The Englisch didn't have a new super weapon; this was nothing more than the deployment of conventional weaponry in a novel, sneaky, way. Perhaps a Gotha squadron could sink the cruiser or send it off? Better still, if he could convince the Grand Admiral to break part of the High Sea's Fleet out of cotton wool, there'd be some naval action – at last.

Förstmann hadn't felt so good in weeks. This information would stop the flow of black rimmed envelopes from Ahlhorn. He invited Burk to join him for a drink in the mess – a high honour: the Führer der Luftschiffe Adjutant rarely drank and then only with those who had his unreserved approval.

Dazed by euphoria and the tension that wouldn't leave him, even when safe on the ground, Manfred followed Förstmann down the great hall towards the corridor that led into the mess. The hall was full of people from all three services. There were a number of civilians there too, friends and relatives of other men.

"Kapitän Harsch?"

His memory reacted long before he could collect himself and, as he turned, the ache which had burned in him all those years burst into flame. She had been beautiful then – but now! The noisy traffic of shouting officers through the great hall vanished and he was back again, back through the years to the day when he had left the orphanage.

The train taking him to the academy had stopped in a little village to take on coal and water. Manfred had passed the time wandering down sunlit streets, squeezing his eyes against the glare from the small whitewashed houses. It had been a moment of immense pride. So what if he was only a boy? The ill-fitting, single-breasted blues they had signed out of stores for him made him a man!

A black shadow moved in front of him, so dark that it was the first thing that he could see clearly – August Neurath. That uniform was unmistakable. He was limping, dragging his feet as though both his ankles had been wrenched. With a cry of delight Manfred ran shouting after his friend. Neurath entered a narrow archway and disappeared around the corner.

When he reached the archway, August was gone. Before him was an arcade that led out into the village square. Manfred ran down the tunnel, but as he did so he noticed a bouquet of camelias, wrapped in gilt paper, lying on the ground. August must have dropped them! He picked them up and ran into the square.

At first he thought that it was empty. And then he saw her – a beautiful girl in gossamer white shimmering in the grandeur of the evening sun. She was alone, sitting in the passenger seat of a shiny new Mercedes parked outside the Bürgermeister's office.

Manfred's bubble burst. Immediately he was aware of the yawning gulf between him and her, the abyssal spaces between aristocracy and poverty. She was that to which he could aspire, but could never hope to do other than serve. Sadly he turned away, Neurath, the flowers, everything, forgotten, but as the bouquet slipped through his fingers he clenched the camelias and madness inspired him. He walked swiftly up to the car.

He approached from the sun so that the glare in the mirror and the fact that he was coming from behind made her unaware of him. He mounted the running board and placed the camelias in her hand. She was startled, jerked and looked up. Her eyes were thoughtful, blue with shadows and lights, and when her face was turned fully towards him he kissed her on the lips. Manfred had intended to leave then, to be back on the train before she could recover, but his foot slipped on the running board, his ankle crashed down hard on the edge of the metal and pain flooded him. He couldn't move, all his strength was needed to hide the agony.

"Why did you do that?"

"I had to," he hissed through clenched teeth.

She opened the door and saw the blood staining his leggings. "You've hurt yourself."

"It's only a graze."

"Sit here with me until you feel better." She opened the door further and patted the seat beside her. "Thank you for the lovely flowers ... Uncle August was going to get me a bunch ... He must have gone back. It is agony for him here."

"Hauptstürmführer August Neurath?"

"Oh, you know Uncle August then? ... I must be wrong. I thought you were not a nice boy."

"I am not a boy. I am a man! I am going to be an officer in the Luftkriegsmarine."

"Zeppelins! ... It's not fair ... I would love to fly a Zeppelin."

"I will let you fly mine."

"Really? ... Really fly it, take the wheels and everything?"

"Of course ... You can fly with me when I am burning London ... You can even drop the bombs, Gräfin."

That was a mistake; at the mention of bombs she became quiet and stared at the morocco leather. Manfred tried desperately to think of something to make her speak again but an insistent moaning whistle commanded him; the train was pulling out.

"It is time for you to go, Kapitän Harsch."

He limped out of the car, but as he closed the door he looked up at her.

"That is not my name, Gräfin."

"I hope not, Manfred. But you are very severe, you surprised me – I will always remember you as my Kapitän Harsch."

She looked at him with a concern that made him ache and her beauty defeated him utterly. It was only when he was back inside the train that he wondered how she knew his name and wept because he didn't know hers.

Kapitän Harsch! He had never so much as whispered about his dream princess to anyone, not even Izzy, so how could this beautiful lady know– unless ...

"You are surprised, Kapitän Harsch ... Have you forgotten me?" she asked.

Guttural with emotion Manfred croaked denial. "No Gräfin ... I am only surprised that you ... remembered."

At that point Förstmann realized that Manfred was not following him.

"Burk!"He turned angrily and then saw to whom his protégé was speaking.

"Ah, Gräfin von Taurlbourg ... What a delight, a pleasure! Permit me to introduce you to one of Germany's more promising heroes, Oberleutnant Manfred Burk."

"Dear Kommodore, you are looking so handsome and distinguished... But Manfred and I are old friends."

"So..?" Förstmann accepted his false promotion and, from the way he looked at him, Manfred realized that he was good for a double now at the very least.

"But of course Gräfin ... your brother. I forgot."

Her brother? Manfred struggled against the confusion but could make no sense of it. A querulous nasal drawl interrupted them."Halgerd, we are all waiting!"

A knot of Army officers had gathered around them. Base stallions the lot of them, Manfred decided; all their braid was silver, there was not a grain of gold among them.

Here were the men who sat behind desks and wrote reports condemning the men in the trenches to death by war, or charges of cowardice. The naval counterparts of these men kept the big battleships safe behind the blockade and sent the airships and lesser surface craft into action.

The one who had addressed them was a thin, haughty little captain of cavalry, a Rittmeister, with drooping eyelids and a long narrow nose.

"Albrecht ... You know the Adjutant, this is Oberleutnant Manfred Burk." Halgerd smiled and seemed proud of Manfred but the Rittmeister was obviously irritated.

"Delighted I'm sure ... Halgerd, we will miss the train."

"Well go then ... Otto can drive me." Her cheeks had flushed slightly and Manfred was thrilled by her anger; it was in his defence.

"Gräfin,"he said, "I'm sure the Fregattenkapitän will agree to my requisitioning a car. I will drive you to your destination ... Besides, you wished to fly an airship."

She brightened, but the gasps of horror all around were universal; even Förstmann was shocked.

"I'm not sure we appreciate your attempts at gallantry ... ahh, Burk, isn't it!" Albrecht sneered.

"I am not interested in your uncertainties, Rittmeister."

"Really, Halgerd I can't say that I approve of your choice of company."

"I do, Albrecht ... I approve very much."

Livid, von Dobberitz tore off a gauntlet. Manfred stiffened. Was the fool going to challenge him?

"Been making a fool of yourself again, Albrecht?"

Manfred recognized the voice, but it was a moment before he knew the immaculate who had just joined them. Jurgen von Lüth was attired in the formal walking out dress of the Luftkriegsmarine. Mamma Ißenquhart had wanted to buy Manfred such a rig, but he hadn't let her. The sweeping night-blue cape with its scarlet lining and the weird, flat, diamond topped pickelhaube always looked like an inverted coal bucket on top of a comedy – unless it was hand tailored by the very best house in Germany. Von Lüth's was and he looked magnificent.

"Herr Adjutant, Oberleutnant. You must excuse us. We've had a train laid on, bad form to keep it waiting. Come along sister."

They left, but Halgerd turned and smiled at Manfred.

Bob Weston woke up with all Manfred's yearning. He found the light switch then groped for a cigarette. This time he agreed with Burk – Halgerd was the most stunning beauty he had ever seen.

Bob had forgotten the dream outside the Burgermeister's Office even though Manfred had not. But it had been different then; he had been only nine and girls a disaster. He had never loved innocently before puberty – as Manfred had. Why was he considering this? Manfred was only a dream. He groped for the packet of cigarettes and his treasure fell off the table onto the bed where its colours were picked out by the light.

Why did he dream of Manfred at all, never mind to the exclusion of everything else? Perhaps he should talk to Susan about the dreams? He lit another cigarette and considered the idea. Now that he was so involved in *Firedrake* he wouldn't be able to give her so much time – not enough to keep her interested in him. But, if he gave her something to be concerned about, she might stick around. Concern was women's thing. They didn't have the strength, nor the will, to compete with men aggressively and it flattered them when a man leaned on them for support.

Was he being fair? Did it matter? Susan confused him. On the one hand she was so mixed up she practically gave herself away. He hadn't seduced her – only exploited her. He wondered if the first seamen to drop anchor off Hawaii had felt the same way when the native girls welcomed them. On the other hand, it was obvious that Sue believed she was going to make a concerned person out of him. Was that what their relationship boiled down to – his exploitation of her belief? Not quite; he wasn't being fair to himself. Otherwise he might have been happier if Sue wasn't monogamous in her affairs and he so personally committed. He would tell her about Manfred Burk. That should keep her available in the rough months ahead.

Just before he switched out the light he replaced his treasure on the table. He still thought of it as such. Was that why he had never married? Because, until he met Susan, he had never found the courage, nor the trust, to tell anyone else about it? He fell asleep trying to imagine what she would say.

"Ever have dreams hon?"

"Please Bob ... It's only eight a.m. ...Go away!"

Major Bob Weston thrust himself past the sleep-haggard wreck at the door and went to sit down by the table in the kitchen.

"I mean a persistent, consecutive series of dreams all about the same person, right through your whole life?"

"I'm having a nightmare right now, Bob!"

Susan Harmon brushed a wisp of brown hair from her face and tried to blink the sleep out of her eyes. If there was anything she hated more about Bob, apart from being always right, it was the way he squared up to the prehistoric morning.

There he was, perched beside last night's unwashed plates, immaculate. His uniform could only have come straight from the press, the gleam on his shoes had to be a hazard and he could only have got that shiny blue jaw by shaving himself with those preposterously sharp creased pants. At last he became aware of the malevolence in her eye and grinned wickedly.

"Sorry to arrive on you like this, honey... Fact is I wanted to ask you about my dreams."

His dreams? So that was it! Stress had given him insomnia. Concern for him woke her up.

"Something wrong at the project, Bob?"

"No! Nothing like that."

"Have breakfast?"

"Yeah!"

"You're worried about nightmares, Bob?"

"No!"

Really, he was infuriating. How dare he come bursting in at this hour, wake her up, get her worried and then come over all enigmatic.

"I see ... You want to be taken off the project and the best way you can think of is to get me to brain you with this skillet."

"No, hon ..." He danced away from her towards the window. "The dreams don't worry me... I was just wondering if they were normal ..." He chewed his thumbnail and stared out the apartment window into the drawn blinds of another block across the street.

Susan tied her robe more tightly around her waist and began to fry up ham and eggs. "Want to tell me about it, Bob? ... I know you think I talk too much – but I've never repeated anything you told not to!"

"I know that, hon ... Besides, you don't talk too much... It's just that we're wearing different glasses. We both see the same things, but their colours and size are different."

He was right about the different glasses, but Susan preferred to think of life as a series of tunnels. Everybody was dimly aware of what lay ahead, but around them was only impenetrable greyness. For the umpteenth time she wondered what she was doing – she and Bob were in different tunnels.

Was it wrong to look for perfection? To wait for the 'one' man? It was if he didn't exist ... But then, what if he did ...? There was something awesome about the concept of one person tailor-made for another. And yet it seemed that God had made women for the express purpose of being the prize – or the victim – and had given men the choice of either award. Should she marry Bob and go it alone in her mind for the rest of her life? Children might grow into friends, but for what? All those years of effort and patience to desert her for other women's children!

Bob was nice, clean, had a good salary and excellent prospects. But he would always fight viciously and without honour to hold the world in the frame he saw it. If she went on too far ahead, he'd cut her adrift.

But would waiting forever for someone who might not exist, be any better? It wasn't as though Bob was pushing her... There was no need. For a moment she felt bitter, used, until she reminded herself that Bob hadn't taken anything she hadn't freely given ... But if he really cared, he wouldn't take her generosity so much for granted. She placed his ham and eggs on the table and turned to get the coffee.

"Honey, I told you ... I've had breakfast!"

"But I asked you *would* you have breakfast Bob!"

"Negative. You asked *did* I have breakfast!"

"Leave it!" She scraped his plate into the garbage disposal unit, comparing the way it shredded the scraps to Bob's hairsplitting mind.

"I keep dreaming I'm this other guy, a Zeppelin officer

in the Great War! ... It's deeper than other dreams; for one thing I always remember them. When this guy hurts, and he hurts plenty, I feel it for real ... And another thing, I never dream the same thing twice – I'm dreaming this guy's life episode by episode and all in sequence."

"A Zeppelin officer? ... Bob, did you have those dreams before Project Firedrake?"

"Before? Look honey, it's because I've had these dreams that I'm the director ... You see the dreams have made me the Army's number one airship expert. I'd written some bumf on them before the New York Zep was even discovered."

"I see."

And in a way she did. Perhaps Bob had powers ... For years, people had ridiculed paranormal phenomena, the aura for a start. But when a militantly anti-spiritual nation like Russia had photographed what they called the 'bioplasmic body' it was time to reassess the human senses.

Was Bob a clairvoyant of sorts? It didn't seem likely. She had two friends who claimed to be witches. They said they had been born with power. But there was no denying they were both better prima donnas than clairvoyants. Susan had attended their séances until she discovered their deceits.

"Bob, could this be genetic, chemical memory?"

"How? My parents and grandparents were American. There's no Kraut in the family tree. Well not recently enough to matter ... If there's a hun in my blood he wasn't around when the Zeppelins were."

"*He* wasn't around." Susan bit back the angry retort that genes and memories were contributed from the female side also. How typically Bob! She made more coffee and listened while he gave her a potted history of Manfred Burk's life and times. There was no doubt about it, Bob's dreams weren't normal and what made them all the more weird was the cold logic that pervaded them – no disintegration into fantasy or chaos, like most dreams. But were they dangerous? They didn't seem to be; it had taken Bob all these years to question their normality and they neither frightened nor disturbed him. And they could not be real, not if Bob were certain that he was mixing up people from both World Wars. Neurath was SS and couldn't have been in WW1. Could he? A dull fear began to gnaw at her. If Manfred Burk was real, had been real – was he trying to come back ... Possession?

"Would you consider seeing a doctor, Bob?"

"A shrink? Are you mad? ... Look hon, in peacetime there are no quick promotions, and nothing for anyone of questionable stability ... If I've gone 'round the twist then I'll stay that way until I'm discovered... Do *you* think I'm crazy?"

"No! ... In many ways you're depressingly normal. And that makes me almost certain that your dreams must be too ... Except ... "

Bob looked hard at her, then shrugged fatalistically.

"I've thought of that too ... I'll accept that depraved persons can become victims of their own depravity. But if there are 'things' out there trying to possess humans, why pick on a grown man? Wouldn't a foetus be easier!"

Susan didn't want to remind him just then that, according to his own story, he had been having these dreams for as long as he could remember ... But the thing was fantastic, too much so. This kind of logic was OK for fireside chats on dark winter evenings – not for everyday life. There must be a simpler explanation. Anything Bob did he did well, to the point of obsession ... Which came first, the Zeppelin or the dream? He must have been subconsciously aware that he was going to be made *Firedrake*'s director before he wrote his articles. She tried to coax him along those lines, but he had stopped listening to her.

When next he spoke it was a monologue, as though she

weren't there.The distant voice reminded her that all aspects of *Firedrake* were classified and then, half way through her unheard assurances, Bob began to tell her a story far more fantastic than any dream.

Accurate dating of samples from every part of the Zeppelin wreck showed that it had lain in the mud off Long Island for at least fifty, and not more than seventy years. But it couldn't have! Because in the New Jersey shed they had the water-logged remains of a 30,000 kilo ship so modern that it couldn't have been built yesterday and was only just feasible today.

The rings, braces, stays and longitudinals of the 230 metre long superstructure were made of beryllium alloys not available to World War One Germany. The sixteen enormous lift bags were made of a low porosity polystyrene derivative so modern that it hadn't a brand name yet. The six engines were all miniaturized diesels, capable of delivering a horsepower that a few years ago would have been considered impossible.

The ship's tattered envelope had also been a modern plastic instead of the original airship's clear doped cotton. And the cells had been filled with helium, a gas not available in commercial quantities outside of the USA or Russia. The whole operation of the ship had been modern also. Helium, being an expensive gas not easy to replace the lift bags were sealed and the gas could either be heated or cooled to realize height, or pumped into storage bottles on touchdown. Susan didn't feel at all confident about technical details and she gave up trying to understand when Bob told her that the ship had been built with a crew/automatic enable. One man could fly her and, although the command car was wrecked, and most of it never recovered, it was certain that it had housed a sophisticated flight computer – a microprocessor.

"So you see, Sue ... The whole thing is crazy."

"I' m sorry, Bob ... Why?"

"Because what we have is the wreck of a ship that we

would be hard pushed to build today ... telling us that it was built by our grandparents ... How? Why?"

"I read the papers when it was raised and, remember, I saw it on display in Central Park. How could you forget that? There's several books in the stall about it, but I thought everybody was agreed that it was a failed World War One mission to bomb New York?"

Bob shook his head. That had been the media's interpretation of the Zeppelin. The Army only began to suspect that something was wrong when the Lockheed team started examining it. He didn't tell her that the initial purpose behind the raising of the wreckage, apart from the disarming of any possible bombs, had been to get the Reds interested. Neither did he tell her why Lockheed were interested, nor that they were building their own prototypes. Instead he stuck to the official handout. America was hosting the Olympic games in two year's time. Fifty years ago Hitler had launched the Berlin Olympics by flying *Hindenburg* and the *Graf Zeppelin* over the stadium. This time the Army would celebrate the occasion with one of their own!

It would catch the public's imagination like oil snatching a flame... How many Russians would die trying to get the damn things to work? Because it was certain they would try to steal a lead in this new race. They had beaten America into space, but America had beaten them to the moon. And nobody, but nobody, except the Germans, had ever made it with airships.

"Bob ... Bob ... Are you listening Bob?"

"Sorry Sue, I got lost there."

"Listen, I'm sure there must be some connection between this Zeppelin and your dreams – have you looked for Burk?"

"Casually. We have no records on him; neither has Germany. Most of theirs were destroyed in the bombings of the last World War."

"Supposing Burk is real, Bob ...?"

"Then I'd start worrying."

"Possession?"

"Perhaps ... God knows ..."

"It couldn't be possession if he is still alive, Bob! He could be ..."

"Only just ... Jesus, hon, ... he'd be ninety ... It'd make no sense."

"Does anything that you've told me?"

He grinned ruefully, shook his head and poured more coffee. Should he tell her about the third wheel? No. Whatever function it had served was certain to have been a mundane one, even though not an immediately obvious one. Susan had enough data to chew on without adding diversionary material. Still, the third wheel was an enigma. It was a steersman's wheel, all varnished wood and polished brass, just like the wheels in the steering and elevator stands. However the latter two had transmission chains parallelling them with the computer and the elevator and rudder lines. The third wheel had only a short chain that must have been directly routed into the flight computer. What purpose had it served?

Bob had wanted to remove the third wheel and its superfluous stand from *Firedrake*'s car, but Bascombe had insisted that it be left there. Somewhere, someone must know what its function was and it would be easier to scrap it later should its uselessness be confirmed, rather than have to install it after the microprocessor had been hardwired in. Doubt gnawed at him. What if the third wheel were only cosmetic – a spare wheel doing nothing? ... Were the Russians playing America at her own game?

The thing would make perfect sense if they had built the Zeppelin, sunk it off Manhattan and then somehow got to him and brainwashed him... If that were true, then no one could help him, neither the army nor Susan.

Was there such a thing as a race yearning? Susan wondered. A cosmic truth that focussed in certain people an expression of universal desire? ... Was the human race as fed up with stress and mediocrity as she was? Could Bob's dreams be a subconscious expression of everyone's desire for the days of magic, splendour and honour, the beautiful times of La Belle Epoque? The times of graceful happy people, when wonderful monsters of polished brass and fiery metal roamed the rails, stately liners cruised the seas and huge airships feasted their passengers on lobster and champagne in the high air between Europe and America? Such things had meant something then. Not like now when everyone had everything yesterday's princes had, and more, yet could enjoy none of it. Bob watched her and recognized the dream in her eyes.

"Don't be a sentimentalist, Sue – those monsters were never safe."He stooped to flick a spot of dirt from his shoe. The shine held his attention, and long after the offending matter was gone he continued to stare at his feet.

Why does he prefer his shoes to me? Susan thought, but she knew why. Sloppy, even when she tried to be neat, she was too disorganized for his ordered horizons. Not that he was anything wonderful. Short and blocky, he would be dreadfully fat when he got older. He was beginning to go bald already and his babyish face was too plump to wrinkle gracefully with age.

But what of herself? She looked well enough now, taller than Bob, swelling only in the right places. But she would grow old – and look it. You needed good bones to wear eternity well.

"What does Manfred look like? Is he a projection of yourself?"

"No – of course not!" Bob was surprised at the vehemence of his denial. He began again. "He's bigger than me, about two metres, not as big as most. Heavyish frame, lots of bone and muscle. OK now, but later he'll have to work to stay trim... His face ... well I'd call it ugly; the jaw's too big and his nose has been broken more than once ... Like I said, he's had his lumps. Guess his hair would be brown, if he'd let it grow. Eyes black, well set but a little too deep and hard ... Guess he'd do OK if only he smiled a piece ... You think that's me Sue?"

"I don't know ... It might be what you wished you were!"

"Aw come on, hon!"

"What are you going to do?"

"I suppose I should see a shrink, or a Padre."

He seemed calm enough and, although she wanted to reassure him, let him hear whatever might make him feel better, Susan was too cautious to do that. This was something she didn't understand at all and an untimely piece of encouragement now might destroy him later. What was difficult to understand was how Bob had lived with these dreams so long without telling anybody. But then he had spent most of his life alone, secretive with his parents, buried in the New England outback with only a crazy old Granny and superstition-ridden country folk to talk to. He had hated school where he had made a lot of enemies and apparently no friends. And once in the Army ...

"Could you afford help, Bob?"

"Cash yes! Career no! There's no way they wouldn't find out, and bingo, I'm packed off to Alaska or some other place where nutty Weston couldn't harm them ... And someone else would put that ol 'Zep together.

Was there any point in stressing that nothing was worth self-destruction? ... But, even if he resigned from *Firedrake*, would these dreams let him be? They seemed to hinge on one, or both, of two possible alternatives: one – Manfred Burk was real and somehow or other there was a link between him and Bob: two – Bob's dreams and the Long Island Zeppelin were connected. Somehow or other, Bob's subconscious had become aware of the airship long before it was salvaged.

Bob wasn't in any position to evaluate these possibilities objectively. So what could she do? One ... she had the library. Two ... being a librarian in a college system with almost universal international affiliations had advantages she would exploit. Three ... there would be more information in the network than there was on any military file and, for someone with more time and patience than the press, there must be more facts. Four ... the first thing that must be done was to confirm, or lay, this Manfred Burk's existence. In the meantime what was needed was reassurance.

"Bob, I'm sure we can work this thing out together! Stay here tonight. That way, if there's a dream we can go over it while it's still fresh."

He was delighted – naturally. For an instant Susan was furious – the arrogance, the complete rejection of her mind. All she had to offer would be in bed – that and a sleep therapy, no more! And was that what the dreams, and the crazy airship, were all about? An elaborate attack on her pity to let him move in? The instant died unexpressed ... Poor Bob, arrogant, yes. But he wasn't anything that devious.

"Must get back, Sue! The super-structure's coming on fine. We got the rings on right at last. Now we're waiting for new envelope gores and lift cells ... Tell you how it goes tonight."

He kissed her and, drawing her head down past his, he whispered in her ear.

"Love you, hon ... You're a 'good ol' boy'."

He was gone and Susan was alone in an apartment in urgent need of sand blasting and the knowledge that worth in a woman could be recognized by a man – but only after he had made her an honorary male. What kind of a world was this? Was anyone at home in it, why did she exist and why couldn't she fit in? These were questions rooted in her childhood.

It had started at school when she realized that, while the boys were encouraged to be interested, obedience was the only accepted norm for girls. Momma and Poppa had never been much help. Perhaps they could have understood, if they had dared, but they had spent all their lives trying to make a 'position' for the family, a position that fed on money, respectability and absolute conformity. After a while Susan learned to hide behind a mask of parroted responses and seeming acquiesence. Later, as her body developed, she had to learn to hide it too. Mother Nature, what a laugh! Nature was a man – and a misogynist to boot. Otherwise why did women have to fight life on two levels, on the one hand to defend their bodies and on the other to command recognition of themselves – their minds. It wasn't so much that society was hostile to women; it resented anyone of either sex who tried to be free. Men had an advantage in their violence, which was denied to women. If a man took on the system he could win respect as a crucified martyr, but if a woman tried there was only rape and shame.

Society was obsessed with dominance. Men dominated each other and accepted domination in every aspect of their lives. Those on top could afford to, and sometimes did, pay lip service to freedom, but their subjects couldn't. They, having to obey, must vent their frustrated leadership on women and children. Of course women contributed to their own servitude; there wasn't a Hitler born who couldn't have been humanized by his mother or sisters ... And women never seemed to support their own, like men did. After all, fifty per cent of the electorate must be women so why were male politicians nearly always returned? Men negotiated with, and were reasonable to, each other mainly because they respected the threat of mutual violence. Women, on the other hand, were an intolerable insolence. They expected rights won not by respect, but by concession. Men despised the unsupported threat of women's minds, while being driven to hunt their bodies. Their intelligence did not crave union with women's as their bodies did so, at best, any relationship between men and women must be a compromise. Why did she bother with Bob, with any man? Because, even though her mind told her she was doomed to disappointment, her emotions insisted that next time must be different. Trust, hope and charity were the trinity of romance, and that was the grail all women followed blindly.

What was so special about Bob? Perhaps it was only his isolation; being a loner he hadn't the arrogant confidence of the pack and that made him more willing to accept her as a person. Would he be different or, as he got older, would he become more like the rest? Men found the 'get the other guy' philosophy quite irresistible. Eventually, when he attempted to dominate her would that be the end of their affair?

Five

Preserve me, Oh God, for I have looked to thee for refuge.

Psalm, 16

The cell was small and filled with wooden things, dark woods that smelled of camphor and other scents, and light woods with polished grain. Prior Constantine loved wood and cloth, anything wrought from the fruits of the earth.

The community, young men for the most part, in spite of the universal decline in vocations, had long ago despaired of dragging their Prior out of the fourteenth century. But Brother Joseph knew him well, knew the little withered partisan who had killed for his country and, unable to forgive himself, had entered the monastery at Bari.

"You are well, Brother Joseph?"

"Yes Father Prior. And you?"

"I too am well, but I wish ... I wish ... Every day I fall further and further behind ... When I was young I didn't care for the world ... didn't realize that Eden is now and not yet denied us ... But now!" He waved to his precious panels and exquisitely carved artifacts. "There will be another war, Brother Joseph;

our agonies were not enough to prevent it ... And, when we have destroyed Eden, God will turn his face from us – as he has from me ... Christ died to warn us, and we won't redeem ourselves."

Brother Joseph stirred uneasily. There was no cure for scruples, only death, or the temporary alleviation of increasingly frequent confession. Fortunately he had no power to forgive, but he could try to comfort.

"God wants friends, Father Prior, not dependants. Joy, youth, delight, even faith are given only to the young. They need them lest they see what lies ahead and give up. You and I are on a higher, sterner road now, and if God is faster than us – he will surely wait for us."

"But we are despicable ... And, Brother Joseph, you and I are heretics!"

"No, Father Prior ... You and I know that we wait in a frail bubble of order. Scientists are beginning to be aware of the chaos that lies without. The real universe is that which you and I must know soon – when we are taken out of this kindergarten."

"Will you be afraid to die, Brother? I must not ... not yet ... I am unworthy."

"There is my quest, Father ... the promise ... If I die before I know, then I will be disappointed ... What I seek, and I hope seeks me, isn't here – I 've sought long enough to know that ... I look for the gardeners, not the garden nor its creator."

Brother Joseph looked out of the Prior cell's only window, a gothic arch with leaded panes that faced west, giving the timber room a panoramic view of the Priory's enclosed garden. Why couldn't they have buried Brother Parvus there? The Priory once owned the sweep of ground that fell away from its outer walls to the harbour of Bari. But that had been in the days when people believed that the priesthood should be rewarded, rather than regard it as a reward in its own right.

Now the Priory only owned the ground enclosed by its walls. Bari had become a huge city.

The Priory's ancient grounds had been engulfed by port expansion and to provide the cemetery, whose pink stone walls embraced the Priory like a ring enclosing a gem. The community had their own plot in the cemetery and it was because they had buried Brother Parvus there yesterday that Brother Joseph would have to flee the priory today.

"Americans called on you this morning, Father Prior?"

"Yes, CIA. Their quickness appals me. I do not fear for myself or the guilty brethren; but I fear for you, Brother Joseph, and the rest of our community ... That brat! Attempted rape in a graveyard – consecrated ground!" The Prior rattled on, whipping himself into a frenzy of indignation, declaiming on the morals of the 1980s like a broody hen scolding the discoverer of her clutch of eggs.

It wouldn't have happened if Brother Parvus had been buried inside the grounds. But then the rape would have been successful and the Prior, and the other old men, did not have the right to protect their ancient grief with that young girl's anguish. Brother Parvus was dead, the times of atonement over, and all that was left was self-revulsion.

Brother Joseph considered his old friend lecturing crossly on the other side of the bureau and knew that he was still running away from himself. Prior Constantine would never regain the brave confidence of his youth until he received the courage to stop running away and endure the truth, and the guilt, when they caught up with him. The realization that one is a mix of good and evil, that virtue needs a disciplined vice to strengthen it, is a fire that tempers the soul. To excuse one's sins is to burn forever. A freezing loneliness shook Brother Joseph and he looked at the wall nearest Brother Parvus' grave. For years the community had nursed him; perhaps their self-respect had been a more urgent invalid than their dead brother had ever been.

Brother Parvus had never sought revenge and yet his death threatened the community more effectively than anything he could have done while alive. They had buried him in the afternoon and Brother Joseph hadn't been able to attend the funeral.

That night, while the sods on the grave still crumbled as they yielded their moisture to the baked air, 'Death' had prevented a rape. Demented by fear, the boy ran from it, a leaping, jerking thing that cleared tombstone and grave as he raced to the city below. The girl huddled on the ground, crying, but not in fear nor horror. Mary, the mother of God had heard her prayer. And when 'Death' stretched out a withered claw to her, she reached out her hand to meet it.

News of the apparition spread through the city within the hour and the foreign press had it before the first flood of the curious began to assemble in the cemetery. The buzz of excited speculation, and the muted thunder of buses arriving and departing, reached into the Prior's cell, interrupting his tirade and Brother Joseph's reverie. The Prior opened a drawer in his baroque desk, pain clouding his face as he drew out a newspaper.

"They raze whole forests to print this rubbish. Have you seen it?" He held up the five centimeter headlines – '*Apparition at Bari*' and '*Young couple see Death in graveyard*' and continued in disgust: "The boy applied for admission into the Order yesterday, and I understand that she's already been turned down by Mother Ursula ... Convinced Catholics, that's what the Church needs, not terrified refugees ... What use is a repentant rapist to us, to any community, to himself for that matter? And what was that stupid girl doing with him in the first place? Mother Ursula should have taken her in – to stop her annoying the rest of us ... What are we going to do Brother Joseph? The Americans are already investigating."

And that was only to be expected, Brother Joseph realized. They were sensitive about Bari and with good reason. It was a pity their concern over old scars must open new wounds. What were the Americans thinking about anyway, how much did they suspect, how much did they know and, above all, was anybody else interested?

General Bascombe considered the newspaper and gulped down coffee to sweeten his sleep-soured stomach. It seemed to be an immutable law that the more stupid the mistake the more vicious and long lasting were the consequences. It was all over the paper – the unwholesome prominence that the Press gave tragedy in the absence of any worthwhile news.

That was what life was all about – managing to climb on top of the mindless and staying there, controlling the situation rather than being controlled! Let the masses revel in the anguish of the casualties. Stories like this one stopped them meddling in politics and kept them doing what they were born for – paying taxes. Taxes that the government needed to implement its strategic and tactical objectives.

APPARITION AT BARI! a headline screamed and lower down in smaller print *Death talks to young couple!* A fatuous heading! Bascombe thought. If the poor creature had said anything, the paper hadn't printed it. That was one of the troubles with the world: indecisive men made vague commitments to political states, like war, and then didn't see them through ... Medical opinion knotted itself splitting the subtle difference between 'letting the patient die' through withholding treatment and 'killing'. In the end, of course, the patient was forced to live – a sacrifice of agony to progress and the reluctance of anyone to make a stand for decency.

He wondered if they still made the M47A1 hundred pound bombs. That question wouldn't mean very much to the destroyed creature haunting the nights in Bari. One hundred tons of those one hundred pound bombs, loaded with Levinstein H Mustard gas, had been shipped into Bari harbour. On the second of December 1943 the Luftwaffe had blown the ship carrying the mustard, the SS *John Harvey*, to pieces. Over one thousand Allied military personnel and Italian civilians had died and the gas had crept into the town.

Someone hadn't been that lucky it seemed. They'd find whoever it was, of course, and the American government would try to compensate him, or her. Interesting question – why hadn't the mustard victim sought relief before? Was the creature's past as badly scarred as its face? The lines from the Bible occurred to the general –*'the fathers have eaten sour grapes and the teeth of the children are set on edge'*. Reports were coming in that the Soviet Embassy in Rome had increased its staff by three. Why? Only a paranoid would imagine that the Reds were interested in the apparition, but paranoia was good for security. Besides, a public reminder of what the Allies had done in Bari way back in the last World War would take the heat off Russian misdemeanours and embarrass the West. The Bari situation should be watched – he'd get someone put on it.

The Priory was too near the apparition to escape investigation, Brother Joseph realized. He was old now, too old to relish the prospect of making a new life for himself; nevertheless he had no choice. Physical seeking was useless; he had done all that years ago and it had become obvious that the questing must be an inward one where that which he sought would hunt him. It didn't matter where his body was except that he could no longer stay in the Priory. Shipping the mustard gas to Bari hadn't been the Allies' sin. It had only been stupid. At the time everyone knew the Germans were stockpiling the stuff and, even though it contravened the Geneva Convention, the Allies had felt it necessary to have a stockpile of mustard gas of their own in Italy for retaliatory purposes, should the Germans use theirs first. No, the sin had been when the Allies withheld the information from the medics that their patients were dying of mustard lesions and oedema. Not that an accurate diagnosis would have been much help. Most people had heard Axis Sally's comment on her nightly broadcast: '*I see you boys are getting gassed by your own poison gas.*'

The Germans had known the truth, the Bari medics had guessed it, but no one knew how to treat the complaint, nor would they until the Allies released treatment details. They didn't until it was much too late.

Where would he go? Panic sent sweaty prickles down his back, but he remained calm. Had it been a mistake to bury himself all these years in the Priory? But if he had taken his chances in the outer world what would have happened to Brother Parvus? The community had nursed him, especially the guilty who had used him as an object of atonement, but only he, Brother Joseph, had given him the will to endure – they had given that much to each other. Had each agonized breath been worth the promise of the next? Brother Joseph couldn't say ... There were other Benedictine houses of course; the Order was distributed worldwide. Surely there must be a house somewhere where he would be safe, where no one would ask questions or spread gossip to outsiders. America seemed to be the best place. The CIA wouldn't expect him to hide there and he could use the pretence of not being able to speak English to hide from the curious, if only for a while. Resolved he turned to face the Prior again.

"We have been good friends, Father Prior ... But when Brother Parvus died, so did my need to stay here!"

"You were good to that poor boy – would that I had been so!"

'Poor boy'! Brother Parvus would have been sixty-six today,

but he had been released two days short of that. Interred in the community's plot in the public graveyard outside the Priory walls, in a grave that was now the centre of world attention, lay a rotting prison. The boy Prior Constantine mourned had been tortured and crippled by Constantine the partisan and his group some forty years earlier. Brother Parvus had forgiven them, but the Prior and those of his group who had also joined the community could not forgive themselves.

There was something about the whole tragedy that had always nagged Brother Joseph and the Prior either would not, nor ever could, answer it. How had the partisans discovered the two Germans in the first place and then, having destroyed Brother Parvus, why had they regretted it so quickly and protected them for so long? Partisan Constantine had killed many men, but he had not killed Brother Parvus – so why did Prior Constantine spend his days in grief for the dead monk and for no one else?

The Prior's eyes filled with tears and Brother Joseph knew that scruples were tearing the old man apart again.

"You are being unfair to yourself, Father Prior. They were bad days and we were the enemy. We are harsher on ourselves than God would ever be!"

The Prior clutched at Brother Joseph's cassock as though to comfort both of them. "Do not leave me old friend ... Wait here with us ...We all wait ..."

"No, Father Prior. We wait for different things."

"Where will you go then?"

"America."

Prior Constantine shifted in his chair, gathering himself to persuade but changed his mind. Any purpose was better than none and Brother Joseph needed a purpose more than anyone he knew.

He opened another drawer and took out a pen, writing paper, envelopes and a cheque book.

"I will send Brother Francis with you. He knows this America ... Besides," he added with a sigh, "It's time to raise more funds. Brother Francis is very good at that."

"Brother Francis? But he wasn't with you in 1943. He's innocent."

"Yes, Brother Joseph, most of our community are. At least one of them deserves to be saved if the worst comes to the worst. Brother Francis goes with you. I'll see what can be done for the rest." The Prior crossed himself and Brother Joseph wondered if the Prior had something in his past, something more serious than the harbouring of two German war criminals.

Six

Has not one of the poets said that a noble friend is the best gift and a noble enemy the next best.

C. S. Lewis, *The Last Battle*

Manfred felt sick as he walked across the dew-soaked grass towards the straining ground gangs. SL 17 was off the docking cars and bobbing sluggishly in the air, restrained by the men on the spiders. Jurgen climbed down the rope ladder swinging out of the command car and walked over to him.

"We'll have to walk her back, Sir." He pointed towards the banks of fog rolling in over the plains. "Lift conditions are atrocious. What with this fog, and low barometric pressure, cells VIII and II are contaminated."

"Sorry, Exec ... This is a priority mission ... Stand the gangs by to cast off."

Jurgen managed a cynical smile which failed to mask the shock on his face. It wasn't fair on any of them, Manfred agreed, but what could he do? He climbed up the ladder into the car and went through the 'up ship' manoeuvres automatically while his mind struggled for some semblance of composure.

A flight of eight ships had been sent out on a raid from Nordholz some twenty hours ago. They had set out on 'route yellow', but were due to return home along 'route black' – directly over the estimated position of the armoured cruiser and its killer sea planes. Förstmann had made it quite clear that their rescue must take priority over every other consideration – even to the extent of taking a ship aloft with air-contaminated cells. But why did it have to be him? There were other commanders; why not one of them? Obvious! They were all aristocrats.

It was one thing to send him, Manfred Burk, out on an 'ascension day mission', but what about his crew? What would they think and, above all, what about Izzy? Manfred wouldn't have been the first commander to develop a suicidal 'throat ache', one that could only be cured by a really big gong, like the Blue Max. Tin was hard to come by in the Airship service; medals were awarded for valour and Zeppelins were only capable of delivering sneak attacks. Izzy, Jurgen and all his crew would know that he could have refused this mission. But he had accepted it, not for any tin he might win but because he knew that only he could do it. There were eight storm-battered ships out there beating their way back home, their crews half frozen, weak and unalert from altitude sickness – surely they counted for something. If Manfred had refused the mission someone else would have been prevailed upon to take it and then there could well be nine torched ships, almost two hundred men burned and on his conscience ... Why? Because Manfred knew he could save them; because the only way to do it was not to search for the scattered armada and warn them off, but to find the cruiser and sink her. A Zeppelin had never sunk a capital ship before; that was an unthinkable combat, rather like sending a snowman out to fight a dragon ... Still, given the present weather conditions, and the fact that he had a good idea where to find the cruiser, he had a chance.

At 10,000 feet Manfred ordered the steersman to shape a course along 'route black' towards England. No one in the car said anything and Manfred was composing himself to break the bad news when the chief shouted up the tubes that more cells were contaminated and suggested dumping the bombs to increase the static ceiling.

"Bombs!" Izzy howled, "but this is a drying out flight – not a mission!"

"We're going after that cruiser!" Manfred informed them and he called down the tubes to the chief that they wouldn't be height climbing today.

"The cells will superheat when the sun warms them up ... Leutnant Graatz, we have four 1,500 kilo bombs on the keel, also some incendiaries. Arm them and have them by for a quick drop."

Rudolf Graatz, the bombardier, climbed the ladder into the ship. Manfred dismissed the steersman and took the wheel. Now there was no one in the car except Jurgen by the elevator stand and Izzy pacing the duckboards furiously .

"He's gone mad," Izzy addressed the plotting stand. "Absolutely mad ... This was to be a drying out flight ... And what is it now? ... A real ascension day mission, I'll bet ... Break out the chestnuts lads – it's bonfire time."

Manfred swung the wheel two points to port and gazed at the glaring white fog below them. The ship was clear of the murk by a good two hundred feet, creaking and groaning as she dried out in the anaemic sunlight. He uncapped the speaking tubes and addressed the whole crew.

"Now hear this ... Now hear this ... This is the commander."

He gave them a simplified, optimistic précis of his orders, emphasizing the rescue element and omitting all reference to the fact that SL 17 had gone over onto the offensive. He recapped the tubes only to realize that Izzy hadn't been listening to a single word; he was still lecturing the plotting table.

"You heard what the chief said? The cells are contaminated. That means that they could explode spontaneously ... Besides, we have a basement instead of a ceiling, air temperature's high, the barometer's low and we have a full bomb load!" He went up to Manfred and stared hard at him. "It's her, isn't it?"

Manfred shook his head, but Izzy wouldn't believe him and turned on Jurgen.

"It's your bloody sister, Exec ... Promise him he can have her ... Invite him home with you ... Anything to make this crazy man take us home – can't you see, she's given him a throat ache."

"Couldn't do that old boy," Jurgen drawled. "Apart from the fact that he's as common as dirt, the Baron don't like fools."

Manfred struggled to contain his anger and called down the tubes:

"Telegraphs, obey bridge ... Mister Kornbloß, I will want a winch by the for'ard loading bay. Also a harness and a thousand metres of rope with a telephone pair spliced to it." Then he sent Izzy aloft to shoot the sun.

"You go in for disposable friends," Jurgen observed when they were alone.

"I need a good Nav."

"I would have done, Oberleutnant!"

"If you are as good as Izzy, then we will both have misjudged each other, Exec!"

"We?"

"Yes – you believe that I am a fool and I consider your navigation to be ahh, inadequate ... Will you still think me a fool when I sink this cruiser?"

"You didn't have to accept this mission, Oberleutnant. Life is valuable and you would throw all of ours away. You volunteered in effect ... That is foolishness."

"Förstmann didn't order me to attack the cruiser. But I know that this is the only way to save the Nordholtz fleet. I also know that I am the only commander, available at this moment, competent to assume this responsibility ... If the performance of my duty is foolishness – then I am a fool. There must be more to life than personal caution. The Nordholtz fleet might burn and we could save them ... Do not accuse me of arrogance – because then you will be a fool!"

"You believe that you have a responsibility to your fellow man, Oberleutnant?"

"Certainly – don't you?"

"Cain asked that question and God did not reply!" Jurgen pointed out.

"Then I will ... Keep us down, Mister. We're going to need all our lift."

Jurgen spun the elevator wheel to drive SL I7 down dynamically. She had been steadily climbing while the sun superheated the cells. Manfred examined the readouts; he must decide on a pressure height soon.

"Nothing is wasted, Oberleutnant, except life itself. Death is a myth – the ultimate disillusionment of the dissolute."

"And what about you, Number One? Are the aristocracy above fear?"

Jurgen considered the altimeter and didn't answer. Manfred called two warrant officers for'ard to take the wheels and beckoned von Lüth to join him at the plotting table.

"Our friends must be attached to the Harwich force ... So, given the conditions at sea, she must be lying, heaved to, here, here, or here ... Nowhere else is suitable."

Jurgen considered the chart and, after an annoyingly protracted wait, he nodded in agreement. "You have X–ray eyes, Oberleutnant – to see her through the fog?"

Manfred dropped onto the stand one of the blow-ups SL 17 had taken of the cruiser. Jurgen studied it and his face grew animated. "It is possible ..."

Manfred climbed into the ship and made his way along the

walkway towards the for'ard lookout's nest. There he compared sightings with Izzy and they agreed on their position. The view was breathtaking. The sun, now high in an unbelievably blue sky, warmed their faces while white hoar formed on the backs of their coats. Below them a swirling whiteness boiled slowly, sending drifting tendrils of mist up into the thundering propellers to be shredded along the rubberized after swims.

"Inspector, have you collected all the tickets?"

"This is no time for joking, Manfred." Izzy was sullen.

"Look, Iz ... This is no wild venture. I've studied it carefully. Besides, if everything is as I predict, if we are torched, then we'll be low enough to jump and close enough to shore to swim ... Quite bracing, this time of the year I'm told."

"Are you certain, Manfred?"

"Izzy, I wouldn't take you on an ascension day mission ... Don't you believe that?"

"Yes – but you'd condemn yourself to one."

"Think of the girls, Izzy ... There'll be so much tin handed out after this that your chest will look like a fruit salad, big gongs, little gongs ... And all the girls love a hero."

"They don't come to funerals though, Manfred."

Both men returned to the führer gondola and SL 17 began her cautious search of the islands off the German and Dutch coast.

The sun was setting and the fog thickening when SL 17 lurched and rolled gently to port. Carefully Manfred eased the ship round in lazy circles, marking the arc where the thermals made her buck, and the whole crew stared into the darkening mist below.

"Smoke on sta'bd bow," the tubes shrilled.

He had been right! The Englisch were using bad coal! The photograph had shown that. Even on the grainy blow-up the smoke and flame could be seen billowing from her three high stacks. Somewhere below them lay a ship, heaved to, but her fires hadn't been drawn; she was staining the mist high above her with eddies of soot. Of course her commander could hear the airship working the sky above him. But he couldn't see SL 17 any more than she could find him ... No need to panic or weigh anchor or draw fires.

"Ready Graatz? ... 'By Chief? ... Exec, 'by to roll the camera?"

A chorus of "Ayes" answered him and Manfred struggled into a padded greatcoat, stuffed a compass into his pocket and climbed up into the ship. In accordance with his instructions Jurgen steered the ship in a wider circle and brought her back towards the smoke stain, bringing her down to 1,500 feet dynamically. Zeitel stood by the ballast stand to drop everything, while Izzy manoeuvered himself into a strategic position for jumping by the ladder leading into the ship's hull. They strapped Manfred into the harness and lowered him out of the yawning loading hatch. Swinging clear over the icy mist, he checked the telephone and Graatz's booming voice answered him.

"Height 1,500 ... Estimated ground speed twenty knots ... 'By on command ... Bursting charges first. A.P. Delay fused ... Gott mit uns, Kapitän!"

Blocks squealed in protest as the winch plunged Manfred, twisting and yawing, into the clammy darkness. On a real Zeppelin he could have made the descent in a proper sky car where the drop could be accomplished from the safety of incredible height and the damn thing would be stable.

If the mission were to end in disaster – he'd draw most of it onto himself. But there was no time for fear or self doubt. Trying to establish a true compass bearing and, at the same time, compensate for the fact that he was swinging on the rope like a yo-yo, commanded all his attention. So much so that when the ghostly superstructure of the high bridged cruiser loomed out of the fog he nearly missed it.

"Port two degrees," he screamed into the field telephone. The rope shuddered spinning him furiously.

"Steer small damn you ... Steady ... Steady ... Bomben ... LOS! UP ...UP."

He saw the shadowy mass of the four huge bombs thicken in the whiteness above him. Everything seemed to have frozen to a crawl. There was a hissing of rain, more like a cloud burst, and icy water ballast drenched him. Then the harness bit into his chest and arm pits. The bombs, bigger and heavier than a man, slid past him. They hadn't fallen long enough to make the air scream.

His ship would surely be high enough and away to for'ard to escape the blast, but would *he*? If the enemy's horizontal armour were weaker than her vertical armour, then the force of the explosions would be channelled upwards and he'd be blown to pieces. But he had gambled on the ship being built to withstand drop shots, so its vertical armour would be weaker and its sides would be blown out.

He had been drawn over the angry glow of the for'ard funnel, and was still being pulled up and ahead by the rising ship and the gang on the winch, when he saw the silhouette of a bomb demolish the after smoke stack and plunge into the cruiser's engine room.

Manfred recovered consciousness over Borkum Island. His ears rang and blood still trickled from his nose, eyes and mouth.

"You'll live, "Jurgen decided.

"The camera ... "Manfred croaked.

"It's all there, Manfred." Izzy was euphoric. "We all saw it ... The whole ship came apart ... like a balloon bursting." Manfred rolled over and vomited bile streaked with blood.

They left him alone, sleeping in a hammock slung between

two flaccid ballast cells and von Lüth worked the ship back along 'route black' to Ahlhorn.

Fregattenkapitän zur See Förstmann was waiting in shed Aladin when the gangs hung SL 17 up. The deputy commander was livid with hours of anger and worry.

"Oberleutnant! ... Where have you been ... What have you done?" Then he saw Manfred, shaken, dirty and blood spattered, and he waved to his aide to assist him to the staff car. Jurgen handed the Kapitän the camera.

"Oberleutnant ... I hope for his sake, for all your sakes, there is something in this to justify this ... this mutiny!"

"Mutiny is a strong term, Kapitän Förstmann ... 'Criminal irresponsibility' ... or perhaps 'valour' might be more appropriate," Jurgen observed dryly.

"A doctor ... he needs a doctor," Izzy shouted .

"Mister Ißenquhart ... I can assure you that your commanding officer will receive complete attention!"

Shaved, dressed and feeling marginally human, although his body still ached all over from the terrible hammering it had received, and his brain still throbbed with the memory of orange fire, black smoke and flying plates and turrets, Manfred presented himself in Förstmann's office. The fleet commander's face was grim and there was no approval in his eyes.

"Well, what have you to say to me, Oberleutnant?"

"I hope the camera will be my log, Sir."

"It is ... You are guilty of the crime of initiative. You were ordered to alert the Nordholtz fleet of the danger. Instead you have severely damaged your command and have cost the Englanders a valuable new cruiser ... Well done Kapitänleutnant."

They had promoted him! All at once Manfred was elated, but why was Förstmann so stern?

"Normally Ka'leut, I should also be empowered to award

you a decoration ... But you know how the Kaiser feels about his British cousins ... You attacked without warning did you not?"

Manfred felt sick again. What good was promotion? He didn't need it – all he wanted was to see Halgerd again ... He still wasn't worthy ... Damn the Kaiser and his crazy outworn chivalry.

"But that cruiser torched our airships without warning, Sir!"

"I told his Imperial Highness that also." Förstmann's stern face cracked into a joyful grin. "And he agreed with me! Kapitän–leutnant zur See Manfred Burk you are commanded to attend a presentation ceremony at the Imperial Palace where Kaiser Wilhelm II will confer on you the '*Ordre pour le Mérite*', the highest award that Germany can confer on one of her bravest sons!"

The wine was thin and bitter; was that because they wouldn't waste good wine on a clod like him? Or was it that at the Imperial Palace they were waging the sternest war of all – the war against reality. Germany was losing the war, eating turnips, drinking ersatz wine and pinning medals on anyone who postponed the finish .

The Kaiser almost wept with emotion when he draped the Blue Max around Manfred's neck and everybody applauded and returned to their closed groups of false gaiety and sour wine. Manfred gulped his glass dry and strode deeper into the press of painted people. "Look at me!" the few grams of cheap metal and gaudy enamel called from his neck, but no one did – they had seen heroes come and die all too often.

He'd cured his 'throat ache', but at what price? Manfred knew that he had killed people before; he knew that every time he had ordered the bombs dropped. But this time it had been different. This time he had heard the terrified scream of the man in the cruiser's crow's-nest when he had seen Burk dangling in the fog over him. The navy estimated that the cruiser had had a crew of over six hundred men – there had been no survivors. All that death now hung around his neck, compressed into a little cross on a blue riband, the *Ordre pour le Mérite*, the Blue Max, and only he was aware of its true worth. Well, the ordeal would soon be over. The press had taken their photographs and been furnished with the prepared official text of an interview he had never given. Already the guests had forgotten him; he could leave as soon as the Kaiser and Kaiserin retired. Then it would be the Bodensee for him and Izzy for a glorious three weeks leave. That was the only redeeming factor in this whole depressing affair. He had been able to requisition a car and Izzy was working on the petrol.

Suddenly the Imperial Palace, everything, was overwhelmed, washed away in the agony of desire that wracked him. Halgerd was here, sitting beside von Dobberitz, two of a larger party, a fact confirmed by the half-filled glasses all around the table. The band had struck up a waltz and Albrecht had decided to sit it out. He could see Halgerd's satin shoe tapping to the music.

"Gräfin, would you honour me with this dance?" And she was in his arms before the astonished Albrecht could object.

"Uncommonly civil of you, Albrecht." Manfred had heard Jurgen use that line and had treasured it. "So glad you could come to my little 'do' ... Pity about the wine!" Delight flushed his face and ruined his dead pan delivery.

Albrecht von Knebel–Dobberitz choked on his indignation, but they were lost in the dance before he could protest. Halgerd laughed; it was obvious that she wanted to dance. Thank God he'd hardly touched the wine. He was able to waltz her across the ballroom with all the vigour and panache that the music demanded and they were both out of breath when it was over. It would have been perfection to enjoy the night air on a balcony but, even in the Imperial Palace, the blackout regulations had to be enforced. They slipped into a dim alcove on the far side of the ballroom. Halgerd's face was flushed and her eyes sparkled.

"Ohh, Manfred ... Did you know, Albrecht doesn't approve of the waltz?"

"Very proper,"Manfred agreed. "His legs might fall off ... I learned an Amerikanisch dance – the black bottom ... Now if the music were right."

"We would be sent home, in disgrace ... The Kaiser would be shocked." She rapped his knuckles gently with her card.

"But would you be shocked Gräfin?"

"No ... I love to dance ... Which would you prefer to be, Manfred, a great hero or a beautiful dancer?"

"One must be both to dance with the fair Gräfin!"

"You are exciting and you wear death prettily enough, Kapitän Harsch – but I am not a prize!"

"My medal? Yes, it is a tombstone of sorts ... which would be mine if I refused to wear it today ... But I promise you Gräfin, I do not rejoice in killing and would not kill if it could be otherwise. And you wrong me. Were you a prize, I would not have to seek your approval of me."

The orchestra struck up a march and he looked at her in invitation but she shook her head.

"I shouldn't have danced with you. My card is full. Albrecht will be most hurt?"

"How can you stand it? ... All these half people, their rituals – their deadness ... Outside in the world it is spring ... Come away with me to the Bodensee?"

It was only a hopeless wish expressed lightly, almost as a joke, so that it could be refused without shock. But her face became wistful. God ... von Lüth, the preposterous Albrecht, all of the Junkers set, were killing her soul and she knew it.

Hiding his excitement, he pressed his advantage.

"Do you know how to cast for trout? Which pools to wait by, and the streams to stalk them in? I have a four berth yacht ... and if you behave, I'll teach you how to take her, right into the wind ... And I promise ... I will ..."

"Will what?"

"Behave myself."

She looked at him questioningly and then the blood began to pound in his head as he saw the animation in her eyes. Everything in the room became tinged with red when she nodded.

From his vantage point in the darkness under the elms, Izzy stared in a despair of horror as the two figures walked purposefully across the starlit square to the aide's park. He was glad that they could not see him and struggled to control his facial muscles before leaving the car to direct them to it. Manfred was almost invisible in his night-blue cloak, but Halgerd, in her white evening gown, stood out like the 'fetch' of a warrior. That she was Manfred's 'death maiden' he was sure. The Taurlbourgs would avenge their honour, and probably do so in a manner that would make the sternest Medici reprisal seem a mild reprimand. What worried Izzy most was that their disapproval would be extended to include him.

Why had she done this to them? Certainly all Germany had gone mad and was engaged in one last fling, the subconscious, or in some cases premeditated, last free act before the slavery of Allied subjugation. It was, he decided, perhaps unfair to expect this spoilt aristocratic brat to behave any differently from the rest of the lemmings.

"Good man, Izzy," Burk slapped his friend's back. "Halgerd, this is my good friend and Navigator, Isador Ißenquhart – call him Izzy for short , it saves breath."

Izzy, terrified, bowed and clicked his heels correctly, "Gräfin von Taurlbourg!"

Oh Yahweh, when will this crazy girl come to her senses and start screaming Rape? But she wouldn't. There was something about her warmth that shocked him deeply. The child was a complete innocent ... How dare she trust anyone, any man, men, so completely!

"Lady, you must try to be patient with my poor demented friend. He has been aloft too long and his brains are addled by cold and height! ... Abducting the nobility's daughters ...Oh Yahweh , why couldn't I have a nice safe war in the trenches?"

Manfred and Halgerd laughed and he opened the back door for her.

Leaving Berlin was difficult; the car had to be driven without lights but, once in the country, it was easier.

"Will your mother object to having me?"Halgerd asked when Manfred explained that they would be staying with the Ißenquharts.

"Not if you convince her that my mad Kapitän has kidnapped you," Izzy muttered.

Sensing his hostility, Halgerd leaned back against the polished leather and stared out the window.

At once Izzy was apologetic, "She will force you to listen to all the woes and itemized misfortunes of our incredibly long list of relatives. Of course anything you tell her will be all over Friedrichshafen in no time. You won't have a shred of reputation left ... And be warned, what you do not tell Momma, she will invent."

"She sounds like a dear." Halgerd accepted his tacit gesture of friendship and leaned forward again. "My mother is like that, the family historian and racial memory."

"All the way back to Adam?" Izzy moaned.

"Oh much further!"

Both men laughed, but Manfred was struck by the way she said it. It had to be a joke, yet Halgerd sounded as though she had meant it.

"Couldn't I pretend to be Manfred's long lost sister?"

"What? Manfred is family to us all these years and only now has a sister?" Izzy laughed. "And even if you could convince Momma, how is the poor lady to sleep at night wondering how an Aryan princess had such a black eyed peasant for a brother?

... No it will be best to tell her the truth and throw yourself on her protection. That way we should be good for one week's peace. It should take her at least that long to come out of shock."

"Manfred, do you have money? We must stop somewhere, I need some clothes."

"Of course, Gräfin."

"No need." Izzy ran his eyes over Halgerd. She was absolutely gorgeous he decided. How did Manfred have such luck? He hadn't shown much interest in girls up to now, nor they in him. Izzy had wondered if his friend were retarded – but now! Manfred scowled at him and Izzy sighed and turned around.

"I have sisters – Sharon is about your size so we should be able to kit you up in something less ... ahh, classical."

The Mercedes cut down and across Germany towards Lake Constance, which the Germans call the Bodensee. They stopped at army depots three times for petrol. The car had been acquired legally, but not so the book of forged coupons Izzy waved under the staff sergeants' noses. While Izzy played the part of a harassed chauffeur, Manfred sat aloof in the back seat with Halgerd and condescended to sign the requisition forms when the tank was full. They stopped to stretch their legs and eat beer, bread and peasant sausage. Izzy phoned on ahead to warn Momma about Halgerd. His explanations began in casual tones that became ever more desperate as the conversation proceeded.

"Make the most of it," he hissed at Manfred when they were alone for a moment. "When her family find you the least you can expect is that they'll leave you with your plums in your top tunic pocket ... I'll help them if they offer me quarter!"

Evening was casting long shadows down the streets of Friedrichshafen when the car entered the driveway of the Ißenquhart household. It was a fine, old-fashioned town house whose previous owners had declined with the rise of industry and the people, like the Ißenquharts, who now controlled it. Izzy's mother, a big, plump middle-aged woman, was waiting for them at the door and looked like she had been hovering there since morning. A teenage boy and girl were playing croquet on the lawn and as soon as the car appeared they ran to it.

"Manfred, can Martha and I borrow the car? Peter and Lottie are throwing a party in Überlingen," Sammy, Izzy's youngest brother, shouted as he opened the door for Halgerd.

"Certainly – but there is only a little gasoline." Manfred could afford to be generous – it wasn't his car.

"Children, children ... Oh what it is to have children with such manners!" Frau Ißenquhart shouted, waving her hands like a conductor in a frenzy, then smothering Izzy to her generous bosom she wailed, "Manfred, such a thing to do. You are a terror. Papa says so and you took the poor child when she had no clothes on."

"Momma, this is Halgerd and she is dressed," Izzy said firmly.

"Yes, for the equator. Oh come with me my poor child and tell me what my wicked boys have done to you. Come into the house and I will show you Sharon's clothes ... Children!" She called to Martha and Sammy who were about to drive off, "Be sure to be back by one or your Papa will have indigestion." She waved her hands in eloquent despair. "Such a man with indigestion!"

"If you run out of gasoline, you'll have to push me back to Berlin," Manfred shouted after them.

"We've got plenty. Sammy sailed to Arbon for it ...We had to get food there anyway," Martha replied, then with a daring crash of gears the two teenagers were off. Halgerd, her face stern with the effort not to laugh, followed Momma into the house.

Papa Ißenquhart returned from his business in time for dinner. If Halgerd had hoped to use the stabilizing effect of the meal to establish some form of harmonious relationship with the family, she was disappointed.

Papa sat at the head of the table, complete with all the orthodox trimmings such as skull cap and prayers and proceeded to demolish a plate of roast pork.

"The pig that we have today did not exist in the time of Moses and therefore can't be an unclean animal. Conversely, the pig Moses knew is now extinct – so there are no more unclean beasts," he explained when he sensed Halgerd's amazement. Prior to the meal he had welcomed her into his household with the same protective concern as Momma, favouring Manfred and his son with disapproving glares.

At the table his displeasure became more specific. "I have been talking to Ruth's father ... Already he is celebrating the birthday of the third grandchild that he does not have! When are you going to marry her, you bum?"

Momma whispered to Halgerd that Ruth Hartstein was the daughter of one of Friedrichshafen's wealthiest families who were also in the cotton and linen business. "Such a beautiful girl," Momma sighed, but her voice lacked any conviction.

"Rich, fat and bad tempered – in that order," Manfred confided.

"But such a good match – for business," Momma insisted.

"There is plotting going on ..." Papa, who hadn't heard, but guessed, what they were saying, glared past the candles into the darkness at Momma 's end of the table.

"Such a man for plots," Momma protested. "We have a guest, Papa, who is here ... Is Ruth here?" she stared up and down the table, craning her neck in a heavy charade, searching for the non-existent Ruth, but Papa ignored her and glared at Izzy.

"Wait until the war is over, Papa ... We'll see what happens then ... Besides I might be killed ... Would that be fair to her?"

"Such a son!" Papa snorted and addressed the whole table. "I spend so much on your education that I cry at night when I think of the furs that your Momma has not! And for what? ... My son joins the Navy – does he become Kapitän of a fine ship? No, he is a navigator in an airborne gas oven. And what is a navigator? He is someone who says he knows where he is and thinks he knows where he is going – this is education? ... For this I spend my money. But when I find him a fine wife and her father's business does he hasten to comply with his besotted father's wishes? ... No, he will wait until the end of the war when everybody is ruined! Marry her now bum, while we still have substance! And if she is to be a widow she will have respect, and we will have grandchildren."

While father and son argued, Manfred, Halgerd, Momma and the rest of the family talked on generalities and the news coming across the Bodensee from Switzerland. But some of Izzy's and Papa's infighting leaked across, especially their urgency to get out of Germany.

"Are you really going?"Halgerd asked.

"Yes!" Momma nodded. "Oh, it will be dreadfully sad, all our friends and our business is here. But the other Germans don't want Jews and, as times grow harder, so does their hate. On Kurfürststraße there is a sign 'nicht fur Juden'. Such a thing, and it is only the beginning. They break our windows and paint hate on our walls! Such a thing, and I never went down Kurfürststraße anyway – the cobbles break my heels."

Halgerd changed the subject. Manfred realized that she was upset. He guessed that, being an aristocrat, she was under the illusion that her class set the behavioural code for the nation. Probably she felt in some way responsible for the harassment of the Ißenquharts.

"Don't think about it," he murmured to her out of earshot of the others. "The aristocracy is the ornament of a nation and can't be anything else, much less its conscience. Swine will always be pigs for all the jewels you stud their hide with."

"You are wise, Kapitän Harsch?" she asked. "Does wisdom make you severe?"

"Perhaps; the more you expect from people, the more they fail!"

"I do hope Sammy and Martha are alright ... Such a drive to Überlingen on their own! ... Suppose there is an accident, a bombing ... Oh, Manfred you should never have let them take your car! You know there will be such speeding ..." Momma complained, breaking the thin thread Manfred and Halgerd had woven between them. Such contacts were rare and had to be spontaneous. Manfred had learned this, along with the value of imperturbable patience. He would not force contact – it would come again.

Three glorious weeks of sunny spring days fled like minutes. By day, Manfred and Halgerd sailed his seven tonner on the Bodensee under constant surveillance from Momma's ubiquitous kin. Neither were they ever alone when they scaled the steep Swiss hills to find small, peaceful villages where wine, bread and cheese were still plentiful. Not that Momma could dominate the hills as readily as she did the lakeside, but her presence was always in the offing, usually in the form of some youthful cousin who 'just happened' to be in the vicinity.

Halgerd affected total unawareness of this benign tyranny and concentrated on enjoying herself. She proved to be an able student and in no time at all she could sail Manfred's yacht on her own.

Manfred's acceptance of this enforced chaperonage was mixed. On the one hand he was glad of it for Halgerd's sake; it had never been his intention that she should be compromised. In Berlin it hadn't occurred to him that he might be harming her. On the other hand he was desperately in love, couldn't accept that they could do anything that was not right and might, had they been alone, have ruined everything.

Apart from being correct, Momma's army was a nuisance. What irritated him most were the other, studiously engrossed, anglers who materialized on either bank every time he tried to teach Halgerd how to cast. She didn't seem to notice them, but it was lucky for them that they didn't laugh at her mistakes. Teaching her to fish had been harder than teaching her to sail, but his patience was rewarded. On their last fishing trip she landed a respectable trout with a fly they had made the night before. The making of that fly should have been a time of togetherness, but instead it had worn Manfred's patience dreadfully. All through the hours that he had helped Halgerd manipulate the silk thread, the bits of oiled wool and the bright feathers around the hook, a red-eyed, jaded Momma had kept up an unbroken commentary about Papa's indigestion and other matters of equal moment. Manfred wondered if Momma slept on the floor outside Halgerd's door – just in case there might be sleepwalkers around.

It had been the only night where they might have been alone together. Usually the whole family played bridge, or skat, until bedtime, and every Sunday night there was a party. As the Ißenquharts had given theirs earlier in the year, the ones Manfred and Halgerd attended were all at friends' houses. The young men adored her and Halgerd spent most of these parties dancing to the point of exhaustion.

Manfred had never wanted to be other than correct, but regretted that they could never be intimate. Life had been too hard for him to be casual about trust. Seduction had not been his intention; he wanted acceptance, not conquest. He tended to reflect the attitude of his surroundings. So, whereas in the mess at Ahlhorn he cursed and drank as freely as the others, with Halgerd he was as circumspect as she expected him to be. She, on her part, radiated an aura which encouraged others to wish to be well thought of by her. Manfred had recognized this gift in successful commanders and hoped that he had it too. At any rate he never did anything to strain the gentle relationship they had built up together and she never encouraged him to.

The Ißenquhart family assembled in its entirety to say "Auf Weidersehen" when the holiday was over. Momma wept copiously, mangling handkerchiefs and moaning, "Such a thing ... such a thing ..."

Papa, who awarded them the rare high honour of staying home from work, was dry eyed, but his voice trembled. Manfred, Izzy and Halgerd said their good byes and left, nostalgia souring the perfect holiday with the acrid dust of the road.

At Bremen, Manfred put Halgerd into a first class compartment and drew the window tight against the clots of soot and clouds of steam. He wanted desperately to say or do something that would impress her eternally, but he could think of nothing that wasn't stupid or weak. He couldn't even ask if they would meet again because 'if' was not a word in Kapitän Harsch's vocabulary. Instead he left the carriage, bought a huge bouquet of white camelias, ran back, gave them to her and kissed her.

"The last time you kissed me, it was you who had to board the train," she said.

"Farewell, Princess ... We are all on standby. There is to be a major push against London, soon ... But I will return."

"Wear this in battle, for me!" She plucked out one of the flowers and placed it in his buttonhole. " ... Manfred, I want to thank you for the most wonderful holiday ... "

"Don't thank me; thank yourself! You enjoyed it. No holiday, nothing, can make you enjoy it. That is most important. There is only one life – it is not for wasting ... Good bye Halgard and thank you for enjoying!" He strode out of the car and stood on the platform until the train crawled out of the station.

The steam was grey with soot, some of it lodged in the camelia – he could never press it now. Automatically Manfred removed his cap and ran the soot off its peak with his thumb. He was about to put it on again when agony cut him from check to ear followed by the sharp crack of the whip.

"Burk! ... I will have you horsewhipped ... You scoundrel!" Spittle wet the edge of Albrecht, Graf von Knebel-Dobberitz's thin lips as he screamed.

Manfred might have laughed at the Count if he weren't rigid with pain and the effort not to show it. Albrecht slapped the riding crop against his high leather boots. Manfred could have killed him, easily, but he was flanked by two burly giants. It was no contest but Manfred managed to hit the two of them before being overpowered and winded by several punches to the stomach.

"Over that baggage," Albrecht commanded. "Bend him over those trunks." He cracked the whip again in hungry anticipation.

"That will be quite enough, Dobberitz!" a cold voice pronounced. The modulation was even and low but the tone was implacable.

Burk felt the hands pinning him over the trunks and mail sacks loosen and he flung them off. The men grabbed for him again but von Lüth rapped their hands away with a silver chased cane.

"Jurgen? ... He must be flogged .. .You must see that ... Look at what he did to your sister!"

"Am I forced to observe what you choose to see? ... You presume too much Dobberitz!" Von Lüth was caustic. "I think you had best leave, Albrecht ... and take this rabble with you!"

Von Dobberitz, followed by his men, left the station, his whip trailing as though it had been used on his own person.

"I suppose, this 'fool', should thank you for his rescue," Burk began, stiff with formality, but Jurgen gestured in dismissal.

"I misjudged you, Burk. No 'fool' cures a throat ache with the Blue Max. But you are not wearing it now? ... Yes ... I think the Baron will enjoy you, Herr Ka'leut ."

"Von Dobberitz thinks ... Von Lüth, I assure you that my conduct with your sister was at all times, ahh ... correct."

"Apart from her abduction from the palace?" Jurgen eyed him expressionlessly. Manfred became stubborn. Anything he might say to mitigate his behaviour would only harm his princess. He picked up his cap, dusted it and turned to go.

"Be under no illusions, Herr Kapitän-leutnant. You were watched ... at all times. And that is why you are still alive ... You see, Kapitän-leutnant, we are all uncommonly fond of her."

Was it true? Had they had him and Halgerd under surveillance? Manfred decided that it must be so. God alone knew what kind of resources a family as rich as the Taurlbourgs could command. But if they had known where Halgerd was, why hadn't they taken her away? And there was no point in assuring Jurgen that he loved Halgerd far more than anyone as cold as he could.

He should leave now and say nothing, but that might imply submission. Carefully he set his cap straight on his head and looked Jurgen in the eye. "'Kapitän-leutnant zur See', if you must be formal, Exec. But there is no need for rank off ship. Only the mission obliges respect."

"True! But you see Manfred, I must respect you!" Burk narrowed his eyes to hide his surprise and Jurgen managed a wintry smile. "Oh I don't like you Manfred ... Not yet. But I do respect you!"

Half an hour later, when Bob had gone back to sleep, Susan still pondered over this latest dream. One thing was certain: whatever was causing them wasn't some object of association. Apart from the clothes he had stood in, and his briefcase, Bob had brought nothing with him ... Or had he?

She got out of bed carefully and searched his uniform for his briefcase keys. There was nothing unusual in it, just some files on *Firedrake* and a short, forty-core computer loom. She stared at the multicoloured harness for a moment, wondering why he needed to carry it around with him. Perhaps it was a security measure? Its removal would immobilize a computer as surely as would removing the distributor cap from a car.

Seven

God not only plays dice but also sometimes throws them where they cannot be seen.

S. W. Hawking

"Quite impressive, I must say! You're doing a good job here, Bob!" General Gerry Bascombe sounded as though he meant it – but then Bascombe's motto was that he meant everything he said.

The tour was going well. The Press were shooting metres of film and they, and the representatives from the Senatorial funding committee, were quite obviously awed by the Zeppelin. That was natural when the size of the ship was considered. Bob had stressed this at the beginning of the tour.

"Ladies and Gentlemen, if you laid out three Boeing 747 Jumbo jets end to end – the line would still fit inside this ship comfortably."

It didn't seem right in these days of jumbo jets and space shuttles that, way back in grandpappy's time, they were putting even bigger things into the air. Of course the whole operation had been terribly expensive. The helium gas alone had run into millions of dollars. It had required kilometres of mirror polythene to cover the hull, 'silver paper' the men called it and in one respect they were right: weight for weight, the stuff was as expensive as silver. But it was a better envelope than the old doped cotton; it was stronger, lighter, weatherproof and sufficiently elastic not to tear when the rings were stressed. There was also the onboard computer and the sixteen lift bags moulded from hydrogen-impervious polystyrene that had to be made in the laboratory because it hadn't yet been put on the market for mass production. Those gas cells might yet prove to be the single most costly item of all. And these were only the hors d'oeuvre on the menu of expenses.

Congress had forced Project Firedrake onto the Army, but the Senate approved the cash and both houses were answerable to their employers – the people. Hopefully this tour would inspire the public by impressing their representatives – the press and the senators. Bob examined the sea of upturned faces, happy faces and sore necks, and he still wasn't happy. *Firedrake* would have both money and time in her favour – but that wasn't nearly enough.

Those who forget their history are condemned to relive it. Whoever had said that had had this situation in mind, Bob thought. Rigid airships were a German serendipity; to everyone else they were a disaster. The only American airship that had an accident-free record, a long life that ended in her being broken up for scrap rather than murdering her crew, had been the *Los Angeles*. *Los Angeles*, ZR–3 or, to be more accurate, the LZ–126, had been built by the Luftschiffbau, Friedrichshafen, for the US Navy and flown to America way back in 1924. The German crew had trained her new owners well and she flew for the Navy until she was scrapped in 1940.

Project Firedrake should have been given to the Zeppelin Metallwerke Friedrichshafen, Bob decided privately. They still had the skills – but where, in the whole world, were they going to find a commander for *Firedrake*? Taking her aloft was going to prove one thing – you could not reduce courage and art to a computer programme.

"Will the ship be ready for the games?" a voice called and Bob answered without his usual caution.

"Certainly – if we can find a crew and a commander!"

"That's no problem ... Airships are still in use," A press man shouted back.

With Bascombe's eyes boring into the back of his neck Bob explained that rigid dirigibles, especially the high altitude 'super Zeppelin', weren't in the same league as the Goodyear Blimp or the semi-rigid types currently in use.

Would anyone notice the third wheel? Bob prayed for an easy time – thanking God there were no experts present. He led the group down the central walkway, dispersing them in small units to look over the six engine cars and the underslung command gondola. Everyone was awed by the cathedral of parted, deflated, gas cells, alloy rings, longitudinals and stays that yawned above them. The upper envelope was painted red on the inside to protect the crew from ultraviolet at height. It added a hellish dimension to the ship's interior and Bob was amused by the hush that came over the tour.

There was a bad moment in engine nacelle five, when a press man asked what had happened to the original motors. Bob had been explaining the advantages of the new lightweight diesels over the World War One MBIVa's.

"What happened to the original engines, Major? I'd sure like to see one of them!"

This time Bob was on his guard and didn't blurt out that these were the original engines, or rather carefully tooled replicas of the sea-ruined motors.

"Scrapped I'm afraid ... Any more questions?"

There were none, so they returned to the command car. They ignored the marvellous technology of the flight computer and the incongruous, functionless steering stand routed midships into it; but they went into ecstasies over the maze of quaint speaking tubes, control lines and brass instrumentation. These were all superseded by the computer, but had been installed as manual fail safes. A Senator wanted duplicates of the steering wheels made as chandeliers. Others admired the binnacle and the Görz bombsight. And then a reporter, whose neck was less tired from straining into the vaulted heights, almost blew the whole thing up.

"Hey! ... I thought this was the real thing ... a refitted war Zeppelin!"

"It is," Bob assured him. "The frame is the original. We believe she is LZ 115 and was commissioned into the German Navy as L 73."

But the reporter was staring at the lintel beam to the rear of the gondola.

"It is the real thing!"Bascombe pronounced and then he too stared at the brass lie.

It was the ship's commissioning plate. On the surface it looked genuine since it was still scored from the barnacles and other crustaceans that had adhered to it on the sea bed. Bob stared at it in horror. It just had to be an elaborate joke. The brass plate was screwed into its mount just over the door struts leading to the ladder, but why hadn't he, hadn't anyone, seen it before?

"A joke, ladies and gentlemen – or rather a sneak attempt to stake a claim! ... Afterall they are refitting this ship and building prototypes of their own... And, in a way, you could say she's been built twice!" Bob was at his most convincing, the Press and the Senators were satisfied, but *he* wasn't and neither was Bascombe.

"I know that the ship came up in bits, Bob, thousands of bits. And I know that you couldn't vet them all – but you should have been there for this one ... Every ship built gets a plate ... Damn it, most of them are cast before the keel is even laid."

Bascombe was sweet reasonableness itself. His office

was comfortable and the martini shaken just right. But Bob was still shaking inside. All the 'ifs' had been reduced to two impossibilities, one of which must be true, and both of them incredible.

One: way back in 1917 the Germans had a technology that the USA didn't have a year ago.

Two: the ship, *Firedrake*, had been built, so to speak, today, found yesterday and flown on a mission the day before yesterday.

If the latter alternative were true, it meant that a missile could be detonated over a target before that missile was even built. Bascombe was as aware of the possibilities as Bob was and Bob couldn't understand why the General was so enthusiastic. Surely this was the dawn of the age of horror where logic and cause and effect, causality, had no meaning any more. He had to stop thinking about this now; there was a more immediate problem – his own fall from grace. He had been so worried about the third wheel that he had overlooked the obvious.

Someone had installed a lintel with the ship's commissioning plate. The results from the lab had come in an hour ago: the plate was as old as the ship. So how could a ship, supposed to have been built by the Luftschiffbau Friedrichshafen over sixty years ago, bear the legend 'LOCKHEED CORPORATION USA'?

A bitter anger choked Bob as he read the communiqué. There was a plum job going back home, the kind of post he'd been angling for all his life and he couldn't apply for it. The commanding officer of the Providence barracks had been wasted in an accident on the firing range and his position was up for grabs. He was in line for it too; that was his division andhe was just the right rank. It was all he had ever wanted, a secure post back home. There was only one snag – *Firedrake.* Sure, he could apply, but they'd never appoint a CO who couldn't take up his duties immediately; neither could he resign from *Firedrake* – quitters didn't get promoted. Could Bascombe help him? Bob couldn't decide which the General would like most – his crawling or turning him down. To hell with pride – he must ask Bascombe anyway.

The General hadn't arrived at his office yet, but he had left instructions with his secretary and she led Bob inside, gave him the file the General had mentioned and retired to the outer office.

Bob was tired and looked it. Normally he carried his impeccable uniform with pride, but today it felt a size too large. He felt like a lobster that has just shed its shell, awkward, timorous, straining to fill its new carapace. He opened the file. Inside was a folder full of almost blank forms. It was a personnel file but, so far, no details had been filled in except for 'Command/s'. Under that column Bascombe had had typed *Graf Zeppelin II.* Pinned onto that form was a sheet with twenty names, all German. Fifth from the bottom was a Hauptstürmführer SS Burk.

Manfred?

What a high kite to fly! Certainly *Graf Zeppelin II* was the last Zeppelin Germany ever built, if it had ever been built. Her predecessors, *Graf Zeppelin I* and the wreckage of the *Hindenburg* had been melted down for bombers by the Luftwaffe. Besides, *Firedrake* had been a wreck long before the Second World War. But what if the dating were wrong – was there some chemical in the mud, or the water, that made the New York Zep seem older than she really was? That might be part of the answer. Perhaps the Nazis had planted their last airship off Long Island just before, or in the early stages of, the War – but that still didn't explain *Firedrake*'s ultra-modern technology. If Hitler's scientists had been that good Germany would have won the war!

Was there any way he could line up that post in Providence? What if he fixed it so that Bascombe had him transferred off the Project? No, that would be worse than quitting. And he'd get himself the boot if he let his mind wander like this. Sadly, Bob shelved his ambition and concentrated on the file.

Blank pages: the folder was an information desert! He flipped through the virgin forms until he found another with typing on it. It was a brief footnote to the effect that *Graf Zeppelin II*, i.e. LZ 130, had never entered service in the Deutsche Zeppelin Reederei, but it had been seen aloft off the coast of England in late 1938, testing that country's radar defences.

There was nothing else, except a memo about her probable commanders 'See note at head of personnel file!' Bob flipped back to the list of names. After each name were the letters 'C.D.' and after others 'P.D.', followed in each case by a seven figure row of numbers. 'C.D.' stood for 'confirmed dead' and 'P.D.' was 'presumed dead'; the numbers were a file code for the source of that information.

Burk was 'C.D.' Bob carefully copied out the file code into his notebook. He sat back in the leather-slung chair, the file still on his lap. It was ironic that, despite all the resources available to Bascombe, Susan had beaten him to the real Manfred Burk. But then the General would have used method and wouldn't have had Bob's dreams to draw on.

It was unfair to denigrate Susan and her 'female logic'. It had produced better results than his 'male method'. Thought was a relatively new field for men. Until the beginning of this century everything had been controlled by force and ritual, two systems that had always obtained against women who had only their minds to fall back on. Was that what feminine intuition really was? The super-efficient process of millions of years of thinking? Susan had found Burk simply by asking Bob the day, and the date, he had been awarded the *Ordre pour le Mérite* – the 24th of April 1917. Twelve hours later she had photocopied the relevant page from the next day's issue of the *Cologne Gazette*. Considering the age of the paper and the poor quality of newspaper photographs of the day, the photograph of the awarding ceremony was quite good.

Susan had been quite taken by the Manfred in the photo. He looked 'so brave and stern'. Every line of him suggested 'strength and indomitable will'. There was a 'wry touch to his mouth that suggested humour', etc

Bob didn't spoil him for her by pointing out that it wouldn't take a giant to stand tall over the crippled, weary Kaiser. And if he told her that Burk's erect posture was nothing more than a heroic struggle against a persistent itch, she would have accused him of being jealous. Burk had been brave, but a committed Aryan never. It had been his tragedy to have been a man of belief in an age of ritual.

Who was this Burk, Bascombe had dug up? Another man certainly. It was a very common German name. Bob stared out the window at the one and only tree in the courtyard. Its leaves were green now, not the pale elfin green of the spring, but the darker, dust weary green of high summer. What would that tree be like come fall? Nothing like the glory of a New England tree! Suddenly he was a boy again, kicking his way through a treasure house of gold and red leaves, fogging the cold air with white clouds of his own breath.

What was he doing here? New England was his home. His soul was held hostage there and would never be released to him no matter where he went. He was an ordinary, not very imaginative man who had been born in, and pledged to, a magic land. The only moderate thing about New England was her people. Colour, splendour, they were for the land – not for her sons. Even his ambition was drab!

He knew that his soul would never be satisfied by, nor allow him anything more exciting than, contentment in life and even that must elude him unless he went home. How long would Susan and he have together?

For an instant he saw everything clearly – saw, but not for long enough to understand. It was one of those brilliant flashes of revelation that flare unbidden only to die before comprehension. For in that instant he saw Susan and, while he started with wonder, the glimpse was gone. And he realized then, with fading certainty, that for everybody in the world there was only self, self and shadows ... And every self wandered through the shades seeking the one to free self from the chains of loneliness... Perhaps the lucky might meet, might comfort each other, try to reach each other through the walls of their prisons, never to succeed, and yet only fail when the will to try did! Was Susan getting anything out of their relationship at all? ... Or did she need anything? Men might rule the world but only women were at home in it.

The door slid open and Bascombe entered the room.

"Good morning Bob!"Bascombe waited for Bob to stand up before continuing, "Sit! No need to be formal here!"

A dangerous man Bob thought, more so because the days when 'the Army let the politicians do the thinking and we do the soldiering' were long past. Bascombe was at all times well informed, fast thinking and predatory and, like all his type, he enjoyed power and the homage paid to same. As a feudal lord, he would have been neither good nor pious, but he would have been fair, after a polemic fashion. Bob was sufficiently awed by him for his respect to show. And the General loved him for it.

"Well, you've seen the file. What do you think?"

"It is possible, Sir," Bob chose his words carefully. "It is possible that what we have salvaged from Manhattan Sound is the wreckage of *Graf Zeppelin II*. However, Sir, I suggest that's not likely ... For one thing the *Graf* was a much bigger ship than the one we've got. Also, it was built too late."

"True ... But suppose they had built a *Graf Zeppelin III*? It would have been smaller because of the shortages. The Nazis failed when they tried to land agents on US soil from U-Boats! As for the dating – they've probably overestimated *Firedrake*'s age."

It was a possibility, Bob thought. But they would never prove it. The vast majority of Hitler's mad schemes had been burnt. And if Germany had wanted to land agents in America he couldn't have devised a madder method. On a radar screen a Zeppelin would stand out like an elephant in a pen of hogs. America knew that Hitler had nothing he could throw at them from the air. And if Hitler had known that we knew that ... Besides, he had used a scheme, just as mad as this, to successfully break the German fleet out of Brest, up the channel, right under the British guns and home! No ... It couldn't be a World War Two Zeppelin. Dating had put the Long Island Zep as older than that ... Besides, Göring had torched the *Hindenburg* and would never have sanctioned the building of another Zeppelin. Bob looked at Bascombe and experienced a twinge of sympathy.

His superior was grappling with a series of insane mysteries and trying to arrive at a sane conclusion. Bob knew that he himself would never have to consciously work out a philosophy to protect his own sanity. He would never need one. In this outer world of chaos anything could happen but, because New England was stable, chaos couldn't touch him. A man could be objective in hell if his heart told him that 'his' universe was safe. He felt quite objective about *Firedrake*. His orders had been to 'reconstruct the wreckage of an airship'. He had done so – efficiently.

Yet nothing could still the sense of wonder and the excitement. *Firedrake* had been in the mud off Long Island for some time before the end of World War One. Yet the date of her commissioning plate indicated that Lockheed had cast it sometime in the 1980s. A joke of course! Except that every feature of the ship insisted that it must be so. The beryllium alloy frame wasn't available sixty years ago and yet that frame, and everything else, had been dated as having lain in the water for at least that many years.

The wreck should have been a pure skeleton with no trace of her cotton envelope nor the ballonets – the lift cells made from membranes of cattle stomachs – remaining. But the wreck had been salvaged with her polythene envelope and polystyrene cells intact, if ruptured. So good had the retentive properties of the ballonets been that they still contained some of the original lift gas – helium.

"Any results on the Bari inquiry, Gerry?"

"No. The Russians are interested too ... Wish to embarrass us with our past sins ... But if the joker pretending to be 'Death' can't be traced to us, they won't find him ... Forget it, Bob. *Firedrake* is not an intricate Red Middle game – they're just as interested to know what's going on as we are."

"But it must be, Gerry! Otherwise there are only two alternatives. Either the Germans built *Firedrake* in the years 1916 or 1917. Or else Lockheed built it recently and sent it on a time trip – back into yesterday."

Bascombe grinned at Bob and shook his head. "Know anything about QED, Bob?"

"Euclid?"

"No, quantum electromagnetic dynamics ... New physics. 'Use it to explain why the universe works ... *Why* mind you. Not how!" The General looked at Bob, but the latter was only barely keeping up. Bascombe was groping in the dark too. Certainly he was beginning to see a light, but since he couldn't see it clearly there was no way he could describe it to Bob.

"It's not my field at all." Bascombe walked to the window, clasped his hands behind his back, drew himself erect and stared out across the city. "QED suggests that anything, and I mean *anything*, 'can' happen ... And what is wonderful is not when an effect *is*, but rather when it is *not* ... All our science, our philosophy, is based on the assumption of causality, that an effect may only be realized *after* the cause ... But we also know that this may not be so; for example – in the vicinity of a black hole. We also suspect that our universe is, in effect, sandwiched between two black holes – those within our universe and the cosmic one inside which our universe is contained."

"Curiouser and curiouser," Bob thought, but then the General wouldn't have been impressed by Lewis Carrol or Alice.

"There is 'Rainbow' ... or is it 'Mirage'?" Bascombe continued, "a project to isolate material from the universe ... The idea being to defeat radar interception of interdictive action on our part. The project is an application of the unified field theory. Work on it started in Philadelphia in the early 1940s, but 'Manhattan' got priority. It's still being kicked around ... Now maybe, just maybe, we've got us a rogue side effect in *Firedrake* ... Trouble is they've buried 'Rainbow' so deep we'll never know."

Bob digested this theory for what he considered to be a decent interval then he picked up the list of names from the table.

"Any luck?"

Bascombe looked at the list and shook his head. "Doesn't seem to be any real Zeppelin commanders left!"

"How will we ever get *Firedrake* off the ground?"

"We've plenty of balloonists and semi-rigid pilots around."

Bob didn't like it. *Firedrake* wouldn't burn a crew to death, not filled with helium. But then neither did *Akron* and she killed all but two of her crew of seventy-six. He tried to sound casual. "What about this man Burk?"

"He's dead, confirmed by Moscow ... How come you picked him, Bob?"

"Common German name." Bob tried to sound disinterested.

"How do you know they've fingered the right one?"

Bascombe shrugged and considered the list. "It's possible ... Get on to it then Bob ... 'Be quite something if you could find him! But remember he was SS so he's certain to be in deep cover."

Eight

The English are now in terror of Zeppelins, perhaps not without reason. I contend here for the standpoint of 'an eye for an eye' but I am not in favour offrightfulness. Also the indiscriminate dropping of bombs is wrong!

GRAND ADMIRAL ALFRED VON TIRPITZ
18–11–1914

"You are certain, Nav? This is London!" Von Lüth shook with fatigue but his voice was as acerbic as ever.

"There's the Thames!" Izzy pointed down to the winding, pearl river below. There was no moon and the sky was mottled with cloud but, here and there, enough stars lit the coal black depths to paint the waters silver.

"That bend marks the eastern boundary of the target area ... They'll confirm that for you soon ... That bank's crawling with cannon."

"Berlin has a river too, Nav. 'Black cigars' all round if we bombed the Kaiser!"

"Willi would understand."

Jurgen left the plotting table and joined Manfred for'ard by the celluloid windows of the 'führer gondola'.

"Are we late?"

Manfred pointed to the calm blackness underneath. It told everything. Eight Luftschiffe had set out from various bases, five from Ahlhorn, the others from various army bases further down the coast. They had been supposed to rendezvous over London and swamp the city and its defences with fire and a blanket attack. They were alone – the others hadn't arrived. Had Burk been late the view below would have resembled a fireworks factory ablaze.

"Lost in the lower stratosphere," Jurgen surmised.

Burk nodded. The fleet of airships had kept their stations fairly well until they were near the coast. At that point Burk had had to leave von Endrath and the others to skirt a localized thunderhead. Those of the armada which were modern 'height climbers' could rise above the disturbance. Beating against a stiff nor'easterly, Manfred had steered his obsolete command around the turbulence and under the massing battlements of cloud over the coast well to the north of London.

Despite the fact that all four Maybach HSLus were delivering maximum thrust, his 180-metre long command was underpowered and Burk had been afraid of being late for the circus. But no haste could override caution. The city must be stalked, struck and fled. Otherwise the fire would be over London and not in it.

Once in a position where he estimated that the wind would carry him over the targets, Manfred rose to 10,000 feet, his ceiling with the bomb load, and closed down the engines. The air was warm and humid so lift conditions were poor, but there was a fifty-knot wind to sweep the twenty-metre diameter cigar of plywood, cotton and explosively flammable hydrogen silently over the city. But now what? Was he to drift past his target and out to sea? Or must he rouse the London defences by trying to keep station over the targets with his noisy engines and wait for the others?

"'By Bombardier ... 'By motors... De-clutch generators ... Aerial, up!" he ordered.

What should he do? The whole purpose of the raid was to start so many fires in the city below as to swamp their fire-fighting resources. If he pressed an attack on his own he would achieve nothing more than destruction of property and the senseless death of many civilians. London would be angered, not hurt – and there would be a full-scale reception committee from the RAC for the other airships when, and if, they materialized.

The best thing would be to show 'a proper caution' and return to Ahlhorn with his bomb load. That would be accepted as correct behaviour in commanders of the aristocracy, whose valour was hereditary. In his case, there was every danger that his caution might be construed as 'cowardice in the face of the enemy'.

Another alternative was to dump his bomb load over Hampstead Heath and report, truthfully, that he had left England ablaze. The weather had been dry and the turf should burn well; the camera would bear that out. It was well known that many commanders who had been decorated for striking terror in the hearts of the English, had confined their 'frightfulness' to the fish or the heath ... In all probability, that was what the rest of the armada was doing right now.

"Bombs armed and 'by,"Graatz called.

"Gun crews 'by!"

"Motors two and four 'by!"

"One and three 'by!"

The voices wailed down the tubes and the engine telegraphs trembled at 'stop'. There was a loud thud and the weight attached to the end of the trailing antenna was stowed in its niche under the gondola's duck boards.

"Our orders are clear and the targets specific ... If von

Endrath and the others chose to dawdle ... let them haul their own chestnuts out of the fire," von Lüth whispered to him.

"Sorry Jurgen, it's not on ... If the strategy cannot be realized then the tactics must be shelved!" Manfred uncapped the speaking tubes and whistled down them to get attention.

"Meine Herren ... We have arrived, but the others have not! We must return."

The whole ship seemed to creak in dismay, or was it relief.

"Luftschiff three points to port," the call came from engine nacelle four and was almost drowned by the gale howling through the open car.

"My God! ... What is that fool doing?" von Lüth shouted in alarm. Manfred joined him by the window and looked up.

"Down man, look down ... The clown must be scraping the roofs."

"Oh, no!" Manfred groaned.

He saw the ship now and the London defences became aware of it too. The black night exploded into a thundering day of brilliant searchlights and roaring flak. The ship was about half a mile away and Jurgen's estimation of its height was exaggerated. It held station at about 3,000 feet, point blank range for the city's AA, sauntering casually over the roof tops, loosing bombs in haphazard clusters. There was going to be a bonfire after all!

"Where does he think he is – on manoeuvres?" von Lüth screamed in anxiety. "Up, up, you crazy sod ... Get up before you roast!"

"He can't,"Manfred whispered in despair. He collapsed his telescope and turned into the car. "It's a Schütte-Lanz, type 'e', like us ... Army. It's doped green, regular Army colours... The poor bastards aren't crazy. They're drifting, stopped with no power. I could see all four screws – stopped dead."

"Why don't they drop everything and climb statically?" Jurgen shouted. "Why the ridiculous bomb drop?"

"They are trying to loose ballast. But they must have been hit ... They are off loading unfused bombs – manually. That's why the drop is erratic, they are trying to avoid detection ... They must be leaking severely, because they're only holding height ... It' s only a matter of time before they're torched," Manfred whispered. A cold hand squeezed his heart and froze his stomach.

Schramm's crew, screaming, falling, burning, broke through the mental barrier he had walled them up behind. No! There must be a rescue!

"Down to 6,000 ... Bomb run, begin ... Herr Graatz, sights for ground speed eight three, height 3,000." It was suicide to close with the city at this height, virtual ground level. But he had to draw fire from the crippled Army ship. So far, the London defences were only aware that there was a ship above them; they hadn't found it yet. When they found SL 17, they'd be occupied – for a while.

"This is it, Meine Herren ... Gott hilf uns im krieg ... Full ahead all."

The motors exploded into life, drowning the clang of the telegraphs, and the ship trembled as she plunged down and across the black city.

A few seconds later the air became a field of arc light. Huge stalks of brilliance sprang from the ground to spear the clouds. The London defences were getting better with each raid, Manfred thought. He had surprised them, but their reflexes were instant. Almost at once the artillery opened up, firing blindly towards the noise above them. That would be a help; it would be some time before the searchlight armers on the ground could distinguish SL 17 from the clouds and only then would the ground fire become accurate. In the meantime the noise of the guns would camouflage that of his motors.

"We're coming in over the docks," Jurgen shouted. "They've found us!"

Searchlights raked the ship and everyone in the command car, except Graatz who was glued to the bombsight ocular, was blinded. The lights swept on aft of the ship, stopped, found her again and locked on. From there on, as SL 17 plunged down to 3,000 feet, she seemed to walk across the city on long legs of light. The thunder of the artillery barrage crescendoed and the nearer misses could be heard by everybody. Once or twice there was a tearing sound as the envelope was ripped and everybody's heart stopped.

"Flares ... Kanone, bear on those lights!" Burk shouted.

But, even as the searchlights found them, their armers were blinded by a hail of magnesium flares. The Spandaus in all gondolas and the look-out nests opened up and some of the fierce beams quenched in explosions of red hot glass.

"Ranging drops!"Graatz shouted. He and Burk squinted down the Zeiss ocular at the puffs of smoke from the ground and set the cross hairs on the negative lens bombsight.

"Eighty-three knots it is!"Graatz muttered.

"Cease fire!" Manfred yelled into the tubes.

SL 17 was inside the firing circle of the warehouse's defences. If the guns elevated any higher to shoot at them the shells would fall back onto the docks and do Burk's work for him. As it was, there would be more damage inflicted on the city as a result of their own unfused flak dropping back on it, than SL 17 was likely to inflict.

"'By camera," he ordered.

"Camera 'by!"

"Run camera!"

"Camera on!"

"They seem to have lost us ... Careless of them." Jurgen indicated the lights which were directing the flak into a distant cloud.

Manfred glanced at the stop watch. Ninety seconds had elapsed since he had started up the motors. The RAC would be in the air now, but there was still some minutes before they could climb to his height.

Rudolph Graatz dropped four 240-kilo bombs at the perimeter of the dock area and their fiery detonations were answered by a crescendo from the ground defences. Again long fingers of light groped for them.

"Main pattern away!"Graatz shouted.

Manfred watched the two huge shadows of the 1,500-kilo bombs slip through the red glow from the bomb hatch and disappear into the blackness below. They would flatten everything, turn it over to expose inflammable material for the 'fire buckets', the rope-bound incendiaries that followed them down. Then the mix of fire and ruin would be stirred by 4,000 kilos of lesser bursting charges.

He was destroying, in seconds, whole lifetimes of patient work. For this he got medals and the labourers despair – God, what had gone wrong with the world? Somewhere ... somewhen ... in the dawn of the world had God, or men, built the future on a flawed truth? Was that why he was here, was that what this war was all about? Would he have to kill and burn, destroying everything until that evil stone was laid bare, rejected, and the world built up again?

There was a dull explosion, peppered with bright flashes and the ground vomited oily coils of orange-yellow smoke. And as the ropes of fire climbed skywards they fell in onto themselves and billowed outwards, scattered by the secondary bursting charges.

"Ohh ... splendid!" Graatz roared, his eye still glued to the ocular, his teeth bared in a savage rictus. "Excellent placing!"

"Stop camera ... Hard'a' port ... 'By for next drop ... Helmsman, stabilize the trim damn you, I want 3,000," Manfred ordered.

Again the gondola was lit up in the brightness of day and the Spandaus and flare pistols opened up on the searchlights.

"They've found us!" Izzy screamed.

Manfred looked at his watch – two minutes. Oberleutnant Wilhelm Schutte began to scream up the tubes that the smoke from the fires below was strangling the motors. Another frailty, Manfred thought. The huge, weak-walled aluminium cylinders were designed to snatch as much oxygen as was available – at height. Naturally the engines weren't fitted with air filters ... Schutte had better be at his best. Grimly Manfred held them in the smoke until they were well away from the burning docks; then he shaped course for their second target, an arsenal.

The ruse worked. Behind them they could see the searchlights stabbing the sky in a futile attempt to find them. He had relied on their assuming that he would use the smoke screen to climb up and away, instead of keeping height and pressing further in. AA gunners lobbed shells into the air, firing at every cloud the beams hit. That was good – the rounds falling back onto the city would pin the fire brigades down. Over the estimated position of the arsenal Manfred looked at his watch again: five minutes. The RAC would be at their height by now. He ordered a few incendiaries dropped with a view to drawing ground fire.

He wasn't disappointed. The air was full of whining shells and his target was clearly pin-pointed on the ground by the circle of muzzle flashes surrounding it. Firework night! The destruction of the arsenal was as spectacular as it was dangerous. SL17, her bomb load spent, hovered over an enormous roman candle that spewed black smoke, masonry and coloured fire everywhere. The surrounding flak and searchlight emplacements were overwhelmed by the blast. For the moment, they were safe.

"About helm ... We go back on the wind ... Attention, all hands ... We are going back to rescue our sister crew ... I will want the walkway kept clear at all times ... Chief, gangs with ladders and grapnels to all cars... Watch to ballast and trimming stations ... It is time the Englanders saw a real circus."

"Permission to man the nets, Sir?" Chief Kornbloß called up the tubes and the laughter of the crew echoed thinly behind them.

Manfred smiled and capped the tubes – morale was good and the ship was in perfect trim to do her creaky best, all surplus ballast had been dropped – with honour ... It was up to God now.

"Manfred ... What are you doing? Get out! Get up, UP and run for home ... We've done more than enough ... We'll all burn, burn and die in agony – and go to hell. Save us Manfred ... Save me ... Long legs Manfred ... Please!" Izzy was hysterical, almost crying in fear. Manfred hugged him and, ignoring everybody else in the car, he tried to calm his friend.

"I can't let them die, lz ... I was here, only a mile away, when Schramm was torched ... I can still hear their screams ... And I could do nothing then, because I was only the Exec ... I am not free, lz, to let them die alone ... Schorn ran from Schramm – but I am not powerless now ..."

Jurgen prized Izzy out of Manfred's arms, strapped a heavy package onto his back and, as Izzy struggled with his surprise, von Lüth thrust a piece of seaming yarn into his hand. "It's a parachute, Nav ... We have sufficient height for it. Stand by the door and, if we are torched, jump, count to ten and pull the cord."

Burk felt the shock of a man, blind from birth, who sees for the first time. Certainly this was the first time he had seen Jurgen. Where was his brutal Junker's contempt for cowardice? Parachute? ... Poor Izzy. He had only a satchel full of charts strapped to his back and the string was merely a loop around the strap. But if he had to find out – well it would be a quicker, cleaner dying. The airships did not carry parachutes. Apart from their being considered by the Admiralty as disincentives to effort, they were impractical. The men would have to wear them throughout the flight and only a few of them would clear the ship if they had to jump. But Izzy was reassured, after a fashion.

"What about you and Manfred?" he whispered to Jurgen.

"We'll have to succeed ... Won't we, Nav?"

"Manfred, please be sensible ... Run for home!"

Burk stared out the for'ard windows. Already the vague shadow of the stricken Army ship hovered ahead and slightly below them. He opened a locker, took out a signalling lamp and smiled crookedly at Izzy.

"Don't jump, until I say so Iz ... They don't particularly like us down there ... And I will not yield, nor run for home, until I am successful."

"Or in flames!" Izzy echoed and shuddered.

Manfred was so frightened that he developed gripe. It was something to be grateful for; the pain, deep in his guts, warded off the terror. The London defences hadn't discovered him again, not yet, and that made each flash from the ground, and every sound SL 17 made, all the more unendurable.

Below him the reception committee were firing and aiming their lights at clouds and the new arrivals. Kapitän-leutnant Joachim von Endrath and the rest of the armada could be clearly seen way to the south, high and climbing away on long legs of light. Well enough for them, Manfred groaned. They had the new height climbers, real Zeppelins that could both run and rise above the RAC. There would be no chance for SL 17 nor the men she was attempting to rescue if there were any planes in their vicinity. The ship creaked as a gust buffeted it and, once more, Burk had a vision of a falling cigar shape wreathed in hydrogen flame.

"Has this manoeuvre ever been tried before?" von Lüth was by his elbow and the fright abated.

"It's going to be done now, Exec!"

"Devilish unhandy ships these!" Jurgen observed, then turned and stood over the helmsman.

Manfred looked at his watch. Eight minutes had elapsed since the crippled ship had been first sighted .

"'By on all lines," he ordered. Then cradling the signal lamp in the crook of his arm he tapped out a message.

"Split your crews ... Position them by gun nests ... Secure lines as we pass ... Climb up to us ... Hurry!"

The reply came after he had repeated the message for the second time.

"We are finished ... Save yourself"

"Hurry, we are nearing your position!" Manfred tapped back.

"Captain to captain ... Go ... Nothing can be done ...We are dead!" the crippled ship replied.

"COMMANDER to Captain ... This is an naval op ... Obey!" Manfred didn't wait to receive any further messages. The time for manoeuvres was now. Slowly, like an ancient stallion being led out to cover a mare, he directed SL I7 over the stricken ship. Once inside the cloud of diluted hydrogen spilling from the Army ship, SL 17's engines began to cough and spray sparks alarmingly. There was a scream in the car and everybody leapt cursing. But it was only the rating Manfred had handed the lamp to. He had burnt his fingers on the hot casing.

"Dummkopf!" Henschell, the Petty Officer on the steering stand, hissed and he stowed the lamp and booted the unhappy rating back to the ladder and up into the ship. All done with one hand on the wheel and not one point deviation from course.

It was a dreadfully hazardous operation. Manfred almost despaired before the Army men succeeded in catching the lines SL I7 was dangling to their upper lookout's nests. Now the problem was to position SL 17 exactly over the other airship and keep her that way. Fortunately the wind was blowing steadily and there were no sudden gusts to tear them apart. Given the poor manoeuvrability of all airships, matching their speeds and killing surplus way-on was an exercise of consummate skill in itself. Now that the two ships were docked, another factor had to be adjusted for. SL 17 was keeping a distance of about thirty feet between her keel and the Army ship's upper envelope. Once in position, the engines could only be used carefully to prevent the huge, four-bladed wooden propellers from smashing on the frames below or fouling in the trailing lines. But as the Army men began to swarm into SL 17 their weight affected her trim negatively and at the same time caused the lower ship to rise.

Twenty-two men, including her commander, rushed up the lines into SL 17. They entered the ship from their own two upper look-outs' nests via the command car and engine nacelle number three. As soon as a man was hauled into the car he was bundled up the ladder into the ship and ordered to lie on the walkway and stay there until the ship could be retrimmed. Manfred was too busy maintaining the ship's separation at the ballast stand to pay any attention to the men being rushed through the car. Most of them managed to gasp a hurried 'thanks', but there were others who could only weep.

By the time all the men were on board and the lines were being chopped away with axes, Manfred had had to bleed off nearly three tons of water ballast. SL 17 was now rising at a little in excess of the one and a half-ton lift the Army ship had acquired once her crew had left. It was certain that, with all that water raining down on them, the Englanders must be in no doubt that there was a Zeppelin above them. But there was nothing he could do. If he stopped loosing ballast, the two thirty-ton ships would kiss and be smashed to matchwood. If he tried to rise a little faster he would only rip out the bow cone and the stern cruciform to which the lines were attached.

Searchlights were already sweeping the sky for them and the control car was swept with brightness and plunged into darkness with each frantic sweep. It was impossible to judge distance in that strobing light; no eye could function in light levels that swung abruptly from night to day. But the long double watches he had stood for Schorn had not been in vain. Half-blinded, he kept SL 17 at her station. Then the flak opened up on them and the air became thick with whistling rounds and the smell of cordite. Panic strove to engulf him and his hand leapt to the breeches.

"Lines away!" Zeitel shouted up the tubes.

Manfred was climbing up and away as fast as he could push his ungainly ship. Tons of water ballast cascaded onto the dying ship underneath them, driving her towards the ground and pouring onto the streets off her doped skin like an exotic fountain.

"Engines, full ahead all ... Helmsman up, up to the attic ... Steuermann, steer north east ... Zeitel, Kornbloß, stow those 'greenbeaks' midships and keep them there ... Get the commander for'ard," he shouted.

"Flugzeug!" A voice screamed from the look out .

"Where?" Manfred shouted but the lookout's voice was drowned by the stuttering Spandaus.

"7,000 Sir and climbing," the helmsman shouted before he could ask what height they had.

"Up ... Get us up ... Loose everything ... Rudolf, torch that hulk!"

The London defences saved them at last. The crippled Army ship had been wallowing above them at point blank range long enough. They couldn't and didn't miss. The sky exploded in a flower of blossoming hydrogen flame and, while the night was made day, Manfred saw the enemy plane bank away in panic. The pilot was obviously inexperienced because he banked in the direction of his own torque and was diving in an uncontrolled spin.

"10,000 feet and climbing," the helmsman sang.

"Himmel, we will make it!" the chief rigger could be heard thinly from the tubes. He must have roared his lungs out inside the cotton cathedral to be picked up so far away.

"Do you hear that, lads? The Spandaus are quiet – the planes have gone ... Mein Kapitän, you insane bastard – you've done it."

The cheers of the men could be heard echoing like an animal roar from the various cars and the stations throughout the frame. For a moment Burk wondered if they were leaking gas; they hadn't sufficient height for the men to be altitude sick. Then the relief hit him too. Tactfully he capped the tube and turned back into the centre of the car.

"*Charts!* ... This is no parachute!!!" Izzy screamed in shock as he struggled out of his comforter and discovered what it really was.

"It was one, dear boy ... When you needed one." Jurgen laughed and helped the embarrassed Nav to stow them back under the plotting stand.

"A course for home, Nav; route white," Manfred ordered and Jurgen's face dropped.

He didn't say anything and Manfred felt a surge of pity for him; von Lüth was not a good subject for below zero temperatures and air sickness. Already his supercilious face was turning blue and his tunic flap was stained from a sudden gust that had thrown his misery back at him. 'Route white' was the longest way home and would add nearly a day to their itinerary, but it would keep SL17 far out to sea, away from the coast and safe from attack.

"Permission to enter car?" a strange voice called from the top of the ladder inside the ship. They looked up as the 'greenbeak' commander slowly clambered down into the car. "Kapitän-leutnant! ... I am Hauptmann Friedrich Schulze, late of Army airship SL-Z XVIII ... She burned well, didn't she, the evil bitch? Saved all our lives too ... Kapitänleutnant, I do not believe it is possible ... there are not the words for me ... or my crew ... to thank you, you and your crew, for our rescue."

"The rescue was made possible by your men's excellent discipline, Herr Schulze." Manfred introduced the captain to his officers and then asked Schulze why, when his position was so impossible, he hadn't landed his command and surrendered.

"Would you have done so in my position, Burk?"

"Certainly. I may not be able to prevent accident, or battle, from burning me and my men. But I would not condemn them to it!"

Schulze nodded and raised his hands in dismissal. "You must be fortunate in your C-I-C, Burk! It is not so with us. Dürr surrendered last year ... I, and all my men have wives and families ... It has been seen that the families of Dürr and his crew, do not prosper ... They will not see this war out!"

"That is not possible!" Manfred was deeply shocked. "It is inconceivable that the Army is that spiteful."

Schulze shook his head vigorously. "It is not the Army Burk ... It is our Adjutant."

"And what, pray, is the name of this paragon?" Jurgen was icy.

"The Rittmeister Albrecht, Graf von Knebel-Dobberitz."

"So ... the ubiquitous Albrecht!" Jurgen turned to the for'ard windows and considered the mist pressing against the celluloid.

"You know him, Burk?"

"He has no cause to love me, Schulze!"

"Have you had every inch of this ship searched?"

"What!"

"I mean it Burk ... You wouldn't be the first."

*

Bob woke up in a sweat of panic. Gradually, he adjusted to the fact that he was Bob Weston, in bed with Susan, and not Manfred Burk aloft in the past in a vicious fantasy about to burst into flame. He wanted to reach out and turn on the light for a smoke, but the nightmare terror still froze him, burying him deep under the duvet, afraid to move lest the fear and the darkness should become aware of him.

Two hours out from Heligoland light the bomb was found. It was quite a simple thing and absolutely deadly. Manfred stared at it for a long time before he could force himself to accept the fact that someone had tried to torch them.

Yes, he had ordered the search and had treated Schulze's warning with every care. But, right up to the moment when Kornbloß had brought the two packages into the control car, he had refused to accept that such a thing could happen. Men did not hate that viciously. In one of the packages there was a brass signal cartridge. The magnesium flare had been removed. Two wires ran into the fulminate, and the charge was fused by a lump of white phosphorous sealed in gelatine. This primary charge had been designed to fire into the second package, about half a kilo of thermite and saltpetre, which would ensure a hot, unquenchable burn. Both packages had been carefully stitched into the inside of the lose folds at the base of cell sixteen.

"It is electrically detonated ... By what?" Manfred asked.

"The wires led to the transmitter, Sir."

Then he was doubly lucky! On one count because he never used the transmitter unless he absolutely had to: all electric machines generated sparks, but the command car was one area of the ship that was not vented by the flues and it contained the transmitter. His second piece of luck had been to arrive over London alone, with no sister ships requesting his position, and the fact that he had had no time to radio an assurance to Schulze.

"It's one thing to know your enemy ... but it will be something else to prove that he did this," Schulze told him.

"I think not!" Manfred's face was a mask of anger. "There is always the duel!"

Jurgen shook his head and assured Manfred that Dobberitz was a considerable swordsman. If Manfred were to demand satisfaction, then Albrecht would have choice of weapons.

Manfred studied the dull, yellow cartridge again and a triumphant smile bared his teeth. "Pencil and paper, Exec ..."

Jurgen produced a gold propelling pencil, ripped a ballast sheet off the pad and flipped the blank side over. Manfred held the cellophane bag close to the red bulb, pressed the transparent paper against the brass shell and read off its serial number "Zeichen gerät § 4628759 ... Got that?"

Jurgen handed the sheet back to Burk who studied it and copied the serial number into the flight log, folding the ballast sheet into his wallet. For once in his life he was going to be grateful to the hoards of pompous bureaucrats! One of them, somewhere, would have issued that signal round ... and it would be there, in writing, to damn Knebel-Dobberitz, in triplicate.

Schulze carried the thermite charge while Manfred and the chief rigger climbed back into the ship. At the nearest loading hatch Kornbloß hurried to undo the clips while the two men hugged death tightly against their greatcoats. Schulze dropped his heavier charge straight down into the greyness, and Burk weighed his carefully before deciding that it was heavy enough not to be caught in the slipstream and pulled into the screws. He hurled it down and for'ard as hard as he could.

Greatly assisted by anti-cyclonic winds, SL17 bore down 'route white' until the Cuxhaven light could be seen off the port bow. They were on the last leg of the mission and soon they would be crossing the German coast and swinging down to Ahlhorn. The whole ship was in high good humour. Already the incredible hardships of flight and the terrors of battle were forgotten; the ship had passed through the jaws of death and soon they would be hung up and on leave. But Manfred was still worried. It all seemed too simple. Why would von Dobberitz go to the trouble of hiding a bomb so skilfully only to forget a simple basic like filing off the serial number? Unless it had been intended that the bomb be found ... and vigilance relaxed.

Was he overestimating his enemy? That would be bad, but not nearly so disatrous as underestimating him. And there was something about the ship, something that was all wrong. All ships had their song, the creaking of the frames, the slapping of the cells and the howl of the air past the hoods and weather-battered skin. Normally SL 17 sang a flat tuneless ditty, in keeping with the fat old duchess that she was. But now, with the sheds only hours away, his command's song had begun to sound like a threnody. SL 17 would never reach shed Aladin ... It all seemed to add up ... There was another bomb on board – the one they weren't meant to find! One thing was certain; he was going to have to power the transmitter within the next ten minutes. Ahlhorn must have the ground gangs alerted and the coastal artillery must be warned of his approach. The flats off Cuxhaven were the graves of too many ships that had surprised their own flak.

"Chief, all men to walkway and 'by hatches ... Engines, high revs. 'By to clutch generators ... Telegraphs to bridge ... Wheels, obey bridge ... Down to twenty feet ... 'By to loose all ballast ... Transmitter 'by for power." He gave the orders calmly and decisively and it was a few moments before the others in the car realized what was happening. All good humour vanished like mist in a desert.

"Not another bomb!" Izzy gasped nervously.

"Best place to find out, dear boy, "Jurgen drawled softly. "I do hope Dobberitz hasn't been tedious ... Cold stuff, the sea this time of year! Everybody here swim?"

"All stations 'by, sir," the Petty Officers called one after another.

"Inflate and tie off enough empty ballast sacks for the men," Manfred ordered.

"Schutte, on my command ... declutch the generators. Full ahead all, maximum revs and everybody over the side!"

"Sir!"

"Lower antenna ... Mister Loffat, 'by to send the following ... Position ... Status ... and landing instructions."

"Thirty feet, Sir!" the helmsman shouted.

"Water wings issued and 'by, sir!"Henschell called.

Manfred waited until Jurgen had given Mark Loffat, the telegraphist Petty Officer, the ship's position and status, before giving the order.

"HT, on ... Transmit message!"

Everyone heard the sharp crack of the 'very cartridge'.

"Fire in cell VII!" Zeitel screamed up the tube.

"Aufgeben!" Manfred howled the order to abandon and threw the telegraphs to 'full ahead all'.

The initial detonation of the signal flare was followed almost immediately by the thumping whoosh of an enormous gas oven being lit. At once SL 17 began to buck and roll under the conflicting forces acting on her. The four 240 horsepower Maybachs drove her forward, straining towards her maximum way on of fifty-four knots.

Ballast and crew poured overboard into the cold North Sea thirty feet below and this weight loss, together with the dynamic lift of her forward way on, kept her bow up despite the instant loss of one-nineteenth of her lift. The crew reacted instantly and with excellent discipline. Most of them jumped from the hatches in the stern and midship walks, while the engine gangs merely dived out of their open windows. Henschell and Zeitel encouraged the men with pushes and kicks, yelling at those caught away from the hatches to stand on the cotton skin and fall through. Doped, the cotton fabric was brittle and they ripped their way down to the sea easily.

"Shall I slip the fuel tanks?" Schutte, the engineer shouted above the roar of fire.

"No ... You'll fire the water! Jump man, that's an order."

"I'm wet already!" came the reply.

The first soft explosion of the gas cell was shortly followed by the real explosion, the deafening blast that occurred when the flames, on burning through the upper envelope, drew the night air into the inferno. SL 17 had managed to climb several hundred feet before she fell by the bow and a tremendous fireball leaped aft of the stricken ship, popping cells and adding their exploding fury to the expanding holocaust.

"Es ist das Ende!" Izzy whispered. Manfred checked that the command car wasn't too high above the water before taking the elevator wheel and shouting "AUS!"

Mark Loffat and Rudolf Graatz smashed out the for'ard window with the camera. At a nod from Burk they grabbed Izzy and dived out into the thundering void. Manfred watched them hit the water and surface, lit all the while by baleful yellow and orange fire.

Everybody had got clear. Manfred on the elevator wheel and Jurgen on the steering stand were the only ones left.

"Tie down the wheel and jump, Exec!"

"And you?" Jurgen secured the wheel and paused by the window.

"I'll jump when the water's clear ... Jump!"

"No, Manfred ... You'll die... I'll stay ... You can't understand ... Pity a rotation's not on ..." Jurgen leaned forward to climb up the steeply inclined car to the helm, but Manfred, waiting until his balance was compromised, lashed out with his boot and toppled van Lüth out the window.

Stupid, bloody Junkers, he thought. Why had they to measure everything in terms of heroic death? Wasn't a good life of infinitely more value? *Rotate*? That had to be a new Junker's word – death was good enough for the plebs, but not for Jurgen! In Manfred's own case the matter was clear cut. He had to save his crew – to hell with honour.

Ten seconds after the detonation of the bomb, Burk was alone on SL 17, struggling with the elevator wheel. It was his intention to keep the ship on a long, slow fall, pushing the hulk forward and up with motors and tail fins against her increasing negative buoyancy as she lost gas. He was assisted in this by the bow-down attitude of the ship which directed the midship inferno aft. However, as the stern cells popped and exploded, SL 17 levelled off. Suddenly she lurched and tumbled by the tail towards the water.

Instantly the envelope above the command car became a chimney for the blaze. For a brief instant, flame jutted from the bow vents in a thundering roar that froze him like a rabbit under a weasel's stare. The plywood roof of the command car began to shrivel and peel back like cellophane under a red hot poker. It began to rain fragments of burning envelope, molten dope, charred plywood and the stinking, sizzling chunks of roast ox gut – the hydrogen-proof lining of the gas cells. Burning dope fell on his back and his great coat caught fire, but as he was reaching for a rope to tie off the wheel it spun free and he realized that the transmission chains to the fins had been burned off their sheaves. There was nothing to keep him on board now. Staggering against the heat and the yellow haze that obscured everything, Manfred ran for the rear of the car and jumped, flinging himself sideways as he did so in order that the wreckage wouldn't pin him underwater.He had just cleared the doorway when cell XIV, over the command car, exploded.

A great ball of yellow-blue fire extended down to the water and, for the eternal moment of his dive, Manfred was in the heart of the flame. Never had he experienced such heat! It was so fierce that it didn't register as fire at all; it was more like being in a bath of crushed ice. Eyes squeezed tight and breath held, Manfred was only aware of being in the water when his hands were driven against his skull; otherwise his body registered no difference in sensation. Flame or ice, the shock was the same. Deep under the North Sea he opened his eyes and saw a roof of red flame above him. A huge spidery claw groped through the bale fires, breaking up and reaching for him. He held the breath in bursting lungs and tried to slow his rate of ascent. Better far to drown than surface inside the blazing hulk!

SL 17's tattered stern ploughed a long white furrow in the black waters before dragging her blazing bows under. Manfred was still submerged when he heard the thunder of her quenching. At the time he confused it with the pounding of the blood in his ears and imagined, when the light above him went out, that he was losing consciousness. Then his head broke the surface and for a long time it was all he could do to snatch air and avoid the guttering oil slicks.

Susan was in a deep sleep. Bob paused, his hand still rubbing his smarting head, and swung his palm down to pat her bottom. But he didn't want to talk about this dream – not just yet, so his hand passed over her and turned on the light.

Manfred had survived – damn it the whole two crews had... But of course he must – dreams couldn't die... Besides, Susan had proved that he was, or had been, *real*! What did that mean he and his dreams were? Was he insane? Possessed? There had been a Burk on Bascombe's list of possible commanders of the *Graf Zeppelin II*. That meant there was a faint chance that he was alive. But was the man on the list Manfred? Were any of his dreams true?

If there were the slightest chance that the man he dreamed about was alive then he must be found. He would be the best man in the world to fly *Firedrake* – perhaps the only candidate. All that would be required of Manfred would be his assistance in programming the flight computer and training a crew.

Bob lit a cigarette. He was quite excited, never realizing that he was sliding down the slopes of obsession, nor plumbing the depths of his own frustration. He dreamed of Burk and shared him, but he could never become Burk.

Nine

The splendour falls on castle walls
And snowy summits old in story:
The long light shakes across the lakes
And the wild cataract leaps in glory.

ALFRED, LORD TENNYSON

The new, thicker, middle cuff rings and the braided shoulder straps clashed with the older gilt. They had promoted him to Korvettenkapitän and his uniform was a reflection of his body, a contrast of new pinkness and old unburnt skin. Manfred entered Jurgen's pullman uninvited. The position embarrassed him; by nature he was an avoider of incidents rather than a confronter. But the situation must be faced aggressively from the outset and there could be no faltering. He, Manfred Burk, the son of a Navy Warrant Officer, had accepted an invitation from Prußia's oldest, most honoured house. There were two ways he could cross the threshold: cap in hand, or with bravura. So there wasn't any choice, not when he loved Halgerd.

Apart from the briefest of recognitions, Jurgen had not said a word and Manfred steeled himself to endure the silence as though he had imposed it. If there were to be any conversation, von Lüth must solicit it. The young Count affected a sublime indifference to Burk's presence. He lounged along his seat, his gorgeous uniform hanging from him in a studied disarray that permitted the velvet lining to flash every time he moved in a flourish of taste and excellence. Not that Jurgen bestirred himself more than to make an infrequent inspection of the ash on his cigar. He appeared to be wholly engrossed in the difficult decision whether to tap it off or let it endure for another puff.

A spasm of contempt and amusement ran through Manfred. He found the paper ethos of the aristocracy hard to understand. For all their vaunted pedigrees, wealth was their pedestal. Yet they affected to despise it. How could any house stand if it rejected its foundations? They were a cold shallow lot, lost somewhere between something and nothing. They dared not live for fear they might enjoy life and become enslaved to it. Halgerd must be rescued from them before their cynicism destroyed her delight.

"Ah there you are ... I was afraid the train had gone!" Izzy, dragging an enormous suitcase and assorted lesser packages, blundered into the carriage.

"Hey!" Jurgen shouted in alarm, swinging his boots to the floor just in time to save them from having a brown paper bag, greasy from hot doughnuts, dropped on them.

"Shouldn't have your feet on the upholstery!" Izzy said severely. "'Damages the fabric – besides the conductors don't care for it."

"A plague on your homilies, Izzy!" von Lüth sat up exasperated. "The world has really gone to hell when a man can't put his feet up in his own train!" He reached up and pulled the communications cord.

"*Your* train!" Izzy was dumbfounded.

"No, the Baron's ... This whole line is his."

"Oh!" Izzy bit into a doughnut, choked and when he had recovered offered them around.

"Can't eat them without coffee," Jurgen decided. A steward entered the carriage.

"You rang, Sir?"

"Yes. Stumpf, isn't it?" Jurgen paused long enough for the steward's gratification at being recognized to register, then ordered him to bring coffee and to tell the engineer to set the train rolling. "Oh, and Stumpf, have this clutter stowed with the rest of the luggage." He pointed to Izzy's disorganized effects. The steward beckoned to others and while they were removing the offending baggage he returned with a silver coffee pot and Dresden service.

"Hey, not that one?" Izzy rescued another brown paper bag from the porters. "Momma made it for us." He grinned at Manfred. "It's fudge – good too, an Amerikanisch sweet."

To Manfred's amazement Jurgen joined in and the fudge was demolished with relish. The Count saw his expression, recognized it and laughed.

"Don't worry, old boy. If I'm letting the side down, there's no one watching – of any importance that is ... Izzy, my dear fellow, you should have sent your mother ... Now, the doughnuts ... and the coffee ..."

"Momma is very particular about the company she keeps!"Izzy returned tartly. "She says she can trace her ancestry right back to Adam and, unlike me, she does not fraternize with people whose pedigree is lost in the informal ruttings of the Middle Ages."

Jurgen and Manfred laughed heartily at the quick riposte. There was nothing forced in Jurgen's delight and whatever reserve the journey had begun with was banished.

The doughnuts finished, they played cards and talked, in unflattering terms, of their brother officers in Ahlhorn. A few hours down the line Stumpf knocked on the door and entered bearing two bottles of wine and a humidor. When he was gone Jurgen poured the light sparkling wine for them, murmuring that it was just the thing to steel their appetites for the 'ordeal feast' that awaited them in Eberheim.

"No rationing at Eberheim then?" Manfred was shocked. It didn't seem right or patriotic that anyone should live in plenty while the nation starved! In Kiel you could buy a girl for a cup of flour – things were that bad.

"Only the initiates fast, Burk ... The masters have made theirs and no longer require that discipline!" Jurgen watched him over the rim of his glass, his eyes glinting with predatory humour.

"You are suggesting that patriotism and valour are the attributes of the lower classes ... But I have seen a lot of your class die too, Jurgen, and I assure you their blood is as red as any peasant's."

"And just as free flowing ... You see, Manfred, only the living are capable of learning. War and death are from the same stable – they rid the world of those who can no longer change."

Millions of people dead! Manfred thought. Between Germany and France a bloody dyke cut Europe from north to south and Jurgen felt only contempt for such enormous strife. Was he right? Surely there must be a purpose to this war? Would God allow his children to slaughter each other by the nation for nothing? A feeling of immense helplessness gripped him. All his life there had only been two alternatives open to him: obey or die. Never once had he any say in the shaping of his country's destiny, much less his own. And then he was angry. He, and everyone else in Germany, was being pushed into the trenches by the people in power, people like von Lüth – and instead of being grateful for all that loyalty, he despised it.

"Why? Jurgen ... The people have given up their very wills to their masters. Why have you failed them so?"

"The world knew that slavery was wrong for about one

hundred and forty years before it was stopped ... "Why did it stop at all Manfred?"

"War?"

"Precisely ... There is a blood penalty to be exacted for change. People knew that slavery was wrong, but only a few stopped it voluntarily. Then it was made illegal and the rest had to be converted by the sword ... Amerika was the schoolroom then!"

"It is ridiculous to compare war with the schoolroom!" Manfred was angry."Children are not killed at school!"

"They will kill each other in the absence of masters ...You of all people will know that, Manfred."

Burk looked sharply at Jurgen. Did he know about the orphanage? Perhaps? After all, Neurath was supposed to be his uncle. At once Manfred felt shamed. There were parts of his life that hurt too much to share with anyone and the fact that von Lüth knew them made him feel soiled. He didn't want to continue this insane conversation any longer, but he had to. Otherwise Jurgen would win – and know it.

"Considering that it was you, and your Kaiserlich set, that got us into this war, how are you going to get us out, and what great lesson is there in all this blood and famine?"

"You trusted us ... You will not do so again ... Oh there will be other men to do the lazy masses' thinking for them, but implicit trust in men or rigid doctrines will never again be respectable. Ritual Man is dying in the trenches. This is the dawn of Thinking Man."

The trouble was that there was a needle of truth in Jurgen's cynical philosophy. But if any of it were true, then Manfred's own life was a lie and all the years of effort a waste to someone else's gain! Rubbish, his instinct screamed at him, but his analytical self insisted that it be examined.

"Don't they grow anything except turnips?" Izzy, who had taken no part in the conversation, suddenly asked. He had been staring out the window at the flat, boring countryside racing past and his question broke the morbid spell that had Manfred in thrall.

"Ah yes. *Sic transit* and all that. To think that our whole war effort rests squarely on the ah ... shoulders of a turnip!" Jurgen answered him mournfully. "What an achievement for a nation! ... Consider the shield, a brown field and emblazoned on it – a turnip rampant! ... There is heraldry in a field of wheat. But our farmers have given us turnips."

All through the afternoon, the evening and into the early night the train rattled eastwards, a brass-bound iron fugitive from the clouds of lignite smoke billowing from her huge stack. Not once throughout the whole journey did the train stop. There were no stations.

Jurgen hadn't been boasting when he claimed the Baron ran a private line. Manfred tried to imagine the order of power, and the fortune, that must be required to lay on extravagance of that magnitude. He tried to draw Jurgen out on this, but the Count avoided further confidences, replying that the Baron had a weakness for steam and machines of grace, and left it at that. Whatever else he might have been coaxed to say was lost when Izzy started a squabble over who should have played what and when. The rest of the journey was whiled away in games of skat until the train cracked steam in the small village station below the cliffs of Eberheim.

A car was waiting for them and soon they were driving, without lights, up the steep zigzagging road that climbed to the Schloß. To one side of the narrow road, huge pines reached into the night, spreading their branches out over the car and denying it even the small light of the stars. On the other side, the ground plunged away abyssally.

"Has he run out of carbide?" Izzy asked nervously, hoping that the oblique question would result in the headlamps being lit.

"No. We follow blackout procedures here. We are too near the front to do otherwise, "Jurgen explained. "Russian soldiers often cross the lines; they are starving. Naturally they can't storm the Schloß. But a car showing lights would be another matter."

"The forest is dangerous then?" Manfred asked.

"I would prefer to call it 'exciting' ... And there is the game!" Jurgen answered dryly.

"What game?"

"Wolves, bear, hart, boar mostly. The Baron is a keen and prudent huntsman. The forest is huge and well stocked."

Manfred had only the vaguest idea as to where Eberheim lay. He judged that they were somewhere in the great Poznan Forest, an eldritch place and one of the last corners of primeval Europe. He regarded the blackness under the trees with rising alarm. Just what was out there slavering in the night? How numerous would the display of glaring eyes have been had they used the headlights? And how could the Taurlbourgs revel in ancient splendour so close to hungry Russia and so far from any military aid? Jurgen had said there were dangers; what measures did the Baron take to protect Eberheim? The Schloß would be easy to defend, but what about the peasants?

"How do your people protect themselves, Jurgen?"

"Our people are all skilled in the things of the forest. To them the beasts are no danger."

"I mean the danger from the Russians. There must be food raids, deserters and scavengers ..."

"Oh that? ... No, we don't have to bother, not with the Russians at any account."

"Well, who then?"

Jurgen seemed to slip into a dream; he stared into the darkness as though it had cast a spell over him. Manfred nudged him and asked again who were the people threatening Eberheim.

"If I remember correctly there is a poem, or something, that goes 'where angels fear to tread', Jurgen quoted dreamily. "What do angels fear anyway? Not people, dear boy. People are more of a threat to themselves than to us ... Our enemies will not concern you."

It was most unsatisfactory. Trying to dig information out of von Lüth required that the answer be known before the question would be considered. But that only obtained with Manfred; with Izzy, von Lüth was quite unequivocal.

"I don't see any lights at all ... Is there any electricity here, Jurgen?"

"Of course, Izzy. But for power only and not for domestic use ... We live the old way here, earthy, virile and Teutonic ... And Manfred ... Death to us is an amusement – if it is also stupid."

A warning? Perhaps. Either way Manfred couldn't think of a suitable question or reply, so he turned away and considered the oppressive darkness. Silence was the only discipline for uncertainty.

The car suddenly lurched past two cyclopean monoliths of pale stone which stood out, wraithlike, in the darkness. Manfred assumed that they were gateposts and his guess was confirmed by the heavy crash of iron as they closed behind them.

At once the darkness lifted and Schloss Eberheim was visible in the moonlight, perched on the edge of the cliff at the end of a long gravel drive. The gateposts marked the outer wall of the castle grounds and the approaches to the Schloß itself were an extensive complex of formal gardens. They looked beautiful in the moonlight against the backdrop of the forest and the mountains, but they were intimidated by the brutal granite structure of the castle. It was a great towering block, square in overall design but, at the same time, built in curved sweeps – there were no corners for cannon to breach the masonry. The windows were sunk deep into the stone like the eye sockets of a skull and that effect was enhanced by the absence of light shining from them.

"Castle Dracula!" Izzy whispered to Manfred. Jurgen overheard and snickered.

"Yes the dear old girl has a severe aspect. When she was built castles tended to come down with each invasion. The Schloß has never been breached; in her day she was the ultimate in defensive architecture. It's not too bad inside; the Baron had boilers installed in the dungeons."

"Hot and cold damp?" Izzy joked weakly.

"Something like that," the Count replied shortly and Burk was amused to see that, although he joked about his home, Jurgen was short on patience with anyone else who did.

Jurgen's youngest brother, Rudi, was waiting for them in the entrance hall and he greeted Manfred and Izzy warmly.

"Well, brother, how goes your work? I trust that the Baron's cellar has not declined like the rest of the country!" Jurgen hailed him and the two brothers embraced.

"Beg pardon Sir ... I'll show you to your rooms ... You'll be wanting to dress for dinner!" It was Petty Officer Zeitel, albeit a changed man. Gone was his midnight-blue rig and green fatigues. Instead, standing behind them, was a civilian in muted, well-cut tweeds.

"Good heavens, Zeitel, what are you doing here?" Izzy shouted in tactless surprise.

"This is my home, Sir!" the Petty Officer answered.

"Don't know very much about your own men do you, old boy?" Jurgen murmured.

"I knew SL17 had been built by public subscription and presented to the Navy ..." Manfred replied, "but I hadn't realized she had been a Taurlbourg gift, or that you had also supplied the crew ... Damn it Jurgen – she should have been your command."

"Oh no!" Jurgen smiled as though enjoying some private joke. "That was not what she was commissioned for ... But you are correct. With the exception of a few extra ratings, our crew are all from Eberheim ... Zeitel is one of our foresters, but once he was a valet and we imagined you'd be more comfortable with him than with one of the others."

Manfred began to get a closed-in feeling. What else was there that he didn't know? Once it had seemed good policy to divorce himself from everything as much as possible. It was enough to know the men's names and their work records; it had been easy to demand excellence from a crew with whom he was not involved. But now it was all wrong. He was completely at the mercy of men about whom he knew nothing, while they knew more about him, and his ambition, than he cared to think. It had been a bad policy and one he would never again repeat.

"Chin up old boy," Jurgen murmured to him. "Virtue is an error profited from! Let us go to our rooms and change?"

Izzy and Manfred followed Zeitel up the starboard flight of polished granite stairs. If the outside of the castle were forbidding, the interior was quite the opposite. There was a degree of starkness about the hewn stone walls which had never been softened by plaster, but the mausoleum-like rooms were warmed by extensive panels of rare polished woods and splendid curtains. The wooden floors varied from burnished mirrors to matt blocks of timber. Huge rough-hewn beams lowered and contoured high ceilings which vanished into the graven oak panelling and rich tapestries adorning the walls. Eberheim was a remarkable blend of military starkness and practical luxury.

In his room, really a small suite, Petty Officer Zeitel laid out his formal undress blues. This was one of a set of three rigs he had ordered for himself on getting the invitation. They completed his wardrobe of formal and informal dress and they represented an extravagance that only someone in von Lüth's social position would ever be able to use.

"Yer'll be keeping yer own company after this ... fer quite a piece,"Zeitel observed dryly when he laid out Manfred's wardrobe.

Burk smiled ruefully and nodded. The Petty Officer was right of course. Kitting himself up had cost him the better part of a year's salary. There'd be no more mercy missions to the girls in Kiel for Izzy and himself for quite some time. He washed, and when he was dried Zeitel stood by with steaming towels and a set of razors.

Manfred considered his reflection in the mirror and tried to decide what to do. Until now he had been able to hide his head under a cap and, although the shortness of his eye brows and lashes looked rather odd, they weren't startling. Not like his head without the cap! The vigorously sprouting bristle was less than half a centimetre long and had reached the stage where it might be considered as anything but hair. His head looked like the mane of a hogged horse; worse still the new growth was more white than black – it was too new for thickness to stabilize the colour.

"Makes yer look like a mouldy billiard ball, Sir ... Best to have it all off," Zeitel informed him when he raised his eyes in the mirror to the petty officer's.

Manfred nodded, sat in the cane chair beside the log fire and watched the flames dance while Zeitel raked his lathered head and face with steel blades. Then he put on a new linen shirt and Zeitel helped to shrug him into the exactly-shaped uniform tunic. The highly polished boots were an ordeal to get on and, once his feet slipped down the final inches to snuggle against the soles, Manfred wondered if he would have to sleep in them or how would he ever get them off again?

Zeitel laid out his medals, ribbons, gloves and dress sword. But there was no way he was going to add disaster to handicap.

It would be bad enough trying to walk in the boots without running the risk of being tripped by the sword.

"I'll carry the Mauser, Zeitel ... No, not the leather, the stock holster ... I have packed an officer's belt. No, that one, the one with the shoulder strap ... That portepee won't do, it's for a sword ... That one."

He looped the colourful tassel around the side arm frog, tightened the belt and ignored the medals. The *Ordre* might impress the Baron, but Halgerd only saw it as a tombstone. Besides, the one thing better than the *Ordre* itself was to affect its display as being of no consequence. He took the buttonhole instead and spread the ribbon through the second button from the top of his tunic. He didn't need the gloves; his hands didn't sweat and there wouldn't be any dancing.

One last thing – there was little point in wearing a side arm unless he showed that it was his weapon. Otherwise everyone would know that he was afraid to carry a sword. He looped the matt, silver cord marksman's lanyard with its gilt shield from his right shoulder to the second tunic button and then stood before the mirror.

Was he ugly, comical or just strange? From the neck down he looked quite military, but that staring head? It looked small with no hair and the black shadows around his eyes didn't improve things at all. The fall in the heart of the fireball had stripped him of clothing and body hair, plunging him into the North Sea as naked as a polished apple.

"Don't worry none about yer head of skin, Sir," Zeitel growled reassuringly. "Yer'll be proud of it when they learns how yer got it."

"Ahh ... thank you, Chief." Manfred fled the room in embarrassment and headed for the stairs.

His bravura almost deserted him as he marched into the great L-shaped dining hall. An old liveried butler flung open the huge counter-balanced doors and announced him formally. “M’lords and M’ladies – Korvettenkapitän zur See Manfred Burk!”

Two paces over the threshold and the iron-studded oak doors whispered shut behind him, the catch fell home with a noisy thud and Burk was left standing indecisively in the shadows.

What to do next? Where was he to sit? These were all silly, pointless fears but, as he stared at the enormous board and the shadowy diners lit by two multi-armed candelabras – the only light in the whole hall, they almost unmanned him.

“Manfred!” Halgerd called in delight, jumping from her place and running to him. Then she saw his baldness and her hand shot up to her mouth. “Oh, Kapitän Harsch ... What have you done to yourself? You look so ... severe!” Before he could answer, she led him to a chair between herself and Rudi and two footmen emerged from the shadows. They pulled the massive, thronelike seat back for him, easing under him as he sat. At once Halgerd began to ply him with questions.

“Halgerd, my dear, where are your manners? You must introduce us to your Kapitän,” an elderly and still beautiful lady in a red gold evening gown admonished her. She was obviously the Baroness. “Sit down dear boy!”

Difficult! He was already seated, pinned against the table by the small tree from which his heavy chair had been carved. Mistake number one ... he should have resisted the footmen and remained standing until invited to sit.

“Mamma, Peter announced Manfred,” Halgerd reminded her.

“So he did! Manfed, this is Karl ...” Starting at the middle and working around the oak massif the Baroness introduced him to the whole table.

Including himself, there were nine people seated at at the table and one unoccupied chair. Karl, who sat across from Burk, was a tall, elfin-built man, so blond that Manfred would have sworn he was an albino until he saw brown eyes staring back at him. A chemical engineer he was, at present, serving as a Captain of Cavalry in General Paul von Lettow-Vorbeck's German East Africa Corps. Younger than Jurgen, but older than the rest of his family, Manfred judged him to be about twenty-three. In contrast, his wife, Eva, was petite, dark haired and solemn. A biochemist, she sat on Karl's left facing Rudi, and looked past Manfred as though she were evaluating a report on him. Jurgen's empty seat was at the bottom right of the table and someone, whom Manfred couldn't see, sat beside the empty chair on Halgerd's left.

Rudi sat between Burk and his mother. The youngest of the family, he didn't have either of his brothers' classic frames, being a little too short for his powerful build. Manfred couldn't see his eyes, but his hair was brown which made him wonder how three men with such widely diverging hair, eye colouring and build could be brothers. Marie, Rudi's wife, was tall and silverhaired, a birch maiden with a shy smile and hazel eyes. She sat between Karl and Jurgen's place – the Baroness introduced her as a biologist. Manfred's nervousness and confusion increased. The Junkers scorned academics, considering Science a discipline to be hired like any other trade. Yet the Taurlbourgs were steeped in it, and in the most modern, esoteric branches of it too, sciences that he had barely heard of. Was this merely a new fashion? Other doubts needled him.

Where was Izzy to sit? He glanced towards the top of the table where an ancient titan, with white hair and enormous walrus moustaches, hunched in a carver beside the Baroness. He wore the old fashioned uniform of a full rear admiral of the Prußian Navy and must have seen service in the days before the Iron Chancellor had unified Germany. Manfred knew he was looking at the Baron. Fierce blue eyes considered him under bushy white brows and the weathered face conveyed no expression save that of immense intelligence and authority. If there was one thing that described the Baron – it was power. He held Manfred's eyes, and Manfred felt lost, drained, no longer aware of the others and incapable of marshalling even the will to break free.

"... Done some growing since I last saw you, boy!"

What was he talking about? ... Could the old giant, like his forest counterpart the great oak, be imposing to the eye but rotted inside, senile? The Baron thought he was someone else. Old, hateful memories stirred and Manfred remembered the pain and the voice, "*Cease this outrage!*"

They had told him there were two men at the orphanage that night, Neurath and an old man who had stopped the beating. Pray God no ... It couldn't have been the Baron! It mustn't be – the shame, the humiliation ... But Neurath was Halgerd's uncle ... He searched for a denial in the steel-blue eyes. But the Baron held him in his stare until Burk could see the amusement there also.

"I hear old Ferdinand is dead?"

"Count Zeppelin Sir? Yes he died last winter ... Did you know him, Sir?" Manfred seized the opportunity to flee old nightmares and dismiss new ones.

"Of course! We hunted together. An Army man though, but no one is perfect. Lost his faith in airships in the end – wanted me to commission one of those damn Gotha bombers instead of one of his Zeppelins."

"Is that why you went to the 'glue potters' Sir?"

"Eh, glue potters?"

"Doktor Johann Schütte's precision death traps. We call everyone who has anything to do with the Luftschiffbau Schütte-Lanz of Mannheim-Rheinau a 'glue potter'! I hope, Sir, that the next time you commission a ship you will approach the Zeppelin Werke."

"Dear me," the Baron chuckled. "I understood from the

War Ministry that the SL class were ahead of old Ferdinand's in design."

"The 'glue potters' are obsessed with wooden frame ships. Neither I, nor any other airship man, care how good their designs are and the War Ministry is only interested in conserving stocks of aluminium. Wood and glue can't compare with metal frames, Sir. SL ships have done less damage to the enemy, and killed more crews, than any other class of airship."

"Don' t worry Manfred," the Baroness calmed his anger. "SL 17 isn't the ship we want, it is only a beginning!"

"Pity old Ferdinand got so angry!" The Baron reached for his stein. "Couldn't see that a Gotha's no good. Wrong machine, wrong war. Damn rattletrap has no grace ... Died young poor fellow."

"He was eighty, Piggy," the Baroness corrected her husband.

"At our age, Theo, that's young," was the tart reply.

Piggy! How could anyone dare to call this terrible man an endearment like that? So the Baron was human! Enormous relief flooded Manfred only to disappear when he realized that the Baron was staring hard at him.

"Dam'n me if the boy isn't bony as a newt," he reflected aloud. "I'll not have it ... It's unnatural ...Why are you shaved like that young man? Are there lice in old Ferdinand's airships?"

"Ringworm or alopecia more likely!"

The affected nasal whine from the bottom of the table came from the remaining diner the Baroness had been about to name before the Baron had interjected. Von Dobberitz here! Shock tingled his scalp, but Manfred was also flushed with anger. He scanned the poorly lit table until he found his enemy, and stared hard at him until the latter looked away. So Albrecht was not only a scoundrel, he was a coward to boot.

"You must excuse my severe cut," Manfred addressed the

whole table. "But I was singed when this maniac put a bomb, a Höllenmaschine, on board my command ... Baron, it was this man who destroyed SL 17."

A deathly silence followed. It took Manfred a couple of seconds to understand that they hadn't heard that he had lost his command ... And that meant that his invitation must have come from Jurgen and not from the Baron and Baroness.

"You torched your own ship ... you coward ... you ... untermench ... Schulze saw it all!" The shake in von Dobberitz's voice confirmed any doubt Burk had left.

"Oh Manfred ... how dreadful! ... And I teased you about your hair ... Are you badly hurt? Was anyone killed?" Halgerd's eyes were enormous.

"No dear sister!" Jurgen, coming in at a side door, entered the pool of candlelight. "Ah Karl – we are all alive still! Do you stay long with us?"

"No, Jurgen, just for the Pronouncement – and the hunt of course!"

"Pity! You and Eva will be complete strangers when this war is over." Jurgen took his mother's hand and kissed it, clicking his heels and executing a flawless bow.

"Ah my dear Mamma ... How is my favourite lady?"

"Poo-poo, you're impossible." The Baroness kissed him lovingly and rapped his knuckles sharply with her fan.

Struggling to hide a smile Manfred imagined himself back in the command car. "I'll want 10,000 feet, Poo-poo ... And Poo-poo, steer small." That would flatten von Lüth for all time if Manfred had been the type of man to use another's private life against him.

Jurgen saw Manfred's mouth twitch. "Control yourself ... or die!" he hissed at him in mock severity and then he presented himself before his father.

"What kept you, boy?" The Baron growled. "Soup must be cold by now – damned bad form ... What's all this about?"

He paused as if struggling to remember the name and Burk wondered whether he had genuinely forgotten, or else was expressing a magnificent contempt, "... Dobberitz here bombing our ship?"

"Cigar don't y'know – had to finish it, "Jurgen explained and sat down. Servants emerged from the darkness to ladle soup and he waited until they were gone before staring at the protesting Albrecht.

"Lying will only postpone our contempt Dobberitz ... We have the serial number of one of the flares. It will only be a matter of time before the person to whom it was issued will be called before a court of inquiry."

"You dismiss my word, the word of a gentleman!" Von Dobberitz, white and trembling with rage pointed at Burk.

But their silence terrified him and Albrecht panicked. Instead of denying all knowledge of the affair, appealing to their reason because there was no real proof, and pointing out Jurgen and Manfred's obvious bias, von Dobberitz began to gobble an impassioned speech about avenging the dishonour done to the Taurlbourgs in Friedrichshafen.

Manfred struggled to his feet, straining to push his chair away from the table until the back of his legs bruised. He was too angry to feel the pain or call von Dobberitz out coherently. Luckily for him Halgerd pulled him back into his chair and poured her soup all over the Count.

The hall was in an uproar; everyone was trying to shout something except Jurgen who ate his soup methodically and affected to be indifferent to his surroundings. Albrecht gaped at Halgerd in shock, his intention to accept Manfred's challenge forgotten.

"Silence!" the Baron growled and was instantly obeyed. Everyone sat down, except von Dobberitz who stood at the end of the table dripping soup and shaking with rage.

The Baron glowered awfully at him with fierce old blue

eyes and then pronounced his judgement. "Albrecht von Kneble-Dobberitz, you are a disgrace to my house and to Germany. You have committed a cowardly treason against the Imperial Navy and you excuse it by calling my daughter 'Hure' ... Begone, Dobberitz – and do not let the hounds catch your scent tomorrow."

Albrecht left the table and vanished into the darkness. He was sobbing. Manfred was left with an inner disgust as though he had been defeated.

"Shouldn't throw your soup at people, my dear," the Baron grunted kindly. "Bad form – and a waste of soup."

"Stops duels though," Karl congratulated his sister.

"Won't a court of inquiry be a bit awkward, right now?" Rudi asked the Baron, who considered it for a moment before nodding.

"The walk will straighten his back ... See to it, boy. A few weeks Elsewhen should be enough, but be sure he's left on the right side."

Rudi left the table and reached the door just as Izzy pushed it open.

"Help ... don't say you're finished already?"

"No, just a small phase adjustment to attend to."

"Got lost!" Izzy apologized as he was led to Albrecht's place. "Ended up with all that weird machinery in the basement!"

"Mein Gott, I'd forgotten about him!" Jurgen groaned, "I hope you kept your fingers to yourself Iz, or Rudi'll want your head – Phase is his watch!"

Murmurs of alarm rippled around the table until Halgerd jumped up and introduced Izzy as her Kapitän Harsch's 'Sancho Panza'. The Baron's eyes glazed in incomprehension.

"The wise servant in 'Don Quixote'," Jurgen explained sotto voce.

The Baron glared at his eldest son, "Damn me, you've been reading boy!"

"Now now Piggy, stop intimidating our guests ... I insist that we are allowed to enjoy our supper." The Baroness patted her husband's leathery cheek affectionately and turned to Izzy. "You are most welcome Isador ... Now don't let them brow-beat you. There are no secrets here... and if they will leave the doors open ... Did you tweak the controls?"

"Oh no, your ladyship!"

"Just as I thought, a polite boy ... I have heard of your people. Friedrichshafen ... they are in fabrics are they not?"

"Yes, your ladyship . My father holds the cotton and linen franchise for the Zeppelin Werke." Izzy was still curious about the room full of machinery, but the Baroness had switched her attention to Burk before he could marshall his questions.

"Manfred! ... Kapitän Harsch indeed! ... No, no, you will call me Theo. I insist ... "She continued with the introductions. Rudi returned as his mother was finishing and she told her guests proudly that he was an anthropologist and sociologist.

"The boy's in Intelligence!" The Baron complained. "Dam'n me if I can see why!"

"Now Piggy, someone has to know what's going on," the Baroness rebuked him.

"Which branch are you attached to?" Manfred asked.

"Army ... forward planning!" Rudi grimaced in distaste. "This war is ahh ... completed ... But plans are being drawn up for the next one – the one Germany means to win!"

"Another war!" Manfred suddenly felt very tired and sick from all the years of terror and effort. "From the way you and Jurgen talk it seems that man is measured from war to war ... Does no one want peace?"

"Peace is deserved– not won!" the Baron grunted.

"War is civilization's cancer" Eva told him."Cancer is a consequence of growth. War is never invoked. It is always present and can only be controlled, never wholly excised ... If the lessons from each war are not learned, then the cancer will progress unchecked and civilization will be overwhelmed."

"Jurgen has suggested to me the possible outcome of this war ... What incalculable benefits will the next one bring us?" Manfred gave up trying to catch an elusive potato and stabbed it with his fork.

"The dawn of homo sapiens, the caring society and the extinction of ritual man," Marie answered.

"Don't imagine I'll care for it," the Baron grumbled.

Jurgen laughed and swallowed a mouthful of wine. "Don't pursue the Baron's star, Manfred. Physics are his delight and the attraction of immutable laws has made his outlook somewhat rigid."

"Nothing wrong with an ordered life – it's what life is all about."

The Baron addressed a second plate of meats and Manfred was left a few moments to himself to adjust to his strange surroundings. The other diners wove an extraordinary web of news, questions and conversation between each other which reached out to include him and Izzy on occasion, but thankfully not consistently. Manfred was left with the impression that the whole family did not meet like this regularly and that the full table tonight was special. Why? For the hunt? ...What was that remark Karl had made – 'The Pronouncement?' Had the whole family been convened to pronounce on him? This suspicion was deepened when he began to realize that they weren't as interested in his replies to their occasional questions, as to his attitude to them. He shelved the idea for future consideration – paranoia wouldn't impress anyone now.

Eberheim seemed to delight in ordeals, both at the table and in conversation. But at least their strange philosophies, futuristic occupations and irreverent insight into Germany's situation and rulers were exciting. Unreal certainly, but there was also a depth to them that was not to be found anywhere in the rituals of the mess at Ahlhorn.

After a while he began to feel at home, if not exactly at ease.

The Baroness provided the only safe haven of conversation. She stuck to personalities, gossip and general niceties while the others were incisive and disturbing – even Halgerd was new. She, Eva and Marie, surprised him by their grasp of the war and their involvement in a world of politics he had not even realized existed.

There was something else that bothered him ... The huge table had been set for ten diners – yet he, Izzy, von Dobberitz and the von Taurlbourgs were eleven ... Izzy had been given Albrecht's place. Where would Izzy have sat if von Dobberitz hadn't been thrown out?

Everyone in Eberheim seemed to be an expert in some field or other. So what was Jurgen's field? For that matter what did Halgerd and her mother do? Omission or censorship? Probably the former; the von Dobberitz affair had confused the whole evening. Perhaps the Baroness was being tactful – there were men who would resent women and subordinate officers better educated than they.

Society, as Manfred understood it, disapproved of people who were curious outside of their prescribed fields of work. The war was becoming increasingly dependent on Science, but people still regarded educated men as unmanly. All the men in Eberheim were warriors, but they seemed to be academics too. It was as though Eberheim sought to defend itself from every variety of assault, while at the same time preserving within its boundaries a microcosm of everything useful and, perhaps, good, in the world. What were Halgerd's, Jurgen's and the Baroness' sciences? And what was the machinery in the basement? What was 'Phase'? What did the machinery do with 'Phase' and 'Rotation'? Jurgen had babbled about not being able to 'rotate' before Manfred had tripped him out of SL 17 ...

From the Baron's remarks it would seem that 'Phase' and 'Rotation' had something to do with this 'Elsewhen'. That was an easy word – another place and another time. Impossible of course! But what if you could rotate in space and time? Would your 'phase' determine your destination and its era? ... No! 'Elsewhen', 'Phase' and 'Rotation' had to be something else, new Junker words for simple realities. He would seem gauche if he asked. Even the straight question – what did Halgerd, Jurgen and the Baroness do? – would make him look foolish, like asking a man you've known for months, what his name is. He had made the same mistake with Jurgen as with Zeitel. Damn it, he should know everything about his own executive officer!

When the meal was over a servant entered with a decanter and a humidor. The Baroness led the ladies into the drawing room, while the men moved up closer to the Baron and the claret. All except Izzy – he followed the ladies.

"So!" the Baron announced. "I am in your debt for the preservation of my son and my men?"

"Hardly, Sir," Manfred answered dryly. "I had my own life to save too!"

"Hah. Very good, very good ... I like that," the Baron chuckled.

"He tells a bad story, Baron," Jurgen interrupted softly. "He confuses modesty with honesty. Manfred stayed on board after we jumped to steer the hulk off us. It is remarkable that gesture only cost him his hair."

The Baron said nothing but, when they began to discuss the hunt that was to take place the next day, Manfred saw him staring at him thoughtfully through hooded eyes as he sat, apparently lost in his old world, in the ornate carver at the head of the table.

"What are we hunting tomorrow?" Manfred asked, breaking away from the cold evaluating eyes.

"The big, one-horned hart – y'know the one, boys? Broken Valley," the Baron grunted. "Beast is old. Should have been culled last season – but it is a cunning animal and may win itself another year yet."

The four men enthused about the promised chase and, once more, Manfred was on the outskirts of the conversation. The nearest he had ever come to a hart was a picture of one. He stared at the dark stone walls outside the pools of guttering light and was able to see the glinting bead eyes of previous harts staring balefully at him from heads mounted on mahogany shields.

"Manfred, come back to us ..."

"I beg your pardon ... I was looking at the trophies on the wall," Burk apologized.

"Can't see them now, but they make a brave display by day. You wouldn't think it now, but the halls get good light ... I was asking what firearms you were familiar with," Rudi pointed to the marksman's lanyard on Burk's tunic.

"Target pistol ... Mauser!"

"Not heavy enough ... How good are you with a carbine?"

"Never tried the light rifle. I'm good with the issue rifle though."

"Too heavy." Rudi answered.

"Shotgun!" the Baron pronounced. "Chain shot; can't have wounded game abroad. With chain you'll kill any thing you hit ... You have ridden I trust!"

"On revue, yes."

"Not the same thing. Not the same thing at all!" The Baron's head sagged in thought, then he turned and shouted into the darkness.

"The Kapitän will mount Helga in the hunt."

Whispered movements followed this announcement then a door opened and closed in the shadows.

"Helga will suit you well enough, boy. It's a good animal, just give her her head."

"What about Izzy, Sir?" Manfred asked.

"He may join us if he wants," the Baron beamed generously.

Manfred had no time to explain that it was Izzy's horse he was interested in.

"Claret finished? Better rejoin the ladies. The Brown Room, isn't it?" The Baron's inquiry was answered by a murmur of assent from the shadows and the five men left the table.

Lost in the embracing luxury of a deeply upholstered, high backed armchair, Manfred toasted his feet with the rest of the half circle around the open log fire. The Baroness was seated by an emboidery frame and Izzy, Rudi, Karl and Halgerd were playing bridge. Jurgen, the Baron and the two girls avidly discussed news and rumours.

They were very excited at the prospect that the Kaiser might have to abdicate and they seemed to be on intimate terms with people whom Manfred had only heard of. He was deeply shocked to realize that many of the Fatherland's gods had feet of clay – some of them very muddy indeed. Although he could only listen to their conversation, he did not feel left out of it. Indeed they kept drawing him into it far more often than he cared, asking his opinion of persons whom it must be treason not to venerate. It would be nice to join the others at cards, to relax in the discipline of the game and rest his imagination. He cast a few meaningful glances at Izzy, but since the latter was winning, he wouldn't take the hint. Damn Izzy – let him worry about his own horse tomorrow.

What was he doing here anyway? Halgerd? Once he imagined that he could rescue her from a life of boring ritual! Eberheim was a turmoil of excitement that made his own life dull in comparison. Her family enjoyed, and were well informed in, virtually all the modern sciences. They were acutely aware of current politics – yet all the while they revelled in the ceremony of feudal aristocracy.

What was Halgerd then? The Baroness hadn't introduced her nor announced her field and Halgerd had never alluded to her work. But she must be an expert in something; the quick way she had prevented von Dobberitz from accepting his challenge could only have stemmed from a highly organized mind.

Poor Albrecht! It was as though he had never existed! No one had so much as alluded to him since Rudi returned to the table and Izzy inherited the Count's place.

The Baron yawned and pulled on a bell sash. Following his movement, Manfred saw a framed picture on a table which had been obscured until the old man raised his arm. Two things about the photograph fascinated him. First it was obviously a photograph, but it was a genuine colour one – not a tinted plate. Second, one of the group of happy young men and women was Halgerd. The Baron saw his interest and was about to pass the picture over to him when a servant brought in cocoa and biscuits.

"The Ministerium – filly's chairman," he growled sweeping a mug of cocoa and a fistfull of biscuits onto the table.

"You are a 'minister', Halgerd?"

"The Ministerium of Delight –mein Kapitän! The ministry is in control of Interface; you could consider that to be a form of philosophical engineering."

The even simplicity of her answer sounded truthful, but surely philosophy was an art, not a technology? Besides there was no such 'ministry' but, since she didn't elaborate, Manfred didn't care to walk himself into a situation that might make him a laughing stock. He was too tired to be subtle; leave it, time would tell him everything. He was more worried than curious; if Eberheim could take coloured photographs why had that technology been denied to the Navy?

The Baron yawned and announced that he was for bed. Somewhere a great clock beat out ten strokes and everyone followed the Baron's lead.

☼

Zeitel was not in the offing and Manfred had to struggle with his boots alone. Damn the man – damn the boots, they swelled his legs inside them like pitched tow. Eventually he forced them off. A cotton nightshirt had been laid out for him and for a long time he considered it before eventually deciding to wear it. Normally he preferred to sleep naked, an unconscious protest against the dreadful, itchy sacks they had been forced to sleep in in the Academy. Still fumbling with the buttons, he entered the bedroom and flung back the heavy green drapes of the huge four poster.

A trap? ... A test? ... He was too startled to decide which.

She was pretty, raven haired, and if she hadn't been naked he might have been able to handle the situation with greater aplomb. She said her name was Gretchen, but all he could do was stare mutely at her while confusion and alarm battled inside him ... What if Halgerd, if anyone should enter the room now... Gretchen was speaking again, her pretty face smiling in invitation while she raised the bedclothes for him to join her ... What had she said? That the bed was warm enough now ... Some bedwarmer!

"Very ah ... efficient I'm sure!" Manfred gasped in reply.

"Kapitän, wouldn't you like to come to bed?"

"Quite ... but my dear ah ... Gretchen, I think it would be ah ... wiser, if one of us left."

Had he hurt her feelings? Hardly – she would be under orders to please him. As Jurgen had said, they did things the old way in Eberheim. The only question now was who had given her these orders – and why?

"Gretchen, I mean you no insult. You are the most attractive ahh ... beautiful girl I have ever ahh ... seen ... But we do not know each other, and that is important," he finished, cursing himself inwardly for having added the last piece and the speech's overall awkwardness.

She got up silently and slid into a nightgown. Then she

smiled at him. "I am glad for you," she said. "You have made the choice to sit with the Baron and not at a lower table ... I hope that you can endure it."

"What do you mean, Gretchen?"

"It is a simple question and most men are afraid to ask it. Do you wish to rule or to serve? The answer may seem obvious, but how many men rule? And, of the few who do, how many are happy with the burden of responsibility? I serve – by preference. Those who would sit with the Baron must rule. Always! Do you understand your choice?"

Manfred pretended to consider the question but his mind was frozen. As she crossed the threshold he asked her impulsively, "Izzy, my friend, is at the end of this corridor. Will you go to him?"

She looked at him for a moment, then seeing no insult nor condemnation in his eyes she nodded. He heard her pad softly down the corridor and Izzy's muted shout: "Christmas Day!"

He closed the door and went to bed. It was a long time before he could get to sleep. Gretchen troubled him; she was the last straw in a mind-numbing load of other straws that must be evaluated.

Zeitel knew about Gretchen – nothing else would explain his valet's discreet absence. But dare he ask him? Who was he, his Kapitän's or his Baron's man? Why had the Taurlbourgs endured the preposterous von Dobberitz for so long only to dismiss him so perfunctorily? What was the room full of machinery that Izzy had discovered, and why was it in some way connected with von Dobberitz's return to Germany? Why did the servants at Eberheim seem to have dual roles, Zeitel, Gretchen, the ubiquitous footmen and Rudolf Graatz, his bombardier and Eberheim's armourer?

Then there was the very curious placing of the Baron's titular sons throughout Germany's command structure: Jurgen, Navy; Karl, the Army; Rudi in Intelligence – all very strategic. And all the time the Baron, all Eberheim, evaluated *him*. Why? Their interest had to be for a reason. Eberheim might convey the impression of triviality but what they thought, said and did seemed to be always of consequence. Perhaps strangest of all were Jurgen's occasional pronouncements. They were either extremely cynical or else a truth uttered by someone too objective to be wholly human.

Bob woke up with much of Manfred's suppressed excitement over Gretchen still bothering him. He turned to Susan, caressed her and kissed her, but she wouldn't respond. He spent a long time in the darkness smoking, thinking and listening to the traffic roaring far below them.

Ten

And if ever I return
All your cities I will burn
Destroying all the ladies in the country-o.

Pretty Peg, A FOLK SONG

Susan screamed in automatic response to the shock. There was no sorrow or fright – these would come later when she realized that it had happened to her and not just to the room. An earthquake would have been more acceptable – it being a directionless disaster. But this had been the work of *people*.

Bob charged out of the lift when he heard her scream and his shoulder slammed into her back as he ran into the apartment.

"Sorry hon ... Ohh shit!" The malevolence of the destruction didn't occur to him until later. All he saw was an indescribable mess that would have to be cleaned up before he could get to bed.

The police were quick and they sifted through the broken, smashed and waterlogged contents of Susan's apartment with a practiced thoroughness. There was nothing here they hadn't seen many times before. Susan had managed to shut off the water hosing out of the smashed bathroom before they arrived and the police helped her and Bob to put the place in some sort of order.

"It's nothing personal against you, Miss ... It's important to realize that ... This particular demolition gang won't bother you again."

Susan waited until the police had gone before breaking down. Bob held her in his arms until the terror spent itself and then assured her there had been nothing premeditated about the break in. This was the work of a bunch of nose-picking teenagers and chance alone had led them to her apartment.

Eventually Susan calmed down, but it would be a long time before she could lose the feeling that somewhere, out there, was another Manson gang, one with a personal interest in her. What would have happened if she had been at home when they broke in?

"Crap like that only hit things because they haven't the guts to stand up to people ... They wouldn't have come near your pad if you were in it," Bob insisted.

But the bright sunny world had dark corners in it now, pools of shadow where reason drowned. Behind his comforting facade Bob seethed with worry and rage. He would like to get the punks who did this and what he'd do then wouldn't be for Susan – but for himself. Susan came under his ambit; they had challenged him by this act. But there was something about it that didn't fit. The violence done to the apartment had been a shade too methodical to be spontaneous. Was this the act of professionals? If so, was it a warning or were they looking for something, something to do with *Firedrake* ... Was this some form of super security check authorized by Bascombe? If the General had been behind all this, there was nothing he could do except roll with the punch – as he had done all his life.

☼

"We aren't a crude people. In fact we delight in subtlety ... Unfortunately, we still believe in the work ethic and some of us get carried away ... Sugar?"

This guy just had to be dangerous. No one made it to Colonel in the KGB by affable prattle alone. Bob gazed at the Russian and wondered why the latter was looking at him with such interest. A few grains fell off the spoon and rattled off the paper doily on the tray. The Colonel was still waiting for a reply.

"Sugar? Surely you have all my preferences on record?"

"Of course Major ... But I am trying to be polite!"

"So you are ... Sorry, two spoons!" He didn't like tea; the Russians must have gathered that he preferred coffee. Still, there was an obvious effort being made in the direction of civility and they probably knew they'd make rotten coffee. Tea was the Russian's long suit when they weren't pickling themselves with vodka. "I'm sure I never implied a want of social grace in you or your countrymen."

It was an effort to keep his sentences short. Bob had always been bad at interviews. He had an overpowering urge to fill all silences with speech. And while his tormentor sat back he would hear himself going on and on.

He didn't know what this comrade, Colonel Lavrenti Bersarin, wanted, but Bascombe had considered it important. To hell with protocol, the Colonel outranked him but let him do the sweating for a change. Enduring the silences, however, was always hard. And of course Bersarin would have to be a professional. Bob studied the pale-faced, slightly freckled man. He reeked of cologne, a rather ineffective ploy to cover his obvious passion for garlic. His face was clean shaven but heavily shaded; he must have to shave twice a day – wet shaves, the man had small flecks of dried blood under his chin. Strange how facial hair seemed to absorb the vigour of a man's head. The Colonel's sandy hair was terribly thin and each weak strand was painstakingly placed over the freckled skull.

"My position is somewhat delicate, Major ... I dare say I could bluster it out and hope that you didn't find out ... But I said 'no, Lavrenti must make a clean breast of it ...' That way will be best. After all, it isn't as if either of us is an innocent!"

What in God's name was the Russian talking about? What was the opposite of claustrophobia? Agoraphobia? Were all Russians agoraphobes? Bob glanced around the room. Normally it would have been considered quite large. But it was so loaded with thick, over-rich carpets, heavy drapes, an enormous, low slung chandelier and countless, crassly ornate, heavy pieces of furniture, that it seemed to close in on him. Or was this just another technique in discreet interrogation? The soft chesterfield suite they were sitting in was enormous. In contrast the paper and lace-clad tea table was intimidatingly frail.

"Naturally we would like to refund any damages to the young lady's property. Unfortunately I cannot see how this can be done without revealing our hand in the affair ..."

So it hadn't been Bascombe after all, nor the commercial world checking up on their investment in *Firedrake*! Why had he never considered the Soviets before? Because it was too uncomfortable to accept that they could reach right into the heart of America. No wonder his first impression of their work had been one of method rather than mania. Perfect tactics of course; make it look like a lunatic had worked the pad over so the police wouldn't suspect the 'responsible' agents of a foreign power.

"Major, are you listening to me – I am trying to apologize!"

This was the creature who had done it? Bob pressed his fingers to his lips and tried to penetrate the affable mask. The faded blue eyes were more cynical than cold and, although he seemed to return Bob's stare, they dared not meet his nor any other eyes. No, Bersarin wouldn't have ordered it. He had only been called in to smooth over a blunder. His eyes were haunted, the eyes of a man forced to do a job he detested – efficiently. There was no point in holding a grudge against the Colonel. No one could despise a man more deeply than he did himself, and Bersarin must have shamed his soul to death years ago. But it wasn't in Bob's power to forgive him, even had he wanted to – it had been Susan who was hurt.

Were these Communist tactics? Take away everything long enough for the loss to register then feed back just enough stolen rights for the victim to grovel in gratitude? Having smashed up Susan's apartment, was an admission of guilt supposed to make him warm to them? Or was it a threat; they'd get what they wanted by leaning on Susan? That would work in Russia – but, by God, it wasn't going to work here! He hoped Bersarin would take the hint as to why he hadn't touched his tea. The Colonel sighed, opened a briefcase on the floor beside his chair and gave Bob six large glossy photographs. They all showed scenes of ruin similar to Susan's apartment.

"Standard procedure," the Russian murmured.Those photos are of civilian homes back East – after your agents had finished!"

It was hard to be self-righteous confronted by evidence like that. Even if it were false there was no way he could disprove it. Bob handed the photographs back.

"Your boys sure left the place in one hell of a mess! Get what you were after?"

Bersarin shook his head.

"Shoot! You want me to get it for you! Well, what is it?"

"Do try the tea, Major. I guarantee that you will not taste its equal outside of Russia."

Mechanically Bob raised his cup. He didn't have to like the set up, but he didn't have to go to war on it either. Perhaps the tea was wonderful, he wouldn't know. A woman's drink and he couldn't tell one blend from another.

"This Miss Harmon, she is your girlfriend? I have a wife and five children ... It's the first thing they make you do ... Single people don't have the same loyalty to the state ..."

"Nice guys shouldn't marry!" Bob tried to keep up a stony expression and Bersarin smiled politely.

"Your Miss Harmon wrote to the Moscow department of War Records looking for information about a certain Hauptstürmführer Manfred Burk. It is very important to us that we find this man."

Jesus! They wanted Burk too.

"Why?" Bob hoped he didn't sound too interested or shocked.

Bersarin shrugged. "Terrible things happened in my country during the last World War, Major. The Germans overran Byelorussia and almost overwhelmed us. It is not the conquest, the treachery, nor the ruin that we will remember forever, but the very special meaning they gave to the words 'cruelty' and 'sadism'."

"So?" Bob finished his tea and declined a second cup.

"We Russians tend to remember the Germans as a race of savages. There were too many of them, and their crimes were too numerous, for us to remember individual acts of barbarism. On the other hand there must be something truly remarkable about a single individual who is remembered so faithfully!"

"What did Burk do to you?"

Bersarin offered the Major a grey-papered cigarette from a rolled gold box. "Do try one, Major; they are quite unique , a blend of Russian and Turkish tobaccos together with a little ... I think you call it 'pot'."

Oh, great; Bob thought. They'd landed him with a Soviet junkie, a spaced out ponce who either couldn't or wouldn't give him a straight answer to a direct question.

"You have proof that Burk is a war criminal?" Bob ignored

the cigarettes pointedly. Bersarin selected one, laid it on the table and put the box aside.

"The Russian peoples have been using pot since Neolithic times. We built our own sauna baths, hollow mounds of branches and turf. When everybody was inside the pot was scattered on the hot stones to mix with the steam. I am convinced that this sensible and age-old approach to drugs is the source of my people's indisputable mysticism, the source of our strength, the strength that has enabled us to endure the unendurable – Siberia, the Germans, Stalin, Beria and Hauptstürmführer SS Manfred Burk."

He lit the cigarette and inhaled deeply. Bob stared at him, no longer caring if his disgust showed.

"Keep your pot, Mister. I'll settle for life any day."

"Yes, but an unenlightened one,"Bersarin corrected him.

"Why do you want Burk, Colonel?"

"For crimes against the people."

There wasn't anything more to be got out of the Russian who had lapsed into a dreamy langour which struck Bob as the most effective dismissal he had ever received. Bersarin stared at the ceiling, heedless of further questions, and even when Bob stood up to go he didn't move. The latter left the embassy in a welter of confused emotions – anger, depression and confusion, the precise state the Russian had striven for.

Why did Russia want Burk? Bersarin considered that question as the blue relaxing smoke poured from his nostrils. There was nothing to indicate that Burk had ever fought on the Eastern Front; the German's war activities seemed to have been confined to middle Europe and the Italian border. But it wasn't Russia who wanted Burk at all; it was Bersarin's own control. He conjured up his superior's evil old face and even the calming influence of his cigarette couldn't suppress the shudder. The philosophy of Marx was wrong. God must exist because his counterpart lived in Moscow and was Comrade

Colonel Lavrenti Bersarin's control.

Everything was going according to plan. *Firedrake* had to be, and would be, stopped. The Soviet Union was exhausted by the ceaseless demands placed on it from the West to match and better their every achievement. Soviet science had answered the challenge at the expense of the people who saw the 'oppressed workers' in the West enjoying standards of living far in excess of their own. Unless Soviet resources could be channelled into consumer goods there'd be civil war in Russia. America and the West must stop throwing challenges like *Firedrake* and the arms race at them.

Burk was important, but he was hardly the key. America could fly *Firedrake* without him; there would be accidents of course, but they would eventually get the airship aloft. So why had his control placed so much importance on Burk? They knew where he was, had known for years... Recently he had been indiscreet, sufficiently so for the Americans to find him soon – but first they had to be made aware that he was alive. Strange how this Harmon girl should be looking for him too! The little lady would never know how near she had come to death. His control did not believe in coincidence, but inquiries had revealed her relationship with Major Weston. *Firedrake* needed a competent Zeppelin pilot and Weston probably talked in bed: the girl was a librarian and just trying to help. His control had decided that she posed no threat to his plans and could be of greater assistance to Mother Russia than she would ever be to her lover. Weston was furious over the raid on her apartment. That was good. His anger would spur him to find Burk, remove him from neutral territory, and his anger wouldn't give him time to see that he was being used.

Bersarin ground out the cigarette. He had followed his control's instructions to the letter; everything was going according to plan. That should keep the crazy old German off his back for a while. Why hadn't the KGB ditched the old man like they had all the other Gestapo officers who had come over to Russia? Why hadn't they bled him dry and replaced him when he had nothing more to teach Soviet security? Above all, what was so special about his control that they had let him rise in the system until he dominated it? An old, evil spider lurking in the 250,000 man strong KGB, the deadliest enemy anyone could have; and who, apart from Bersarin and less than a hundred officials of the party, had ever heard of him or even knew of his existence?

Eleven

When now he saw himself so freshly reare,
As if late fight had nought him damnifyde,
He woxe dismaid, and gan his fate to feare:
Nathlesse with wonted rage he him advaunced neare.

E. SPENSER, *THE FAERIE QUEENE*

Zeitel woke Manfred at six in the morning. He carried a box of razors, soap, a bowl of steaming water, and had two hone leathers hanging from his belt.

"Bravely done, mein Kapitän," he growled as he loosened the stubble on Burk's head and face with a hot towel.

"What's that, Chief?" Manfred yawned.

"Yer knows damn well, Sir! ... Mister Ißenquhart sends his compliments and instructs me to inform yer that he'll suffer on in bed."

"I see!"

He wondered if Gretchen had still been in Izzy's bed when Zeitel called him. The Petty Officer's remarks confirmed that he had been part of the plot to put her into his. All the same, he wasn't going to let the Chief know what had happened. Let him find out for himself.

Later, kitted up in twill breeches and a green corduroy jacket, both with cowhide inlets and reinforced panels, brown leather boots and gloves, he made his way down into the great hall. At first he didn't recognize it, it was so choked with people. The L–shaped room was demarcated at the angle; around the tables in the horizontal part were mostly peasants and servants identifiable by their leather garb and homespun shirts. The tables in the vertical arm of the 'L' were a maelstrom of the upper elements of Eberheim. Both groups were breakfasting heartily on red beef, wholemeal bread and sufficient small ale to displace a battleship.

"Ah, there you are old boy ... Had a rough night what?" Jurgen greeted him.

"No, Jurgen, I slept well ... Good God man, how can you breakfast like this?" Manfred, who was used to a roll and a cup of 'ersatz' to start the day, was revolted by the heavy board in front of him.

"Oh, I advise eating. It's the last meal you'll see 'til sundown. Here, follow me; I'll beat a path to the table for you. This style of eating is all the rage; they call it a 'running buffet'."

For the next ten minutes Manfred endured the deafening cacophony while he methodically forced himself to stow away slices of cold beef, so bloody it could only have been licked with flame, and downed two tankards of thin sour ale.

"Who are all these people?" he shouted.

"Oh cousins, kin, friends, local peasantry – anyone who wants to hunt. The Baron keeps an open house ... Don' t ask me to introduce you; most of them are looking for an 'in' to fob me off with some dreadful daughter or sister."

"And you're too young, I suppose," Manfred laughed.

"For marriage, certainly," von Luth was deadly serious. Then his eyes twinkled and he searched Burk's face for signs of fatigue.

"Didn't overdo it last night I trust? ... Gretchen was the

Baron's idea. He thought you might prove to be a little too 'Teutonic' for Halgerd."

"Good old feudal hospitality?"

"Something like that old boy ... There are no prudes here; remember the caring society must also be promiscuous."

"I sent her away, Jurgen!"

"You, what?" von Lüth's face was inscrutable.

"Morning all ... Mother! how could anyone face a break fast like that!" Izzy bruised his way past them and helped himself to an enormous plate of meat.

"Thought you were sleeping on, Iz." Manfred greeted him.

"No ... Gretchen had to go ... By the way, thanks!"

"Is he saying what I think he is?" Jurgen gasped.

"We're getting married," Izzy informed him. "You could spend your life looking for a girl like Gretchen."

"You gave her to Izzy!" Jurgen accused Manfred.

"I thought he might be lonely."

"You really are priceless, old boy! "Jurgen choked. "If she does marry Izzy, the Baron will have to honour his promise and set him up in Eberheim. He promised her a holding and a husband of her choice if she'd do your bidding. Oh God he'll love that." Jurgen collapsed in paroxysms of laughter but when Manfred and Izzy invited him to be more explicit he waved them away and staggered, laughing, into the crowd.

"Are you really going to risk your neck with that lot?" Izzy asked.

"Certainly ... Aren't you?"

"Not likely."

"She's a lovely girl, Izzy. Generous too – you could do a lot worse."

"Don' t I know it ... Thanks again Manfred!"

There was no sign of Halgerd, or others of the family, in the riot of shouting, beer-swilling hunters so, taking steins of bitter thirstcutting ale, Manfred and Izzy went out into the inner yard where the horses were being saddled. The sky above the castellated walls was pink and gold. It was the only peaceful scene in the otherwise bustling panorama of Eberheim.

The courtyard was a melee of horse, hounds, ostlers, grooms and handlers. To add to the confusion, screaming children played around the stamping feet of the massive seventeen-hands-high hunters and the shaggy bellies of the baying elk hounds.

"Manfred!" The voice was strong as distant thunder and it reached him through the din with the same effect. The man was big, about forty, and he brushed his way through the press towards him effortlessly. His brown hunting dress was very different from the rig he had first seen him in, and he was no longer a giant. But the generous face was the same, the pain in his eyes was gone and he walked confidently. Manfred pushed his way forward.

"August Neurath ... I am delighted to see you again Sir."

"*Sir*! ... You idiot Manfred."

Neurnth hugged him like an old comrade and only then saw Jurgen gesture and shake his head. Comprehension followed by dismay chased across his face, but when he held Manfred by the shoulders at arms-length he was smiling again.

"And Halgerd? How are things between you and her?"

"She is well." But their relationship – what could Manfred say about that?

"She's for you lad; Delight and Honour are a matching set! But nothing worthwhile comes easy – and you will know that."

Whatever else Neurath might have said was lost in a crescendo of cheers, baying, whinnying and stamping hooves, as the enormous double doors in the west wall groaned open. The Baron, at the van of a host of men and gaily dressed women, strode into the yard.

"I must speak to old Hildemar before the hunt,"Neurath apologized. "He made me Warden of the East Marches and there have been incursions ... We'll meet again Manfred." He disappeared into the crowd which milled about the yard in confusion.

With the arrival of the Baron everybody began to mount up, each one shouting down the other to get the grooms to tighten a girth, adjust a stirrup, or run a martingale. The hounds, rank from their enforced fast, deafened Manfred with their baying. The old Baron was hoisted ponderously into his saddle by a team of red-faced, grunting, ostlers and he slouched astride his mount like a ruptured sack of turnips while they secured his saddle and irons.

"Helga is ready, Sir," a boy's voice shrilled beside him.

Turning, Manfred saw yet another of his erstwhile crew grinning happily and reeking of the stables. He conducted a quick mental roll call and found him.

"Brück, isn't it! What are you doing here?"

The boy grinned. "I was a stable hand before the call up ... It's great to be back, Sir!"

Brück led him to a prancing monster. Manfred stared up into the wild whites of her eyes with an apprehension that verged on alarm. She was a powerfully built bay whose prominent curved spine proclaimed that she was no longer a filly – but whatever her age Helga was certainly no hack. Her broad impressive forequarters indicated tremendous heart and lung capacity and therefore endurance, while the sparks rung from the cobbles by her hooves, and the lashing of her night black tail, announced her impatience to be off. She was fully clipped except for the black mane and, although the morning was cool, she had begun to lather where the reins, pinned by the martingale, slapped her arched neck. Brück gave Manfred a leg up and, having tightened the straps, walked him round in a circle, eyeing Burk critically to ensure that he was riding low and even.

"Keep her on a loose rein, Sir ... She's got a soft mouth and is used to a plain snaffle. I gave her a half twist for you – so don't saw at her."

Manfred suppressed the urge to put Brück down. Damn it all, it wasn't as though he were a complete amateur. He'd be as stiff as a board after today, but that would be from lack of practice, not the want of experience.

"Good hunting, Sir." Brück vanished into the press and Manfred began to guide Helga to the rear of the meet. He couldn't find Izzy, but Karl rode up to him, slid a well-oiled shotgun into the holster over Helga's right foreleg and thrust a belt of paper cartridges into his hands. He warned Burk not to take Helga into Broken Valley which had been named for the tangle of rock and briar that filled it. Deer could negotiate it, but a horse would break its legs.

"Stay behind the Baron after the draw, Manfred ... If you or anyone breaks ahead of the Master, ohh boy!" He made a gesture of cutting his throat before driving his heels into his mount's flanks and plunging towards the gates. The cheering of the crowd and the ululations of the hounds intensified. The Baron raised his horn and flourished it vigorously. Fever gripped the horses and Helga began to buck and prance in excitement.

A crack of light split the black logs of the north gate. The drawbridge was already lowered and Manfred could see yellow waterlilies and venom green scum on either side of it in the moat. The Baron wound a long blast on the horn and immediately Helga exploded under Burk, surging into the flood of horse.

The whole forest was alerted to the hunt by the clangour of iron-shod hooves booming over the railway-sleeper bridge. For a while Manfred was swept along by Helga into the forest – a total passenger – but after a while he began to gain some degree of control. Riding her was like running before a gale. There was nothing he could do to conquer the force, but with skill he could guide and use it. For all her strength and eagerness, Helga was a comfortable ride, being too big to make sudden jerky movements. With her soft mouth she steered easily provided he did not attempt to run her too far off what she determined to be her mean course. She seemed to appreciate the etiquette of the hunt too and, once Manfred was assured that she wouldn't break ahead of the Baron, he let her have her head, only keeping enough rein in hand to pull her up if she stumbled over a root or hole. Riding her was like sitting in a comfortable rocking chair; her pitch and roll were much smoother and rhythmic than the movements of a ship. Soon all fear was gone and he was enjoying the hunt immensely. The hart, which had been driven towards the Schloß the previous day, was scented by the hounds after a short beat and, almost at once, the hunt became strung out with only the strong and the determined up front with the Baron.

Those who, like the Baroness, had come along purely for the social occasion, returned to Eberheim after the first hour, to be joined later by others with green mounts spent from sustained excitement. Helga took a middle course and kept Manfred at the rear of the hunt proper, but well ahead of the tiring stragglers.

The one-horned hart was a cunning beast which had laid false trails and doubled back on its spoor on other occasions. It employed impenetrable thickets and obstacles, laying trails that seemed to lead into them only to double back deeper into the forest. Helga was too wise to gallop wildly after the impulsive hounds; rather she cantered along the hunt's mean course, stopping to graze now and then while others wasted their energies beating a stubborn thicket from which she knew the hart had doubled back. After the first worrying beats where Helga rested and the less experienced hunters lathered themselves into a frenzy, Manfred accepted that his mount knew what she was doing and was pleased to let her command events. He concentrated on taking in his surroundings, enjoying the forest and the heady mountain air, invigorated by the astringent scent of pine rosin.

All morning they hunted through the trees, occasionally breaking into areas of cultivation that seemed to mark the edge of the forest. Then one saw the trees looming on the horizon, and the fields of cattle, corn and ricks of hay were diminished to what they were – islands in the tree ocean of Eberheim. The hart did not favour the cultivated areas and only entered them to use water to lose the hounds. On a few occasions it led them through timber house villages, no doubt with a view to deadening the hounds' noses with the stench of man. It could not be expected to realize that the villagers would tell the hunt where it had gone, but in one respect its strategy was effective. On being warned of the hunt's approach by the sight of the hart, the villagers would flock to greet their liege lord and the hunt with tankards of ale and slabs of apple bread, while the children clamoured to water the horses.

Towards noon, Helga closed the gap and bore Manfred into one of these villages to join the Baron who had arrived with his fieldmasters and a reduced hunt of twenty horses. Women in white caps, red blouses and black skirts ran to them with steins of ale. Manfred seized one gratefully, suddenly aware of his raging thirst. Over the rim he saw Neurath and the Baron roaring with laughter at one of the hunt who had walked his horse to the pond for a drink. The animal decided to roll in the water and nothing its howling rider could do would stop it. Eventually the man had to leap from the saddle and stand knee deep in muck with a red, furious face while the horse wallowed and kicked happy legs into the air.

"Are you enjoying yourself, Manfred?"Halgerd asked, her image distorted by the steam rising from both their mounts.

She smiled at him over her tankard. She had changed mounts earlier on and now sat astride a blowing chestnut whose lungs worked its flanks like a bellows. She looked very competent and, at the same time, beautiful, in a black hat and jacket, both stained, as were his, by the sticky amber blood of the forest.

"Yes," he gasped and slapped Helga's neck affectionately." I can honestly say that I have never done anything quite so ahh ... active as this ... You will agree that this sport requires a pitch of such size and fixtures," he waved to take in the whole forest, "that it would be unreasonable to expect it to be included in the amenities at Ahlhorn."

Halgerd laughed, finished her ale and handed the stein to a convenient small boy. "We seem to have lost a few people," Manfred observed.

"I should hope so; if the Baron didn't set so hard a pace we should all be trampled at the kill – if there is one. My money is on the hart again this year."

"I don't see the Baroness or Eva or Marie." Manfred stood up in his stirrups and looked around the group.

"Eva lost a shoe in the fen and Marie's saddle tree broke, so they're out of it. As for mother, she's gone to guide von Dobberitz home. It will take him weeks and I don't imagine he'll ever understand."

"He'll kill her," Manfred shouted in alarm.

"Oh no, Mother's too well protected – she can rotate at will."

"I've been meaning to ask you, what is this 'rotation', and also 'phase' and 'interface'?"

"They are terms which attempt to describe multi-dimensional effects in three-dimensional terms.

"What do you mean?"

"Consider this universe to be one of many, an infinity of alternate relativistic states, coexisting in one multi or omniverse. Mother's our cartographer; she translates the viable phases of Elsewhen. Jurgen's a navigator; he determines the rotation necessary to get there. The rest of us, the ministerium, determine the interface. Elsewhen can be fragile and, where there have been incursions, hostile."

"I don't understand ... August mentioned incursions?"

"Eberheim explores other philosophic and relativistic states.This involves the setting aside of so called natural laws and the invocation of higher ones. Not all the relativistic states love God. Elsewhen is at war with itself ... This is the war we want your ship for."

"What?"

The Baron finished his tankard and tossed it to one of the village girls. He belched loudly, smacked his lips in satisfaction and drew his sleeve across his froth-sodden moustache, then he sounded another blast on his horn and galloped off after the distant baying. Halgerd and the others dropped everything and plunged into the forest after him. Helga paused long enough to raid a nearby pig trough, then carried a bewildered Manfred after them at a deliberate canter. 'Elsewhen' ... 'a war'... 'an airship'? Dear God, Halgerd hadn't even said which side she was on.

Manfred and Halgerd met once again as the day was slipping into evening. She was too excited by the progress of the hunt to return to their previous conversation and since he was still trying to digest what she had said, seriously or in jest, he was wary of returning to the subject. But there was one thing he had to find out.

"Which side is Eberheim on?"

"Think, Manfred. Only one side can love!"

Then it was back to the hunt. It was her opinion that the hart was done with trying to throw them off its trail and that this was probably its last deception before it made its final run for Broken Valley. The deception in question was a huge amphitheatre of briar and thorn, a dark green island in an ocean of black trunks rising from a carpet of pine needles and rotted cones.

At some time in the past a huge tree had fallen, clawing down its neighbours with it, which in turn felled others. This ruptured the branch ceiling, allowing the sun to light this oasis on the otherwise lifeless forest floor. It was this, the very density of the forest, that made passage through it so easy. The towering trunks were spaced well apart and the lower branches had atrophied and fallen off in the lightless zone under the canopy of the upper branches. Only fungi grew on the dark floor.

"I hope for his sake he hasn't tired and run for home. He's near now, but not near enough to outrun the hounds," Halgerd confided.

"Why do you hunt if you pity your victim?" Manfred asked.

"I enjoy the hunt, but not a kill ... Oh, they've beaten the cover. He's not here... Come on, we must kill him before the hounds do."

"By all means do, dear sister ... Else it will be quite spoiled for the table." Jurgen, who had ridden up to them unnoticed, grinned at them.

"You ... You've no soul, only senses,"Halgerd riposted and was off after the hunt in a storm of churned up loam and pine needles.

The hart did not attempt a direct run. As the forest grew darker with the falling sun it proceeded, surely but deviously, towards its territory via every obstacle and diversion it could find. Although a large animal, it seemed to penetrate with ease thickets that barred or tore the hounds, and leapt the thorn laden branches of fallen trees insurmountable and impenetrable to the horses. Always the hounds flung themselves into the deepest parts of these sunlit tree graves where briar, hawthorn and bracken warred slowly for the light. But when the hounds emerged bleeding and burred the hart had gone.

"The hart is making for Broken Valley. Why don't you simply head it off instead of letting it run you in circles?" Manfred asked Rudi.

"We hunt; we do not set ambushes!" was the terse reply.

After the sixth, time-consuming beat the hunt veered to the left, but Manfred, after consulting his compass, decided that Broken Valley lay to starboard and with tremendous difficulty, and much assertion of will, he managed to force Helga to shamble to the right and away from the hunt at a surly trot.

He was just about to sue for peace and let Helga gallop back to the others, who were now only barely audible, when the hart burst out of a dead thicket to his left. It was a splendid creature. One enormous branched antler sprouted from its left forehead and pointed away from Burk towards Broken Valley but, where the antler from its right forehead should have sprouted, there was only a bald pucker of ancient scar tissue. In its youth a hunter must have gouged the bone and growth centre away with a shot that maimed, yet taught the beast caution. Head up, breath steaming from flared nostrils and saliva dribbling from quivering jaws, it stared at Manfred in a moment that seemed to last forever. Its rust-red flanks heaved with each gale of breath, scattering burrs, thorns and broken twigs of dead pine from its matted, unscathed pelt.

What luck! Manfred thought. Wouldn't it be really something if I killed you! His hand touched the stock of his shotgun and all at once he understood Helga's murderous quiet. She was frozen, a gun platform. He knew that he could bring the gun up and fire before his quarry could get out of range, even if the hart bolted now. And then he remembered that Halgerd wanted the hart to live. Some wish! If he let the beast go then she would never know because no one would ever believe him. To kill it would impress the Baron. His hand tightened on the stock, then grunting a good humoured oath he let it go.

"Go Hart. Make your run – nothing can stop you now," he shouted.

With a parting flash of whiteness, the hart displayed its cream furred rump and was off, bounding for the twin hills that marked the entrance to Broken Valley.

"Wait, Sir Stag!" Manfred shouted after it. "An escort ... I will be your escort!" Then whooping loudly he unholstered the shotgun and swung it around his head, imitating an American Indian he had once seen in a comic book, and dug his heels into Helga. He nearly fell off; as it was he lost a stirrup and spent so much time with his head bowed trying to reinsert his foot that he missed the point where the hart leapt off the path. He was much too near the fallen tree to avoid it when he looked up again. He had forgotten how intuitive Helga was to the hunt and when he had lifted his legs to urge her on she had surged ahead at a full gallop while his legs were still wide apart .

The tree was enormous and since it had fallen in darkness there was no shroud of vegetation to hide the savage palisade of broken branch arms radiating from it. Frozen in horror Manfred felt Helga cram way on and gather herself up under him. Surely the crazy horse wasn't going to jump ... It was six feet high at its lowest point if it was an inch. Frantically Manfred scanned the obstacle for a way around it, but there was none. The great torn up gout of earth that had been the tree's roots contained him on one side, and the other was an impregnable wreckage of broken branches.

There was only one answer: Helga was going to run under the trunk – she couldn't be insane enough to risk disembowelment by jumping. When she did he would be swept off, skewered on the thick, jagged stumps of broken branches... And it was too late now to do anything except throw himself along her neck, grip the martingale and bury himself in her black mane. As he flung himself forward her neck came up with her shoulders, smashing into his face, throwing him back and Helga took off.

Again, like the moment of confrontation with the hart, time crawled during the split second of flight. Manfred was still falling backwards as Helga rose over the deadly wooden spears, black hafts that were corpse-white where they were broken, and the inside wood, seasoned, dead and shot with fungus, glinted balefully underneath them. Relief and gratitude to the splendid horse flooded him when Helga's rump caught him and thrust him forward again. She had cleared the obstacle and had begun the descent. But Helga had saved his life twice, the first time when she had cleared the tree, the second time when she had thrown him back on her rump. And Helga threw her head up before he could realize this, up and up, beyond the pumping stump of her neck, up until the reins were wrenched from his fingers and her head fell into a thicket on the opposite side of the place that had exploded in a double detonation of violet-rimmed spears of yellow flame. The horse spasmed under him and the thrashing corpse crashed into a carpet of pine needles on the other side of the fallen tree. Manfred, slack jawed with shock, kept on going.

He understood what had happened when there was more flame and another double explosion, the first when his hand squeezed the shotgun stock and tripped the for'ard trigger. His finger kept on squeezing when his shoulder and the stock hit the loam and ploughed a deep furrow in the forest and the second barrel went off, tearing the gun from his hand. Pine needles, loam and rank pulped toadstools were driven deep into his clothes and mouth, shovelled into arm and collar openings by the force of his slide, and down his throat while he cried out in fear. Someone had emptied both barrels of a shotgun at him. That person still had his gun and Manfred's was gone.

Trembling with shock Manfred staggered to his feet, pulled two waxed paper cartridges out of his belt and looked for his gun. Then he heard the 'clack' of another gun's breech being snapped shut. He saw his gun only ten feet away and was staggering towards it when the man stepped out onto the game path from his ambush in the pit where the fallen tree had been rooted. Manfred recognized him at once, Matrose Schiller who had sailed under him on SL 17 from the date of her commissioning. He must be another of the Baron's men ... Was this how the Baron had intended Halgerd's problem to be settled? ... And he had walked right into the trap, so willingly and in so much hope.

Manfred's fingers closed around his gun and he broke it open, fumbling to extract the spent cartridges and slide in the new rounds. Schiller's gun was still dribbling smoke and as he brought it up to his shoulder Manfred knew that it was already reloaded and that he would never get his own gun up in time. He stood up, his gun loaded but not closed. Schiller lowered his slightly. There was a frenzied disturbance in the thickets behind Schiller's ambush site, but neither man paid it any attention– a bird, frightened by their presence beating through confining briar and bracken to be away. Manfred tried bluster.

"This is mutiny, Schiller ... Put up the gun man, or else you will hang!" He tried to force as much authority into his voice as his shaken body would permit. There was always the hope that Schiller would respond automatically to a command long enough for Manfred to close and raise his own gun. It didn't work. Schiller levelled the gun at his stomach and with his eye lying along the barrel he spoke.

"I am sorry, Kapitän. I really am, but nothing can save you ... You could say that by doing this I have invested all my silver to turn it into gold ... So you see, I must kill you."

"The name of your banker, Schiller ... You owe me that at least!"

"The Graf von Dobberitz ... We had plenty of time to secure the deal when I drove him from the Schloß. Good bye, Kapitän. I truly am sorry ..."

Schiller's knuckles whitened in the trigger guard and Manfred leapt to one side and swung his gunup. There was no way he could avoid death, but there was just the chance he could take Schiller with him if he could stand against the screaming panic that was unmanning him, clawing at him to run, to squirm through the thickets and burrow through the loam to safety. What a way to be carried back to Halgerd – shot in the back, bled to death, his final scream plugged with the black earth.

The bushes between the two men parted and the hart emerged onto the game path. It had plunged into the forest to avoid the fallen tree and, by happy accident, was completing its detour in time to prevent murder. It froze when it saw Manfred, then shied and ran down the path towards BrokenValley. Immediately on turning it saw Schiller, but this time it did not leap away. Safety was a short distance up the path and this man was in its way. The hart, normally a non–aggressive creature, was now desperate, its stamina spent and the hounds could be heard in the far distance. Lowering its one horn it charged up the path, causing Schiller to curse in fright and jump aside. That was all the time Manfred needed. He brought his gun up.

"I am almost tempted to let you blow your head off."

Jurgen's voice was conversational. "The barrel man ... It is not a spade, yet it is clogged with earth ... Very careless ... Schiller, you will go now."

Trembling with relief Manfred watched Schiller's face crumple in horror and the gun fall from his nerveless fingers. Manfred quickly broke his own gun open and considered the loam-choked barrel ruefully. Not only was it blocked, but in the fall the barrels had become bent. The shotgun was quite useless for anything other than suicide.

"No, Master," Schiller was pleading. "I have served you all these long years, faithfully ... He is not of us, why do you favour him for your servant ... Do not send me away, I beg you."

"Get out, Schiller!" Jurgen's face hardened in disgust. "You have chosen another master and there is no longer an obligation between us. I see only greed in you – go sate it elsewhere."

Schiller waited, his face white with grief, until Jurgen had pronounced his doom. Then, picking up his gun, he turned towards Broken Valley. His back was towards them so his body hid the gun as he brought it up. Seven paces on he blew his head off.

"The fool!" Jurgen hissed, more to himself than to the horrified Manfred. "Neurath was right; there have been incursions." He slumped on his horse in deep thought, ignoring Manfred, the dead Schiller and the still twitching Helga.

"Thank you, Jurgen ... You saved my life," Manfred gasped when he had mastered himself.

"Is it possible to save a life? ... I think not ... It is only possible to influence direction ... Perhaps our accounts are settled now, Manfred. You cannot dream how inconvenient it would have been for me to have burned with SL 17!"

A horn sounded in the distance and Jurgen became rigid in the saddle. It was a different sound from the one the Baron had wound during the hunt, deeper, more urgent, a note that would travel for miles and miles commanding attention.

"Interface control! A Rotation now? It can't be us they seek!" Jurgen spoke to himself and wheeled his horse around. He called to Manfred.

"I must go back. Don't dwell!"

"Wait, I have no horse. Let me mount behind you ... Jurgen, I don't know the way back. What about Schiller? You can't just let him rot here ... Jurgen!" But the Count was gone and Manfred was left at the entrance to Broken Valley half way between a dead man and a dead horse while night thickened in the forest.

Eberheim must be at least twenty miles away and he must walk – but in which direction? He consulted his compass and decided that the Schloß lay to the east. Wait a minute; he was a fool ... Schiller couldn't have walked here – he must have a horse nearby.

Finding the horse was no problem, but catching it was something else again. Schiller had tethered it to a tree, but the horse had grown impatient and broken its reins. It was grazing on bark when Manfred discovered it. At first he worried about how to repair the reins, but after a while he began to realize that he might not have to solve that problem because, try as he might, the horse would not let him catch it. It was content to torment him by maintaining a gap of some twenty feet between them. For the next half hour Burk wheedled it with rare tussocks of grass, green pine cones and fronds of bracken – all to no avail; the horse expressed sufficient interest in his offerings to keep Manfred trying, but all the time it led him deeper and deeper into the forest. Then, when it had got so dark that he had difficulty in seeing it, the horse threw up its head, gave a derisive whinny and galloped off to its warm stable. There was nothing else for it, Manfred conceded bitterly, he would have to return on foot, but he promised himself a secret visit to the stables if he ever made it back.

Again he consulted his compass and estimated his course from the luminous instrument. He had memorized a map of the forest last night and he reckoned that he was about twenty five miles from Eberheim. The trouble was: he needed to know his exact position if he was to reach the Schloß and not pass it by on a correct but parallel course. To get a bearing he needed to shoot a star, but if there were any in the sky this night they were cut off by the branch canopy above him.

On the verge of tears from fatigue, frustration and shock he searched for a high, climbable tree. It was not as easy as he had hoped; few of the forest giants had low-growing branches but, after a long search during which he consoled himself by imagining the thrashing he would give Schiller's horse, if he ever managed to find it again, he found a suitable tree and climbed it.

His clothes were ruined by sticky amber resin by the time he reached the upper branches. Worse, thousands of dead pine needles had poured down the back of his neck and up his sleeves, pricking and itching him abominably. The tree was no longer the rock-fast pylon it had seemed to be when he had begun to climb it. Towards the top, its thinning stem creaked and swayed in a high wind that tossed the upper leaf canopy of the forest.

Shooting two stars and hanging on at the same time was extremely difficult; he had to read the star's angle with the pocket compass/sextant in one hand and consult his watch with the other. In the end, his patience almost exhausted, he succeeded in roughly estimating his position. From now on, it should be possible to shape a course for Eberheim by compass alone. He began the slow descent of the tree. It was worse than the climb had been; then there had been the glow from the sky to silhouette the branches ahead of him but, going down, there was only absolute darkness. He had to grope his way to the ground by feel. Ten feet from the ground, and it could have been a hundred for all he knew, he slipped and fell, yelling all the way.

"You really shouldn't play monkeys if it's going to make you hysterical, old boy!"Jurgen called from the darkness.

There was a hiss, the small explosion of a match and Burk, already winded, was blinded by the light from a carbide lamp. How had Jurgen found him? Cold wetness pressed against his hands and hot slobbering tongues on his face answered that question – the hounds. He was amazed that they could hunt the hart so savagely, yet track him so gently.

"I was shooting a star, Jurgen," he gasped tartly.

"How very ingenious of you, dear boy ...Well, you'll know the form then – just keep going west south west and, if you're brisk, you'll be joining us for breakfast."

"You can't leave me here ... Let me up behind you." Manfred yelped in alarm.

"Can't oblige, old boy ... As you can see I' m already overballasted." He swung the lamp up and, for the first time, Manfred became aware that someone was slumped behind Jurgen, gripping his waist with torn pallid claws. Manfred stared at the semi-conscious form for an age before he recognized it as Neurath.

August was horrifyingly changed, by age and by agony. Lunatic eyes, pain raddled, ancient from suffering, stared from the puffy wasted face of a boy some twenty years younger than the man he had spoken to that morning. His soft, yellow riding boots were hardened and caked with the blood that still welled from their rims and, all at once, Manfred became aware of the terrible stench of burnt flesh.

"We were all caught in the rotation," Jurgen said quietly. "He will be well again when I get him back, but in the meantime ... it is unspeakable. The body tends to resonate near its times of maximum trauma. That's why I owe you so much ... all the crew owe you ... had you not spared us on

SL17 we'd all be burning now!" He shut off the water to the lamp and the flame hissed, guttered and went out.

"Couldn't catch Schiller's mount then?" Jurgen was his normal, caustic self again. "Must see to that! The Baron's mad enough as it is over Helga – won't do to lose another horse."

"The horse will find its own way home. They do it all the time," Manfred protested.

"Can't rely on that ... Too risky, wolves and bear about, y'know ...Well, I'll tell Zeitel not to wait up for you ... See you tomorrow."

At this point Ncurath began a weak, terrible moaning. Nothing human, just animal overtones of something driven way over its threshold of agony and despair.

"Hang on old boy – we'll have you back before you know it," and with a muffled thudding of hooves on the loamy soil von Lüth was off.

Hell had never touched Manfred so closely before and for a long time after they had left he stayed, sitting where he had fallen, unwilling to press into the unknowable night and frozen with horror by what he had witnessed.

Twelve

And on the eighth day God waited ...

The man from 'Silicon Valley' obviously loved his work. But he feared it too. No one would smoke so heavily and aggravate his ulcers unless he was under permanent stress. Bob and his team had worked under the guidance of the microprocessor expert for a month, which had raced by like a week and exhausted them like a year's effort.

"Y' know, this is all new now ... But it'll be obsolete the minute we insert the first chip – what the hell, it was obsolete on the drawing board," Max Cogan, the expert, told him.

"Hardly matters here," Bob answered.

True. And Bob felt a deep sympathy for Cogan. What a hell of a life it must be just to keep abreast with man's discoveries, never mind keep on top! It must be hard to sell gear to big business knowing, on the one hand, that the product was the best 'now' and, on the other hand, that his rivals would have better rigs on the market by the time the job was done. Cogan should have rested his feet on this one ... But he couldn't. Years of worry had turned the computer salesman into something akin to a rocket booster – to burn and thrust his product forward until he was wasted and his cargo receded ahead of him.

Bascombe joined the two men in the command car, his face

softened by the green, red and yellow LEDs of the control board.

"Is this all there will be?"

"Yes, General. From here the computer has access to all functioning parts of the ship. All we need now is a flight programme."

"That is in hand." The worry gnawing inside the General made him snap the reply more brusquely than he had wished. He corrected it with a wide smile. "'Your company computerizing the Lockheed units too?"

"The prototypes, yes ... Like you General, they are building, or rather have built, conventional rigid dirigibles for flight tests and as an exercise to capture public interest and confidence ... They have started work on the oblate version. Sub contracts will be awarded when your ship is worked up to their satisfaction."

The General grinned and tried to imagine how much the civil aviation gang were paying Cogan for details on *Firedrake*. This time the military was going to use private industry to fight the war for them instead of vice versa. It had been their idea to force *Firedrake* on the Army in an attempt to get the government to underwrite the development costs. The Army must place all contracts for *Firedrake* with them and, for every part the Army ordered, they would make several. This way, they were able to assemble their own *Firedrake* prototypes at minimal cost. But the whole point of *Firedrake* was to force the Reds into competition and that was a bill the civil aviation gang could carry. Once they went commercial it would be up to them to stay ahead of Russia, and the armed forces could buy commercial airships and modify them for military use as they had the 747 Jumbos and other civilian aircraft.

Lockheed and its partners had been successful in getting the Army to build the prototype, but now they found themselves locked in fierce competition among themselves.

Not only that – suppose a rival company like Boeing got an airship aloft before they did? The General had been careful in his selection of civilians with access to *Firedrake*. Corruption wasn't an evil to be eradicated, it was a weapon to be deployed. Cogan and the other civilians with access to *Firedrake* could be trusted to sell to anyone who could buy. Security was like a beautiful, stupid dame – desirable and wholly irrational. Those who understood security could manipulate it; those who didn't were trapped by it.

Soviet scientists might dismiss lighter-than-air transport for the mare's nest that it might well prove to be, but their logic wouldn't be heeded once Russian security learned that the Lockheed, Boeing and Supermarine companies, to mention but a few, were cutting their throats to develop it. *Firedrake* was going well and was already burning more fingers than the General had initially hoped for. To hell with the tactics, he had been bitten by the spirit of competition too. The civil gang had tried to make use of the Army, draw it into a race it had never wanted to compete in in the first place. Well by God, the Army was going to win it! *Firedrake* would be in the air long before Lockheed, or any of the others, could find anyone to take their versions up. Bascombe would win that triumph for the Army and the taste of victory needled him with delight and worry . . .

Worry because he hadn't quite got it all tied down yet. For years the commercial world had robbed the armed forces of the cream. They could pay. They could, and did, offer salaries to the few 'experts' available who made a career in the Army a laughable alternative. But what money couldn't buy, blackmail would secure. Bascombe had found his expert, a hunted man whose past made him absolutely the General's – Hauptstürmführer SS Manfred Burk. But Bascombe hadn't collected yet and the Reds were after his man too.

Standards must be slipping in the Kremlin. It wasn't like the Reds to put all their eggs in an open diplomatic basket.

They had come right out into the open and demanded that the General's prize be handed over to them to stand trial for war crimes. *Firedrake* must be causing a great deal of panic to make a system that was devious by choice behave so naively. The Reds amused him and he was wholly conscious that he owed them a great deal. If Russia didn't exist at the technological level she did, then he'd have been lucky to have made the rank of chicken colonel, never mind a general.

Running Burk to ground had been one of the few recent CIA successes. As political assessors that organization had proved to be a disaster, but as head hunters they justified their existence.

No records of Burk's activities between the years 1918 and 1930 existed. He had joined the SS and there were some indications that he had done so to escape from Royalist execution squads. The German Navy had more or less mutinied towards the end of World War One and quite a few airship crews had burned their Zeppelins in their sheds to avoid being sent out on any more suicidal missions. Burk had probably been one of these. After the Kaiser's abdication he would have been found guilty, most likely in his absence by a kangaroo court, of dereliction of duty and sentenced to death. Throughout the Second World War Burk had never left Western Europe. He had joined the Waffen SS as a technical advisor and his age excluded him from combat until 1944. In that year, after Count Stauffenberg's unsuccessful attempt to assassinate Hitler, Burk, assisted by men from the SS Charlemagne, succeeded in rescuing one of that division's officers, a certain Major Neurath, from the Gestapo.

That rescue, together with the Gestapo's failure to recapture Neurath, had cost a certain SS Oberführer his career and had got him transferred to the Eastern Front. Perhaps the Russians did have a valid crime to accuse Burk of because that SS Oberführer had been captured by the Reds, had joined the

NKVD and risen from there to a position of enormous power in the KGB. That SS Oberführer was Colonel Bersarin's control.

Burk, Neurath, and the remnants of the *Charlemagne* had fled to Italy in six tanks. There they had severely mauled an American Sherman division, and were believed to have been annihilated themselves. In fact Burk, and one other, had escaped, fled south and taken refuge in a Benedictine Priory in the Italian city of Bari.

Burk must be as old as sin by now, Bascombe decided. He could have died in the Priory and never have been discovered if it hadn't been for that God-sent 'apparition' in the graveyard beside the Priory. A routine investigation had uncovered the fact that the monks had been harbouring at least two War Criminals – Germans, Burk and another now deceased.

Why did the Reds want Burk so bad? Simple! They, like the USA, had no experts in rigid dirigibles and whoever got Burk would have an edge on the other. Secondly, and more serious for the Kraut, the KGB had informed the Kremlin that Burk was a War Criminal and they, enslaved by their brutal myopic system of rigid authoritarianism, had accepted his guilt unquestioningly. Burk was guilty of War Crimes now, not because he had committed any but because the infallible Soviet courts had pronounced him to be a criminal. And, as everybody knew, the one thing the USSR did not make was mistakes – apart from the one of putting a revenge-crazed, ex-Gestapo man in charge of national security. That had been the Nazis' fundamental weakness which had cost Hitler the war – their weakness for prizing vengeance above everything – even victory.

It was only when Moscow insisted that Burk be turned over to them, and after the State Department had requested proof of his guilt, that the Politburo became aware that the KGB's resources were being exploited by a senile old Nazi to hunt down the remnants of the Stauffenberg plot. Lovely! The General cracked his knuckles with glee. Projecting a front of keen interest, but still wrapped in his thoughts, Bascombe let Bob and Cogan lead him through the ship describing how the automatics worked and tracing the control lines. Both subordinates were very excited by the lift conservation systems. The General forced himself to pay attention – an acknowledgement seemed to be in order.

Helium was a gipsy element. Earth's gravity couldn't hold it, and free helium in the atmosphere wandered off into space. Held dissolved in certain rocks, it could not be classified as rare, but the quantities required to lift the ship, some two million cubic feet of gas, couldn't be wasted like hydrogen. In *Firedrake* the cells were closed, each one containing an inbuilt heating element and a feed to a compression flask. The ship derived its lift by inflating the cell, and its boost by heating the gas. To descend, air was ducted around the cell to cool the gas, deflate the cell, and a compressor fed the helium back into the flask. All these operations, together with the engines, the cantilevered fins and all other ancillary functions were controlled by the computer and had a manual override option. Cogan was right; everything save one had been done. All *Firedrake* needed now was a commander.

Bascombe endured the tour with seeming enthusiasm. Let the acolyte from Silicon Valley have his sweets – and stay sweet when Burk was delivered to him. It would be up to Cogan to compile a flight programme ... But Burk would be half senile by now! Would he remember his skills? He would have outlived them by up to half a century.

Later, when the tour was over, Bascombe thanked Cogan and left, waving to Bob to follow. Mustard gas, the General thought. Obsolete as a weapon, yet if it hadn't been for mustard, and that accident in Bari, the 'apparition' would not have been investigated nor Burk discovered. The two men walked across the cracked tarmac of the disused airfield. Grass and weeds had burst through the asphalt years ago and now the strip was more brown, from dead grass, than grey. If it were ever to be used for planes again the whole runway would have to be relaid. But that airstrip had been laid when the Japanese were throwing something less lethal than the yen at the States, laid over the rolling lawns that had served the older airship shed. And what a shed! Bob loved it dearly. From a distance it reminded him of a New England barn; at evening a man could walk into its shadow and never reach the door before the sun set. More than twice as big as the airship hung up inside it, the shed, nearly half a kilometre long, sprawled across its circular turntable and drew itself up into the sky, a massif of raw wood and PVC sheeting.

"I like it, Bob!"Bascombe decided. "The computer's small and doesn't change the lines of the ship or the layout of the car ... And we'll be in the air weeks before Lockheed, and the rest of the competition, get theirs programmed."

"If we can find someone to fly her," Bob reminded him.

"*Where*, Bob, not *if*. We already have a name ... All we have to do is find him!"

"Who?"

"Haupstürmführer Manfred Burk! Who else?"

"But we can't use him, General, even if we find him. The Ivans want him and, with all this detente, we'll have to hand him over."

"Certainly Bob. But only after he's trained our man!"

"What if he claims political asylum, General?"

Bascombe smiled, flashing his teeth like a cat watching its food approach. There was no need to answer that one. Bob hated anyone to accuse him, evenly tacitly, of innocence. He knew these things happened, but they shouldn't. If a law or a procedure existed, then it should be adhered to or scrapped. No one could be comfortable in a world where there was no certainty to fall back on. Besides, the Burk he dreamt of, and the Burk the Russians wanted, did not correspond ...

"General, why do they want Burk?"

"A vendetta – Burk allowed himself the luxury of a live enemy."

"Huh?"

"Bersarin's superior was sent to the Stalingrad front by Burk."

"And a Nazi now runs the KGB, General?"

"No – just a department ... Grow up Bob – Moscow wouldn't waste that sort of talent ... Come to think of it – neither would we."

"But none of ours could swing the State behind his personal revenge."

"This one can – as long as it suits his master's jackboot tactics and paranoid strategy ... Don't weep for Burk – the bastard was SS too, remember!"

Mercy for the merciless sword? That bunch of silver-studded supermen had taken their orders direct from Hell. They could be classified, yet never understood much less forgiven – why, why, had Manfred joined them?

"Do you think we'll find him? Alive I mean?"

Bascombe laughed. He was sure Burk was alive: why else were the Russians so eager to get him? The General reached into his tunic and handed Bob a large manilla envelope.

"The 'apparition of Bari'! We struck paydirt! ... There's a plane standing by to fly you there Major ... These are your papers and an extradition instrument for one Brother Joseph, alias SS Haupstürmführer Manfred Burk ... Bring him back quickly and quietly."

The General emphasized that Bob was, as far as possible, not to request the assistance of the authorities. Of all Italy, Bari held the most bitter memories. Not so much as a result of the accident which poured flesh-withering mustard gas into the town way back in '43, but because of the Allied cover-up to hide their breach of the Geneva Agreements, and the consequent death and disfigurement of victims denied the correct treatment. If America tried to extradite Burk officially the chances were that someone would inform the Soviets and Bascombe didn't want that to happen until he was finished with the man.

Bob took the envelope hoping that Bascombe had left him enough time to call Susan and cancel their date. He handled the brown paper gingerly and felt defiled. This was a disgusting treachery and the fact that he would do it under orders made him no better than the man who hammered in Christ's nails.

"It doesn't seem right, General!"

"What?"

"The Ivans wanting Burk so bad. Atrocities are nothing to them. Stalin and Beria buried more Russians than Hitler or Himmler ever did ... Why are they so insistant about this man?"

"That's not your worry, soldier."

"Oh but it is, Sir." Bob was embarrassed by his own vehemence. "Especially if he's squeezed, then handed over ... I never believed we were all that good – but I hadn't reckoned on being a bastard ... We can't just hand him over ..."

Bob faltered. The General grinned at him savagely.

"I know, Boy! ...It's not fair ...Well, fairness is a man-made concept that sits easy on all you peacetime rookies. Me – as far as concepts are concerned – I'm into demolition! Besides, if they get Burk, the Reds are bound to compete with us in airships. And that's what *Firedrake*'s all about!"

"And what about honour?" Bob insisted.

"A set of rules, made by the folk on top to contain the ambitious underneath ... It looks good in print Major, but you can't live a book ... Humanity is a mess of thinking monkeys, Mister, nothing less – and certainly nothing more. And if you don' t like it I'll have your resignation now!"

But Bob wasn't that brave, nor that committed. They parted, the General to his quarters, Bob to the airport and the waiting plane.

Thirteen

I saw pale Kings and Princes too,
Pale warriors, death-pale were they all;
They cried –"La belle Dame sans Merci
Thee hath in thrall!"

La Belle Dame Sans Merci J. Keats

The fall from the tree had stopped Manfred's watch and he soon lost all track of time. After a number of falls, scratches and bruises, he acclimatized to the darkness and developed a method of proceeding that minimized collisions with trees and prevented him falling when he stumbled on roots, or tripped in holes. Adopting a gait similar to that of airship men groping along an unlighted walkway, he explored the ground with his foot before resting his weight on it. The process was automatic and he soon began to make good progress. He avoided the invisible trees and plunging too deeply into thickets, by sweeping ahead with his arms, the left one sweeping horizontally to detect trunks, while the right arm worked vertically to catch briars or low branches, just as they would in a ship to feel for cells and ratlines. Because he was able to perform these manoeuvres automatically his mind was free to think.

'Rotation'! What was it? ... Izzy had found a room full of machinery – the 'Interface room' they had called it at the table, and it had something to do with this 'rotation'. Halgerd's explanations made no sense. Science was magic explained, not vice versa. They had had to 'rotate' to expel von Dobberitz from the Schloß. But what the hell did it mean? Some form of defence? To defend the Baroness against Albrecht? Against incursions? What incursions? Schiller's corruption by von Dobberitz had been treated as an 'incursion' by Jurgen, but Schiller had been human, not a demon as Halgerd had implied ... But what had happened to August? He had first reported the 'incursions' so what had happened to him?

There was something very strange about Eberheim, about the district and the people. Judging from the behaviour of the peasants and the guests at the hunt they seemed to be unaware of the war; it was as if they hadn't been touched by the suffering – were totally unaware of it ... And that was impossible ... Neurath's agony, Gretchen, von Dobberitz, Schiller and the disturbing conversations – they all added up to something that made their strangeness more than curious – it was frightening.

And what was his position in this weird pantheon? An incredible intuition prompted him that he was a student, that they were teaching him something. But to what purpose? His damnation, salvation – or just their own amusement? But that had to be wrong. He had never met an aristocrat, nor any of the Junkers' set, with a free mind. They affected to disregard the rules, which confused commoners like himself, until one got up close and saw that they had their own rituals which enslaved them more certainly than any conscripted stubble hopper.

So why was he in Eberheim? ... Because the Baron was a doting father, so besotted with his daughter that he would take the pains to reveal Manfred as an awkward lout against the background of Eberheim and her family, rather than cause her the pain of his horsewhipping and, if he persisted, death? Or was this some recognition for having saved his son's life? ... And what crazy ideals motivated Jurgen? He had tried to remain onboard SL17, acting as though he could not die but, while Neurath groaned his agony, Jurgen thanked him for having spared him ... Was there a connection between mortal agony and 'Rotation'? Jurgen had said that the body 'resonated' near the times of its maximum trauma. What was more traumatic than death? No, torture must be more traumatic than a natural death. And, August wasn't a ghost! ... But he couldn't concentrate. His thoughts were interrupted by starts of fear when the forest night life sounded off near him.

It was an impossible situation. He could not see the scuffling creatures and had no way of knowing whether the paddings and snappings on the carpet of pine needles were caused by a large stealthy beast, or by rodents digging for grubs. That was the difficulty with the forest floor – it amplified small noises and muffled heavy ones. The night sounds above him were unnerving too, not like the unbroken cacophony of a tropical jungle. Here in the black woods a painful, fearful, silence was the norm, punctuated at infrequent heart-stopping intervals by movements, crashes, the moaning clucking of woodcock and pheasant and the shriek of hunting owls. Once there was the soggy chomping of teeth and a large body heaved out of the leaves and pine needles to blunder in alarm across his path.

He had shaped an unsteady but persistent course for several hours, during which time his mind oscillated from aroused panic to deep reflection, then a stab of alarm again at the next noise, when a cold wetness pressed against his right hand on one of its downward sweeps. He shouted in alarm and threw himself backwards.

"Auf ... Verdammt Wolf ... "

Maybe it wasn't a wolf. It could be a boar or, worse still, a bear to splinter his ribs, crush his spine and gnaw his face. Padding noises were all around him now and, as he staggered backwards, he tripped over a root and fell. Heavy bodies leaned on his chest as he sprawled along the ground. A slobbering tongue caressed his face, filling his mouth when he opened it to shout, then a joyous baying almost burst his eardrums and he nearly wept with relief – the hounds had found him again. The carbide lamp spluttered noisily flooding Halgerd's lovely face in its harsh light.

"Manfred ..." Her voice was full of concern and then she saw him stretched out, slack jawed, struggling with the affectionate hounds. She burst out laughing.

"Oh poor Manfred ... I' m sorry the hounds startled you, but I had them hunt silently lest you think there were wolves after you."

Flaming with embarrassment at the ridiculous image he felt sure he was presenting – a sort of resin and pine needle rag doll, as against a tar and feathered effigy – Manfred staggered to his feet and patted the nearest shaggy heads to convey a 'no hard feelings' attitude to the hounds .

"You have enormous skill, Manfred!" Halgerd was serious now. "Jurgen is hugely amused. He thought you would get lost."

"How is Neurath?" Burk changed the subject, his voice uncertain as concern for his hurt benefactor, and irritation at von Lüth, battled for dominance.

"He is well now ... It should not have happened, but when the alarm went up the watch rotated to a preset setting. He should have checked. That setting was Uncle August's ... Come on, mount up behind me; we'll be in time for supper."

"Halgerd ... In God's name, what is this 'Rotation'?"

She laughed but all the time her eyes were fixed on him in compassion.

"I could not explain it to you now, Manfred, it would take too long. In essence, this is an isotropic universe that obeys the perfect cosmological principal and is homogeneous. Do you understand any of that, Manfred?"

"No!"

"Neither are you meant to,"Halgerd sighed. "Look, the Universe isn't lawful, never was, never will be ... Absolutely anything is possible and, being possible, must be, and that is the ultimate absolute. Our local three-dimensional universe is deformed by the multi-dimensional one in much the same way as a two-dimensional sheet can be wrapped around a three dimensional object."

Was she right? Manfred had no knowledge of the universe and had never considered it except as a backdrop for stars and navigation. But he could listen to her forever. Understanding wasn't necessary; it was enough to hear her voice, store the words and try to learn their meaning up ship on some lonely watch.

"Limited by three dimensions, our bodies can never experience the whole of reality – but we can guess at it. We can draw a graph of reality on a piece of paper and the result is a cross section of the 'omniverse' that looks like the Englisch flag– the Union Jack."

Curious! Manfred thought. Did that explain how little England had such an enormous empire – their happy adoption of the symbol of reality for their flag?

"Omniverse?" Manfred struggled with the term.

"The multiverse, the whole of reality that comprises of this universe and an infinity of others... Look, you exist in the 'here' and 'now'. That means that, as you move into the 'future', an effect is available to you only after you have initiated its cause – you can't have a house without first building it. However, although you are confined to the future and causality is very real to you, remember that you can't see where you are going.

All your perceptions lie in the past. Your only experience of reality is your history and a view of space that recedes from the Now the further out you look.

"But 'phase', 'interface', 'rotation?" Manfred stumbled.

"Those terms apply to Elsewhen – another time and place. Rotation must be accompanied by a shift in phase, either into another relativistic state – another universe, or into another time and place in this one. Once a phase has been selected, and a rotation made, 'interface' – the ability to survive in the alternate state without affecting its own or Eberheim's integrity – becomes a major consideration."

"But none of this explains what happened to August!"

"Usually there is no penalty, apart from the loss of perception, when one leaves the omniverse and confines oneself to a single plane, a universe. However it is not wise to occupy a here and now that has the same phase as a previously occupied one. Only the very disciplined may do so and not despair because the body will resonate with the dominant phase. Uncle August was caught unprepared when we were forced to rotate suddenly and a phase resonance with a near fatal experience overwhelmed him."

"I don't understand, Halgerd ... Back on SL17, Jurgen said he couldn't 'rotate'– yet he doesn't seem to regard what could have been a terrible death as anything more than an inconvenience."

"It would have been, for him and for all of us. Uncle August's trauma isn't mortal; only a tremendously disciplined mind could dominate the body then. Mother, or the Baron, could, but my brother's isn't of that order. And we need Jurgen – for the bridge."

"Ahh ... the bridge?"

"For our ship, Manfred. Tomorrow's ship for yesterday's voyages. An airship is particularly suitable for Elsewhen. The one we want will only be built after lesser ones have been flown and their deeds accomplished. The bridge is necessary to span two points of the 'here' and 'now' in this phase.

"But, why? ... I don't understand any of this, but you did say Elsewhen was meaningless – so why do you want a ship?"

"Elsewhen, at zero time, is only meaningful to God. To us it translates as a shift into another relativistic state and its option of positive or negative causality. Unassisted, man may not leave the crèche – the quadrant of reality offering him movement in space down times that lead away from the beginnings. Eberheim has the freedom of all quadrants of reality and would explore them."

"But why do you need a ship?"

"An airship will permit us to observe without being observed ... There is a war in progress and, like it or not, we are all front line troops."

"But the war won't last much longer Gräfin ..."

"Not this war. The real one – the war that polarized creation and has been waged ever since Time and Space became one. We are children of Truth, Manfred. It is not intended that you understand – yet. But children must acquire wisdom and the battlefield is a poor crèche ... Some place, Elsewhen, had to be made for us. A place where law seemed to exist, where causality encourages us to think, to seek God and grow in generosity. The real universe would terrify us and be as healthy as Flanders under bombardment by both sides would be to an infant."

"Perhaps there is no time now for understanding," Manfred insisted. "Just tell me what happened."

"They were looking for you ... And you must not go back to Ahlhorn until the Baron has spoken to you ... We had to rotate – go Elsewhen."

"And Neurath?"

"We adjusted the interface ... I never would have believed that someone not born to Eberheim could find his way through these woods so well – you are over halfway home Manfred."

He took the hint and dropped the subject. He was too tired and anyway Halgerd wasn't making any sense. He scrambled awkwardly up her huge mount behind her.

They set off at what, to Halgerd, was an easy canter, but to Manfred it was hell. He had never ridden bareback before and now he was seated far back over the animal's hindquarters where motion was extreme and the only aid he had to remain onboard was Halgerd's slim waist. His pride insisted that he must not announce his inexperience by holding onto her tightly. To make matters worse, Halgerd kept talking to him and he was forced, to distract himself from the all engrossing subject of staying on, to answer her.

They had only gone a few paces when Manfred became aware of an even more difficult problem. He was being tossed rhythmically up and down on the horse's rump as it cantered. In itself that was normal and posed no problem; what did was the fact that each time he rose he was thrown forward, down towards the hard, high rise of the back of Halgerd's saddle. Recognizing the problem and its painful consequences in time, Manfred concentrated the last reserves of his mental resources on controlling his descent. He had almost succeeded in getting it all together when Halgerd suddenly asked him, "Why did you send Gretchen away last night? I always imagined that men found her irresistible."

Didn't she know? Was she completely unaware that he was in love with her? At that moment the horse stumbled and Manfred, distracted, was thrown off balance and came down hard, slamming his groin into the back of her saddle.

The knowledge that she must be aware of what had happened did nothing to improve the situation. He could feel her firm, hard waist trembling in suppressed laughter as his arms spasmed around her in agony. For an eternity he froze, rigid, battling with the waves of pain, denying himself the comfort of rolling up and nursing his hurt.

When he could think again he realized that his hands had worked themselves upwards to cup her high yielding breasts. He stopped himself in time from snatching them away; chance had won him an advantage, the next move was hers. Gradually he let his fingers explore, then regretfully he allowed her to reposition his arms chastely around her waist.

"I see you have recovered," she observed. "Hold onto me tightly if you don't want to have another accident – I'm not made of Dresden you know ... Honestly you men are so vulnerable ... What happened to you?"

"I didn't know you knew about Gretchen," he gasped.

In the silence that followed Manfred became afraid that Halgerd had dismissed him as a prude, until she spoke.

"Yes, I had forgotten how little charity there is in your world. The best of you would give, but all fear to receive ... We are different here and delight in the joy of other people. Sex is not love, but there can be little love without it ...It is a gift Manfred, not a penalty ... Do I shock you?"

"Amazed, confused yes ... Did you know about Gretchen?"

"At the time, no. Jurgen told me about her this morning. I would not have tried you so grievously, and I would have been disappointed , for all our custom, had you lain with her."

"It could be that my tastes areGreek," he observed sourly.

"Oh no, Kapitän Harsch – not you ... I feel your burn and it is for me."

"Yes!" He said simply. "Will you marry me Halgerd ?"

Again there was a long silence that endured until the dark outer moat of the Schloß glinted in the moonlight through the thinning trees. She halted the horse to a walk and turned to look at him.

"Leonardo da Vinci loves his portrait of the Mona Lisa. This is possible because he, in his three-dimensional universe, may reduce himself to a two-dimensional one ... But what if the painted lady loved him?"

"How could she. He would be beyond her comprehension," Manfred offered.

"Yes. Were he to lay his hand on the portrait, all she would see would be five ovals, the interface of his finger prints on her two-dimensional world ... But she could aspire to him even as we aspire to God ... I see and understand you, Manfred, totally. You are my delight and I love you. But you cannot see me at all."

"But I do not have to know you, Halgerd ... It is enough for me that I feel so complete with you. Love does not need absolute comprehension."

"No, but it demands trust and trust is shared best between equals ... There is a greater gulf between us than you dream, Manfred. It is one that you must bridge because it would end in bitterness, for both of us, were I to carry you across ... You are very beautiful Manfred, true and innocent – a child. But children can be hurt, their innocence withered ... I am a child of Eberheim and that is no place, but a condition of those who have stood true. We, I, are the hardest way of all, because men love the worthy, while God loves indiscriminately. I love you Manfred, but you must reach me. Because only then will we love each other and our eternity be meaningful!"

The horse was clattering over the iron-trussed bridge and Manfred waited until they were in the quiet of the yard before replying, proving that he hadn't understood a single thing she had said. He slipped off the steaming, froth-lathered mount and before the ostlers had reached them he had lifted her out of the saddle and kissed her fiercely.

"Very well, my Dresden princess; we shall be like that – two figurines on either side of the mantel ... You did not refuse me and that is enough. Here I am disadvantaged, an inept clown in a strange circus. It is in the air that I am king and I will ask you again – there!" He kissed her again, ecstatic with the passion she responded to him.

"What about the Baron?" she whispered in mock fear when he released her on the arrival of the ostlers.

"I'll pay the bride price, say twenty horse! – No, by God, you're worth at least double that ..."

"Will you two stop mauling each other – bad form, before supper," Jurgen, who had observed the whole scene from the shadows of the great door, called out irritably, adding as he ground out his cigar, "And speaking of supper, old girl, we can't begin without you ... For God's sake Manfred, hurry up and dress." He strode into the hall, Manfred and Halgerd following meekly.

Fourteen

Saint Augustine asked the right question: "Does freedom come from chance or choice?"
And you must remember that quantum mechanics guarantees chance.

FRANK HERBERT, *THE JESUS INCIDENT*

Chief Petty Officer Zeitel became the grim airship man again when Burk told him about Schiller. While Manfred gave himself a quick wash in a china basin, the Chief left the room and headed for the stables where Schiller had been quartered. He returned just as Burk was struggling into a shirt, an envelope containing a thousand marks in his hand.

"It used to be thirty pieces of silver," Burk observed. "Still I'd like to fancy myself as being more valuable."

But Zeitel was taciturn and made no reply. Later as he shaved his Kapitän's head he muttered in bewildered tones, "I don't understand it ... A traitor ... Here?"

"I believe there were people looking for me!" Manfred said. Zeitel answered automatically, before he had time to think of what he was saying, "Yes, they want everyone back at

Ahlhorn I imagine ... But of course we weren't here for them."

"What do you mean, Chief? Not here? "You couldn't miss the Schloß!"

"Of course not, Sir ... Your tunic Sir ... The Baron will be most impatient by now."

Burk struggled into the tight fitting jacket, resolved to go deeper into the Chief's remarks when he was less pressed for time. Whatever happened, he had better go back to Ahlhorn fast. Desertion wasn't a particularly healthy charge to have to answer – not now when Germany was losing.

"They'll be mounting your head on the wall, along with their other leather-brained trophies, "Izzy hissed at him as soon as he had left his room. Relief from worry had turned his little friend vicious.

"Didn't see you at the hunt, lz!"

"Didn't attend ... Thank's to you I have other distractions. Can't see how I can avoid this one though – the one where the Baron gets you over his precious horse."

He explained that the Baron was furious over Helga and would entertain no excuse for her death. The only help he could give Burk was the knowledge gleaned from a day of chatting up old ladies that the only thing the Baron would not tolerate was weakness – especially in his quarry.

"Then I have no option but to go over onto the offensive," Manfred whispered, more to himself than to his friend. "Listen Izzy, he must fire the first shot ... Will you draw it for me?"

"Help! Why is it always me? I'm in your debt – for Gretchen, but you'll owe me, if we're both killed. Very well, mein Kapitän, I'll give you an 'in', but after that I'll be off and away – understood!"

"I think it would be bad manners to keep them waiting any longer," Manfred answered and pushed the heavy doors apart.

The supper was a hostile affair compared to the previous one.The diners spoke but conversation did not flow easily.

Everyone sat around the outer edge of a pool of guttering light and whereas, apart from Izzy and himself, no one appeared to be uneasy, the meal was an introverted one.

The Baron sat in his great carver, Englisch fashion, with both hands on the table, a glowering death to all spontaneity, and everybody else ignored him and retired into themselves. For his part Burk sat erect well into the shadows and observed the full academy-learned etiquette, one hand on the table, the other on his lap. He studied the angry old man covertly and realized that, although the Baron seemed to have fixed him in a relentless stare, it was only a mask. The old man's eyes were fixed on the darkness outside the circle.

Was this then another elaborate charade? Constraining himself to a show of indifference, Manfred forced himself to consume a huge plate of cold meats. When the coffee and cheese were served, Manfred nodded imperceptibly to Izzy. This might not be the time, but it was the only place; if there was to be a war then the presence of the Baroness and the ladies must limit the Baron's field of action.

"Has Karl left us?" Izzy asked the Baroness in a loud voice.

The Baron twitched in disbelief and his eyes snapped back into focus.

"Yes Isador," the Baroness replied. "He boarded the train this evening. I do hope he has remembered his sunburn oil. I believe it is very hot in Afrika ..."

"Left us ... US? What do you mean! ... How dare you associate your snivelling self with my family, you preposterous little upstart!" the Baron roared, venting his pent-up spleen in an explosion of terrible outrage .

"Piggy, how can you be so, so petty. "The Baroness's eyes flashed and her high cheek bones rouged with anger.

"Baroness, please," Manfred interrupted gently, then, staring hard at the Baron, but actually focussing on his eyebrows to avoid the old fierce eyes, he continued, "Izzy spoke on my order, Baron, so your displeasure is for me and not him. I regret the loss of your horse, but I will remind you that whereas Schiller was one of my crew, he was in your employ."

The Baron stared hard at him for a long moment, disbelief and outrage written on his leathery face. Finally he puffed his moustaches and roared. "You dare to correct me, in my own home ...You, Burk are either a liar or a great idiot ... What did you come here for – apart from the destruction of my stables that is?"

Senile! Was that it? Was the old man senile? If so he was finished. Nothing could be accomplished now, neither by running nor standing his ground – all would be grist to the age-demented rage ... And senility was the one factor he should have considered and hadn't. So, with nothing to salvage save bits of his own dignity, he must finish it as he had started.

"I could play games and remind you that I am here by your invitation," Manfred intoned in his best official voice, the cold emotionless one he reserved for his peers in the engineering or ordnance branches who had failed him. "But I came here for your daughter's hand. Nothing more, nothing less, Baron!"

The Baron looked at the tense faces all around him then burst into harsh baying laughter. "Men, have these dogs driven out of my house," he roared:

"You've done it again, Manfred," Izzy screamed and tried to run from the room. Shadows detached themselves from the curtains and pinned him.

Burk turned to face his adversaries, but they were on him before he could rise. He struck out twice then was bundled, along with Izzy, unceremoniously out of the room. It was so humiliating that it took all his strength and concentration not to weep. It was the shock of course, he knew that. But why must the body betray him in shock with tears? He couldn't even speak, shout a defiance, because he knew his voice would break. Perhaps silence was the only show of strength left to him, but what would dignity mean to this whole crazy house that seemed to insist on nightly degradation? Yesterday von Dobberitz; tonight himself. If women feared rape, then this was what men dreaded – the display of absolute helplessness in front of the princess he so adored and needed to impress.

Struggling was as futile as speech, so he remained still throughout the ordeal while he was bundled roughly down the long halls of Eberheim. Izzy was not so dignified. He yelled, kicked and tried to break free. Irrationally Burk felt all his anger direct itself on his friend. "Why couldn't you have told the despatch rider we were here!" he shouted at him.

"What rider?"

"One was sent here, from Ahlhorn ... They want us back. Zeitel told me and if you had received him, as it was your duty ..."

"A despatch rider! In this fog?" Izzy's voice cracked with the vehemence of his disbelief.

"It was sunny all day," Manfred insisted.

"Like hell it was ... The fog came down at noon and only lifted when that man with the shattered legs and burns was brought in ... A real stinker it was! You couldn't see your nose."

Elsewhen! That's what Halgerd had said 'rotation' was all about ... Did she mean that the machinery in the dungeons could site all of Eberheim anywhere at any time? ... No, that was impossible, against all principles of physics and reason ... Except that she had also said the universe was essentially lawless. He didn't have long to consider these points. Doors scraped, locks clanged and they were, or rather he was, in the Brown Room again.

The men released him at the threshold, pushed him in and drew the doors closed behind them. Behind him, receding down the corridors and muffled by the heavy doors, Manfred could hear Izzy's wails grow thinner and eventually cease.

✲

"Gretchen will comfort your friend, Manfred." The Baroness seated in a tapestried armchair, clacked her fan shut and waved him to an empty chair by the fire.

"Come in boy, chair's there ... Time we had a talk." The Baron poured a goblet of claret and handed it to Manfred whose hand accepted it for him while his mind reeled. Jurgen grinned at him sardonically and Halgerd was looking very happy. Eva, Marie and Rudi stared at him frankly, but approvingly. The only person who seemed unaware of his entry was Neurath. He was wearing the familiar silver ornamented black uniform, but the black leather boots were standing on the hob while Uncle August toasted white-socked, and manifestly healthy, feet in front of the fire; no longer was he the dying twenty-year-old, but a hale, fit man closing on forty. He wrapped his hand around his glass and, still ignoring Burk, he spoke into the fire, as though confirming a consensus reached by the whole room while Manfred was still in the corridor.

"Civic courage and a deal of good sense ... You always could see the man in the boy, Hildemar. .. He'll probably make it." He tossed back the dark wine and turned sideways in the chair to face Manfred.

"On graduation day, are you leaving school, or beginning your career?"

No answer. Manfred heard the question but everything was still a chaos. He was so confused that he couldn't know whether he was angry, embarrassed, or just going mad.

"The trouble with graduation is that the act is sometimes painful and the student must make the transition alone ... You helped me in mine Manfred, a student may help another. But I am a graduate and may not assist you in your ordeal; besides, as you saw with me earlier today, graduates who return to their years pay a penalty as severe as graduation."

Manfred sat down stiffly and carefully, as though he expected the chair to be pulled away from him. And all the time he was thinking furiously. What were they at? This whole charade, including the frosty dinner, was obviously a well-rehearsed performance and not just an attempt to gloss over the Baron's studied tantrum. Senile! Far from it; the old man was manipulating him, stressing him and studying the responses. So far, he seemed to have done well. But must Manfred Burk resign himself to degradation with aplomb? No, never! Anger exploded. How dare these accidents of fortune torment him as a spoilt child would a patient pet! He could leave now – cast their god-play in their teeth and retire unbowed.

But where did Halgerd stand? Was she just playing with him too? Or was there the chance that something deep and meaningful lay behind their contempt and manipulation? One thing was certain – if he stood on his honour and left he would never know. He would lose her and if there was a lesson to be learned from this weird tuition he would deny himself that knowledge.

"Dearest, I know you ... But·the Baron insists on proof."

He searched her eyes for reassurance. But the room, lit only by the fire, had dilated them black, huge, alien.

"Any animal can be brave through stupidity or want of the freedom to be otherwise ... But only a man can endure humiliation without loss!" the Baron grunted.

It all had to be deliberate and the party must have removed to the Brown Room even as he and Izzy were being rushed out of the dining hall ... But why?

"Dignity is the refusal to accept shame." Eva, Karl's wife, spoke. She did not look at him, nor move her eyes from her embroidery frame and the quickly darting needle. How could she work in that light? "It is the asset that makes all virtue credible ...And that is why dignity is always the first thing that the weak man seeks to destroy in others. For if he fails to crush another's dignity – then he must acknowledge him as his master!"

What were they doing, saying? Manfred tried to remember that he was very angry, that the Baron had flouted the essential rules of hospitality ... But wonder, and an enormous sense of unreality, wouldn't let his anger flower.

"Do you understand what we are saying, Manfred?" Halgerd asked.

Did he? He shook his head. "Am I to understand that this an apology?"

The Baron laughed hugely, shaking the vast chesterfield he sat in so that the fire danced in the disturbance.

Manfred's cheeks reddened, but before he could express his anger the Baron fixed him with his eyes.

"Does the schoolboy demand an apology from the master who beats him?"

"Not if he accepts the master as his master." Burk was surprised at his own quickness.

For a moment both men stared at each other. The Baron eyed him with the amusement of one enjoying the spirit of a colt, while Manfred's held all the defiance and uncertainty of one about to be broken in.

"Von Dobberitz accepted shame." Jurgen roused himself from a study of the sizzling logs and poured himself more claret.

"I never liked that boy – he had sneaky eyes," the Baroness agreed. "Piggy, what on earth possessed you to consider him?" The Baron grunted and didn't release Manfred from his stare. Eventually he spoke. "You want my daughter ... Now the first and perhaps the only question I have for you is, why?"

"Because I love her!" It came out automatically, unconsidered, and even as he said it he knew that it was trite ... But what else could he have said? He did love her, adored her. Surely that must be obvious ... But why, the Baron had asked *why*!

"Love! ... An admirable stimulus, an execrable goal ... Love feeds on hope and is choked by its realization." The Baron dismissed the whole subject and returned to his wine.

They were running rings around him. It was just one more hunt in 'the Season at Eberheim'. Manfred felt the fury boil within him. He had sworn to accept battle, but on his own terms and he had never considered that words must be his weapons. In such a conflict, the orphanage and the Navy were poor arsenals. He knew how he felt and what he wished to say, but he hadn't an adequate vocabulary to express himself in words. Yet they challenged him to try and mocked him as he drowned in his own ineptitude .

"You know quite well what I mean, Baron." His voice sounded icy calm, belying the turmoil in his heart. "I love Halgerd and if she loves me enough then there will be little need to play semantics with you."

"Do you like her Manfred?" the Baroness asked.

That had to be another trick question otherwise its stupidity was stunning – how could anyone love someone and not like them?

"Happens all the time, boy," the Baron answered and once more Burk felt terribly depressed and not a little frightened at the ease with which they read him.

"Love is the acquisition of an ornament for oneself. Once acquired it is fit only for the trophy room. To like someone, on the other hand, is to wish for a friend."

That wasn't fair ... He had thought of Halgerd too. Of course she would have to make a sacrifice, that of accepting him. But, once committed, his life was for her alone, as it was now.

"Worship, infatuation ..." Eva paused, but this time she looked at him. "Consider: God has offered us nothing greater, nor less, than friendship. On the other hand, the best we can offer him is love and, failing that, worship."

They were crushing him and it wasn't fair. Or was it? All his life he had striven to be correct and had never once really questioned the rituals of civics, German style. It wasn't enough to follow the mummeries of society with absolute obedience – Eberheim demanded conviction. To them he was little better than a spoilt child ... Was he? They had him doubting himself now.

"You are a child, Manfred, and a dear boy too ... But all children are sweet. It is only the special ones who remain so." The Baroness smiled at him approvingly.

A vestige of calm reasserted itself. Although they had him down and confused, especially by their tricks of seeming to read his mind, it became obvious what they were trying to do –force him to renounce Halgerd by reducing him in her eyes, and his own, to the level of an idiot ... And that could only mean that Halgerd loved him, that they couldn't part her from him and must induce him to leave her.

"I do Manfred ... But it is no use my loving you, if you do not know me. I am forever, and my friend must be too ... When, if, you ask me again, then we will both know ... I have been, and will be, true, but now come your times of striving. If you prevail then the answer is yes! If not ... Lots of boys fall in love with their governess."

Her voice was strong, but it had an ache in it that upset Manfred deeply. Did she imagine that there was anything, even Hell itself, that he would not cross to reach her. And why these veiled allusions? In the yard he had promised to wait until she would let him ask again. Women underestimated men's patience; as a force it was rarely invoked, unlike theirs, but when called on it was inexorable.

"I do not know what you are trying to say!" He felt every bit as lost as he knew he sounded.

"Of course not!" the Baron's gruffness carried undertones of approval and something akin to expectation. "It is not yet possible for you to comprehend Eberheim, what it is, what it means to us who are of it, or to the few who have won it ... But what you must know is this: Halgerd is no Brynhild to forsake our halls for you. If you are to lie with my daughter then you must win a place in Eberheim ... So, Manfred, I give your strivings my blessing and there is always hope ... But we are not many. We are the hardest way."

For some time Manfred had nursed a suspicion, something derived from their remarks, their attitudes, and at the same time so unnatural, that to speak it must make him at one with any primitive savage. Once more the suspicion was driven to the fore and, in his confusion, he voiced it. "Are you telling me that you are not human – that you are the gods, the dead, or something else?"

The Baron roared laughing, tears coursing down his walnut cheeks like the first streamers of rain on a sunbaked mudflat. "Not human! ... Ahaa! Haa! ... Haa ..." When he calmed down he directed his attention to the claret, calming the heaving of his massive shoulders with deep draughts.

Jurgan shifted in his chair and addressed the others. "Not a bad guess, all things considered. I told you before, ol'boy, death is more conceptual than actual ... Operator 'J' and all that, y'know – the math thing, useful in calculations but not realizable ... People grow, 'course some wither a piece ... We're human though ... Question is, what are you?"

There was a butcher once who wouldn't sell a woman half a rabbit because he didn't like splitting hares ... A silly joke, but Manfred felt like that woman, confused by a power that he had invoked – a power that played with him and with words, twisting him and them into some ridiculous pun. What did they mean by being human! Had they a contempt of the term because the world, like Burk, drew its authority from posturing cretins who had started this war and now strained to sustain it and themselves? That was humanity, and it didn't make Jurgen any better a man for all that Eberheim protected him from the degrading futilities of staying alive with some semblance of dignity and direction. Let Jurgen derive his definition of humanity from Eberheim. He, they, were protected. His condemnation of the rest of humanity was little better than that of a beggar's son for the source of the bread on his father's table.

How was he, Manfred, to draw worth from Jurgen's well, when he and every other stubble hopper in Germany were its very source. His fingers groped for the buttonhole, his Blue Max ribbon ... Here it was meaningless and he would have cast it into the fire to emphasize the fact. Then he remembered all the allusions to children. To reject the award by destroying it would be impulsive – childlike. A man would put it away.

The tunic button slipped open under the pressure of his fingers. Must he surrender everything to them? ... No, by God, if Halgerd was for winning, then Eberheim was for storming! Besides, worth recognized, from whatever source, was still merit. And the whole crew of that Englisch cruiser had died to win him his tin. The *Ordre* made him a walking memorial to them. To reject it would make him no better than a casual murderer. Re-securing the ribbon in the buttonhole, he fastened the button and let his hand drift back to the arm of his chair. Useless; the Baron had been watching him.

"You must enjoy this war, boy!"

"No, Sir!"

"Don't lie to me, boy ... The reluctant are not decorated. You must have striven for the *Ordre*!"

"Yes Sir, but for position only; just as your ancestors must have soiled their hands – the most noble tree has its roots in dirt."

"You know nothing of Eberheim, boy, save what we choose to reveal. Ambition then is valid – regardless of cost?"

Manfred struggled hard to master anger and the dam of

his despair and frustration held. Still his voice trembled with emotion. "Of course it is not ... But is there any other way? ... You rule us and waste us for your pride, allowing us existence only as pillars for yours ... What choice do you leave me, and all the others? To deny you and die – that is defeat; to serve and hope the defilement won't corrupt us – that is surrender; or to obey and win – that way is the only hope of change and the establishment of reason."

"You don't believe that this war is a holy one then?" the Baron snapped at him, "a conflict waged against evil by good and pious princes so that, in the spirit of those noted wordsmiths, the Amerikaners, this is 'the war to end all wars'?"

"No." Manfred's control slipped from him and his answers to their attack were wild with battle. "This is a stupid war, the inevitable folly of stupid men with absolute authority! ... Was the fatherland attacked, invaded? Had our rulers struck out against an irredeemably wicked enemy? No, the world was a happy prosperous place now rent apart by fools."

A stillness filled the Brown Room after his outburst. Ashamed, he suppressed the urge to modify his stand, to back down with placating explanations – his position was too weak for self-destruction. He looked at everyone in turn. Halgerd seemed pleased and yet aloof in a beauty and peace that took her way beyond him. The others were unreadable, set in attitudes of comfort, lost in their own thoughts. The only person to move was Neurath and he only to dip the end of a cigar into his glass and light it from the fire.

"Do you believe in free will, Manfred?" the Baroness asked him suddenly.

He calmed down and considered the question. The stock religious answer was yes – but was it all? In the main men performed acts, both good or evil, because they were expected of them. Was the man who hammered in Christ's nails evil or dutiful? And when King John signed Magna Carta was that a good deed, or simple coercion? How had a man free will when everything depended on his environment? Men were judged good or bad citizens by their society. The executioner who decided that execution was murder would be himself executed were he one of a firing squad ... And a man of that calibre would be so far above the rest of men as to be considered superhuman. No, damnation or salvation were beyond the average man's choice. The times of his birth must decide the place of his eternity.

"If it exists it is very limited," he answered.

"Then if there is no free will how is war or peace determined? What allows civilization to progress?" It was Eva this time.

"I do not know. Momentum, God?"

"Consider this," Rudi spoke carefully. "When you think of the numbers of qualified people who failed, what made people like Bonaparte, Bismarck or even Lenin succeed? And again, consider the phenomenon of global spontaneity. Why did slavery become so universally unacceptable? Why are women only looking for suffrage now and why in so many countries all at once? And why was the desire for this war so universal?"

Manfred struggled in his chair uneasily. Were they trying to make him recant? Perhaps there was limited free will in individuals which was a cumulative force in societies. If that were so, what made society better than the mob?

"I believe that we are guided by God. But some of the things you suggest are hardly divinely inspired," Manfred hedged.

"Curious," Jurgen drawled, his eyes hooded as he considered his cigar. "God made the universe, created it, not built it. Matter therefore is unnatural to God which suggests that He is inimicable to it. Apart from the initial programme for a universe, and the subsequent consequence of intelligent life, His hands must be ... ahh, tied. I imagine that God may only influence the direction of his creation with difficulty."

"What about Jesus Christ?" Manfred asked. "Do you not believe that he is God with the enormous influence he has had on the world?"

"Of course, ol'boy ... My point exactly. Consider the Old Testament; for the most part it is a history of the house of David that culminates in the realization of the most perfect human being that is realizable – the Mother of God. She and only She could, and did, make the interface between God and creation possible."

Manfred digested this. It was typical of Jurgen that he would couch the most sacred truth in sardonic terms, but Manfred could find no flaw in what he had said except the despair at the idea that God must leave him more alone than he could bear.

"If God may only observe and not interfere, someone must be influencing us ... Your examples insist on that."

"His servants do." Halgerd spoke calmly but with a hint of defiance.

"But all the suffering, the pain, the war?" Manfred objected.

"Wrong angle," the Baron grunted. "Human misery is not inflicted on mankind. It is averted, controlled so that the maximum lesson may be learned from the least destruction ... We are for development, not extinction."

It made a startling form of sense after all their allusions to children and the schoolroom. Was the Earth an academy and all its peoples students? ... It seemed correct. What else would explain the weird situation where men did wrong while meaning well? For all the war, tortures and acts of barbarism, the human race always seemed to draw virtue from chaos and grow more enlightened with each generation. Why were people getting better instead of worse?

"Germany will lose this war soon," the Baron continued. "And being the loser will become the scapegoat for the lesson which this war teaches – that unquestioned authority is wrong. Germany will seek to justify herself in the face of world condemnation by plunging ever deeper into blind authoritarianism ... But whereas the lesson from this next war – that racism is wrong, will be in no doubt, the subsequent direction of society is in the balance." He looked at Manfred fiercely and Burk became aware that they were all looking at him.

"There is something I can do?" Disbelief raised his voice.

"Precisely ol'boy!" Jurgen leaned forward confidentially and replenished Manfred's glass.

As he sipped they told him about the despatch rider who had tried to recall SL17's crew to Ahlhorn. A new super-Zeppelin had been commissioned into the service with a specific mission in view. Burk would only have a month to work her up.

"You are to be her commander, mein Kapitän!" Jurgen dripped irony.

"You are disappointed?" Manfred accused him.

"Yes, dear boy. Had it not been for your interference, culminating in the present inquiry about von Dobberitz's attempt to sabotage our last command, dear Albrecht would have commanded this mission ... It was to be an Army one, but it has been transferred to the Navy."

"What is this mission?"

"To bomb Amerika, or to be specific, New York," Rudi said quietly.

Rudi was in Intelligence, so he must know ... It was the most sensible piece of strategy Manfred had heard of in a long time. Amerikaner troops were flooding France with inexorable waves of men and material ... To them, war was fun, good business because they imagined their fatherland to be invulnerable ... But if Amerika were bombed – it need be only one strike and not necessarily a heavy one – Amerika would panic! They would withdraw their troops to defend the homeland and Germany would rally for a final push on the spent French and Englisch ... But why had they wanted von Dobberitz to fly the mission? He would be fortunate to sail to Greenland! The truth smote him like a punch to the heart; Eberheim wanted nothing less than failure!

"Look at it this way, Manfred ..." Neurath spoke to him persuasively, leaning over the arm of his chair to face him. "If you have a class of children and, in it, one group who do something wrong – what happens?"

"The master corrects them," Burk answered.

"Ah yes, but what happens if the master wishes them to learn, really learn?"

Manfred thought hard on that one. Forget the orphanage; there they were beaten on whim. But at the Academy? There had been classes there, and beatings for lessons not learned correctly, but the lessons had faded with the welts. Not so experience learned on the training ship where you found things out for yourself and endured the laughter of your peers while you groped.

"The master will allow the group to be instructed by its own error in front of the whole class."

"Quite so!" Neurath leaned even closer to him. "Now, what happens if, in this class, there is a group who persist in their error?"

"The master must interfere, else this group will always be the butt of the rest and never learn."

Then he had it! Realization poured into him, crushing him like the burst waters of a dam engulfing a town below it. And their arrogance appalled him. Including himself, there were nine people in the Brown Room and, except for himself, they presumed to direct the course of the world. Aristocrats, it was natural for them to consider themselves to be the best. But there were other aristocrats and doubtless better people.

"No, Manfred ... We are of you, not above you. We only

guide, brighten, dilute hate and disarm disaster. We do not presume to rule." Halgerd wiped the bitterness from his heart and again he felt helpless before their ability to read his mind.

"Only your face, dear heart – and your soul!"

Dear heart! She had said it before, but it was meant. Warmth glowed in him. He addressed himself to the Baron.

"I presume Germany is this delinquent group, the world the classroom and Eberheim the master?"

The Baron shook his head. "Don't settle for a mare when you can have the whole stable, boy! God, however you worship him, is the master. Eberheim is a tutor."

By appointment or assumption? Manfred wondered. The Englisch assumed that they were divinely appointed to impose civilization on their colonies. Germany was more humble, being content to rape hers.

"There is an alternative we have not discussed," Neurath interrupted him. "So far we have given freedom of movement only to the master ... But our delinquent group may, if it is strong enough, kill the master and the rest of the class."

Manfred was shocked. He looked at Rudi, but the latter nodded in agreement . "There will be another war Manfred. The department I work in is planning it already ... If Amerika suffers grievous loss in this war they may be reluctant to involve themselves in the next one ... And Germany will fall first in that war where man pits himself against monster."

What did they want him to do? Become traitor and saboteur? Besides it was all talk and confusion ... Certainly Förstmann would give him a new command, but they insisted that they knew not only what type of ship it would be, but also his sailing instructions ... Still Rudi worked in Intelligence. Didn't he? His emotions seethed through him like a rip tide, demolishing logic and instinct, tearing him down into a maelstrom of bewilderment. He looked to Halgerd for guidance. He would do anything she prompted, but she turned her face aside and wouldn't influence him. Having made him her slave she now denied him instructions.

"So you had von Dobberitz groomed for this mission? What did you buy him with?"

Halgerd's shoulders twitched and instantly he regretted saying that. Until he realized that she was laughing and then he was angry again. Who was she laughing at? Him?

"Really! Jurgen sounded quite offended. "I cannot imagine how you could think that we had to offer that vain idiot anything except the command. He was certain to fail!"

"And I'm not?" Burk wanted to add "with you as my number one," but he didn't. A remark like that wouldn't achieve anything more than to shut Jurgen up – and he wanted him to keep on talking. To talk until some sense emerged.

"Fact is ol'boy we can't, won't actually, move without consent."

"Whose?"

"In this case yours ... You see Albrecht virtually guaranteed that we wouldn't have to act."

"You want me to sabotage this mission!"

"No, Manfred,"Halgerd reassured him. "There will be sacrifice enough for you in the years ahead – what Germans will rightly call 'the dreadful peace' ... What we require of you now is that you execute your duties faithfully ... But you have told us that the world is sick, perhaps to the point where it may not recover unassisted."

'Insane' would have been a better word. There was something about people that made peace oppressive and attracted them to war. War drew from people what peace dissipated – loyalty, friendship, unselfish dedication and co-operative effort. All mankind's greatest technological discoveries and social advantages had come out of wars ... And that was the sickest reality of all. If nothing subversive were expected of him, then he could afford to submit to the slippery philosophies of Eberheim. On the grand scale of things Halgerd was right: men, having walked themselves into a mess tended either to blame others, or pray to God for help. But what if they were right that God could only intervene in his creation with great difficulty? That would make sense of some form of intermediate agency ... But Eberheim? ... Still they weren't asking him for worship, or belief, – just a simple invocation.

That must be it – help couldn't tender itself unasked. That would translate it into interference. Neither could help be offered for the asking – that would be coercion. Perhaps he was about to make the greatest of fools out of himself, but the only sense the whole crazy evening seemed to make was that they wanted him to ask them for help – on his own behalf, or on behalf of all mankind? And if the evening had been nothing else than an elaborate joke, the baiting of a peasant ... But that would have made Halgerd a part of it ...

There again, perhaps it was neither of these possibilities and the only enigma to the evening's proceedings were the limitations of his own intelligence and information – but then it would be Halgerd who would be disillusioned. He re-examined the storm of facts and allusions and reached the same conclusion even when he firmly put aside the bewildering role Eberheim suggested for itself. But he couldn't dare to commit himself without further confirmation; too much was at stake. It was one thing for the Baron to force humiliation on to him and Izzy; it was quite another for him to invite it on himself.

"Gräfin, you must know that it is no great thing to ask me to do my duty, for I always have. Neither is it anything new to wish an end to this war, for only peace is wholesome. And you hint that something great is expected of me before we can be together ... I will do anything for you that is honourable, and not if it is not, for I will not dishonour you, even though you command it ... Dam 'n it all Halgerd, if I didn't truly love you, I'd agree to any price."

Halgerd smiled at him wistfully and murmured, "Our halls are for the high minded only, Manfred. I am not to be bought. But when you match me love for love then we will be ours."

"Getting back to the analogy of the school ..." Neurath was abrupt, as though dreading the sentiment threatening to disrupt the evening, "What options are open to the well-intentioned pupils, assuming they are not strong enough to sit on the delinquents? They can't appeal to the master, not if he has withdrawn."

Manfred considered the problem. "They could, perhaps, ask a senior class for help – the prefects?"

"And would the senior boys impose order on their own initiative?" the Baron cut in.

Manfred entered into the spirit of this weird game that took him right back to the naval academy. "Not if the master has ordered them not to. But they might intercede if the junior class asked them to."

Silence filled the room. Manfred was certain that the almost tangible expectancy was real and not prompted by the conclusion he had reached earlier. He could beat around the bush all night and get no further clarification

... They were waiting for him to invoke them. A small thing, involving no treason, cowardice, nor any apparent commitment on his part... Yet, at this moment, he almost wished that he was in the heart of the fear over London again ... Would Halgerd laugh too?

Very slowly, he raised himself from his chair, staggering slightly as one of his legs developed 'pins and needles'. He straightened his tunic, turned to face the Baron and flung him an impeccable naval salute. "Grüß Gott, Herr Baron!"

The old man acknowledged him by the slightest tilt of his head.

"Herr Baron, on behalf of myself and er, the whole German nation, ahh, the whole world... As a citizen of this same world I command , no, ahh ... I ask, I plead that you and yours act, to whatever extent lies in your power, to halt this war. To prevent, or at least minimize, no, contain, any subsequent one, and to direct the human race on the way to peace!"

Idiot! His mind hissed at him. They will split their sides laughing at you! He wanted to look to Halgerd for reassurance, but pride locked his neck. Let them laugh; it could only hurt him, but if that were the way they saw others, then they would be their own destruction. But Halgerd ... she couldn't be like that, could she? Inside, he felt himself tearing apart.

Then the Baron was speaking again, his deep, dry tones rattling off the stone walls and pushing Manfred's doubts away with their sincerity and solemnity.

"Herr Kapitän, is there some way in which you would limit our power to act?"

"In no way, Herr Baron!"

"Very well, Herr Kapitän. I accept your mandate from the people, since you are of the people and since you have appealed to me of your own free will ... Do you confirm that you ask this of your own free will?"

"I do, Herr Baron!"

Then the room was filled with applause. Everybody was on their feet and Halgerd led Manfred out into a conservatory.

"That was well done, Kapitän Harsch!"

"It was nothing, Gräfin ... They were only words, any actor could have said them and delivered them better!"

"Yes dear heart – but he wouldn't have been you!"

"I would like to do something better for you, Gräfin! ..."

She looked down and did not speak. Manfred reached out his hand, cupped her chin and tilted her face to his. She was weeping.

"What is the matter Halgerd?"

"Do you really want to be with me, Manfred, forever?"

"Yes!"

"Then I am weeping for you, Kapitän Harsch ...Oh Manfred." She leant against him, buried her face in his tunic and burst into deep wracking sobs.

He hugged her to him fiercely, gripping her as though to choke her tears.

"Hush my dear one ... There is nothing to weep over!"

But there was, and she did. Later he would understand.

"If you really want to be with me, Manfred, then it will be the hardest thing," she told him when she had composed herself again. He tried to hug her, to kiss, not talk, but she would not let him. "Jurgen, Rudi, Karl, I, all the others, even the Baron, have all had to walk the same stern way to Eberheim ... But if you can do it Manfred ... It will be worth everything." Her voice shook slightly as she tried to force some of her customary gaiety into it. "You must return soon, to your ship, your new command ... Do not forget me, Manfred ...Be true to me, but above all to yourself ... And never doubt that I shall come to you ...If you remain true and do not forget ... Do not fail me!"

He couldn't reply. At that moment the Baroness came into the conservatory and brought them into the Brown Room for a rubber of bridge.

It was after midnight when Manfred went to bed and before dawn broke that same morning he, Izzy, Jurgen and the rest of SL 17's crew, had boarded the train for Ahlhorn.

Bob woke up in an agony of loss. He switched on the light and for a long time regarded the sleeping Susan, weeping because she wasn't Halgard and broken by the certainty that no woman ever would be.

Fifteen

King Sigtrygg asked, "How did Skarp-Heden bear the burning?"
"Well enough to start with," replied Gunnar. "But in the end he wept."

NJAL'S SAGA

The first thing Bob wanted to know when he saw the ruins was: how the hell had Bersarin found out? It had been one thing for Bascombe and Susan to arrive at Bari independently; the former had Military Intelligence, the CIA and the tacit cooperation of the Italian authorities, while Susan had the microfilm library and Bob's dreams. So how had the Soviets found Burk and beaten Bob to him by one whole day?

They were still digging bodies out of the rubble, black matchstick things such as a child might draw with a wax crayon. The corpses had lost too much of their humanity for pity and they were too badly charred to be obscene. Still, Bob recognized that his lack of emotion was due mostly to disappointment. Forty four monks and God alone knew how many civilians, all gone along with the monastery and much of the quaint graveyard.

Susan ... have you been indiscreet? ... Manfred, why

didn't you kill your enemy years ago – you must have had the chance? Bascombe could go to hell. As soon as he saw what had happened, Bob had declared himself and demanded co-operation from the officials.

The Italian Captain in charge of the investigation met Bob in the monastery.

"Of course it wasn't an accident Major. However we will insist that it was one."

"Oh?"

"Certainly Major ... You have your troubles in the States, but they are only gangsters ... Here we have terrorists. You may publicize your gangsters – they don't threaten your government – but we must deny the terrorists. The nation would have panicked years ago had we been truthful."

Bob would have liked to tell this gold-toothed, swarthy man who had really organized the massacre – Colonel Lavrenti Bersarin. But apart from being impolitic such a move would be dangerous to himself on the grounds that what he knew he must have a hand in. Italian jails were no rest homes.

"Are you certain that this is a hit and not an accident?" he asked the Captain.

"Sure I'm sure, Major! Look, liquid petroleum-gas tankers are not permitted on this circuit. In Italy we have the best roads in the world and traffic runs freely. Why would a rig that size squeeze itself down this narrow tire track and park just outside the monastery?"

"Suppose the driver wanted to go to a ball game? It would be a safe place to park!" Bob suggested.

The Italian shook his head and ground out the cigarette butt. "Follow me Major ... I'll show you!"

They walked through the now cool wreckage of the monastery towards what once had been a walled garden. The LPG tanker must have leaked a lot of gas before it was ignited. The explosion had blown the tanker into barely recognizable pieces and the huge puddle of burning gas had raised the temperature of everything in the vicinity of the monastery to several thousand degrees. The explosion had torn down the walls and the fire had demolished the wreckage.

When all the bodies had been recovered it would be possible to say how many had died but, without dental charts, no one could ever identify them.

The remains of two walls of a room that had led into the walled garden still stood. The room they contained, or what was left of it, was blacker than the surrounding mess.

"This was the Prior's cell" the Captain told him. "The Prior collected wood sculptures – anything made from wood, as you can see." He pointed to the thick cakes of cracked carbon littering the floor and peeling from the bits of wall left standing. "The Prior had had everything in his cell treated for fire. That's why he's in better shape than the rest of the community."

The Captain pointed to a dense black mound in the corner by the walls. Even though he had been told that it was a body it took Bob some moments to accept it as such.

"Examine him Major ... You'll see what I mean!"

Bob stooped over the pathetic thing. Then he straightened, ran into the seared garden and was sick. Later he asked the Captain if he could take some photographs. The Captain looked at him with the same disgust a visitor at the zoo might reserve for a vulture eating: necessary but revolting.

"Sure ... I've been ordered to co-operate ... Just remember that this is an 'accident', right?"

"These won't be for publication, Captain ... They'll go down to Records."

Bob tried to make it as fast as he could. The whole thing turned his stomach, not the destruction nor the mess, but the knowledge, spread over this whole 300-metre diameter slaughterhouse, that mankind could be, and was, something really special.

Afterwards, in a bar by the airport, the Major and the Captain washed the oily soot from their throats with a carafe of wine watered with aqua minerale.

There was no way the two men could ever be friends, or even companions – they were too different. Not in race, creed nor ideology, but in method, and method was the root of discord. It was not difference that drove men to hate, but the subtle mismatch of similarities. The Major and the Captain believed in the same things, but whereas the former was an ordered idealist the latter was an untidy cynic. Each would be glad to see the other go.

"If you do get a positive ID on my man you will let me know?" Bob stood up to leave.

"Of course!" The Captain remained seated and poured out the last of the wine. "You know Major, Italy is full of German war criminals and we will not disturb them ... We are not the same men that Julius Caesar commanded. We cannot bear arms as well as you, nor burn for revenge for so long!"

"This isn't revenge Captain!"

The Captain's raised eyebrows in disbelief, then he turned from Bob to his wine and the view of the airport. Bob collected his overnight bag and joined the queue to board his plane.

"What the hell happened back there, Mister?"Bascombe asked as soon as Bob crossed the threshold of the General's office.

"Bersarin, or his goons, got there before us, Sir!"

"OK, so who's the canary?"

"Probably me, General, or rather my girlfriend."

Bascombe said nothing, but he glared at his subordinate – an action rehearsed over the years to demolish a man with his own fears – it was far more effective than any reprimand. Damn that loud mouthed bitch to hell, and that's exactly what he'd make her life! She'd wrecked *Firedrake* ... No, *he* had! He'd recognized the risk and hadn't acted on it.

Bob knew what he had in the photographs and wasn't to be intimidated this time.

"If you don't like the way I work, General, you have the whole army to replace me from!"

"I like your work, Mister ... It's your mouth that worries me! ... Who's your girl been seeing ... How much did you tell her?"

Bob told him how Susan had found Burk by searching microfilm of old German newspapers. One of them had run a list of SL17's entire crew and Immigration had traced a descendant of one of them, a New York businessman. Susan had interviewed him in his colonial-style farmhouse home in New York State. At first he had refused to see her, but a few days later he had telephoned her and made a date. Someone had sent him a package containing the paybook and war decorations of his deceased great uncle, one Lieutenant Isador Issenquhart. The package was postmarked Bari, Italy, and Samuel Issenquhart, the New York importer, was curious. Susan had assumed that Manfred and Izzy had been living in Bari and that, on his friend's death, Burk had sent his effects to his nearest relative. She hadn't made the connection with Brother Joseph in the annihilated priory.

"So, why run hot foot to the Commies?" Bascombe demanded. "What's with your girl? ... There's nothing on file about her being political?"

"She isn't, and she didn't ... The bastards were on to her though – took her pad apart after she'd written to Moscow for information on Burk. But that happened *before* she met Sam Issenquhart, Sir."

"The boy's a fool!" Bascombe buried his face in his hands then shouted at Bob in exasperation, "Why didn't you report this to me immediately?"

"I was sure you had ordered it – it's your style, Sir!" He added after Bascombe apologized, "I didn't see the point."

Bascombe considered this for a moment then asked, "You stopped overnight in Rome before going to Bari?"

"Yes, I couldn't make an earlier connection, Sir."

"And you told her where, and why, you were going!"

"Yes!" Bob's defiance confirmed his blunder.

Bascombe gave him a wintry smile then said suddenly, "Who put the pad together again?"

"Bari, Sir?"

"No. Your girl's flat."

A look of anger and deep shock transformed Bob's face "You don't think ..."

"No Mister. It is you who aren't thinking ... Consider! The girl's home has been taken apart, the lady is distressed. And then along come these fatherly decorators, reasonable rates and a shoulder to cry on. A clean up of that order would take time – long enough for a very deep bugging."

"Oh God ..." was all Bob could manage.

"The telephone would have been tapped of course. Civvies wouldn't recognize a bugged phone if it repeated everything back to them!"

"I'll check out the flat and the decorators too." Bob jumped to his feet.

"Sit Major ... That bug could be a useful feed. You get on over to New York and find this Issenquhart guy before they do. Convince him that a vacation out of town would work wonders for his lifespan – I can't afford a Bari here."

"I'll go right away Sir ... Sir?"

"Yes Major."

"What about Bersarin?"

"I may send in an advice note for his immediate expulsion ... But he still has time. Don't you go sightseeing until after you've done the job!"

"Yes Sir!"

He stood up again and Bascombe rose too but, instead of returning the Major's salute, the General went over to the mini bar and mixed them both drinks.

"One for the road? Bourbon?"

Bob preferred Scotch and Bascombe knew it, but the General didn't consider Scotch to be an American drink.

"What will we do now, Sir? Now that Burk has gone to ground again!"

Bascombe almost choked on his drink and shot Bob an angry glance. "Burk's been wasted ... Hasn't he?"

Bob savoured his brief moment of superiority before placing the snaps he took at the Priory on the table.

"Only forty-four bodies inside the Priory! Two got away, Sir."

Bascombe shuffled through the snaps until he came to the one of the Prior's remains. He stared at it for a moment before dumping them all back into the envelope and gulping back the last of his drink.

"Shit! And to think our streets are full of trash, apologists for the Soviets ... Glad I brought you in with me, Bob – sure you're soft but you'll do! ... By God I'll have Burk this time, and I don't give a damn how much ass gets broken. This guy's been tortured ... eight fingernails gone! Now why did they stop there – unless he talked? He told them Burk was gone and they wasted the whole place to make us think Burk was dead."

"Sam Issenquhart, the guy Sue interviewed in New York State ... Burk must have sent him the parcel from Bari. The Red's have guessed that's where he's gone – no wonder they want us to think Burk is dead! So they really think they can make a snatch in America, Sir?"

"Y' know," said the General, "that's what religion is all about really – a formula for a static universe."

"Huh?"

"The 'apparition' ... Y'know, 'Death saves Couple from Coupling' and all that, and a few weeks later the monastery where 'Death' appears gets razed ... They'll all blame God, of course ... Be quite something for our Godless opponents – to be responsible for filling the churches again! ... What Order were these monks?"

"Benedictine."

Bascombe laughed sourly. "And they wear an all black rig ... Imagine one of them bouncing out at you at night in a graveyard ... Quite cramped his style I should imagine." The General chuckled.

"You still talking about Burk, Gerry?"

"No ... That randy wop ... Seems he's been damaged permanently. He want's to become a monk. The girl's trying for a convent ... Come to think of it, what woman wouldn't – if she knew what we were really like."

And that was a damnable thing, Bob realized ... Men feared punishment instead of anticipating reward. Fear of hell filled the churches, not gratitude for heaven and now. And God was female – all God's works were creative, a begetting and not a destroying ... So God gave man woman, to learn how to love God? Was that why Christ was male – because women, the instrument of salvation were already saved?

"You're not listening to me, Bob."

"I'm sorry, Gerry. I' m not fully awake yet, didn't get much sleep last night."

And since the General knew all about Susan, he was pleased to misunderstand.

A corporal drove Bob to New York. It would be quicker than flying and, besides, he might need the discretion and manoeuvrability of an army vehicle to snatch Burk – if he could get to him before the Russians did. The corporal had a lonely job; his passenger sprawled across the back seat and slept throughout the journey.

Sixteen

By the noon–day brightness,
And by the night when it darkeneth!
Thy Lord hath not forsaken thee, neither hath he been displeased.
And surely the Future shall be better for thee than the past,
And in the end shall thy Lord be bounteous to thee and thou be satisfied.
Did he not find thee an orphan and gave thee a home?
And found the erring and guided thee,
And found thee needy and enriched thee.

Koran. Sura XCIII. – The Brightness

In the weeks that followed, Halgerd and Eberheim occupied Manfred's mind for as much time as his new command would permit. Certainly she had all his dreams but, by day, the new ship made demands on him that would have broken a lesser man. Even von Lüth's imperturbability cracked on occasion: little things in the main, but an awful lot of them, any one of which could be lethal. Like the day cell VII sprang a leak. On the old SL 17 that would have posed no problem; the riggers would have slapped on a patch and that would have been that. SL 17 had had a clear-doped skin but, as well as having flues, her upper gores had been undoped – porous. This had caused problems in rain as the cotton took up water and SL 17 had become heavy but, on the other hand, it had meant that if a cell sprang a leak the gas would escape out of the ship.

The new ship had five coats of cellon mixed with silver painted all over the outside of her skin, and a coat of red ultraviolet insulation inside. As there was no escape for the leaking hydrogen, the men inside began to strangle and the gas had access to electrical wiring and hot engine nacelles. Manfred had sweated blood that day as he shut down all power and grounded the ship by juggling her in the air on valves and breeches alone. And there had been the day when the experts had raved to him about the marvellous engines.

There were seven of them, super compressed MBIVa altitude engines. The experts hurled a litany of figures and statistics at him while showing him around the streamlined power eggs to which the engine cars had been reduced. In essence the new ship was capable of speeds of seventy miles an hour at 19,000 feet.

They showed Burk the oversized cylinders with their aluminium pistons pointing to their total of 1,074 horsepower. Then they stood back and waited for their laurels. Manfred pointed out that the exhaust stacks were too short, that they would vomit smoke and flame that would be seen for miles. The exhaust stacks were to be lengthened. He answered their cries of 'reduced power?' with a shrug and then told them he wanted the seventh engine, the one at the rear of the command car, to be resited or removed. He told them no orders could be heard down the speaking tubes with the engine at full throttle.

"Engine noise won't interfere with the telegraphs, Kapitän," an expert objected.

Burk told him that he didn't use anything electrical in flight and silenced their protests by pointing to the roll of honour – all the crews who hadn't come back. They agreed to remove the seventh engine and, by that stage, were too depressed to be offended any further when he called the designer of the 'power eggs' a sadistic lunatic. They were air cooled and therefore open to the high, thin air. No engineer could work there and hope to escape frostbite.

But apart from small design considerations, Manfred felt there was something more seriously wrong with his command – something that he couldn't put on a report because it was a thing that all seamen knew and dared not be seen to believe.

This was the first ship he had ever boarded that had no 'feel'. It was as if she were dead or had never been born. There were happy ships whose 'feel' sweetened the sourest crews, and killer boats – craft that waited to suicide and take all hands with her. But this ship was nothing at all. Manfred would have enjoyed a 'happy ship' or defied a 'killer', but this ship ...

Sailing her posed other problems. Conceived in haste, ignoring all considerations except height and speed, she was very difficult to handle. Being little more than a lengthened version of the slower height climbers, she was frail, unstable, difficult to trim and had an enormous angle of moment. On the other hand she could climb like a bird with scorched tail feathers – climb to heights where water and oil froze and the only thing to run freely was the men's blood – from their noses, eyes, ears and mouths.

He and Jurgen worked her up over the Baltic for a month and then Manfred was called to the Führer der Luftschiffe to receive his sailing orders.

The orders came in two envelopes, one to be opened at dawn the next day in the command car when the ship was aloft. The other set of orders were to be opened when they had reached the position designated by the first set of orders.

The FdL did not like Manfred and tried to hide the fact. Since the feeling was mutual Burk didn't attempt to make things any harder for either of them. He did ask if anything had been done about Albrecht von Knebel–Dobberitz.

"Nothing yet, Kapitän!"

"Really ... Sir?"

"We can't find him, Burk!"

Manfred wondered if the man were glad. The Führer der Luftschiffe was a snob and must resent having to press charges against one of those he worshipped, and for what – a junior captain who, like the FdL, was a nobody striving to become a somebody? Manfred would have gladly traded the high honour of being seen off by the chief himself in preference for the kinder, lower ranking Förstmann ... But then Förstmann was of the old school, an officer, a gentleman and a humane if stern human. This would not have been the first time old Förstmann had refused to send a crew out on an ascension day mission, but it was the first time he had been overruled, and by the FdL, in person.

Doubtless Berlin had taken precautions to insure that Burk wouldn't be coming back this time, but any murder was justifiable if it could be transmogrified into an heroic sacrifice by the proper observance of pre-mission protocol! The first thing Manfred would do when he upped ship would be to have her searched with a fine-tooth comb.

The FdL offered him a glass of sherry but refused to discuss the mission or Burk' s orders. Manfred felt smug and fought to preserve an impression of ignorance. Forewarned was forearmed, and he had had the ship stocked with inflatable rafts, the full rig for abandoning at sea. The FdL didn't know that yet and wouldn't until the bills came in from Kiel.

The briefing over, the FdL stressed that the mission was "of the utmost importance to the waging of the war" and that Kaiser Wilhelm II had given it his personal endorsement.

"And we mustn't fail him Burk, must we?" He walked with Manfred to the door.

Manfred left the administration complex just as his new command was being walked back into shed "Alma", one of the two bigger sheds on the fields of Ahlhorn. Her envelope had torn again; he could see the tablecloth-sized tears of brittle skin flapping in the wind as the gangs struggled to ease her through the doors onto the trestles within. Someone had gone ahead and painted the legend 'L 73' on her bow cone, and again on her cantilevered tail sections just above the huge black Deutsches Kreuz. The FdL would die of angina if he saw that. This was supposed to be a nameless ship on an unknown mission.

To hell with them all, the ship had no soul – let it at least have a number. But, even with a painted fin planted in Central Park, the Amerikaner head-hunters would be hard pressed to avenge their bombed city on a Navy that had never commissioned an L 73. If it wasn't in print, it didn't exist. Dear God, keep my own and Halgerd's papers in your wallet, he prayed.

"What was it this time?" he asked Jurgen who had walked over to report to him.

"Ice thrown off the screws! It ripped the after-swims. A seventy knot head wind did the rest."

"I want the torn gores replaced; stitching won't do and, this time, I want the after-swims reinforced with rubberized paint."

"I've already seen to that, Manfred ... When do we go?"

"We 'up ship' at first light tomorrow."

Reaching down strong anti-cyclonic winds, L 73 arrived at the designated co-ordinates over the Atlantic a good two hours ahead of schedule. Manfred drew the second envelope, the one containing their battle orders, from an inside pocket of his greatcoat and considered the plain manilla envelope.

"Clear the car ... Exec, take the wheel ... Izzy, on the elevators." He issued the command distantly.

The two Petty Officer Steersmen climbed up into the ship closely followed by the telegraphist.

Alone in the car except for Jurgen and Izzy, Manfred broke the seal and studied the instructions. He read the two page set of orders twice before crossing to the helm where he calculated their exact lift-to-ballast situation. Yes – they had enough useful lift to realize the primary objectives ... But lift-off conditions had been poor and the secondary targets now lay well outside of L 73's present endurance; he was free to deploy his initiative – especially for the end game.

Carefully he evaluated all he knew about Amerikan history and its present political environment. Germany had weighed up his faithful service and unquestioned skill and judged him to be expendable... The extraordinary thing was that they had included von Lüth with the pawns. But a clever pawn could make it to Queen so where did L 73's eighth square lie? Was there anything he could do to accomplish the mission and save all their lives? He consulted the charts and his memory carefully before making his decision. Then he re-read the orders and checked their authenticity before passing them on to Jurgen, taking the wheel from him while he read.

"An ascension day mission!" Jurgen shrugged. He handed the instructions back to Manfred but Izzy grabbed them, stepping away from the wheel to read them. Jurgen howled and seized the spinning wheel, flinging his weight behind it to bring the ship back on course.

"Bomb New York! ... "Izzy screamed. "Bomb the Statue of Liberty, the Chrysler Building, the Waldorf Astoria, Carnegie Hall, Minsky's ... They can't do this ... I've relatives in New York."

"I imagine the Kaiser hasn't been made aware of that, Izzy, "Jurgen said gravely.

Manfred's shoulders heaved and he struggled not to laugh.

Not that Izzy would have noticed. He carried the orders over to the plotting stand and tried to chart a course for their targets and read the rest of the instructions at the same time.

"Did you see this, Manfred? ... Did you read this?" Izzy howled. "After we bomb New York the cretins want us to run inland as far as we can, exposing ourselves over as many cities... Oh good Jerusalem, they've even plotted a course for us! Last city Los Angeles, and we're supposed to strafe it ... What will the Amerikaners be doing all this time? That's what I want to know – selling tickets to see us fly by?"

"It would be quite an occasion," Jurgen murmured. "The Amerikaners are culturally deprived – they don't have Zeppelins ... Be rather a shock to see us, I'd imagine."

Izzy wasn't listening. He was working himself up into a fever as he neared the end of the instructions. "The Deutsches Bund will help us land at a secret field that has been prepared. They will break up the ship, hide us and the pieces, then have us shipped home ... What is this Deutsches Bund, Manfred?"

"The thirteen-odd million Germans living in Amerika."

Manfred's answer was offhand. He was too busy thinking. Doubtless there were Germans in Amerika loyal to the Kaiser, and it was certain that he could dock L 73 unobserved in that huge continent. After all, the rendezvous with the Bund was to be in some place called the Mojave Desert.

"There is a Bund alright ... But I imagine you'll find that the Kaiser may raise enough support to destroy L73, and us! Anything more elaborate, such as shipping us home in secrecy, would be unrealistic ... I'd consider another option." Jurgen recovered the orders from Izzy while he spoke.

"There's this place in Mexico ... Acapulco!" Manfred began seriously but his face broke with a smile. "Beautiful beaches

I'm told. So much better than a bullet in this Mojave Desert!"

The full implications of what they were saying struck Izzy and, for once, the enormity left him speechless. Jurgen had called it an 'ascension day' mission, a suicide one, and he had accepted that on the face value of what L73 was expected to achieve. But Manfred and Jurgen were worried about being murdered on the completion of the mission ...

"Speak up there ... We can only hear the Nav!" Graatz's voice, sounding like a barrow load of gravel being off loaded, called down the walkway into the car.

It was only then, as a horror sweat prickled his forehead, that Manfred realized the speaking tubes had been uncapped all the time. If the men had heard half of Izzy's indignant rantings then they had heard too much. He called the Warrant Officers back into the car and took Jurgen with him into the ship to address the crew. He told them everything, except his reservations and the fact that a holiday in neutral Mexico for the duration of the war hadn't been on the original agenda. If the men's apathy and weariness were anything to go by, then they hadn't heard very much. He couldn't do anything about his crew's sickness and fatigue, but there was one little spark he could kindle for their spirits.

Jurgen's alarm was wonderful when he realized that his Kapitän was handing out Iron Crosses, second class, to all the ratings, and first class to the Warrant and Petty Officers. A commander was permitted to make awards in the field – one or two and very infrequently. Manfred was dishing them up to the whole ship ... Admiralty would never confirm them. He closed his mouth when it struck him that if they survived the Admiralty would be forced to endorse anything that Burk did.

The weather was kind to the ship throughout her long passage across the Atlantic – kinder than she was to her crew. The engine car gangs were plagued with mishaps and breakdowns – motor failures, overheating, piston seizure, broken wrist pins, snapped shafts, sheared reduction gears, oil clogged or salt corroded cylinders, blocked fuel lines, dirty fuel, transmission failures – nothing unusual. But that was why the seventies class were so superior to the others; they had more engines, so no matter what happened, short of the simultaneous failure of everything, the ship always had power and way on.

One hundred and thirty hours out from Ahlhorn, L73 ran into a deep rolling bank of fog. Jurgen stood watch in the command car while Manfred and Izzy were asleep in hammocks slung between the rings inside the ship. Jurgen smiled as the steersman drove the ship into the clammy darkness. Zeitel and Henschell saw his smile reflected in their read-offs above their wheels and smiled back. Then it became too dark to see anything as L73 rotated from the here and now into the there and when.

There was something terribly wrong! Manfred snapped awake and swung out of his hammock, or rather, he tried to. But it didn't swing away under him when he flung his body out. Not so strange really when he discovered that he wasn't in a hammock, but in the lower berth of an aluminium double bunk. A practical joke, it had to be; L73 didn't have any bunks. Jurgen, or Graatz more likely, must have rigged one up and sneaked him into it while he slept. So what had woken him up? And then he became aware of the unnerving silence and the crazy rolling, yaw and pitch of the boat. L73 shouldn't toss like that, not if she were under way. And that explained the silence: the engines, all of them, were stopped.

"What the hell' s going on here! ..." he yelled and ran down the walkway, pausing only to punch Izzy awake.

Two things struck him as he clattered down the ladder into the command car. Izzy had been snoring himself hoarse in another double bunk and he had been greatly assisted in his race to the car by a railing. A railing on the ladder connecting the command car with the inside of the ship! ... A railing that had never been fitted because of the weight penalty and L73's role as a strategic bomber ...

He hadn't time to reflect on these anomalies because it was Christmas day in the command car – at least that's what the thing occupying the centre of the car first suggested. Not that it looked like a tree, but it had more coloured lights than any Christmas tree Burk had ever seen. It was a mahogany desk about the same size as the plotting table, only considerably deeper, wider and completely overlaid by metal panels encrusted with hundreds of illuminated buttons, meters, small levers, knobs and lights of every colour in the rainbow. There were quite a few lights flashing and, since these were all red, Manfred was sure that the thing, whatever it was, was malfunctioning. Had he been confronted with it back in Ahlhorn he could not have comprehended it. Now, shocked and close to panic, it frightened him. Where was Jurgen, where was the watch? There was a round, green glass port set to one side of this invading stand which turned a green beam on him rhythmically. Was this some sort of infernal hypnotic device? A murder machine to subdue his mind and send him overboard with the rest of the watch?

Without thinking, Manfred eased a fire axe off its brackets and plunged the head into the green eye which exploded with awesome violence, filling the car with acrid smoke. Choking, he swung the axe into the table again and again. It shrieked, sounding a horrid alarm, loud, ugly and insistent. Roaring in fright and anger, Manfred flung himself at the table and, with the superhuman strength given to those beyond desperation, he wrenched it off its floor brackets and tried to heave it out the for'ard windows.

The celluloid panels that served as the car's windows should have torn in his hands like thin plywood. But he couldn't smash them even when he swung the axe against them until his tunic was soaked with sweat that ran in small rivulets between his shoulder blades. The panels were scratched slightly, no more.

Sobbing for breath, Manfred dropped the axe and seized the desk and wrenched it clear away from the deck. Splintered wood and a snake's nest of brightly coloured cables whipped at his boots and he believed that the car itself was attacking him. Maniacal vigour gave him the strength to push, push until blood spurted from torn fingernails, push until he had the infernal machine out the rear of the gondola and swinging above the sea twinkling a thousand feet below. But the command car still shrieked at him and the desk still clung to the ship, held there by a dense spider's web of multicoloured wires. Through eyes that still saw everything tinged in red, the colour of his blood, rage and effort, Manfred imagined that he saw the thing hauling itself back onboard, winching itself up by the wires. Howling defiance, he began to hack at them with the axe. The table lurched and the evil noise strangled in a shower of sparks and the stench of burning lacquer.

"What are you doing, Manfred ... What's going on?" Izzy wailed from the portal above the ladder.

Manfred pointed to the dangling table and, certain that his friend was trying to dislodge a bomb, Izzy ran into the car, grabbed another axe and began to hack with him. With the desk gone, and the noise over, Manfred could think clearly again ... He checked the wheels. "Gott in Himmel!"

There were three of them. The two natural ones were set on the correct course and altitude – so why was L 73 losing height? The third wheel, in the centre of the car, trailed torn cables ripped from the desk. It was locked off and he couldn't budge it. He clawed at the ballast stand only to roar in amazement. None of the breeches or ballast levers responded to his hauling on them. The levers moved alright but nothing happened.

"In God's name what is going on here? Where is the watch? Where's Jurgen? ... Where are the engines?" Manfred left Izzy gibbering into the tubes and raced up into the ship.

It was deserted. Henschell, Zeitel, Kornbloß, Loffat, Schütte, Vlob, Brück and the men, the whole crew, were gone. Every power egg was deserted. Shock after shock pounded him until he was incapable of registering surprise and his voice, hoarse from responding automatically, fell silent. But his body drove him with blind will long after his mind had surrendered to incomprehension. He didn't have to be as good an engineer as Schütte to know that the engines in the power eggs were not the same as those with which they had sailed from Ahlhorn. But he would have to be at least as good as Schütte to get them started up again – they were of a kind he had never seen before. They burnt a heavier oil than petrol and seemed to require no electrical ignition.

Stumbling back to the command car, he slipped off the walk way and was thrown flat on his face by an immensely strong and strangely elastic envelope. Where his feet should have ripped through brittle cotton, this stuff bounced him back onto the walkway. With no engines running to power the generators, there was no light inside the ship so he couldn't examine the new skin. He didn't have enough curiosity left to do so anyway.

Back in the car he found what was left of his crew. Izzy had called them for'ard on the voice tubes. There were only seven souls left onboard, he, Izzy and five cadets, seven people on a ship so fundamentally modified while he slept that none of them had the faintest idea how to sail her! Perhaps that machine he had flung overboard had been some form of central control? If that were so then everything was over. Even if he could unlock the third wheel, and learn what it did, it wouldn't work anymore.

"Where are the rest of my crew?" Burk was cold and distant.

"I don't know, Sir," one of the boys stammered. "I was off duty, asleep ... We were all asleep when it happened!"

"What happened?"

"Sir?"

Manfred hit him, hit him hard before he was even aware of his intention to do so. The boy stood stock still to attention, a trickle of blood forming under one nostril and an angry red weal painting his livid face. Manfred was instantly ashamed. Izzy was shocked and a protest gargled in his throat only to die in a gasp when Manfred waved him to be silent.

"Kadet, MikäI. I should not have struck you. Your conduct has been correct and it is I who am at fault. Forgive me." The boy struggled to reply then burst into tears.

Pain and shame were everyday events to a sixteen-year-old, and Burk guessed that he wouldn't see that birthday for several months yet, but he was still too young to defend himself against kindness.

He looked at the altimeter again and saw that L 73 must hit the water soon.

"Gentlemen ... We must abandon ship ... Now remember, when we are rescued, our story is that we are all U-Boat men and none of our officers survived the Waßerbombs."

The inflatable life rafts slid through the hatches easily, trailing mooring ropes as they fell astern. Two of the boys slid down the ropes and stood by to secure the lowered provisions and navigation aids, food, water, flares, compasses and sextants, and then the rest of the cadets climbed down, extra blankets strapped to their backs. Izzy swung down into one of the rafts only to shout in despair when Manfred cast off the lines without entering his raft – his demented friend was going down with his command.

At that moment Manfred had given no thought to his own fate. He was overwhelmed by a sense of loss, failure, both to L73 and the Baron and, above all, Halgerd. The absolute confusion as to what had happened drove every consideration out of his mind except the final one. He must scuttle the ship, obliterate every trace of its existence. That part of his orders he could attend to, and must, because the only thing the German high command would fear above success and its consequences would be the discovery of the unsuccessful attempt.

Methodically he replaced the hatch cover, secured the dog clips and retired deep into the ship. He was calm when he raised the signal pistol and pointed it at the base of a midship gas cell. Time slowed to a crawl when he squeezed the trigger and felt the departing flare kick his wrist up. But instead of a shroud of agony, the purification of his guilt in the pain of hydrogen fire, the flare sizzled and was extinguished. Gas poured into the ship. He couldn't smell it but it carried a metallic taint from the gasometer. Again he squeezed the trigger and another cell ruptured and put out the flame.

Something quite insane was laughing, filling the dimly lit cathedral inside the ship with its wild paeans and, as he staggered up and down the ship putting flares into all the cells, spilling lift and shrieking at them to ignite, he recognized that the laughing lunatic was himself. He ran out of flares and clicked off the empty chamber countless times before that futility registered. Neither was he aware that he was close to asphyxiation and deeply drunk on the gas now almost wholly displacing the air inside the hull.

Weaving drunkenly, he made his way back to the command car for another box of flares and he was half way down the ladder before he noticed that the water was up to his armpits. So gently, like an egg being lowered into cotton wool, L73 settled on the calm waters. The command car and engine nacelles went under first. But Manfred had ruptured all sixteen gas cells. As they bled empty, the ship's 150,000 pounds, laden dead weight, would press on the ocean, the skin would rupture and she would sink to the bottom.

The immersion of the führer gondola struck Manfred in his gas-intoxicated condition as hilarious. Gone were all thoughts of what had happened and what he had been trying to do. He swam around in the half-filled car singing and trying to find the soap.

Above the rear portal, where the commissioning plate should have been mounted and hadn't been because L73 had never been commissioned into the Navy, a shiny new plate caught the light and dazzled him. He swam towards it, drawn to its brightness like a moth to a flame. It bore the legend 'LOCKHEED CORPORATION'. Manfred's English was poor. He thought the new commissioning plate translated into 'Look' 'Heed' and that must mean the soap he was looking for.

"No soap every day, Keeps everyone away!" he sang.

Paralyzed by his own wit he drifted out of the command car where an ocean current drew him away from the ship. He was still singing when Izzy pulled him out of the water. There was this strange ribbon of multicoloured wires twisted around Manfred's foot. Izzy ripped it off and threw it into the sea.

Bob was fully awake – instantly and in a frenzy of inspiration ... His treasure...

He snapped on the light and ran to his briefcase, pouring its contents onto the bed so that a sheaf of notes fell on Susan's foot, waking her.

"... What is it, Bob?"

He held out the strap of ribbon wire to her in a hand that shook.

"Oh, your computer loom! That's a stupid way of switching it off; anyone could replace it." She buried her face in the pillow with a final, muffled wail, "Look at the time ... Go back to sleep, Bob!"

Seventeen

Deceptive features of uncanny spirituality and entirely perverted beauty, like a Renaissance cardinal.

DR BERNHARD WEHNER,
ON HEYDRICH'S DEATH MASK

It was cold this deep under the subway. The hot Moscow sun hadn't reached far enough into the earth and concrete to warm the dreary office and its ancient occupant.

The man, frail with age, stooped over a filing cabinet and had to use both shaking hands to extract the folder. Eyes watering from cold and age, but full of purpose, fixed themselves on the clock. They were the only outward signs left of the driven spirit trapped behind them. Bersarin would have sent his report by now ... But these sub-humans weren't efficient and, in spite of every effort he and Müller had made, neither the NKVD nor the KGB would ever hold a candle to what the Gestapo had been! He turned the pages of the file while he waited for the decrypted text of Bersarin's report to be delivered when and how this new generation of spoilt brats saw fit. Life had always kicked him in the teeth ... In the days when he was young enough for power, Müller had had it all and he had never been anything more than Gestapo Müller's lieutenant.

Now that Müller was dead, and he was old and useless; these untermenchen – his pupils – were too soft to either use him or kill him. Once he could have rubbed the world's nose in its own foulness, towered above it as Himmler had, and levelled everything in a welter of fear. But, like Bormann, he had chosen influence rather than glory. His dreams were over now and he was nothing to anyone but an obscure General of the Red Army, long retired from the active list and the head of a department of the KGB that was little more than an archive. Emeritus rewards from a people, the majority of whom had never heard of him and whom he despised! Nothing mattered now except to finish. He found Bersarin's previous reports and reread them.

The Harmon girl had located and interviewed a Samuel (Sam) lssenquhart who had offices and a penthouse in New York City and a colonial farm in the State. This man would be a grandnephew of the Jew he had laid a road over in 1942, in the heat and dust of the Byelorussian sunflower fields. The Jews were laying roads across the black earth and tall golden fields and those who collapsed, and could not be revived, went into the asphalt boilers. What was it like to have a road for a grave? Ißenquhart had been unconscious when he had been plunged into the boiler but he had revived as the flesh peeled from his bones.

"Gretchen!" he had shouted, a greeting to a dream that had taken away his death agony.

Later that day, Kaltenbrunner had personally rebuked him for his carelessness in letting a prisoner escape on a despatch rider's motorcycle. The rider had been a girl and in the side car there had been a man in work-force uniform, bearing the yellow star and Ißenquhart's serial number.

The Military Police had chased the fugitives for several

miles until the motorcycle had entered a small copse. It had never emerged and the most intensive search had failed to locate it or the rider or passenger.

After a painstaking investigation he had been able to present Kaltenbrunner, who had succeeded Heydrich as head of the SD, with a list of all the staff and the labour force. No one was missing. But a despatch rider's transport and side car had been stolen. It was a pity that he hadn't had Ißenquhart stripped! That way he could have presented Kaltenbrunner with the uniform and serial number. A naked ghost could not have been identified and he could have covered up the loss of the motorcycle.

The Jew intrigued him. In all the hundreds of thousands of lives he had signed away and, in some cases, had personally terminated, Ißenquhart had been the only ghost. It would appear that the rest of the family had left Germany for America before Crystal Night. Judging from Bersarin's reports they had done very well for themselves.

It was a pity the Politburo had found out so soon. The old General leafed through the folder until he found the form from Moscow authorizing him to go ahead with Sam Issenquhart. Bersarin was efficient. He had placed him under deep surveillance, as deep as that accorded to the Harmon girl, intercepting his mail, checking up on his friends, and he had managed to tap the interview as successfully as he had wired her apartment.

The interview had taken place in a restaurant and, apart from confirming that lssenquhart had received the package and fed this information to Miss Harmon, it had been hostile and uninformative. lssenquhart had been suspicious of the girl, was insecure about his family's pre-American history and incurious about it. In the end, by dint of playing up to his pride, while assuring him that she wasn't bait for a marriage trap, Issenquhart had relaxed sufficiently to tell her about the package from Bari. The old General's trap was sprung. He had hidden that package from Müller, the Gestapo, the NKVD and the KGB for nearly forty years, hiding it for the day he could use it to get Burk for himself.

Bersarin must be taken care of now. Neither the KGB nor the CIA would guess that the Colonel had inserted that package into the US Mail and he mustn't live to tell them. The package had contained Isador Ißenquhart's Navy pay book and a shallow handful of faded ribbons and chipped medals. But the postmark had been Bari, Italy. Bersarin should have dealt with the monastery by now and, as far as the CIA and the KGB would be concerned, Burk was dead. It had been necessary to manipulate the CIA and the KGB. They had forced Burk out into the open and, now that he had fled his sanctuary, it was important to call his hired dogs off ... Bersarin would have made quite sure that Burk had left the Priory for America before opening the cocks of the LPG tanker. Now the CIA and the KGB must believe Burk to have perished, his ashes unidentifiable from those of the community. But would this Miss Harmon be sensible enough to let the past be? He hoped so; the time had long passed since he had derived any pleasure from killing fools.

Everything went round in circles and it seemed that airships were important again. People with no right, no claim, on Burk wanted him! But Bersarin would have done his work well and, as an agent, he was used up. It was time for the General to leave his deep headquarters and go to America himself – for the endgame. But first Issenquhart must be induced to leave the city. His farm would be the best place to trap Burk.

There was a knock on the door and the courier entered before the General answered.

"General Sir, the decryption!"

Once they wouldn't have dared to send anything less than an officer, and one in uniform at that. He glared at the young, plainclothes policeman who had entered with Bersarin's latest report. But the boy, who was from the country and as thick as a U-Boat bunker, didn't see his displeasure.

"It is cold Sir. I will have them turn on the heating."

Cold? No, it had always been cold. Cold in his father's beautiful house – the one that had never been his because the Allies had sold it to a Jew who had demolished it. Cold on the long walk down a bitter life, a shadow building works of mist, works without meaning in a world peopled by aliens! Cold until he had found his purpose. Purpose lit a flame inside him that sustained the illusions other men wove of love, hate and fear.

Once he had hated – but he couldn't sustain it. And, once, life had given him a choice – the only real choice he had ever known – his purpose or power.

"Do not. I am not cold!"

"You must sign the receipt, Sir." The boy waited until his superior had done so before giving him a sloppy salute. "You need heat, Sir. At your age people need heat! I will see to it. Mother Russia looks after her old!" With that well parroted party slogan the boy left him, left him to the inner fury of patronized decrepitude. Thank God he still had power to run his own department.

What would he do when his purpose was realized? Die? Everything else was already dead and now only his will held him to this era of mediocrity and degraded wonder. Thinking of his own death cooled his anger. Would he die in disgrace, weeping terror to God while his body wept blood and urine as had Heydrich and Beria, Stalin's Chief of Police and head of the NKVD? He had lived in obscurity long enough not to die of it, as had Müller, and the days of power were over.

He opened Bersarin's decrypted message and ran the columns of letters into his own decoder. He read the decyphered message twice before filing it away with the rest of the material. Then he consigned the whole file to the paper shredder, waited for the spaghetti pulp to emerge and burned it. The Burk case was all but closed. Bersarin had played his part well to ensure that his wife and daughters might enjoy Soviet prosperity! What would happen to them now wouldn't be the Colonel's worry anymore. The old General unlocked his dycrypting machine, took it apart and let the pieces fall into a drawer, clattering over his passport and the money he had requisitioned for America.

America! A very suitable place for the end game – a place of chaos. He struggled into his greatcoat smiling in derision. It seemed you could lose anything in America. The story had broken in time for the early edition of Pravda. It seemed that when staff, reporting for duty on one of the Lockheed prototypes of *Firedrake*, had opened the hangar doors they found the shed empty. Between the trestles on which the huge airship should have been resting they found a box. It contained Lockheed share certificates to the value of twenty million dollars and an instrument transferring them back to the company. The shareholder had been a certain Baron Hildemar von Taurlbourg, a man every intelligence agency in the world was confident didn't exist.

Struggling to free the lining of his heavy coat which had snagged on an epaulet, Albrecht Graf von Knebel-Dobberitz left his office, locked it and took the lift up to the ground floor.

There was a dead monk in the doorway, a little corpse lost in a black habit. For a moment Bob's heart stopped only to race again when he turned the body over. Two monks had got away from Bari; this one couldn't be Burk – he was too young.

Samuel lssenquhart the Third lived in a beautiful old manor that had once been a farmhouse in the rural heart of New York State. Or had lived! Nobody had really meant him harm at that stage. It was just that, when they tied him to his chair and gagged him, they had stuffed his handkerchief a little too far into his mouth. There was another body in the lounge, a slav-featured man with a small, blue-grained hole between his eyes, his finger still trapped in the trigger guard of a Nagan revolver that reeked of cordite. By warning Issenquhart, Bob had killed him. Bascombe had guessed wrong – they had waited for Issenquhart at the farm and not at his city penthouse.

A faint groan spun Bob around on his heels. A fourth man, the front of his shirt soaked in blood, was lying under the antique bureau. Colonel Lavrenti Bersarin had never been an impressive figure and he looked even less so now. There was a hole in his chest, starting high but reaching deep down into the aorta. There was nothing Bob could do to staunch that high pressure bleeding and an ambulance wouldn't reach him in time. He lifted the receiver and began to punch the nearest hospital's number. There was no tone from the machine – Bersarin, or his goon, had wrecked the phone.

"You are late Major!" Bersarin's whisper rattled horribly.

Bob drew a rug over the soaked carpet beside the Russian, knelt on it and held the man's head in his lap. "I was late in Bari too! That was your work?"

"I should deny that Major, but I am too near death. We could have spared them had we found Burk there – or here! But I didn't – and they are mad with youth, a young department with no tradition and everything to prove ... I should have known that I was being hunted too." Pink foam choked him and Bob wiped it away.

"I know you killed Issenquhart. Who was the monk?"

"No, it was the KGB. My control wanted Burk alive. Boris was my man, but we are both KGB ... I forgot that, I was stupid. It's just as well that I am dying ... I will not live to see them punish Sonia."

"Where is Burk?" Bob couldn't feel sorry for a man who

had ruined so many lives just to spare his family. If the human race wasn't so damned scared all the time, and did what was right whatever the cost, then hard sites like Russia would collapse. An easy philosophy; Bob wasn't married.

"My control will follow me, Major!"

"I know that. Perhaps we won't be so damn co-operative with his next stooge. Where's Burk?"

"Boris tried to kill him – should have ... But he had the one weapon to which there is no defence. Why do we want him? Do you know why I am dying Major?"

"Where is he, Colonel? Did you harm him? Where is Burk?"

But Bersarin had passed the point where pain, or reason, meant anything anymore. His eyes glazed as he slipped into the last dream where the mind tries to comfort the dying body. "War criminal ..." His body twitched with weak laughter. "We don't hunt war criminals, we employ them. My chief is ... But he surprised us – there is no defence to horror ... Tania, here is an American doll for you ... Ludmilla, come to Papa ... Sonia ..."

Repressing his disgust, Bob examined the dead man's wound. In the end he decided that Burk must have entered the room swinging an ice pick and bearing a gun. He must have buried the former in Bersarin at the same time as he shot Boris. Some co-ordination for a nonagenarian!

But no ninety-year-old heart could endure the stresses Manfred had endured today – and must still be enduring – on the run, friendless in a strange land. If he died Bob would never know what had happened to him and Izzy because he wasn't dreaming about them anymore.

His treasure had been the cause of his dreams. Relaxed in the vibrating seat of the car while the corporal battled with the traffic, he thought of his last one. Susan had seen his treasure before! How? When?

"Where did you see it?" He had jerked the duvet off the bed forcing her to sit up to recover it.

"Where do you think – they're everywhere. The library is full of them. I saw that one when I emptied your bag on your first night here. I had hoped to find something that was causing the dreams." She was cross and sandy-eyed with sleep.

"This loom was around Manfred's foot when he lost his ship off Manhattan Sound in 1918. I pulled it out of a rock pool under a Long Island pier when I was eight."

"And the dreams started after that?"

"Yes."

They had both stared at the brightly coloured cable strip. Bob's dreams made some sort of sense now. What were the properties of this object that was anything up to three quarters of a century old on the day it was forged?

Manfred had destroyed the computer and the loom had become tangled around his leg. Bob had been the only other person to come into intimate contact with it. His treasure was obviously imbalanced in time. Was the link between Bob and Manfred some form of energy bridge bled from the harness as it regressed in time? If that were so, then there was a harness missing somewhere on *Firedrake* ...

He had sent Susan into the kitchen to make coffee and when she returned he was gone. There was an empty socket in the third wheel's pedestal. His treasure fitted it exactly but, since Manfred had destroyed the original flight computer, there was no socket for the other end of the harness. Why had he plugged his treasure in just then? And why had Bascombe chosen that exact moment to inspect *Firedrake*? The General hadn't seen Bob install the loom, but there was no way he could recover it. Bascombe had been looking for Bob. Lockheed were making thinly veiled accusations about an Army involvement in the theft of their ship and there was still no news about Burk.

He would need a power screwdriver and a lot of time to regain his treasure and his dreams now. The command car flooring had been installed during the General's meeting and the duck boards had been screwed down over the cable-runs.

Eighteen

God, thou great symmetry,
Who put a biting lust in me
From whence my sorrows spring,
For all the frittered days
That I have spent in shapeless ways,
Give me one perfect thing.

Envoi, A. Wickham

It was raining when Susan left the library, but not heavily enough to call a cab. She was glad. Walking sorted out her thoughts and crystallized them in a confidence she couldn't realize any other way. Walking gave her the solitude she needed to work up the courage to go back to her apartment. The fear, every time she turned the key and stepped across the threshold, would not go away. She would be alone in the corridor and God alone knew what was lurking in the darkness inside.

What had happened to the world? There never was a time in its history when so many people were so well-to-do or so vicious. Crime was as old as man. Once it had been a profession but now it was being done for kicks. You could buy your life, safety, from a man motivated by need, but what could you do against people who destroyed without need?

Why had they smashed up her apartment so viciously? Were she a witch in the middle-ages,and her apartment a cave of magic, their violence would be understandable. Why hadn't they just taken the money, or whatever it was they had been after, and left? But they had ripped up everything, blocked the drains and flooded the place, smashed the pictures and smeared ... She wouldn't think about it. It made her sick – not the actual mess but the hate.

What was the point of life at all if people were so malevolent! Not that all people were. In all the vast pantheon of lives there were a few who redeemed the whole. Bob? No, he was decent enough, but only because others had convinced him of it – the few like Manfred Burk who invoked honour, and a society that paid lip service to it. Bob could have been anything from a martyr in a Roman arena to a camp commandant in Nazi Germany – anything provided he fitted in with the crowd.

Manfred was the feudal dream-quest of a world embittered by cynicism – the good and pious prince, a liege lord fit to repose trust and faith in. Evil was charismatic; its practitioners had to employ intelligence to pervert reason. The good, on the other hand, more often than not, were dull. Manfred had championed honour in a world so stifled by compromise that virtue was made as suspect as vice.

Susan had been content with her image of Manfred, accepting it as she would any other dream, until the night Bob broke their date and told her Burk was in Bari. He was alive, real, and she had to meet him. Where could a man hide in a big city? There were people everywhere and, given the decades Manfred must have stayed there, someone was bound to discover him eventually – a contemplative Order seemed to be the only solution. Driven by her faith-need she had sent a letter to every monastery and religious institution in the city. Would he reply – dare he? Halgerd had betrayed him – left him to age and exile in a world that hunted him. What manner of man would he be now? Bob's dreams – their dreams – had ended once he had placed the loom in *Firedrake*'s third wheel stand.

A surge of fury gripped her. How dare Bob have done it ... She had been useful to him as a sort of wall, something off which he could bounce his problems. He only endured the irritation of her thoughts for as long as he needed his wall. But, the first idea he had, he was off and doing without consultation. Thanks to his impetuosity, his chauvanism and his stupidity, the loom and the dreams were lost forever. Couldn't he have guessed that the loom had always been meant for *Firedrake* and never for him! Once he had given it to the ship he would never get it back. General Bascombe had entered the command car the moment Bob had finished installing the loom. The General hadn't seen him doing it; he had taken Bob back to his office and when he was free again the loom was inaccessible: other equipment had been installed over it. What was wrong with men? The best of them spent their lives looking for magic and, if they found it, they spent what time was left them attempting to demolish it.

Firedrake was magic and they couldn't see it. To Susan the matter was very clear. Eberheim had wanted a ship and hadn't wanted Manfred to bomb New York. Halgerd had told Manfred that they could rotate to any place at any time, so it was obvious what had happened. The Lockheed Company had now built an airship which, since it was a copy of the New York Zep, was a copy of an Eberheim design and therefore the Baron had a right to it! Eberheim took the Lockheed airship and rotated it back into 1918, swapped it for Manfred's L 73, leaving Manfred to ditch his new command into the sea off Long Island. Later Bob would discover a piece of its flight computer and, later still, the Army would raise the Lockheed airship and call it *Firedrake*. Lockheed would copy it and the time loop would have been completed once Bob gave the ship back its missing loom.

Bob hadn't treated her ideas seriously, wouldn't even discuss them, and his attitude, together with his behaviour over the loom, was driving a deep rift between them. The dreams were over and, unless she could meet Manfred, she would never know anything more about him. Would that be best? To leave him an idealistic prince, or strive to know the disillusioned ancient? Was that the formula? She and Manfred were in love with the unattainable – he with Halgerd and she with him. Bob was the trouble now. He no longer had anything to offer, yet if she cast him off now she would be a kind of hooker, having sold herself for a dream rather than money. Perhaps there was nothing else to do except to ache and endure. Endurance, hope and intellect– that's all women ever had.

To date the human race had lived by, and under, the physical strength of man. Was that the reason for all the anger and the violence? A sort of survival of the fittest, Darwin on a mental plane, where the unfit weeded themselves out on drugs, or waged war on the force they were unfit to comprehend? If that were so then God help women. Because it would get a lot rougher before getting any better.

She did her shopping in the supermarket on the ground floor of her apartment block. Some men were fitting the new order nicely to themselves, she thought, and a slow resentment burned as it did every time she did the shopping. Bob had no objection to her working; he encouraged it. But although he made free with her and her flat, he never lifted a finger to help run it. Except on the night when it had been wrecked. He had been very good then. Some men were good in crises because, for once, they stopped thinking about themselves.

It was difficult to get the door of her apartment open. She was carrying two bags and had to leave the door open behind her while she dumped the food in the kitchen. As she did so she heard the door click shut behind her and the light snapped out. A great flood of ice seemed to rush into her stomach and her legs couldn't hold her up. They were back and this time the wrecking would be done on her.

"Please do not be alarmed, Miss Harmon!"

The voice rattled and grated as though the speaker were unused to speech and had difficulty pronouncing words. She couldn't scream. She couldn't breathe; her mouth worked and saliva dribbled down her chin, but her lungs only sipped the air – enough to keep her alive, but not to scream.

"You wrote to me ... I had to turn off the light so that you wouldn't be alarmed ... I, I am deformed!

Visions of a blind rapist suggested themselves to her. There was a switch on the wall, by the electric kettle. Carefully, so that her trembling hands wouldn't slap the tiles, she felt for it. Could this creature hear what she was doing?

Oh God ... Help me ... Please! she prayed. She found the switch and the light flooded the apartment. And then she was three people: one cold, remote, evaluating the other two, the room, everything. Another agonized in pity for what she saw. While the third person, herself, her body, heaved great ragged gusts of air into her lungs and screamed her throat raw.

It was late when Bob reached Susan's apartment. A smell from way back in his childhood tantalized him and he paused with his finger over the buzzer. Good old apple pie, with cloves, lots of them and raisins! His mouth watered and he prayed that she wouldn't make a mess of this meal. He leaned on the buzzer.

She was shaking like someone who had just been hauled off a power line, delighted to be alive and yet unable to express it because her body was still in shock.

"He's here, Bob ... He's here ... Please Bob, please ...".

Something had upset her and, whatever it was, it was obviously still in the apartment. At best Susan didn't express herself very well and there was no point in waiting for her to get it all together now. He pushed past her while she clung to him, trying to pull him back, to warn him.

There was a priest in the room, a monk all in black. He wore the scapular and soutane of a Benedictine, the same rig as the dead priest in the Issenquhart place. But this one had his back to him, was rising from a chair and had the cowl up. The priest was old, had to be ancient, but his frame had no stoop and there was nothing else to tell if he were even human, never mind his age. In Greek mythology, Medusa the Gorgon was the most terrible spectacle the eye could behold, but she had only been a myth and not the terrible travesty of carnage and despair who turned to greet him. Susan thought Bob wonderful in his calmness, not like her; she never imagined that he was too shocked to move.

The priest was an outcast, a leper to every sense, even to pity. The thin, hideously translucent purple shim that stretched over the white skull and phosphorous-blackened face bones, wasn't flesh. It was the obscene best that a shattered body could do to cover and protect a face that had been burned and shot away. No nose, just a ragged purple hole. No eyelids to blink the tears away from those age-faded eyes which, like his nasal cavity, streamed constantly. But the most hideous aspect of that face was the mouth. There were no cheeks or lips. The whole upper and lower jaw was bared. The teeth, miraculously perfect, grinned in a permanent rictus from their setting of purple gum and knotted strands of scar tissue that held the jaws shut and allowed them to chew after a fashion.

He had no ears, just small shrivelled holes in the pulsing wrap of scar tissue that covered the head. The creature raised its hands – in a gesture of greeting or to hide his terrible face?

Bob couldn't guess. But the hands were as ruined as the face. He had a right hand, of sorts – a three-digit claw that was gloved for decency. His left wrist terminated in a black iron hook ... a savage looking thing – the thing that had killed Bersarin. Bob was certain about that, he didn't know how? He was just certain!

"Major Weston, my name is Manfred Burk. I am from Oldenburg." The thing tried to execute a stiff bow.

Mechanically, Bob nodded back, but it was a body courtesy, not a conscious civility. Burk's voice was a travesty too. With no cheeks and a damaged throat, speech hissed and slobbered between those enormous fangs. Perfectly normal teeth of course, but they looked big with no lips to cover them. The man had difficulty with his speech and couldn't manage the sounds B, F, M , P, or V: they all translated as E.

It wasn't enough that no eye nor ear could endure him, but Burk stank as well. The damage hadn't been limited to his face and hands. There had been deeper, more cruel hurt done to him under the black cassock. Whoever had sewn back his spilled insides had been competent enough. But whatever plastic tubing or synthetic insides that had been available in the 1940s weren't adequate now. They leaked, denying Burk the friendship of even the deaf and blind. Already Susan's apartment stank faintly of excrement.

"Jesus!" Bob whispered. It was all he could say for a long time.

"Manfred likes apfelstrudel ... I'm making it for him."

Susan sounded so calm – then she burst into tears.

Bascombe surprised Bob. Whereas *he* had stood frozen before Burk, whispering God's name over and over before bolting to the phone for the General, Bascombe didn't turn a hair. Bob had to admit it – the General had style.

It wasn't a natural charity. Bascombe had had to cultivate the warm candour he now displayed so well. He strode into the room, paused ever so slightly when he saw Burk, and dumped two carry packs of beer and a bottle of bourbon on the table.

"Burk, isn't it? Bascombe's the name ... Call me Gerry!"

"Thank you, General. I regret the trouble I am, and have, caused. I have read the newspapers. You have raised my Luftschiff!"

"Ours! US Army's now!"

"Natürlich!"

Bascombe cracked four beers, laughed and passed them around.

"Ms Harmon, isn't it? Bob never stops talking about you." Untrue! "Call you Sue? No formality here ... My, that pie smells good."

He sat down, raised the can to his lips and considered Burk carefully. Manfred raised his hook to pull the cowl over his head. "No need mister ... I've seen boys come back from 'Nam a lot worse than you ... First thing is to have you prettied up a piece ... We got a ship we want to know how to fly."

Burk nodded and didn't try to hide any more.

Gradually, slowly, the horror receded. The meal was a retrograde step since Burk couldn't eat without slobbering and the effort caused an unbroken stream of mucus to issue from the twin craters where his nose had been. Even drinking was an ordeal for him since he had neither cheeks nor lips to seal his mouth.

They tried to make him not talk too much. The remnants of his jaw muscles weren't up to it, but talk he did – monosyllabically, economically, mostly about World War Two and after. He and a Sherman tank had collided escaping from Germany over the northern borders of Italy. An Italian doctor had patched him up – after a fashion. The tanks and the remnant of the Charlemagne never marched again.

"Izzy got you to the monastry in Bari?" Susan prompted.

Burk shook his head. "No, August ... Izzy was dead. Partisans raided the doctor's house where I was repaired. I was too near death for them to bother with me – but they tortured August, for amusement – there was nothing we could tell them. Later, some of the partisans came back. Took us to Bari to the Priory and stayed with us. He never forgave himself – Prior Constantine."

"That's what happened to him!" Bascombe slapped the photos Bob had taken at Bari on the table and Manfred examined them slowly.

"He who lives by the sword shall die by the sword! Guess that applies to torture too. They tore out eight of the poor bastard's fingernails. Why did he wait 'til then to sing?" Bascombe asked.

Manfred wept, but whether in grief or because it was a natural condition of lidless eyes, the others couldn't guess. Then he pointed to the charred wood on the ground in the photo. "See, that was a rosewood bureau. You can see most of the woodwork is intact, if charred. But the bureau is smashed."

He turned to the picture of the mutilated corpse and whispered to it, "Ach, my poor friend. They could have tormented you to your death, and you would have welcomed it as pain from God, the dear, forgiving God you feared so much. But they learned that, didn't they? And once they began to smash your wood – what need for your poor nails then?"

Susan felt sick and fled into the hall.

"So Brother Parvus was August Neurath, and not Izzy?" Bob asked him, ignoring the interest Bascombe showed at his mentioning names that didn't occur on the General's file. And Burk was answering them. To hell with Bascombe ... Bob had to know.

"Who was August Neurath then?" he insisted.

"Royal Neurath ... He got the name 'Royal' from the Royal Tigers, tanks he deployed so well. He was a brave, honourable man and a dear and loyal friend."

"You visited his grave the night this happened?" Bascombe's tone silenced Bob, and the General slid the paper with 'Apparition at Bari' in front of Burk.

"Yes General. I am the 'Death' they mention. I stopped that rape. I had thought to say Aufwiedersehen to my comrade in the safety of night. That was the first time I had been outside the Priory walls in almost forty years ... Perhaps I should have stayed."

"It's you they want!"Bascombe reminded him. "The Reds wouldn't have spared your brethren – they had to cover up their visit."

"No, General. They knew where I was all the time and they spared the community all these years. I killed them by my flight."

"They couldn't have known!" Bascombe insisted and instantly regretted it. The old fool was half senile, over-tired and dangerously near to croaking on the spot. Humour him, don't wear him out defending his idiotic fears.

"In his last letter to me, Prior Constantine informed me that Miss Harmon had circulated a query to all the religious houses in Bari. In it she mentioned that someone had sent Izzy's paybook and medals to his great nephew. I do not believe that your CIA have done this General."

"No. It was Bersarin and his goons who set you up," the General agreed.

"You and Brother Francis were staying at a local retreat house here when Prior Constantine wrote to you. You found Sam Issenquhart's address and you went straight to him," Bob finished for him.

Burk nodded. Brother Francis had entered the house first, protesting to Manfred that their uninvited entry was wrong. But Sam Issenquhart was dead and, as soon as Brother Francis had realized that, he had descended on the armed

Boris, scolding him in typical Italian style. Boris had shot him but, as he tried to get off his second round, Manfred's hook had deflected the revolver and sent the bullet into the Russian's head. He wouldn't have killed Bersarin had the Colonel remained still, but Bersarin was groping in his jacket – for a gun? Burk's hook was as lethal as an ice pick! Now he was friendless, a murder suspect in a strange land and all he had was Susan's address.

"It's been hushed up – there'll be no investigation," Bascombe promised.

"Do not imagine that I fear for this time-trap, General." Burk pointed to his dreadful body. "My body has been a penalty to me for more years than I care to remember. But I had to wait and not know why, or for what. And then you gave me back my ship. I will always be grateful to you for that."

Vitamin B, that's all that was wrong, Bascombe reminded himself as he stared at the old, tired, pain-wracked ruin. He summoned a field ambulance.

"Two ships," Manfred rattled. "One for yesterday and one for forever."

A senility trip, Bascombe decided ... Nothing that massive doses of vitamin B and a lot of surgery wouldn't correct ... But in the meantime the old guy was jaded – dangerously so. He wouldn't let Susan or Bob question him further, but he allowed them to assist Burk into the ambulance.

Military hospitals the world over have the same problem during peace time. They have the best equipment and the most competent staff, yet they get little opportunity to realize their skills or potential. Soldiers, seriously ill, are sent to civilian hospitals. But Burk was a military secret, a small, unimportant one, but nevertheless not for release to a civilian hospital. And so he got a better overhaul than he might have expected to receive under other circumstances.

Surgeons, both plastic and conventional, who up to now had never been allowed to work on anything more serious than blisters, acne and the occasional fracture, were allowed to loose their pent up skills on him. But time was a consideration that limited them seriously. *Firedrake* must be taken aloft soon and no one could say for certain how many years, weeks or days were left in Burk's ancient ruin.

He should have died when he took the hit. The doctors were unanimous in their disbelief that he was alive at all. He was impregnated with shrapnel that they didn't dare disturb now.

The shock his body must have endured when he had stopped the tank should have been well above the limits that the body could endure. And, with each fresh discovery, the belief in guardian angels, held by some of the medics, became a certainty. The old man had been pulverized to death almost forty years ago, but no one had told his body that and it kept on holding itself together.

There wasn't much they could do for the claw. It still functioned as a hand although there was only a thumb and two fingers. They could have replaced the hook with a shiny new, functional prosthetic arm but, once Burk realized that the whole ship had been computerized and could be run, virtually on one finger, he refused. The partisans had surprised August while he was forging the hook for his unconscious, dying friend. They had smashed August's legs and spine with the red hot hook, tempering it in his blood ... That hook was too costly – he would not discard it.

The surgeons gave him a silicone face, expressionless, inhuman, but quite pleasant to look at, almost serene. And this mask meant that he could talk again more clearly and eat or drink so that the mouthfuls didn't dribble through the teeth down his chin. And of course he had a nylon scalp of grey hair and plastic ears. Neither did he stink any more, that had been one of the first things that had been attended to.

Bascombe was pleased. He had the Kraut wrapped around his finger in an untieable knot of gratitude and the B shots seemed to work also. The old guy was lucid, even intelligent, and there was no more talk about 'my ship'.

All the while Bob and Susan waited impatiently to talk to Manfred alone. They had failed to accept Burk the leper, and now circumstance wouldn't give them time with Manfred the cyborg. Susan froze when she heard Bob's inhuman description of his condition: *A robot is a smart machine. An android is a robot built to resemble and mimic human beings. A cyborg is a human being modified by surgery, or machine parts, to mimic a robot.*

Bascombe had ordered Bob to make certain Susan didn't get near to, or hear anything about, Burk any more. As far as the General was concerned, he wouldn't have trusted her even if she and Bob were married. But, since there was no need to have her in on the project, he excluded her. No attempt had been made to debug her apartment because there was no need. Since Brother Francis' body had been identified as Manfred's and cremated, Moscow must believe him to be dead. Besides, without Bob to feed her, Susan was no threat. Bascombe's weakness lay in the fact that he, and America, had been a little too successful and for too long. He dismissed Susan as a threat, as a piece on the game board, and never considered that she might still play a role as a pawn.

They took Manfred through the ship as she lay hung up in her huge hangar. For a whole month they taught him how to operate the computer console and made him memorize the circuit layout. There would be no possibility of Burk taking the ship up before he knew how to handle her.

At first Cogan, the engineers and the construction gangs had been amused by Burk. Of course there would be nothing that 'ancient mariner' could tell them, although his anecdotes on prehistoric aviation might be amusing. But after his first tour through the ship their tolerant amusement changed to anger and then grudging admiration. The old man had it all together upstairs. He had forgotten nothing and he reminded them they hadn't built anything into *Firedrake* that the Luftkriegsmarine hadn't thought of, or wouldn't have implemented, had the technology of the eighties been available to Germany back in 1917.

"What you have done, Meine Herren, is realize old dreams," Manfred told them. "Do not imagine yourselves as modern visionaries. And you have made mistakes ..."

He listed them and Bascombe enjoyed the discomfort of his experts. For the most part they were little things that emphasized the difference between an airman and a draftsman. He complimented them on the excellent de-icing facilities installed in the hull and then pointed out that, if they didn't install a system to knock dust off *Firedrake*'s upper envelope, several tons of it would accumulate and the ship would be blown away together with the dust on walk out. Furthermore, although the airship's frame had been tested in a wind tunnel, Bascombe's experts had not estimated the ship's internal stresses accurately and had secured the lift bags in a manner guaranteed to rupture them in a storm. Manfred was quick to point out existing chafe marks, showed them which rings to re-site, and re-designed the gas cell anchorage. Chastened, the gangs went back to work.

Bob knew that Manfred had no idea what the third wheel in the command car was for. Bascombe was disappointed and at the same time suspicious – if Burk didn't know what the wheel was for, why hadn't he ordered it taken down? The third wheel and its stand were heavy and Manfred had already criticized *Firedrake* for carrying too large a weight penalty in the form of safety railings, bunks, the galley, the central walkway and too many leisure appointments for the crew. Bob suggested that, since Burk was a seaman of the old school who navigated by sextant and skill, it might be possible that he didn't know what the third wheel was for because he had refused to dabble in new-fangled navigation devices, leaving that job to his watch officers. The General accepted that theory for the moment. Manfred was too involved in devising a flight programme now to be distracted on what might well have been a point of petty pride.

Burk's sessions with Cogan were the hardest part of his involvement with *Firedrake*. Neither man had the slightest understanding of the other's field: still, a computer was an idiot and its input a programme for one. Once Manfred understood that fact he treated Cogan as a simpleton and gradually the software was compiled.

Bascombe knew that Cogan was selling *Firedrake*'s software to Lockheed and the other companies involved in commercial airships. True, Lockheed had suffered a setback with the theft of one of their prototypes, but they had at least one other and the race was on. Although the strategy of *Firedrake* was to get the commercial world to take the burden of airship development away from the Army, Army pride was now at stake. The General wanted *Firedrake* aloft before anyone else got theirs out of the hangar. To ensure this, Bascombe saw to it that every minute of Burk's time was spent in work and rest. Bob wanted to be alone with Manfred, if only for five minutes. But the only time Manfred was alone was when his escort returned him to his quarters. He was an old man – a very old man, who was being worked too hard and needed uninterrupted sleep. The General had given express orders that Burk was not to be disturbed. Bob could have ignored them, of course, but then he would have had to face the General the next day. The project was almost completed, and Bob's part in it over, and he didn't want Bascombe to have him transferred. If he waited, an occasion must arise where he could get the old German alone. Bob was good at waiting, but the trouble with waiting is that it takes time.

The decorator called on Susan at eleven. She was surprised to see him, but the man explained nervously that he was leaving town on another job and wanted to know if she was happy with the work on the apartment. He was a kind man. Probably he was lonely, no wife, otherwise why did he dance around so insecurely and why was he so desperate to please? She invited him in for a cup of coffee and showed him the work his team had done; it seemed fine to her. She said so and he practically jumped for joy. He told her of all the jobs he had done to date and admitted that the vandals were a major factor keeping him and others of his profession in business. The poor man! He seemed so completely inadequate he commanded mothering like a cute kitten. She asked him about his next contract. It seemed that he had been called on by the Army to furnish and decorate quarters near an old army airfield for an elderly German. The décor period was to be the Thirties.

Manfred Burk! Who else could it be! It didn't seem important to try to be disinterested. She made his describe the rooms, where they were and what he was doing them in. Had he met his client? No! The disappointment was terrible. Would he meet him? The decorator didn't imagine so. For a moment despair wracked her. It was so unfair that this pathetic little man should have access to the only person in the whole world she really needed to see, and that she be denied.

There had to be some way she could use the man, or his information – God was not a sadist. He must have sent him to her for a purpose. The man couldn't slip Burk a message for her, or tell her anything about his movements; what had he been sent to her for? What had made him ring her bell?

... RING! ... That was it.

"Is there a telephone in the room?"

"Why yes, Miss – a very nice one too – genuine reproduction period piece."

"Never mind that. What's the number!"

He gave it to her and she never realized that there was something wrong. She had been too eager. Anyone but a trained con-man would have become suspicious and backed down. But Moscow had wanted her to have that number.

She called Manfred that night. She was very excited, so much so that she forgot to tell him who she was. But she did say that she wanted to talk to him about Halgerd.

Apart from Izzy, no one had mentioned that name to him for over forty years. How could this excited, almost hysterical, girl at the other end of the phone know? He agreed to meet her in the Zeppelin shed the next night and, very carefully, so that she would remember in spite of her excitement, he told her how to get in without alerting security. He made her repeat the instructions to him and, satisfied that she had got it right, he replaced the receiver firmly. A full minute later Susan got her receiver hung up correctly and it was only then that the listeners in the Soviet embassy let their's click.

Interesting! What or who was Halgerd? They would have a whole day to find out before the case was dealt with. Why? The team in the embassy didn't know and had been conditioned not to care. Two copies of the telephone call were typed up and the original was delivered to a very old General of the Reserve. He read it, put it in a paper shredder and ordered all copies of it to be destroyed. In another room of the embassy another department of the KGB destroyed the duplicate – after they had encrypted it and wired it to Moscow.

Nineteen

Though I am old with wandering
Through hollow lands and hilly lands,
I will find out where she has gone,
And kiss her lips and take her hands;
And walk among long dappled grass,
And pluck till time and times are done
The silver apples of the moon,
The golden apples of the sun.

W. B. YEATS

"Can't sleep, Sir?"

Manfred turned and saw the big corporal step from the shadows and walk up to him. The soldier had a pleasant smile, but his eyes were hard. A veteran, Burk decided and this meeting was no accident; the man had been detailed to guard him, or was he there for his protection? Nothing about this place was obvious. Everybody was very kind, but then Manfred had been co-operative. They had given him a batman, a big strong, patient man who seemed to have an uncanny understanding of the problems of old men. He had said he had had an invalid father, and then Manfred had discovered that he had once been a male nurse in an insane asylum. What would his batman, or any of these people do, if he ever said no?

The camp was a prison, albeit a comfortable one. It was also a game, a make-believe situation where the loser would be the first person to admit that this was a prison. They hadn't posted guards by his door, nor had there been any sign of one in the building; but only once had he stepped out of the prefabs onto the ancient runway. Well, two could play that game. If it was bad form for Manfred to accuse the corporal of being his warder, then it must be equally difficult for the man to reveal himself as one.

"I cannot sleep, Corporal ... It is a beautiful night. A walk to the ship and back again should help."

The man fell in beside him, uninvited and very casual, as if it were the most natural thing in the world. And Manfred couldn't think of a single thing to send him away. Of course he could order the corporal back to his post, except that he was at his post. Bascombe had been at pains to insist that Burk assume an equivalent of his SS rank, another civility, but of what worth? At this stage in his life Manfred would have preferred to be called Herr Burk rather than Captain. He had fought in two World Wars, achieving middle rank in two services, only to lose everything in the subsequent periods of peace. The only recognition the SS had given to his World War One Naval rank had been to admit him into the Waffen SS as an Untersturmführer, a second lieutenant. At the end of World War Two the SS was banned and those who had served in it were stripped of rank and pension rights. Now he was an Army Captain again, but in a different type of war. And Halgerd? She had promised him that she *would* come ...

Manfred felt all his years and suffering bear down on him, an oppressive cloud of despair and a torment of nostalgia. Of what use now for Halgerd to come? Always he had been willing to die for her, but he had never imagined that she would command him to live – or how hard that had been. That didn't matter now; the Amerikaners could be as kind and as clever as they liked, they still couldn't ward death away from him for much longer. And then what would have been the purpose of his long life of mediocrity and pain? The same as August's, he tried to remind himself. Royal Neurath had been born in Bavaria, fought in the Charlemagne and died in Italy. In all that time he had never heard of Eberheim, nor Halgerd. Like Manfred he had never married and had no family – so how could he be Halgerd's uncle? Did all that come afterwards? The reverse causality of 'Elsewhen' made perfect sense of a niece being born decades before her uncle. He remembered his meeting with August in the courtyard of Eberheim just before the hunt.

"August Neurath ... I am delighted to see you again, Sir!"

"*Sir*? ... You idiot Manfred," August had hugged him warmly. "And Halgerd? How are things between you and her?"

"She is well."

"She's for you lad; Delight and Honour are a matching set. But nothing worthwhile comes easy – and you will know that."

There had been ghosts in Eberheim then, three of them, preview people in a real world, Manfred, Izzy and von Dobberitz. Perhaps Manfred could look forward to Eberheim after his death, but then August Neurath had faced forty years of long, hard dying without ever having heard of the place. Manfred had tried to tell him, but he wouldn't listen to children's fables. The despair that haunted Manfred was: when August had seen him in Eberheim he had greeted him as a newcomer – did that mean he had been forsaken, that he would never see Eberheim or Halgerd again?

Some of the old fire returned and burned the clouds of despair away, or rather lifted them a little. He didn't want Halgerd to see him now, not ever. But he did so want to see her. Perhaps she had aged gracefully, like her mother.

The affairs of the body were so important to the young ... But if he could look into her eyes again he would see her, see the real Halgerd, even though she be locked in a dying prison as he was. But could he ever see her face without her seeing his? Better that there be no meeting. But he would like to hear about her, how she had fared. And this young girl, Susan Harmon – the girl he had fled to, had said she wanted to talk to him about her. If she knew Halgerd's name, then perhaps she could tell him what his life had been all about. But would this big corporal let them talk? Manfred examined the man. Perhaps he could kill him ... one swing with his hook. But in all his years of killing and war, he had never murdered anyone – he couldn't do it now.

The great silver ship wallowed on her trestles like a whale in clear waters. Above her, xenon lamps flung cold light that scattered off her skin and flooded the shed with a brightness that, while intense, lacked the life of sunlight. Closed circuit cameras followed Manfred and the corporal as they walked around the vast ship.

"She's a real beauty!" the corporal whispered.

"A firedrake," Manfred told him. But he didn't tell him that firedrakes were for beauty and not for greed. Too many men had built airships for war and had been burned for their presumption. But the firedrakes would come back again in a new age of steam and sail when the last aeroplane had burnt the last Iitre of petrol.

They reached the steps leading up into the command car and Manfred paused with his hand on the rail. Now was the time to get rid of the corporal. But how? If everything had gone according to plan Miss Harmon should be waiting for him, up inside the ship, hiding behind the folds of number twelve cell. Every day the shed was cleaned by contract staff and, since the project hadn't been a top security one, security checks on outside contractors was slack. If nothing had made them suspicious, no one would notice a cleaner who had arrived for work late and started to sweep under the trestles. Again, he had hoped that no one would notice that one less cleaner left the shed than had come in. The security detail at the shed gates was changed shortly after the cleaners arrived. Susan should have passed the new shift when she entered and they, provided nothing alerted them, would pass out the old roster unaware of the addition. ... And then everything was solved for him.

There was the noise of a jeep being driven very fast and men began to scramble into the open doorway. They lined themselves up like a row of tiny teeth in a yawning black mouth, through which moonlight poured like light entering an enormous gullet. Then the jeep could be seen racing and bouncing across the broken runway like a jumping bean on a hot plate. The soldiers stood their ground, for the most part certain that this was another of Bascombe's snap inspections. And then the security check-point vanished in a roar of flame and a splash of orange fire. The men strung across the doorway brought up their arms and Manfred's corporal ran to join them. Burk climbed up into the command car.

"Manfred, I'm terribly sorry. They must have bugged my phone." Susan's voice was flat with defeat. She stood by the ballast stand while her captor barred the exit with his pistol.

"Will you murder this child too, Albrecht?" Manfred knew who he must be even though age had changed von Dobberitz beyond recognition – old, withered, an emotion-spent husk.

"Would it serve you, Manfred? How far do I, and the other pawns, have to fall to lustre your virtue?" He holstered the gun and gestured to Susan that she was free to go.

"I won't go, I won't let you kill him!" She moved stiffly, positioning herself between Burk and his enemy.

"Little girl, you are young and pretty and that will lend you power for a while. But here you will find only death unless you leave – quickly."

"You could always call your thugs off." Manfred held his hook out towards the fighting at the doors." They have finished with me here. I will go with you to Russia, von Dobberitz."

"Yes Manfred – it is time for us to go. And we will leave together ... You see – those aren't my men. The Kremlin has decided it doesn't want to extend the arms race to include Zeppelins. Also we are both an embarrassment to them: they accepted my evidence that you were a War Criminal. You are guilty of innocence and I of abuse of power, and since they can never admit to error, we must both be liquidated."

"Their orders are to destroy us and *Firedrake*?"

"It's good to know your mind hasn't deteriorated like your body, Manfred."

"Don't listen to him, Manfred. He's lying. He'd die too," Susan shouted, stammering in a rush of explanation, "he got sent to the Russian front for something you did – he hates you. Bob told me all about him."

"Stalingrad?" Manfred asked.

Von Dobberitz shook his head. "Too late for that. Yes, I assumed responsibility for 'Royal Neurath's' escape; indeed, I was responsible for it – you will concede that there were very few guards around. Besides, it had become necessary for me to change sides. The KVD seemed to be a better place for me to continue to protect you."

Manfred's mask couldn't register shock but his hook jerked and tore his tunic. "Protect me?"

"I looked for Eberheim too. All these years I have watched over you – made your life my purpose and when they come for you, I will be there. I even protected Neurath too, in the belief that his charmed life must keep you whole. But the fool almost killed you."

"August saved my life!" Manfred spoke quietly but his conviction was absolute.

"He was battle crazy and included you in his folly. Six

Tigers against a whole American division! He had become too dangerous a comrade for you. I changed all that."

"You? What do you mean? The partisans crippled August."

"On my orders. Prior Constantine's subsequent behaviour was quite predictable."

"You' re mad, Albrecht. That poor man spent his days in an agony of remorse."

"True, he was my agent. But he thought he had escaped me and his remorse walled the three of you up in that monastery where your every move could be observed ... I believe he got quite upset when Boris told him. He was dying then of course."

Manfred's mask stared out the window emotionlessly, but his crippled hand tore at his hook in distress. "You are a savage, von Dobberitz, a lunatic from hell. No wonder Eberheim would have none of you. All your cruelties, and for what?"

The Count's shoulders collapsed and tears coursed down his enormous nose. "They threw me out Manfred and they kept you! And when I got home the war was over. Oh how I hated you, and I could have killed you in those days of power. I followed you – everywhere. But you couldn't find Eberheim either, could you?"

"No. I had a star fix. I searched those co-ordinates on foot and by air, but there was only forest there. No one in all Germany had ever heard of Eberheim or the von Taurlbourgs. Not even August!"

Von Dobberitz nodded, blew his nose and was calm again. "I could never understand how you let yourself become involved with that mad child Neurath. Boys were never your weakness."

"When I met 'Royal Neurath' in 1942, I recognized him, in spite of his youth," Manfred's voice was remote. "I thought I could reach Eberheim through him, but he knew nothing of the place. I tried to tell him – after you crippled him and forced him to become Brother Parvus. But people can't believe in dreams when they have no hope."

"You nursed him; I knew you would, and your loyalty tied you to me. You're deluded Manfred, mad! Neurath was nothing. What could he know of Eberheim? True, he was of some value to me, but not to you, nor to himself."

"Did you ever meet the Warden of the Eastern Marches?" Manfred asked.

"I saw him, but he left the room when we came in."

"That's hardly surprising – considering what you did to him."

"You mean ... Look, Manfred, we've very little time left ... Talk sense."

"August Neurath, the Warden of the Eastern Marches, snubbed you in Eberheim."

"That was a forty-year-old man. 'Royal Neurath' was too young to have been even born then."

"You do allow that we were both at Eberheim, yet it has disappeared – as though there never was such a place?"

"Yes, Manfred, I have to."

"Then you may as well accept the fact that one of the reasons they threw you out was because of what you did to August." Manfred waved his hook in emphasis."He was Halgerd's uncle! Didn't the Baroness tell you?"

"Uncle?"

Von Dobberitz walked for'ard and watched the battle. It would be over soon. Most of the defenders were dead, including Manfred's corporal. In the darkness outside the doors bulky objects were being hauled into position. Moscow wasn't going to leave the Amerikaners a rouble's worth of salvage. He groped inside his coat in a fever of excitement and pulled out a flask of red vodka.

"Drink with me Manfred, you too, Miss. Please accept friendship from me." His voice broke with pain and Manfred was anguished by the little boy lost he glimpsed behind the watering eyes. Von Dobberitz had murdered Izzy, August, thousands of others and had hounded him to this day. Was all that to be forgotten?

"Don't Manfred," Susan warned.

Then Albrecht was pleading, "Intercede for me, Manfred, please. We have both wasted our lives – you in hope and I in despair. You must not condemn me for I made you and might have been you."

Manfred took the bottle and drank but Susan refused.

"Halgerd couldn't possibly have loved you," she yelled at the Count. Albrecht looked at her and some of his old cynicism returned. "It was not Halgerd I loved. Be thankful, little girl, that you are in an age where you are safe to make a mistake like that! When I was in the SS and, later, in the NKVD, they gave me all the pretty girls – girls like you, to interrogate, because they, and you, have nothing to influence me with."

"You are a monster!" Revulsion overcame her fear.

"No, little girl. It is not for you, with your ability to relate to 'the other', to condemn me – for your ignorance is vaster than my own."

"Condemned? No – pitied? There was hope for me with Halgerd. But surely you saw that Jurgen despised you!" Manfred was harsher than he meant to be.

"Did you think I burned your ship for you? You were nothing to me – until they threw me out of Eberheim. Ach – that was then, Manfred. All I want now is forgiveness. Perhaps Eberheim never existed. And in this world of children, you and I are so alone – so alone Manfred."

But Burk didn't hear him. He recognized the shadow outside the shed doors and once more he was back in Ahlhorn wrestling with a ship and the blue fire of hydrogen. He activated the computer and punched a programme that would get the ship aloft. But even though he turned the cell heaters on to maximum it would still take five minutes for them to inflate to a free lift.

"Oh my God! ... What's happening?"

Susan screamed as a hollow cough sounded from the night and the last defence at the shed doors was engulfed in a river of flame. The flame thrower vomited again, a low-toned detonation, but this time the flame was oily black from the withered men it fed on. Then the pit of the fire hose swung towards *Firedrake* and the flamethrower ground over the ashes into the shed.

Manfred stared down into the ignition vortex of flame and the bile of disappointment rose into his mouth. He would never see Halgerd again.

Susan had once lost her balance on the bank of a pond. A small piece of earth had given away and she had begun to tumble and nothing could arrest her fall unless she took a step forward, a step which would have put her into the pond anyway. Instead she had chosen to fall. The lake had been shallow and cold, but what she remembered most of all was the enormous length of time it had taken her to heel over into the water. It had been as if time itself had slowed to a crawl. The same thing happened now. Flame bellied from the hose, leapt out towards them and then began to slow down until it stopped. Everything, including herself, her own breathing, was stopped. Before her Manfred was still hunched over the control board and the rush of air that threw her hair forward, the air to feed the angry flame had grown still and yet her hair hung out and in front of her stiff, like a picture of a flag on a windy day.

Something was moving – the ship. She tried to turn her head to see what was happening and found she couldn't even roll her eyes. But soon enough it became evident what was taking place. A team of men in green overalls were walking the ship out onto the airfield. Out past the frozen flame the ship swayed, out into the moonlight and the small hard stars, out past the other ship, a second ship which was being walked in.

The second ship was smaller than Firedrake, a leaner more weather-beaten affair with enormous black crosses painted on the underside of its silver fins and bearing the legend in bold letters taller than a man was high: L73. An evil red light shone from her open cargo doors and, glinting in this hellish lustre, she could see the nose cones of dozens of brass-cased bombs, fat stubby bombs like the ones they showed in cartoons. The second airship was docked and hung up on the trestles in front of the flame thrower, and the gang began to walk out to *Firedrake*. She could feel the ship tremble and buck against the stay ropes as the men boarded her.

Then the night exploded with noise. Only it wasn't noise, it was the happy sounds of greetings ringing out in a desert of silence. She recognized Izzy from his photograph. He entered the ship with a tool bag in one hand and a metal box under the other arm. He shouted a greeting to Manfred, blew a raspberry at von Dobberitz and dumped his load at the base of the computer and the third wheel.

"Interface module – one off," he announced and began to unscrew the duckboards.

An exquisite girl in white organdie rushed into the car and ran towards Manfred. At the moment she entered Susan could move again and so could Burk. With an animal cry of shame he tried to hide his face, brought up his hook to cover the mask. Only the hook had become a hand again and the mask was the very earnest face of a youth in his twenties. The grey wig was gone, replaced by a close shaven bristle of brown hair.

Then he saw himself in the rear view mirrors of the car and he fell into her arms shouting "Halgerd ... You came ... I knew you would," and he sobbed like a child.

A hand rested on Susan's arm and she looked into the face of an immaculate – a sweep of night-blue cloth lined with scarlet, all topped by the most ridiculous looking helmet she had ever seen. It seemed to be black enamel with gold piping and flashes and vaguely resembled a teacher's mortarboard. He looked past her at von Dobberitz and everything about that tired, evil old man collapsed – except the fire in his eyes.

"Still making a fool of yourself, Albrecht?"

"No Jurgen – I graduated to killing them!"

"Yes, Izzy told us all about that."

"I will not accept shame for killing the Jew ...What I am and what I do was never mine to choose. The role of teacher was forced upon me."

"Some 'teacher'! Remind me to bring you an apple – a poisoned one," Izzy hissed as he prized the duckboards off their joists. He located the free end of Bob's computer harness, plugged it into a socket in the metal box and slipped the lot into the space under the third wheel. "We can rotate now– check the setting."

Jurgen released Susan's arm and locked the third wheel off. "Disengaged Nav ... You may switch on."

Izzy closed a switch on the box and began to screw the duckboards back onto their joists.

"Are you not human and without humanity, von Dobberitz?"

An enormous old man with walrus moustaches yellowing at the tips like old ivory heaved his way down the ladder and addressed himself to the Count. He was followed by a lady of great grace and similar age. Both of them ignored Susan as if she weren't there.

"Well done boy!" The Baron patted Manfred's shoulder. "You've some more growing to do yet – but you've done with pain. Twenty is a good age for love but power begins at forty."

If Manfred heard him he didn't acknowledge it.

"You will not dismiss me any more, Baron," von Dobberitz insisted. "No – I was denied humanity ... But you knew that all the time, didn't you Herr Baron? Eberheim's flowers bloom fair and no one sees the filth they are rooted in. What I will know is, was I made evil? I know you used me because you, and all your virtuous concourse, would be meaningless if I, and despair, did not menace you ... You used me ... You owe me!"

Von Dobbcritz matched the Baron's ferocious glare with hungry eyes and a terrible patience that seemed to draw the Baron's force to feed his own withered soul.

"You're not the boy I threw out, von Dobberitz!"

"No, Baron – he could have been quite different had circumstance been instructive, kinder – he died."

"You are wrong, Count! Eberheim neither employs nor forges evil ... Nor would you know anything about evil since you are only grief – nothing!"

"Could Eberheim heal me, Baron?"

"Certainly."

"Then I demand that you do!"

"Demand ... You *demand*!" The Baron exploded into hoarse guffaws of laughter that shook the whole car and hurt Susan's ears.

The thunder squall of mirth ended abrubtly and the Baron, calm with suppressed humour, asked, "On what do you base this preposterous demand, Albrecht?"

"On your debt to me!"

"Very well. I will concede that if I owe you anything then I owe you something."

"Your subject, one Isador Ißenquhart stole a motorbicycle from me back in 1942 – I believe you still have it."

"What? ... That rattletrap – I had forgotten all about it." Again the car shook with laughter.

The Baroness put an end to the game. "You are quite right, Albrecht. You have been used and you are owed – but not by us. Come, we will take you to your destiny."

Jurgen took Susan's arm and she looked up. "It's time for you to go Miss Harmon!"

She couldn't resist. There was something about the man that, in spite of his comic dress, commanded absolute obedience. She let him lead her down the ladder and asked, "Don't you realize von Dobberitz is a homosexual – that he loves you and that's why he tried to kill you and Manfred!"

Jurgen marched her across the broken concrete towards the edge of the field and waited for such a long time before answering that she was startled by his objective monotone.

"Have you read the Bible, Miss Harmon?"

"Yes."

"Then you will be familiar with the Parable of the Talents. Manfred was dealt the full five. Albrecht only two. All in all they have both managed nicely."

Again the feeling of powerlessness engulfed her, numbing her mind and will to the extent that she couldn't think of the questions she yearned to have answered. They walked until the shed was a small shadow in the night and Jurgen released her arm.

"We must leave now, lady. So far there is no record of your presence here and if you go home at once you will not be suspected of having played any part in what is to come."

He turned to go, but when he had released her arm it was as though he had also freed her mind. She grabbed his cloak.

"Wait, Jurgen ... You mustn't go ... I've so many questions ... What's happening? Where is Eberheim? Who are you, the Baron, Halgerd? Why did Bob dream all this?" She couldn't ask any more, the awe and dumb inadequacy returned and she couldn't conquer it. "Please!" she whispered before her voice froze.

Jurgen looked at her and he seemed incredibly distant. "Lady, there are no answers here; Truth and Time cannot coexist. This life is a quest and not for answers. But you might seek Eberheim too, now that you know of it. Do not! This much I will tell you so that you will seek a less stern way. Eberheim is a collector of fine pieces. It will never be available to anyone but the very best."

With that he turned and walked back towards the shed. Something flew out of his cape as it swirled about him and fell into a tussock of weeds at Susan's feet. She picked it up automatically, without being aware of having done so and ran after the Count shouting.

"I will find Eberheim! I will – you cannot stop me ... Jurgen!"

But the Count was gone and she was alone on the edge of the field.

Slowly, with the grace of a ballet dancer, *Firedrake* hovered and nosed into the wind. Susan ran after it, waving, sobbing and shouting her will to follow them until the ship was only another faint star in the sky, a point of light speeding under three wheels towards Eberheim, two set on direction and height, the third shaping a course Elsewhen, just a few points south of west in Time.

In the old days when a king was born they announced the fact with a public fireworks display. So now that Manfred was reborn to his youth, to Halgerd and to Eberheim the night was made day in a fiery brightness of noise and flame. Time flowed again and closed the loop around L73. The flamethrower hit the ship that had set sail to bomb America over sixty years previously. A ship containing nearly two million cubic feet of hydrogen and sixteen thousand pounds of bombs.

Epilogue

Bob helped Susan stow her gear on the luggage rack and then stood back in the carriage, wishing that the train would pull out quickly. Strange that he could have been so involved with Sue once and now all he wanted was for her to go. Not that he had wanted her to throw over her job, her apartment, everything – it was just that he had begun to feel inadequate in her company and, although she had eased up on her silent accusations, he still felt guilty, About what? He wanted her out of his life because it was just about to begin and she didn't fit into the new order. He would forget her faster than he had forgotten any other girl, mostly because he was ashamed of being so grateful to her for leaving him. A gratitude that couldn't care for the way she was wrecking her career, and didn't dare to care lest she reconsider and stay. He was a louse, but a free one.

Firedrake had changed a lot of things. During the long months the court of inquiry had sat, Bob sweated as Bascombe took, and gave, an awful lot of stick. It would have been so easy for the General to dump the blame on Bob and the rest of his staff. What Bob didn't know was that Bascombe had been promised the post at West Point he had always wanted if he kept the court of inquiry 'tidy'. Susan had stood by Bob while he had sweated and now that it was all over she was leaving him.

'Poor security and sabotage' was the eventual verdict of the court. The former was blamed on the General and the latter wasn't specified since the loss of *Firedrake* was nothing compared to the CIA's loss of face. The world must never know the Reds had hit the airship, nor how easily they had done so. Bascombe's silence, and his dismissal from the project, had been secured by his horizontal promotion to West Point. That must have really meant something to the General because, within hours of his transfer coming through, in a gesture of unprecedented consideration, Bascombe had secured the post at the Providence barracks for Bob.

"You always said you wanted to go home, Bob. So scram!" the General had told him. The Army had secured Bob's silence too. The only people *Firedrake* had destroyed were Burk and Susan. Chivalry nagged him to do something while caution screamed at him to leave.

"Where will you go, hon?"

"Oh, around ... Don't worry about me Bob. This is something I've wanted to do for a long time." Her hand dipped towards her pocket, but she snatched it away before he might guess that she had something there. Bob had thrown his treasure away; she wasn't going to let him steal hers.

It was only after *Firedrake* had vanished into the stars that she had become aware of the cold weight in her hand. It was a pocket compass-sextant. The needle kept station on a fixed bearing when she twisted the instrument, but it didn't point to the north. It was an artifact of Eberheim; would it lead her there? What would Jurgen say when she returned it to him?

The train lurched before pulling out. Bob, unshaven for the first time she had known him, scraped her a hurried kiss and scrambled out of the carriage onto the platform. He watched the train pull out, comparing its disappearance down the tunnel to a form of negative birth process. He was being left behind and yet, with Susan gone, he had been reborn. She didn't trust him anymore, but neither he nor any member of the court of inquiry suspected that she had been at the shed on the night of the bonfire. To him and Bascombe, *Firedrake* had ended with a black matchstick thing studded with ancient shrapnel, the half melted twists of medals and the heat discoloured iron hook that had once been Manfred Burk.

The ship that had mysteriously blown up should have been the one raised off Long Island. But it wasn't – neither was it *Firedrake*. *Firedrake* had always been a contradiction. It should never have existed and now it didn't. Neither did *Firedrake* have any point now that Burk was dead. Lockheed, Boeing and the others would continue to develop a commercial airship, but the Army was finished with them. Perhaps in the peace of later years he could figure out what had happened. He would go to Providence and find that peace.

Printed in Great Britain
by Amazon

63102338R00187